Lost in his arms

Cass broke the kiss. His eyes were bright sea blue, pupils wide and black. I stared at him, stunned, consciousness slowly returning, which he must have seen in my face because he pulled back.

He cleared his throat. "Stop?"

Shaking my head emphatically was wrong. A mistake. Certainly, so was me flipping up the arm rest and moving closer. Which resulted in Cass pulling me right into his lap.

I took my hands out of his hair (warm at the roots, frost cold at the tips) and reached down. What was I doing? I was doing exactly what Cass was, and my fingers folded on his as he pulled the lever to recline the seat and BOOM I was lying on him and his hands were all over my back, then swirling my hair aside so he could put his open mouth on my neck.

Oh my God. Cass Somers had lightning-fast reflexes and some magic potion coming out of every pore that dissolved self-control, caution, rational thought.

It was all gone and the only thing I could think was that it was the best trade I ever made.

Other Books You May Enjoy

WHAT I
THOUGHT
WAS TRUE

by Huntley Fitzpatrick

speak

An Imprint of Penguin Group (USA)

SPEAK
Published by the Penguin Group
Penguin Group (USA) LLC
375 Hudson Street
New York, New York 10014

USA * Canada * UK * Ireland * Australia
New Zealand * India * South Africa * China

penguin.com
A Penguin Random House Company

First published in the United States of America by Dial Books,
an imprint of Penguin Group (USA) LLC, 2014
Published by Speak, an imprint of Penguin Group (USA) LLC, 2015

THE LIBRARY OF CONGRESS HAS CATALOGED THE DIAL BOOKS EDITION AS FOLLOWS:
Fitzpatrick, Huntley.
What I thought was true / by Huntley Fitzpatrick.
pages cm
Summary: "17-year-old Gwen Castle is a working-class girl determined to escape her small island
town, but when rich kid Cass Somers, with whom she has a complicated romantic history, shows
up, she's forced to reassess her feelings about her loving, complex family, her lifelong best friends,
her wealthy employer, the place she lives, and the boy she can't admit she loves"
—Provided by publisher.
ISBN: 978-0-8037-3909-3 (hardback)
[1. Social classes—Fiction. 2. Dating (Social customs)—Fiction.
3. Family life—Connecticut—Fiction. 4. People with disabilities—Fiction.
5. Old age—Fiction. 6. Islands—Fiction.] I. Title.
PZ7.F578Wh 2014
[Fic]—dc23
2013027029

Speak ISBN 978-0-14-242395-0

Printed in the United States of America

1 3 5 7 9 10 8 6 4 2

For you, John, for more than twenty years of your love, faith, and friendship. For all the moments when I despaired of Cass or Gwen or Nic, and you said softly, "I like them." For all those distracted hours of mine when you picked up the slack. Picking up groceries, taking kids to ballet . . . those things never show up in romantic novels. But they should.

For you, K, A, R, J, D, and C, the Fitzpatrick six . . . who love books and beaches and summer. What I know is true? You are the best things that have ever happened to me.

Chapter One

Nothing like a carful of boys to completely change my mood.

There's a muffled expletive from inside Castle's Ice Cream, so I know Dad's spotted them too. A gang of high school boys tops his list of Least Favorite Customers—they eat a ton, they want it now, and they never tip. Or so he claims.

At first, I barely pay attention. I'm carrying a tray of wobbly root beer floats, foil-wrapped burgers, and a greasy Everest's worth of fried scallops toward table four out front. In a few weeks, I'll be in the rhythm of work. Balancing all this and more will be no big deal. But school got out three days ago, Castle's reopened full-time last week, the sun is dazzling, the early summer air is sticky with salt, and I have only a few more minutes left in my shift. My mind is already at the beach. So I don't look up to see who just drove in until I hear a couple of whistles. And my name.

I glance back. A convertible is parked, slanted, taking up two spaces. Sure enough, Spence Channing, who was driving, shakes his hair from his eyes and grins at me. Trevor Sharpe and Jimmy Pieretti are piling out, laughing. I whip off my Castle's hat, with its spiky gold crown, and push it into the pocket of my apron.

"Got a special for us, Gwen?" Spence calls.

"Take a number," I call back. There's a predictable chorus of *ooo*'s from some of the boys. I set the tray down at table four, add soda cans and napkins from my front pockets, give them a speedy, practiced smile, then pause by the table where my brother is waiting for me, dreamily dragging French fries through ketchup.

But then I hear, "Hey, Cass, look who's here! Ready to serve." And the last boy in the car, who had been concealed behind Jimmy's wide torso, climbs out.

His eyes snag on mine.

The seconds unwind, thin, taut, transparent as a fishing line cast far, far, far out.

I jolt up, grab my brother's hand. "Let's get home, Em."

Emory pulls away. "Not done," he says firmly. "Not done." I can see his leg muscles tighten into his "I am a rock, I am an island" stance. His hands flick back and forth, wiping my urgency away.

This is my cue to take a breath, step back. Hurrying Em, pushing him, tends to end in disaster. Instead, I'm grabbing his ketchup-wilted paper plate, untying my apron, calling to Dad, "Gotta get home, can we do this take-out?"

"Not done," Emory repeats, yanking his hand from mine. "Gwennie, no."

"Gettin' slammed," Dad calls out the service window, over the sizzle of the grill. "Wrap it yourself, pal." He tosses a few pieces of foil through the window, adding several packets of ketchup, Emory's favorite.

"Still eating." Emory sits firmly back down at the picnic table.

"We'll watch a movie," I tell him, wrapping his food. "Ice cream."

Dad glances sharply out the take-out window. He may be brusque with Em from time to time, but he doesn't like it when I am.

"Ice cream *here*." My brother points at the large painting of a double-decker cone adorning one of the fake turrets. Yes, Castle's is built to look like a castle.

I pull him to the truck anyway and don't look back, not even when I hear a voice call, "Hey, Gwen. Have a sec?"

I turn the key in Mom's battered Bronco, pressing hard on the gas. The engine revs deafeningly. But not loud enough to drown out another voice, laughing, "She has lots of secs! As we know."

Dad, thank God, has ducked away from the service window and is bent over the grill. Maybe he didn't hear any of that.

I gun the car again; jerk forward, only to find the wheels spinning, caught in the deeper sand of the parking lot. At last the truck lurches, kicks into a fast reverse. I squeal out onto the blazing blacktop of Ocean Lane, grateful the road is empty.

Two miles down, I pull over to the side, fold my arms to the top of the steering wheel, rest my forehead on them, take deep breaths. Emory ducks his head to peep at me, brown eyes searching, then resignedly opens the foil and continues eating his limp, ketchup-soggy fries.

In another year, I'll graduate. I can go someplace else. I can leave those boys—this whole past year—far behind in the rearview mirror.

I pull in another deep breath.

We're close to the water now, and the breeze spills over me soft and briny, secure and familiar. This is why everyone comes here. For the air, for the beaches, for the peace.

Somehow I've wedged the car right in front of the big white-and-green painted sign that marks the official separation between town and island, where the bridge from Stony Bay stops and Seashell Island begins. The sign's been here as long as I can remember and the paint has flaked off its loopy cursive writing in most places, but the promises are grooved deep.

Heaven by the water.

Best-kept little secret in New England.

Tiny hidden jewel cradled by the rocky Connecticut coast.

Seashell Island, where I've lived all my life, is called all those things and more.

And all I want to do is leave it behind.

Chapter Two

"Kryptite the only thing," Emory tells me, very seriously, the next afternoon. He shakes his dark hair—arrow straight like Dad's—out of his eyes. "The only, only thing can stop him."

"Kryptonite," I say. "That's right. Yup, otherwise, he's unstoppable."

"Not much Kryptite here," he assures me. "So all okay."

He resumes drawing, bearing down hard on his red Magic Marker. He's sprawled on his stomach on the floor, comic book laid out next to his pad. The summer light slants through our kitchen/living room window, brightening the paper as he scribbles color onto his hero's cape. I'm lying on the couch in a drowsy haze after taking Em into White Bay for speech class earlier.

"Good job," I say, gesturing to his pad. "I like the shooting stars in the background."

Emory tilts his chin at me, forehead crinkling, so I suspect they aren't stars. But he doesn't correct me, just keeps on drawing.

An entire day after running into the boys at Castle's, I'm still wanting a do-over. Why did I let them get to me this time? I should have laughed; flipped them off. Not very classy, but

I'm not supposed to be the classy one here. I should have said, "Well, Spence, we all know that with you, it *wouldn't* take more than a sec."

But I couldn't have said that. Not with Cassidy Somers there. The other boys don't matter much. But Cass . . .

Kryptonite.

An hour or so later, our rattly screen door snaps open and in comes Mom, her dark curly hair frizzing from the heat the way mine always does. She's followed wearily by Fabio, our ancient, half-blind Labrador mix. He immediately keels over on his side, tongue lolling out. Mom hurries to push his bowl of water closer to him with one foot while reaching into our refrigerator for a Diet Coke.

"Did you think about it some more, honey?" she asks me, after taking a long swallow. Caffeinated diet soda, not blood, must run through her veins.

I spring up, and the old orange-and-burgundy plaid sofa lets out an agonized groan. Right, I should be making decisions about what to do this summer, not obsessing about the ones I made yesterday—or in March.

"Careful!" Mom calls, waving her free hand at the couch. "Respect the Myrtle."

Emory, now scribbling in Superman's dark hair, heavy-handed on the black marker, offers his throaty giggle at the face I make.

"Mom. We got Myrtle from Bert and Earl's Bargain Basement. Myrtle has three legs and no working springs. Getting off Myrtle makes me feel like I need a forklift. Respect. Really?"

"Everything deserves respect," Mom says mildly, plopping onto Myrtle with a sigh. After a second, she crinkles her nose and reaches under the cushion, extracting one of my cousin Nic's ratty, nasty sweatshirts. A banana peel. One of her own battered romance novels. "Myrtle has lived a long, hard life in a short time." She swats me with the gross sweatshirt, smiling. "So? What *do* you think—about Mrs. Ellington?"

Helping Mrs. Ellington. The possible summer job Mom heard about this morning, meaning I wouldn't have to keep working at Dad's again. Which I've faithfully done every year since I was twelve. Illegal for anyone else, but allowed for Nic and me, since we're family. After five years, for sure, I could use a change from scooping sherbet, frying clams, and slapping together grilled cheese sandwiches. More than that . . . if I'm not handling Dad's at night, I can help Vivien on catering gigs.

"Is it for the whole summer?" I plop down, stretch back gingerly. If you hit her the wrong way, Myrtle lists like the *Titanic* before its final dive.

Mom unlaces the shabby sneakers she wears to work, kicks one off, stretching out her toes with a groan. She has daisies delicately painted on her big-toenails, no doubt the work of Vivien, the Picasso of pedicures. On cue, Emory leaves the room in search of her slippers. He would have gotten her the Coke if she hadn't beaten him to it.

"Through August," she confirms, after another long draw of soda. "She fell off a ladder last week, twisted her ankle, got a concussion. It's not a nursing job," she assures me hastily. "They've got someone coming in nights for that. Henry . . . the family . . . just wants to make sure someone's looking out for her—that she's getting exercise, eating—not wandering off to the beach by herself. She's nearly ninety." Mom shakes her head as if she can't believe it.

Me neither. Mrs. Ellington always seemed timeless to me, like a character from one of those old books Grandpa brings home from yard sales, with her crisp New England accent, straight back, strong opinions. I remember her snapping back to some summer person who asked "What's wrong with him?" about Em: "Not as much as is wrong with *you.*" When Nic and I used to go along with Mom on jobs, back when we were little, Mrs. E. gave us frosted sugar cookies and homemade lemonade, and let us sway in the hammock on her porch while Mom marched around the house with her vacuum cleaner and mop.

But . . . it would be an island job. A working-for-the-summer-people job. And I've promised myself I won't do that.

Rubbing her eyes with thumb and forefinger, Mom polishes off her soda and plunks the can down with a tinny clink. More tendrils of hair snake out of her ponytail, clinging in little coils to her damp, flushed cheeks.

"What would the hours be, again?" I ask.

"That's the best part! Nine to four. You'd get her breakfast, fix lunch—she naps in the afternoon, so you'd have time free. Her son wants someone to start on Monday. It's three times what your dad can pay. For a lot less work. A good deal, Gwen."

She lays out this trump card cautiously, sliding the "*you need to do this*" carefully underneath the "*you want to do this.*" Whatever Nic and I can pull in during the summer helps during the Seashell dead zone, the long, slow months when most of the houses close up for the season—when Mom has fewer regulars, Dad shuts down Castle's and does odd jobs until spring, and Em's bills keep coming.

"What about her own family?" I ask.

Mom hitches a shoulder, up, down, casual. "According to Henry, they won't be there. He does something on Wall Street, is super-busy. The boys are grown now—Henry says they don't want to spend their whole summer on a sleepy island with their grandma the way they did when they were younger."

I make a face. I may have my own thoughts about how small and quiet Seashell can be, but I live here. I'm allowed. "Not even to help their own grandmother?"

"Who knows what goes on in families, hon. Other people's stories."

Are their own.

I know this by heart.

Emory bounces back into the room with Mom's fuzzy slippers—a matted furry green one and a red, both for the left foot. Reaching out for Mom's leg, he pulls off the remaining sneaker, rubs her instep.

"Thanks, bunny rabbit," Mom says as he carefully positions one slipper, repeating the routine on the other foot. "What do you say, Gwen?" Mom leans into me, nudging my knee with hers.

"I'd have afternoons and nights free—every night?" I ask, as though this is some key point. As if I have a hoppin' social life and a devoted boyfriend.

"Every night," Mom assures me, kindly *not* asking "What's it matter, Gwen?"

Every night free. Guaranteed. Working for Dad, I usually

wind up covering the shifts no one else wants—Fridays and Saturdays till closing. With all that time open, I can have a real summer, do the beach bonfires and the cookouts. Hang out with Vivie and Nic, swim down at the creek as the sun sets, the most beautiful time there. No school, no tutoring to do, no waking up at 4:30 to time for the swim team, none of those boys . . . Running into them yesterday at Castle's was . . . yuck. Out at Mrs. E.'s, the farthest house on Seashell, I'd never have to see them.

I can practically smell my freedom—salty breezes, green sun-warm sea-grass, hot fresh breezes blowing over the wet rocks, waves splashing, white foam against the dark curl of water.

"I'll do it."

It's an island job. But only for one summer. For one family. It's not what Mom did, starting to clean houses with my Vovó, her mother, the year she turned fifteen to make money for college, still cleaning them (no college) all this time later. It's not what Dad did either, taking over the family business at eighteen because his father had a heart attack at the grill.

It's just temporary.

Not a life decision.

"Hon . . . did your dad pay you for your days yet? We're running a little behind." Mom brushes some crumbs off the couch without meeting my eyes. "Nothing to worry about, but—"

"He said he'd get it to me later in the week," I answer absently. Em has moved from Mom's feet to mine, not nearly as sore, but I'm not about to turn him down.

Mom stands, opens the fridge. "Lean Cuisine, South Beach, or good old Stouffer's tonight? Your choice."

Gag on Lean Cuisine and South Beach. She stabs the plastic top of a frozen entrée with her fork, but before she can shove it into the microwave, Grandpa Ben saunters in, his usual load of contraband slung over his shoulder, Santa Claus style. If Santa were into handing out seafood. He pushes one of Nic's sweat-stiffened bandannas to the side of the counter, unloading the lobsters into the sink with a clatter of hard shells and clicking claws.

"*Um, dois, três, quatro.* That one there must be five pounds at least." Excited, he runs his hands through his wild white hair, a Portuguese Albert Einstein.

"Papai. We can't possibly eat all those." Despite her protest, Mom immediately starts filling one of our huge lobster pots with water from the sink. "Again I ask, how long will it be until you get caught? And when you go to jail, you help us how?" Grandpa's fishing license lapsed several years ago, but he goes out with the boats whenever the spirit moves him. His array of illegal lobster traps still spans the waters off our island.

Grandpa Ben glares at Mom's plastic tray, shaking his head. "Your grandfather Fernando did not live to be one hundred and two on"—he flips the box over, checking the ingredients—"potassium benzoate."

"No," Mom tells him, shoving the tray back into the freezer. "Fernando lived to one-oh-two because he drank so much Vinho Verde, he was pickled."

Muttering under his breath, Grandpa Ben disappears into the room he shares with Nic and Em, emerging in his at-home mode—shirt off, undershirt and worn plaid bathrobe on, carrying Emory's Superman pajamas.

"Into these, faster than a speeding bullet," he says to Emory, who giggles his raspy laugh and races around the room, arms outstretched Man-of-Steel style.

"No flying until you're in your suit," Grandpa says. Em skids to a halt in front of him, patiently allowing Grandpa Ben to strip off his shirt and shorts and wrestle the pajamas on. Then he cuddles next to me on Myrtle as Grandpa fires up a Fred Astaire DVD.

Our living room's so small it barely accommodates the enormous plasma-screen TV Grandpa won last year at a bingo tournament at church. I'm pretty sure he cheated. The state-of-the-art screen always looks so out of place on the wall between a cedar-wood crucifix and the wedding picture of my grandmother. She's uncharacteristically serious in black and white, with the bud vase underneath that Grandpa never forgets to fill every day. It's a big picture, one of those ones where the eyes seem to follow you.

I can never meet hers.

Lush, romantic music fills the room, along with Fred Astaire's cracked tenor voice.

"Where Ginger?" Emory asks, pointing at the screen. Grandpa Ben's put on *Funny Face*, which has Audrey Hepburn, not Ginger Rogers.

"She'll be here in a minute," Grandpa tells him, his usual answer, waiting for Emory to love the music and the dancing so much that he doesn't care who does it.

Em chews his lip, and his foot begins twitching back and forth.

My eight-year-old brother is not autistic. He's not anything they've mapped genetically. He's just Emory. No diagnosis, no chart, no map at all. Some hard things come easy to him, and some basic things he struggles with. I wrap my arms around his waist, his skinny ribs, rest my chin on his shoulder, feeling his dark flyaway hair lift to tickle my cheek, inhaling his sun-warm, little-boy scent. "This is the one with the funny song, remember? The sunny funny-face song?"

At last Em settles, snuggled with his favorite stuffed animal, Hideout the hermit crab, in his arms. Grandpa Ben won him at some fair when Emory was two, and he's been Em's favorite ever since.

I nudge aside Fabio, go outside to the front steps, because I just can't watch Audrey Hepburn being waifish and wistful. At nearly five eleven, nobody, no matter how nearsighted, will ever say I'm waifish.

Squinting out over the island, over the roofs of the low, split-level houses across from ours—Hoop's squat gray ranch, Pam's dirty shingled white house, Viv's pale green house with the red wood shutters that don't match—I can just barely catch the dazzle of the end-of-day sun off the water. I lean back on my elbows, shut my eyes, and take a deep breath of the warm, briny air.

Which reeks.

My eyes pop open. A pair of my cousin's workout sneakers are inches from my nose. Yuck. Eau de sweaty eighteen-year-old boy. I elbow them off the porch, onto the grass.

The screen door bangs open. Mom slides down next to me, a carton of ice cream in one hand, spoon in the other. "Want some? I'll even get you your own spoon."

"Nah, I'm fine." I offer a smile. Pretty sure she doesn't buy it. "That your appetizer, Mom?"

"Ice cream," she says. "Appetizer, main course, dessert. So flexible."

She digs around for the chunks of peanut butter ripple, and then pauses to brush my hair back from my forehead. "Anything we need to talk about? You've been quiet the past day or so."

It's ironic. Mom spends most of her spare time reading romance novels about people who take their clothes off a lot. She explained the facts of life to a stunned and horrified Nic and me by demonstrating with a Barbie and a G.I. Joe. She took me to the gynecologist for the Pill when I was fifteen—"It's good for your complexion," she insisted, when I sputtered that it wasn't necessary, "and your future." We can talk about physical stuff—she's made sure of that—but only in the abstract . . . Now I want to rest my head onto her soft, freckled shoulder and tell her everything about the boys in the car. But I don't want her knowing that anyone sees me like that.

That I've given anyone a reason.

"I'm fine," I repeat. She spoons up more ice cream, face absorbed. After a moment, Fabio noses his way through the screen door, staggers up to Mom, and sets his chin on her thigh, rolling his eyes at her beseechingly.

"Don't," I tell her. Though I know she will. Sure enough, Mom scrapes out a chunk, tapping the spoon on the deck.

Fabio drops his inches-from-death act and slurps it up, then resumes his hopeful post, drooling on Mom's leg.

After a while, she says, "Maybe you could walk down to the Ellingtons'"—she wags the spoon toward Low Road—"say hiya to Mrs. E."

"Wait. What? Like a job interview? Now?" I look down at my fraying cut-offs and T-shirt, back at Mom. Then I run inside and come back with my familiar green-and-pink mascara tube. I unscrew it, flicking the wand rapidly over my eyelashes.

"You don't need that," Mom says for the millionth time, nonetheless handing me her spoon so I can check for smudges in the reflection. "No. I pretty much told her you'd take the job. It's a good one. But I don't know how many other people already know about it. And such good pay. Just get there, ground floor, remind her who you are. She's always liked you."

This is why, three minutes later, I'm toeing on my flip-flops when Grandpa Ben hurries out, his shock of curly white hair tousled. "Gwen! Take this! Tell Mrs. E. they are from Bennie *para a rosa da ilha,* for the Rose of the Island. *Mando lagostas e amor.* I send her lobsters and love."

I look down at the moist paper sack encased in Grandpa's faded rope-mesh bag, from which a pair of lobster antennae wave menacingly.

"Grandpa. It's a job interview. Sort of. I can't show up with shellfish. Especially alive."

Grandpa Ben blows out his breath impatiently. "Rose loves lobsters. Lobster salad. Always, she loved that. *Amor verdadeiro.*" He beams at me.

"True love or not, these are a long way from lobster salad."

One of the lobsters is missing a front claw but still snapping scarily at me with its other one.

"You cook them, you chill them, you make the special sauce for her to eat tomorrow." Grandpa Ben thrusts the bag at me. "Rose always loved the *lagostas*."

He's aged in the years since Vovó died, more so since Dad moved out and he moved in. Before then, he seemed as unchanging as the figureheads on a whaling ship, roughly hewn, strong, brown as oak. But his face seems to sag tonight, and I can't stand to say no to those eager chocolate eyes. So I bundle the mesh sack onto my wrist and head down the steps.

At nearly six o'clock the early summer sun is still high in the sky, the water beyond the houses bottomless bright blue, glinting silver with reflected light. There's just a bit of a breeze, and, now that I'm out of range of Nic's shoes, the air smells like cut grass and seaweed, mingled with the mellow scent of the wild thyme that grows everywhere on the island.

That's about all we have here. Wild thyme, a seasonal community of shingled mansions, a nature preserve dedicated to the piping plovers, and the rest of us—the people who mow the lawns and fix and paint and clean the houses. We all live in East Woods, the "bad" part of Seashell. Ha. Not many people would say that exists on the island. We get woods at our back and can only squint at the ocean; they get the full view of the sea—sand tumbling all the way out to the water—from their front windows, and big rambling green lawns in back. Eighty houses, thirty of them year-round, the rest open from Memorial through Columbus Day. In the winter it's like we year-rounders own the island, but every spring we have to give it back.

I'm halfway down Beach Road, past Hooper's house, past Vivien's, heading for Low Road and Mrs. Ellington, when I hear the low clattery thrum of a double lawn mower. It gets louder as I walk down the road closer to the water. The rumble builds, booming as I turn onto Low Road, where the biggest beachfront houses are. The maintenance shack on Seashell—the Field House—has these huge old stand-up mowers, with blades big enough to cut six-foot-wide swaths in everyone's yard. As I pass the Coles' house, the sound stutters to a halt.

And so do I.

Chapter Three

At first I just have to stare, the way you do when confronted with a natural wonder.

Niagara Falls.

The Grand Canyon.

Okay, I've never been to either, but I can imagine.

This summer's yard boy has climbed off the mower and is standing with his back to me, looking up at Old Mrs. Partridge, who's bellowing at him from her porch, making imperious sweeping gestures from left to right.

"Why can't you folks ever get this?" shouts Old Mrs. Partridge. She's rich, deaf, and Mom's number one candidate for undetectable poison. Not only are all the people who work for her in any capacity "you people," most of the other island residents are too.

"I'll work on it," the yard boy says, adding after a slight pause, "ma'am."

"You won't just *work* on it, you'll do it *right*. Do I make myself clear, Jose?"

"Yes." Again the pause. "Ma'am."

Old Mrs. Partridge looks up, her mouth so tight she could

bite a quarter in half. "You——" She jabs her bamboo cane out at me. "Maria! Come tell this boy how I like my lawn mowed."

Oh hell no. I take a few steps backward on the road, my eyes straying irresistibly to the yard boy.

He's turned to the side, rubbing his forehead, a gesture I recognize from Mom (Old Mrs. Partridge can get a migraine going in no time). He's in shorts, shirtless . . . broad shoulders, lean waist, tumble of blond hair bright in the sun, nice arms accentuated by the bend of his elbow. The least likely "Jose" in the world.

Cassidy Somers.

Oh, I should keep backing away now instead of what I actually do, which is freeze to the spot. But I cannot help myself.

Again.

Snagging the shirt draped over the handlebars of the lawn mower, Cass wipes his face, starts to mop under his arms, then glances up and sees me. His eyes widen, he lowers the shirt, then seems to change his mind, quickly hauling it over his head. His eyes meet mine, warily.

"Go on!" Mrs. Partridge snaps. "Tell him. How Things Are Done. You've been around here long enough. You know how I like my lawn. Explain to Jose here that he can't just mow it in this haphazard, higgledy-piggledy fashion."

I feel the sharp edge of a claw nudge under my arm and slide Grandpa Ben's bag to the ground behind me. This is bad enough without lobsters.

"Well, *Jose*," I say firmly. "Mrs. Partridge likes her lawn to be mowed very evenly. Horizontally."

"Horizontally?" he repeats, tipping his head at me slightly, the smallest of smiles tugging the corner of his mouth.

Cass. Let's not go there.

"That's right," I say. "Jose."

He leans back against the mower, head still cocked to the side. Old Mrs. Partridge has caught sight of Marco, the head maintenance guy on the island, making his final rounds with the garbage truck, and temporarily deserts us to bully him instead, railing about some hurricane that'll never make it this far up the coast.

"*You're* the yard boy on island this summer?" I blurt out. "Wouldn't you be better off—I don't know, caddying at the country club?"

Cass lifts two fingers to his forehead, saluting sardonically. "This year's flunky, at your service. I prefer yard *man*. But apparently I don't get a choice. My first name has also been changed against my will."

"You're all Jose to Mrs. Partridge. Unless you're a girl. Then you're Maria."

He folds his arms, leans back slightly, frowning. "Flexible of her."

I've barely spoken a word to Cass since those spring parties. Slipped around him in school, sat far away in classes and assemblies, shrugged off conversations. Easy when he's part of a crowd—*that* crowd—striding down the hallways at Stony Bay High like they own it all, or at Castle's yesterday. Not so simple when it's only Cass.

He's squinting at me now, absently rubbing his bottom lip with his thumb. I'm close enough to breathe in the salty ocean-scent of him, the faint trace of chlorine. Suddenly that cold spring day is vivid in my mind, closer than yesterday. *Don't think about it. And definitely not about his lips.*

He ducks his head to see my eyes. I don't know what mine show, so I direct my gaze at his legs. Strong calves, lightly dusted with springing blond hair. I'm more conscious of the ways he's changed since we were kids even than the ways I have. *Good God. Stop it.* I shift my gaze to the limitless blue of the sky, acutely aware of every sound—the sighing ocean, the hum of the bees in the beach plum bushes, the distant heart-beat throb of a speedboat.

He shifts from one leg to the other, clears his throat. "I was wondering when I'd run into you," he offers, just as I ask, "Why *are* you here?"

Cass is not an islander. His family owns a boat-building business on the mainland, Somers Sails, one of the biggest on the East Coast. He does not have to put up with the summer people. Not like us—the actual Joses and Marias.

He shrugs. "Dad got me the job." He leans down, brushing grass cuttings off the back of his leg. "Supposed to make a man of me. School of hard knocks and all that."

"Yup, we poor folk make up in maturity what we lack in money."

A flash of embarrassment crosses his face, as if he's suddenly remembered that, while we both go to Stony Bay High, I don't have a membership at the Bath and Tennis Club. "Well . . ." he says finally, "it's not a cubicle, anyway." His sweeping gesture takes in the gleaming ocean and the swath of emerald-green lawn. "Can't top the view."

I nod, try to picture him in an office. I'm most familiar with him near the water, poised to dive into the school pool or, that one summer, hurling himself off the Abenaki dock into the ocean, somersaulting in the air before crashing into the blue-black water. After a second I realize I'm still nodding away at him like an idiot. I stop, shove my hands in my pockets so violently I widen the hole in the bottom of one and a dime drops out onto the grass. I edge my foot forward, cover it.

Done with browbeating Marco, Old Mrs. Partridge tramps back up the stone path, points at Cass with a witchy finger. "Is this break time? Did I say this was break time? What are you doing, lolly-gagging around? Next thing I know you'll be expecting a tuna sandwich. You, Maria, finish explaining How Things Are Done and let Jose get to work." She stomps back into the house. I step away a few paces. Cass reaches out a hand as if to stop me, then drops it.

Silence again.

Go, I tell myself. *Just turn around and go.*

Cass clears his throat, clenches and unclenches his hand, then stretches out his fingers. "Uh . . ." He points. "I think . . . your bag is crawling."

I turn. Lobster A is making a break for it across the lawn, trailing the mesh bag and Lobster B behind. I run after it, hunched low, snatch up the bag, and suddenly words are spilling from my mouth as freely and helplessly as that dime from my pocket. "Oh I've got this job interview, sort of . . . thing, with Mrs. Ellington—down island." I wave vaguely toward Low Road. "My grandfather knows her and wants me to make lobster salad for her." I shake the lobsters back into the bag.

"Which means I have to, like, boil these suckers. I know I'm a disgrace to seven generations of Portuguese fishermen, but putting something alive into boiling water? I'm not— It's just— I mean, what a way to go—" I look up at Cass, expressionless except for one slightly raised eyebrow, and clamp my mouth shut at last. "See you around," I call over my shoulder, hurrying away.

Nonchalant. Suave. But really, are there any nonchalant, suave good-byes that involve unruly crustaceans? Not to mention that the Good Ship *Pretense of Nonchalance* sailed several blatherings ago.

"Will I?" Cass calls after me. I pick up my pace but can't resist a quick reverse look at him. He just stands there, arms still folded, watching me scurry off like some hard-shelled creature scrabbling over the seafloor. Except without the handy armor.

Chapter Four

I keep speed-walking down Low Road, my thoughts racing ahead of my feet. The yard boy is everywhere on island, all summer long. Cass will haunt my summer the way he preoccupied my spring.

I hear a sound behind me, rubber on sand, skidding. I turn, my breath catching. But it's just Vivien, bouncing over the speed bump on her old-fashioned, sky-blue Schwinn with the wicker basket, legs kicked out. She looks, deceptively, like an ad for something wholesome. Butter. Milk. Fresh fruit. Her glossy brown hair is caught up in pigtails that don't look stupid, her cheeks glowing in the heat.

"Hey!" she says. "Your mom told me where you were going. Wanted to say good luck."

"I thought you were meeting up with Nic."

Vivien flushes the way she always does at Nic's name, the thought of Nic, the sight of him. Yes, things have shifted, rearranging our childhood trio into something different.

She shakes her head. "I talked him into applying for the island painting and repair gig. He's interviewing with Marco and Tony right now. If that works out, please God, he won't have to rely on Hoop's connections to get sketchy painting jobs all over the state." She rolls her eyes. "That was a good idea... why?"

"Hoop's an idiot," I say. Nic's best friend and partner for the summer in the house-painting business, Nat Hooper, can make a disaster of anything, and Nic is far too good-natured to stop him.

I hear the *zzzzzzz* of the mower starting up again. It takes all my concentration not to look back over my shoulder. Did Vivien see Cass? She must've.

"Hey, want to work a clambake with me Friday night?" Vivie asks. "Mom and Al are catering a rehearsal dinner. Ver-ry fahn-cy. It's on the Hill—okay with that?"

"Absolutely. Nic up for it too?"

"Oh, for sure. We've got the bar covered, but low on waiters and servers. Hoop's not sure he can make it—might have 'a hot date with a special lady.' Although I'm thinking the special lady is digitized. D'you know any other guy who'd be willing?"

I can't help shifting my eyes down the road. Vivien trails my gaze, and then stares back at me with a little crinkle between her eyebrows.

"Have you seen this year's yard boy?" I ask, wary.

"Yup." She watches my face. "I gave him the gate code when he drove in to report for duty this morning."

"You didn't think to mention it to me? No warning text? Nothing?"

"Oh shit, sorry." Viv lowers her heels to regain bike balance. "I tried once, but you know how cell reception sucks here." She sneaks another look over her shoulder. "I should have kept trying."

I follow her eyes back to the Partridge house, where Cass has dutifully returned to mowing the lawn. Horizontally. Shirt off again, hair gleaming in the sun.

My God.

"What, Gwenners? Thinking of asking Cassidy to be a spare set of hands?" She tips her head at me, eyes twinkling.

"No! What? No! You know my policy. Hands *off*. Avoid at all cost."

Vivien snorts. "You sure? Because you're getting that glazed look that leads to bad judgment, impulsive decision-making, and a walk of shame."

Even though it's Vivie, no real criticism there, I can feel my face go red. I look down at the ground, kick aside a pebble. "There were only two actual walks of shame."

Vivien's face sobers. She flings her leg over the bike and knocks back the kickstand, moves closer. "Cassidy Somers . . . right here on the island. Just . . . watch your step, Gwenners. Be careful with yourself." Her fierce expression is so at odds with her sweet face and my childhood nickname that I want to laugh, but there's a little twist in my stomach too.

We all can't be Vivie and Nic.

My cousin and my best friend have been an item since we were all five, when I ceremonially performed their wedding service on Sandy Claw Beach. Since we were more familiar with boat launchings than weddings, I bashed them both on the knees with a bottle of apple juice.

How many people, honestly, get the guy they've loved all their lives treating them like they're rare and precious and deserving of adoration? Hardly anyone, right?

Still, there's a big gap between that and some unseemly scuffling in the sand.

Or a bunk bed.

Or a Bronco.

"Gwen!" Vivie snaps her fingers. "Stay with me, here. Remember your promise. Want your dad to catch you rolling around on the beach again, like with"—she hesitates, lowers her voice—"Alex?"

I cringe, turn my back on the Partridges' lawn. Then I hold up one hand, resting the other on an imaginary Bible. "I remember. From now on, I will not, no matter how tempted, get even close to a compromising position with someone unless I love them and they love me."

"And?"

"And unless we've passed a lie detector test to prove this," I finish obediently. "But I have to say, *that's* going to be awkward. Carrying around all the equipment, setting it up . . ."

"Just stay out of the sand dunes. And far away from those parties on the Hill," Vivien says. "When it's real love, no equipment necessary. You just look in their eyes and it's all there."

"Go apply for that job at Hallmark *right this instant!*" I swat her on the shoulder. She ducks away, kicking the bike back into gear, laughing.

I wouldn't pass the lie detector test myself if I didn't say that, oh, I want what Vivien and Nic found without even having to search. I give one last look over my shoulder at the back of Cass' uptilted head, as Mrs. Partridge once again bellows at him from the porch.

Chapter Five

The Ellington house is the last one on the beach—big, turn-of-the-last-century, graceful, stretching along the shore like a contented cat in the sun. It's got weathered dove-gray shingles and gray-green trim, two turrets, and a porch that sweeps three-quarters around, like the tail of a cat cozying close.

Taken with all that, the carport where Mrs. E.'s Cadillac is parked looks so . . . wrong. There should be a carriage house there, an eager groom in livery waiting to take the reins of your horse.

I walk up the side path to the kitchen door, wondering if this is the correct thing to do. You never know on the island. Half the houses Mom cleans welcome her in the front and offer her a drink, the other half insist she go around back and take off her shoes.

Toeing off my flip-flops, I look down at my feet, wishing for a second I had dainty ones like Viv, or that my nails were decorated with polish and not a Band-Aid from stubbing my toe on the seawall.

Mrs. Ellington's glossy oak side door is propped open by a worn brick, but the screen door is closed. "Hi . . . ?" I call down the shady hallway. "Um, hello? . . . Mrs. Ellington?"

A television murmurs in the distance. A porcelain clock shaped like a starfish ticks loudly. From where I am I can see the gleam of a silver pitcher on the kitchen table, a tumble of zinnias glowing in it. I put my hand on the screen door, poised to push it open, then hesitate and call out again.

This time, the TV is immediately silenced. Then I hear *click/ thump, click/thump* coming down the hardwood floor of the hallway, and there's Mrs. Ellington. Her hair's whiter and she's holding a cane, one ankle tightly wrapped in an Ace bandage, but she's still beautifully dressed, pearls on, smile broad.

"Gwen! Your mother says you are Gwen now, not Gwennie. I'm *delighted* to see you." Propping her cane against the wall, she pulls open the screen door, then holds out both hands.

I slide my bag o' lobsters down behind my back and take her hands, her skin loose and fragile as worn silk.

"So you're to be my babysitter this summer! How it does come round," Mrs. Ellington continues. "When you were tiny, I used to hold you in my lap on the porch while your mother cleaned. You were a dear little thing . . . those big brown eyes, that cloud of curls."

There's a note of melancholy in her voice when she uses the word *babysitter* that makes me say, "I'm just here to be—"A friend? A companion? A watchdog? "I'm just here to keep you company."

Mrs. Ellington squeezes my hands, lets them go. "That's lovely. I was just getting ready to enjoy a nice cool drink on the porch. How do you like your iced tea?"

I don't drink tea, so I draw a blank. Luckily Mrs. Ellington steams ahead. "It was quite warm this morning, so I made a big batch of wild cranberry, which should be perfect now. Personally, I adore it cold and very sweet with lemon."

"That sounds good," I say, glancing around the kitchen. It looks the same as when Nic and I were little—morning-sky-pale-blue walls, appliances creamy white, navy-and-white checked cloth on the table, another Crayola-bright bunch of zinnias in a cobalt glass pitcher on the counter.

When Mom makes iced tea it's a two-step process—scooping out the sugary powder and mixing it with cold water. Mrs. Ellington's iced tea is a production involving implements I never knew existed. First there's the bucket for ice and special silver tongs. Then the lemon and another silver thingie to squeeze it. Then a little slanted bowl to set the tea bag in. Then another little bowl for the squeezed lemon.

Mrs. E.'s blue-veined hand opens the cabinet, flutters like a trapped bird, hovering between two glass canisters. After a second, she selects one, the one with rice in it. The one I know from years of coastal weather must contain the salt. Rice keeps salt from sticking in the moist heat. She places it on the counter, starting to screw off the top.

I put my hand on top of hers gently. "I think maybe it's the other one."

Mrs. Ellington looks up at me, her hazel eyes blank for a moment. Then they clear, clouds moving away from the sun. She touches her fingers to her temple. "Of course. Ever since that silly fall I've been all in a muddle." She shifts the canister back onto the shelf, takes down the other one.

Then scooping the sugar into a silver canister . . . and some sort of scalloped spoon . . . This process was obviously designed by someone who didn't have to do their own dishes. Or polish their own silver. Mrs. Ellington again asks me how I like my tea, and I want to say "with everything" just to see how it all works. But I repeat "Cold and sweet," so she removes a frosted-cold glass from the freezer. She blends sugar in the bottom and finally pours tea for me, then does the same for herself.

"Let's have this on the porch," she suggests.

I start to follow her, but remember Grandpa Ben's gift. Just in time. One of the lobsters is again crawling for its life, this time scrabbling down the hallway toward the back door. I hastily snatch it up and put it, indignantly waving claws and all, back into the soggy paper bag.

I'd have expected Mrs. Ellington to be horrified, hand pressed against her heart, but instead she's laughing. "Dear Ben Cruz," she says. "Still setting those traps?"

"Every week all summer." I open the refrigerator, shove the bag in, hoping that Houdini the lobster and its cohort will be stupefied by the cold before I have to slay them. I pass on Uncle Ben's message, translated entirely from Portuguese.

Mrs. Ellington sets down her cane again to clasp her hands together. "Lobsters and love. Two essentials of life. Do come with me to the porch, Gwen dear—if you wouldn't mind carrying the glasses? There we can discuss the *other* essentials of life."

The porch too—just exactly the same—all old white wicker furniture with the worn, teal-colored hammock swaying in the breeze. The Ellingtons' wide lawn fades into sea oats, sand, and then the azure ocean. To the far left is Whale Rock, a huge boulder that looks exactly like a beached humpback whale. At high tide all you can see is the fin, but the water's low now and almost the entire rock is visible. The view's so stunning, I catch my breath, with the feeling I always have when I see the prettiest parts of the island—that if I could look out my window at this all the time, I would be a better person, calmer, happier, less likely to get flustered with school or impatient with Dad. But that theory can't really work, because Old Mrs. Partridge up the road has one of the best views on the island—I mean of the water, not of Cass Somers—and it doesn't sweeten her disposition at all.

Mrs. Ellington clinks her glass against mine. "Here's to another sunset," she says.

I must seem puzzled, because she explains, "My dear father's favorite toast. I'm quite superstitious. I don't think I've ever had a drink on the porch without saying it. You must answer 'Sunrise too.'"

"Sunrise too," I say, with a firm nod.

She pats me approvingly on the leg.

"I imagine we should negotiate our terms," Mrs. E. says.

Damn. I stammer out something about the salary Mom mentioned—she must have been wrong, it had to be too good to be true—and Mrs. Ellington chuckles. "Oh, not money. That's all been settled by your mother and my Henry, I suspect. I meant terms as in how we will rub along together. I haven't had a . . . companion before, so, naturally, I need to know what you enjoy doing and you need to know the same about me, so we don't spend the summer torturing each other. I must say . . . it will be good to be around a young person again. My grandsons . . ." She trails off. "Are off, living their lives." For a second, all eighty-plus years show on her face as her usual smile fades.

I have a flash of memory of some big party she held for one of the grandsons. His wedding? Twenty-first birthday? Big tent. White with turrets. Almeida's catered. There were fireworks. Nic and Viv and I . . . and Cass . . . lay on the beach and watched them burst and glimmer into the ocean. A private party with a public show. Like the ocean, no one owns the sky.

After a moment, she continues, resolutely. "As they should be. Now, do tell me all about yourself!"

Uh . . . What "all" does she want to know? The kind of "all" I tell Viv is different from the "all" I tell Mom, so God knows what the "all" is to someone who might want to employ me, and . . .

As if hearing my mental babbling, she again pats me on the knee. "For example, how do you feel about the beach, dear Gwen? Like it or loathe it?"

Does anyone on earth hate the beach? I tell Mrs. Ellington I love the ocean and she says, "Good then. My friends—we call ourselves the Ladies League, but I believe there are others on the island with less flattering names—the Old Beach Bats comes to mind . . . Anyway, we like to swim every day at ten and again at four—just as the light is shifting. Sometimes we make a picnic and have a day of it. The beauty of age—we really don't need to worry about sunscreen and we can linger all day." Her eyes get misty as they look out over the water, her wrinkled face softening with a dreamy expression that makes it suddenly clear how beautiful she must have been back then. The Rose of the Island, indeed.

For the next half hour we cover Mrs. Ellington's likes and dislikes, from her favorite and least favorite things to eat—"If you ever make me egg salad I shall reconsider my good opinion of you"—to her views on exercise—"I shall like good brisk walks when this silly ankle recovers but when *I'm* in the mood. I don't wish to be prodded"—to technology—"You won't be perpetually typing on or answering your cell phone, will you? When I'm in the presence of another person, I want them present."

I guess I pass the test, because Mrs. Ellington finally pats my hand and says, "Good then. Our new regime will start on Monday." She beams at me, lowering her voice. "I was dreading this. I am a creature who enjoys solitude. But I think, bless fortune, I may be lucky in my employee."

I thank her, and then remember I have to cook the lobsters. Hell. *Does she even want me to do this now? Or am I dismissed? If I am, can I leave her with living lobsters? Should she even be using a stove?* Nic got a concussion playing soccer in middle school and he was out of it for days. I'm about to ask her what she'd like me to do when there's a knock on the screen door, forceful enough to rattle the loosely nailed boards. A voice calls, "Uh—hello? Seashell Services!"

"I wonder what that can be." Mrs. Ellington's eyes brighten as if a visit from the island maintenance crew is cause for excitement. "The hydrangeas aren't due to be pruned and we had the lawn mowed only yesterday. Do let's go see."

Though her back is as straight as ever, her gait is so wobbly, despite the steadying cane, that I waver behind her, trying to be on both sides at once to break her inevitable fall.

"Hullo?" the voice calls again, slightly louder. More recognizable.

"Com-i-ng!" sings out Mrs. Ellington. "Do come in! My progress is gradual, but we will be there in good time!"

I wish her progress were nonexistent, because far too quickly we reach the kitchen, where, yes, Cass is standing, looking particularly tan against the dainty ruffles of the sheer white curtains.

"My dear boy!" Mrs. Ellington says.

How has he managed to be her dear boy after just one day spent mowing her lawn? Does she remember him from that one summer? Old Mrs. P. didn't.

"Gwen, dear. This is Cassidy Somers, who will be keeping the island beautiful for us this summer. Cassidy, this is my new"—she hesitates, and then continues firmly—"this is Guinevere Castle."

I wince. Concussion or not, Mrs. E. recalls my whole, real, hopelessly romance-novel name. Which I never use at school. Or anywhere. Ever.

Unfazed, Cass extends his palm cheerfully. "Hello again, Gwen."

I ignore his outstretched hand. "We've met," I say, turning quickly to Mrs. Ellington. "We know each other. Um, not that well. That is, we're not friends. I mean . . . We don't have that much in common . . . Or know each other at all, really. We just . . . we go to high school together." I conclude these ravings, not looking at Cass, and wait miserably for Mrs. Ellington to decide I'm a lunatic.

Instead, she smiles gently at me. "Schoolmates. How lovely.

Well, then, I do believe our gentleman caller could benefit from some of our iced tea. Will you do the honors, Gwen?"

I nod, opening the freezer to scoop out the ice and, with luck, cool my blazing face. Grateful I don't have to mess with all the silverware, I pour tea into an iced tumbler and hand it to him, trying to avoid any contact with his fingers. Which means that the sweaty glass nearly crashes to the ground. Good thing Cass has fast reflexes.

Mrs. Ellington flutters next to him, apologizing for not asking if he takes lemon and sugar.

"No, just as it pours is great. Thanks."

"It is terribly easy to become parched in this heat," Mrs. Ellington says, "particularly when in the throes of physical exertion. You must feel free to come by my house at any time to get something tall and cool."

Cocking his head at her, Cass gives her his best smile. "Thank you."

He chugs the iced tea. I watch the long line of his throat, look away, wipe my fingers on my cut-offs. My palms are actually damp. Fantastic.

"Perhaps a refill for him, Gwen? Now, dear boy, why *are* you here? If it is in regard to the bills, those all go to my son Henry."

"It's not that," Cass says swiftly. "I'm here to boil your lobsters."

My head whips around sharply.

"We've been looking to expand our list of services," he continues, calm and reasonable. "Competitive times and all that." His eyes cut to mine and then away again.

36

"Really?" Mrs. Ellington moves closer, as though he's a magnet with an irresistible pull. "How so?"

"Well . . . um, seems as though the yard boy usually just mows and weeds. And"—Cass takes a long slug of iced tea—"I think . . . there's room for more. Dog walking. Grocery runs. Um . . ." He looks up briefly at the ceiling as though reading words off it. "Swimming lessons."

"Enterprising!" Mrs. Ellington exclaims.

Cass tosses her another smile, and then continues. "When I saw Gwen here heading over with your, uh, dinner, I thought it might be a good time to show you my technique."

"You have a *technique?*" Mrs. Ellington clasps her hands under her chin, a happy child at a birthday party. "How accomplished! I wasn't aware there was any such thing with regard to lobsters."

"Technique might not be the right word," Cass says. "Where's your lobster pot?" He asks this with total assurance, like every kitchen in New England has such a thing. But yes, Mrs. Ellington does, the exact same huge, spattered black-and-white enamelware one we have at home. He pulls it out of the cabinet she opened for him and takes it to the sink, totally at home, practically toeing off his shoes and kicking back on the couch.

"You know," I say, struggling to keep my voice level, "I can do this. You don't need to—"

"Sure you can, Gwen. But I'm here."

I think my eyes actually bug out. *Him* being *here* is exactly the problem. But this is still sort of a job interview; it's not like I can arm-wrestle him for the lobsters.

He fills the pot with cold water and sets it on the stove, turning the gas up high, talking rapidly all the while. "Technique implies finesse—or skill. This isn't really that. It's just . . ." He fiddles with the knob, concentrating on lowering the flame. "Some people get bothered by the idea of cooking something alive, you know. Plus, lobsters can make that screaming sound—I've heard it doesn't really mean anything, and their nervous systems aren't well-developed enough to feel pain—their brains are the size of a ballpoint pen tip, but . . . it can still bother some people."

Oh, yes, thanks for rescuing me, Cass. I'm just so squeamish.

I don't *want* to kill lobsters. But I *can.*

"Indeed," Mrs. Ellington says. "I always made a point of leaving the kitchen when Cook boiled lobsters. Or chopped the heads off fish." She shudders reminiscently.

Cass flashes that melting smile at her again. All charm—the kind that pulls you in as surely as a hand in yours, and can hold you back just as firmly, leaving you wondering which is real, which Cass is true. As I think this, he glances over at me, straight into my eyes this time, and I'm taken aback by the expression in his. Readable for once, not guarded the way it's been since March.

Direct.

Deliberate.

Challenging.

I turn away, open the refrigerator, take out the bag of lobsters, pulling it close to my chest. He reaches for it and I hold on tighter. He pulls, gently, looking at me quizzically to see if I really will challenge him for possession of a bag of shellfish.

I let go.

"Thanks, Gwen." His voice is casual. "So, yeah, some people put the lobsters in the freezer for a while to numb them out. But that doesn't seem all that much more humane than the heat, does it?"

He disentangles Grandpa Ben's rope-mesh sack and sets the wrinkled brown paper bag that was inside it on the table. One huge claw immediately gropes out, clunking on the wooden island. Despite a stint in the Sub-Zero, Lobster A has not lost its mighty will-to-live.

"They say," Cass continues, dipping his hand into the bag, "that if you kill the lobster too far ahead of time, it gets all tough and then it's no good for eating."

He twists Lobster A right and left to avoid its clinging claws. "Look away, Gwen."

I'm not used to the note of command in that laid-back voice and instantly fix my gaze out the window on the beach plum's fuchsia blossoms, then shake myself. "I can handle this," I repeat to Cass. Then, trying to sound brisk and casual: "It's in my blood, remember?"

"There," he says, ignoring me. "Just a quick knife to the brain and then into the very hot water. No time to feel a thing."

Mrs. Ellington claps her hands. "That does relieve my mind. It seems to work. No waving claws. None of that awful sound."

"I'm done now, Gwen. You can look." It's an aside. Quiet, not mocking.

"I *am* looking," I mutter, feeling suddenly adrift.

"These guys are, what, one-and-a-half-pounders? So fourteen minutes or so." He reaches for the egg-shaped timer on the stovetop, deftly twists it. "I can stay and take 'em out if you like."

I clear my throat. "You can go. I'm fine. I'll take it from here."

"You are a marvel, young man!" says Mrs. Ellington. "I am delighted by Seashell Services' new policy. Dare I hope you also clean fish?"

"I do whatever needs doing." Cass flicks me a quick glance, then grins at her again, that wide, slightly lopsided smile that creases the corners of his eyes. "Thanks for the iced tea. It was the best I've ever had. See you later, Mrs. Ellington."

He crumples the soggy brown lobster bag and tosses it to the trash can. It bounces off the side. Without looking at us, he scoops it up, drops it directly in, then turns down the hall.

His "Bye Gwen" is so quiet it's barely a whisper. But I hear it.

"What a kind young man," Mrs. Ellington says. "Handsome too."

I examine the lobsters bobbling in the water, now vivid red and motionless, and stare at the ticking timer. With ten minutes to go, I pour Mrs. Ellington more tea and start on Grandpa Ben's sauce. She watches, bright-eyed and interested, murmuring occasional comments. "Oh yes, of course. How could I have forgotten the sour cream? Dear Ben Cruz had this down to a science."

I'll have to ask Grandpa Ben how it is that Mrs. Ellington knows his secret recipe for lobster salad. Sauce finished, I dump the rosy lobsters into a colander, running cold water over them and hoping it'll cool me down too. I feel weirdly off balance.

"These will be perfect for lunch tomorrow," I tell Mrs. E.

over my shoulder, trying to sound breezy. "Unless you want them for dinner tonight, in which case I can make a butter sauce. Or hollandaise."

"Oh no!" she says. "I want Ben's lovely sauce with chilled lobster. I will make do tonight. In fact." She cocks her head, then calls out, "*Joy!*"

Just as I'm worried she's lost her mind for real, the door opens and a tired-looking woman in hospital scrubs comes in from the carport. "Yuh-huh, Mrs. El? I'm here."

"Well hello, Joy! This is Guinevere Castle, who is to keep me out of mischief during the day. Gwen, this is my night nurse. Joy, will you show her out? I find myself a bit fatigued with all the excitement of the day."

Joy leads the way through the porch hallway into the carport, hauling her gray hoodie off over her head and hanging it on a hook on the wall. "So you're the babysitter."

That word makes me uncomfortable. "I'm here to keep Mrs. Ellington company during the day, yes."

Joy grunts. "You'll be getting the same amount of money I am, without medical training. Makes no sense. That son of hers has more cash than brains, if you ask me."

I don't really know what to say to that, so I stay quiet.

"She needs a trained nurse twenty-four/seven, after a fall like that. Could easily have been a broken hip, and at her age that can be the beginning of the end, but the family just won't accept it. I got no patience with them."

Maybe you shouldn't work here then, I think, and then want to scratch the thought out. Here on island, how many of us have a choice, really? Joy opens the latticed screen door to the carport and I walk out, grateful our shifts won't coincide much.

Outside, I halt, listening. Over the soft roar and shush of the waves, I hear the lawn mower thrumming again, farther down Low Road. Even though it's the longer way home, I turn uphill in the direction of High Road.

How am I going to get through a whole summer of constant Cass? I'll have to ask Marco and Tony what his schedule is . . . Right. "Tony? Marco? Your yard boy's a little too hot for me to handle, and now he's getting on my nerves too, so if you wouldn't mind ordering him to wear a shirt? Grow some unsightly facial hair, pack on a few pounds, and stay clear of Mrs. E.'s? Thanks a bunch."

I pick up my pace, and then turn into the small, beaten-down clearing in the Green Woods at the bend in the road. Maple trees arch and curl their branches over me, making the path a tunnel. The air smells earthy and tangy green. These woods have been the same for hundreds of years. When we were little, Nic, Vivie, and I used to play a game where we were the Quinnipiacs, the first people to live on Seashell. We tried to tread soundlessly in the forest, one foot in front of another, not even snapping a twig. Now a turn by a twisted branch, then another by an old stone shaped like a witch's hat, and I'm out in the open again, by the rushing creek that runs into the ocean, cleared only by a bridge so old that the wood is silver and the nails rusty dark red. I climb to the apex of the bridge, look down at the water, clear enough to see the stones at the bottom but deep enough to be well over my head. I shuck off the T-shirt I'm wearing over my black sports bra, kick off my sneakers, climb to the highest point of the bridge, and jump.

Chapter Six

The water is an icy shock, stripping away any fears or feelings. I blast up toward the surface, emerge, take a deep, gasping breath of air, then plunge back down into the cold depths, push off from the pebbly bottom, flip toward the surface, turn on my back, eyes closed, lazily breathing in the difference between the icy water and the still, summer air.

Rising in me, I know, is what I've been trying to avoid. For months. I open my eyes, let the memory lap at the edges of my thoughts, then close them again, and give in.

They call it the Polar Bear Plunge, which doesn't really make sense because it's held in the spring—and here in Connecticut, polar bears are pretty damn scarce.

But ocean water in March in Connecticut is the stuff of hypothermia. And the Polar Bear Plunge is Stony Bay High Athletic Department's big spring fundraiser. There's always a bonfire, and the cheerleaders and the PTO bring hot cider and yell encouragements as the athletes run into the icy water. Parents and people from town show up—to bet on who stays in the water longest, who will swim out farthest. This year, since Vivien was cheer captain and Nic was on the swim team, which

I'd been timing for all year, I got up at seven a.m. and went with them to watch.

The morning was blinding bright and extra cold. There'd been one of those freakish heavy coastal snowstorms the week before, and patches of snow still drifted in the tall sea oats. I wanted to stay in Vivien's warm car with the heat on nuclear, but Nic was in swim trunks and Vivie wearing her skimpy cheer outfit with only Nic's sweatshirt pulled over it. So I got out and stood by the bonfire in the name of supporting the football team, the field hockey team, the soccer team, the baseball team, the basketball team, and the swim team.

Plenty of show-offs all around, stripping down and striking muscle or cheesecake poses to hoots and whistles from the well-bundled crowd. Hooper, though small, was speedy and mighty confident for a skinny, pale guy. Ugh, and he was wearing a Speedo. Gross, Hoop.

I clasped my fingers around a foam cup of cider, blowing into it to feel the warm steam on my face, then heard a rustle of movement next to me, felt this prickle of awareness across my skin, and turned. It was Cass. He'd shucked off his parka and shirt and was now unbuttoning the top of his faded jeans, revealing navy swim trunks.

I expected him to be out putting on a show like the others. Even Nic, hardly an exhibitionist, swirled his sweatshirt on a finger with a grin before tossing it to Vivien. But Cass was alone, quietly undressing. Right next to me.

I assumed he didn't realize who I was. I'd grabbed Mom's parka on the way out the door, and with the hood tipped up I had all the sex appeal of the Goodyear Blimp.

He hesitated, then kicked his pants and the rest of his discarded clothes into a pile farther from the fire.

"Bet on me, Gwen?"

I looked at him. Shivered. Shook my head.

"You should. Nic and Spence are the flashy ones with all the strokes, but I'm all about going the distance. And endurance."

"I'm not the betting kind." I took a sip of my cider, breathed in the apple-cinnamon-scented steam, added quietly, "Good luck."

He opened his mouth as if he wanted to say something, then shook his head and loped off. I tried unsuccessfully not to follow him with my eyes as he strode through the crowd, but . . . Those nice shoulders, the V of his upper body tapering down. I mean, it was purely aesthetic. Who wouldn't look?

The opening air horn blasted, shrill, ear-splitting. Everyone plunged into the water. Jimmy Pieretti, ever the comedian, was wearing a yellow-and-white polka-dot bikini, although I couldn't imagine where he found one that fit. Nic got delayed by Vivie's good-luck kiss. There was a lot of splashing and yelling and swearing.

"Quit your bellyaching and focus!" Coach Reilly bawled through his bullhorn. Through the crowd, I saw Cass dive into the water, then slice through the surf, shoulders and forearms flashing in a fast crawl. Yes, there were chunks of ice. I marveled at some people's school spirit. You couldn't have made me take that plunge for anything less than world peace or having Emory's medical expenses paid for life.

I walked down closer to the water, where Vivien was jumping up and down with the other cheerleaders.

45

"Shake it, shake it, Stony Bay. Swim it, swim it, all the way."

About twenty kids had already lurched back out of the water toward the bonfire. Nic was sticking it out, but he looked crimson with cold. Jimmy Pieretti was evidently going for "Longest Time Underwater" because I could see his enormous legs sticking out in a headstand as the crowd shouted, "Jimbo, Jiiiiiiiiiimbo!" He had to top two hundred fifty pounds, but that wasn't enough insulation: his toes were blue.

Coach, a bunch of parent volunteers, everyone was watching, but I still found myself counting heads, scanning the water. By the shore my whole life, I'd grown up knowing what the ocean could give, then take away in a flash.

Where was Cass? He was popular, but no one was chanting his name the way they were for Jimmy or even Hoop, who had dashed out of the water to throw up on Coach Reilly's shoes.

Where was Cass? Someone could easily have drowned in this noisy, yelling crowd, without anyone noticing.

I ran to the edge of the water, shielded my eyes from the bright sun dazzling off the waves, seeing black spots dancing in front of me. But no blond head. The race had been going on for at least five minutes, maybe more.

"Coach. Coach! Where's Cass Somers?" I pulled at his sleeve as he raised the bullhorn again, my voice panicky. "Can you see him? Do you have binoculars?"

"Which one of you morons spiked the cider?" Coach bellowed. "You guys are disastrous. What the hell!"

I yanked at his sleeve again, and he turned, face ruddy against his thick black hair. "Not now, Gwen." He tried to sound gen-

46

tle. Coach had always been good to me, maybe because my dad's restaurant donated food and ice cream for the beginning and end-of-year rallies. "Got a public relations disaster here. If the PTO finds out about the cider, we can kiss this fund-raiser good-bye."

"I can't see Cassidy Somers. He's in the water somewhere." I tried to haul Coach with me into the waves, which were HOLY FROSTBITE frigid. My skin felt like it was being peeled off with a thousand knives carved from ice. Coach remained motion-less, a red-faced Rock of Gibraltar. So I yanked off my parka, tossed it to the sand, waded in up to my knees, my waist, my armpits.

"Gwen! What the hell are you doing?" Vivien shouted. "Are you insane?"

Now everyone was back on shore, except me, in my cling-ing jeans and soggy hoodie, and there was a splash and Cass surfaced right in front of me, eyes wide and blue, hair plas-tered over his forehead, darkened to shifting shades of amber and gold by the water. He gave his head a shake, tossing his hair out of his eyes.

"I . . ." My teeth were chattering. My whole body was trem-bling. Cass too was shuddering so hard, I could feel his legs buck against mine. "I thought you'd drowned."

He didn't say anything, just reached out and wrapped an arm around my waist, stumbling as he tried to steer me to shore.

I was shaking and he was breathing hard and fast. I wasn't sure who was holding up who, but he'd been in the water lon-

47

ger and I had the sense that I was towing him. Coach wasn't even watching us, having headed up to the bonfire to cuss out his wayward team.

"I th-thought you'd drowned," I repeated when we got to land. Vivien was holding out one of the big quilts from the back of her mom's car. Cass's fingers swiped at it, but didn't close. It was me who grabbed it and shook it open, reaching for his waistband to pull him close to me under the quilt. Smack against him, I could feel his heart racing.

"Thank you," he said. "I w-w-wasn't drowning, but if I had been, that would h-h-have been an awesome rescue. As it was, it was plenty am-m-mazing." His breath was white in the frigid air but felt warm on my face and now I was conscious that my hands were tight on his cold waist and I was practically thigh to thigh with Cass Somers.

Coach came over at this point. "You aced the distance and length record, Somers. Maybe the personal stupidity one too."

Cass nodded, game face, neither gratified or abashed. Then he looked over at me. "Can we g-give G-Gwen the Lifeguard of the Year award, Coach? She *w-was* trying to save me."

Coach snorted. "All you two need saving from is your own foolishness. Didja even kick off your shoes, Castle?"

I wiggled my wet toes in my hiking boots. "N-no."

"Glad you're not on my team," Coach huffed. "You gotta think on your feet." He scanned the beach for Mrs. Santos, the school nurse, but she was bent over Hooper, face concerned.

Coach sighed. "Always that guy," he said. "Scat, kids. The bonfire's not going to do it for you. Go someplace warm. And lose those sopping clothes, pronto."

48

I *was* someplace warm. Cass's arm was tight around my shoulder. It was thirty degrees, tops, but I felt hot.

"Can you drive me home?" he asked. "I came here with Pieretti and I think he's w-wasted." In addition to the chattering teeth, his voice sounded slurry.

"Well, that was a given," I said. "Can't you be the designated driver? Or, oh, were you drinking too?"

"N-no. My lips are j-just numb. B-but frostbite may be setting in." He held one whitish blue hand outside the blanket, flexing it gently, wincing. "I can't feel my fingers. Doesn't seem safe to wait. Jimbo's car's got a stick shift. Hang on."

He disentangled himself from the quilt, and my arms, and walked slowly up the beach toward the bonfire. Vivien immediately scooted to my side.

"What's going on?" She gathered the quilt folds around me more securely. "What's up with you and Sundance?"

"Nothing. I thought he was d-drowning. He wasn't." I gave a short laugh. "End of story."

"I doubt that." She ducked around to the other side of me as Cass returned, carrying his clothes and Converse.

"All set," he said. "Thorpe is d-driving Pieretti home. You can drive me—can you handle a s-stick? Pieretti can grab it when he sobers up. Then I'll bring you home."

I found myself saying only, "I can drive a stick," concentrating on pulling Mom's parka back up. After lying on the cold beach sand, it felt like an ice pack.

"Cool." He put a hand on my down-covered back, steering me to Jimmy's car up in the beach parking lot.

It was a Kia. Why did huge Jimmy Pieretti have the smallest

car in the world? I squelched my way into the driver's seat, shivering again. I'm sure my lips matched the navy-blue vinyl seats.

"Here." Cass tossed the keys to me. I snagged them in midair, and he smiled at me, the sidelong curl revealing his dimples, crinkling the corners of his eyes, taking his face from perfect to real. When I turned the keys in the ignition, he snapped on the hot air, which blasted glacial currents at us.

"It'll heat up in a minute."

"That's okay. I'm f-f-fine."

"Gwen, you're a Popsicle." He dropped his clothes in my lap. "P-put these on."

My face heated instantly. "I c-c-can't do that!"

He folded his arms. "Want me to do it f-for you?" He flexed his fingers. "As soon as the numbness and tingling go away . . . But I thought you m-might not wanna wait that long."

"It's fine. I'll just change later." I notched up the heat a few more degrees. It seemed to get even colder.

"C'mon. I can't have your f-freezing to death on my con-science." He said all this in a flat, logical tone without glancing over at me. "Just change."

"Here?"

"Well, I th-thought you might like the privacy of the back-seat, but whatever my fearless rescuer w-wishes."

"You want me to take off my clothes in the backseat?" I echoed, like an idiot.

"C-can't get warm if you just put the dry clothes on over wet ones," he told me, still in that serious, scientific way. "So, yeah, d-ditch yours, put on mine. I'll wear my parka over my suit. It's fine. But do it fast. I'm f-freezing." He shuddered.

His clothes were faded jeans, a black turtleneck, thick woven gray wool socks. Sandy, but not dripping wet or icy cold. I stumbled over the stick shift and into the backseat, unzipped Mom's parka, then halted, my eyes flicking to his in the rear-view mirror. "No looking."

"Damn. I was hoping you'd forget about the m-mirror. No problem. I'll just shut my eyes. I'm getting kind of warm and drowsy, anyway. Must be the hypothermia c-coming on."

I tried to move quickly. My drenched hoodie made a wet slapping sound as I yanked it over my head and onto the back-seat. My fingers were too stiff to undo the clasp of my bra, so I just left it on. Though I'd forbidden Cass to do so, I couldn't avoid a glance in the rearview mirror. Fantastic. My hair stood out in icy-dark Medusa curls, my nose was red, and my lips, yes, blue with cold. I'd never looked more bedraggled in my life. I shoved myself into Cass's clothes and stumbled back over the seat.

Cass did indeed have his eyes closed; his head slanted back against the headrest, his black parka bundled around him. There was a silver strip of duct tape on the shoulder, starkly bright against the black. He looked pale. Had he really gone to sleep? Into a hypothermic coma? I bent over to take a closer look.

He opened his eyes, smiling. I caught my breath. He moved in infinitesimally closer, dark lashes fluttering closed, just as Coach rapped hard on the window.

"C'mon, you two clowns. Get a move on. This isn't a drive-in movie."

We were silent after that as I pulled out of the parking

lot, through town, following Cass's mumbled directions. He reached out, flexing his fingers, then drumming them against the dashboard.

I tried to drive resolutely but couldn't resist a few stolen glances.

Always when he was doing the exact same thing.

It was strange. Like a dance. One I'd never done.

"First left up here," he said. I turned onto one of those quiet, tree-lined streets with wide, paved sidewalks and generously spaced houses with their rolling lawns. So different from the scrubby twisted pine bushes, crushed clamshell driveways, and shoulder-to-shoulder ranch homes of my side of Seashell. "You turn down this road." He indicated a right onto a drive with a sign that said "Shore Road."

I couldn't help but gasp when I saw the house. It was unlike anything I'd ever seen . . . Modern, but somehow old-fashioned, built along the long strong lines of a sailing ship, a schooner, a clipper ship—something majestic poised to conquer the sea. One whole side of the house was bowed out with a narrow rail around the second story, high and proud, jutting like the prow of a boat.

"Wow."

Cass tilted his head at me. "My uncle designed it. That's what my parents were building—that summer."

"It's amazing. This was where you went? When you left us?" Then I winced because . . . because the Somerses were on the island for one season. It's not like they abandoned us. Me. But Cass didn't blink.

"Yeah. My brothers still rag on me because I mostly got

52

to grow up here and they were already off to college. Down there"—he pointed down the low hill, grass turning to sea grass, tumbling softly down to the ocean—"there's a good stretch of beach. Just ours. It's beautiful. I'd like to show it to you. But not now. We'd both freeze."

A mansion. No one could call this anything but that. Not a house. An estate. It reminded me a bit of Mark Twain's house, where we went on a school field trip once. But that was built to look like a riverboat, and this could only be a sailboat. The yard had all these big trees, a wrought-iron bench under a willow, a fountain even. It looked like something from *Perfect Life* magazine.

A mansion and a private beach.

I did not belong here.

"I'm glad you didn't drown," I said, at the exact moment he said, "Thanks for wading in after me."

"It was nothing," I added, just as he said, "Gwen—"

We both stopped. His eyes were the darkest, purest blue. The ocean in winter.

"Look . . . My parents are going away tomorrow for a week. I thought I'd live the high school cliché and have a party. Will you come?" He'd somehow moved closer again, smelling like the best of the coast: salt water, fresh air.

I leaned toward him without meaning to, without a clear thought in my head, and he bent forward and kissed me. It was such a good, sweet kiss—a simple press of the lips at first until I opened, wanting more, and he was ready. No jamming tongues or bumping teeth. Just one smooth delicious glide and then a rhythm that made my insides jangle and had me tilting against him, gasping for breath, then diving back for more. We kissed for a long time—a long, long time—and he let that be it, only brushing his hands into my hair and gently grazing my neck with his thumbs.

"Will you come?" he repeated.

I looked back at his house, that huge house. I'd never heard of Cass having a party. Who would be there? Spence Channing. The people Cass hung out with at school. Jimmy Pieretti, Trevor Sharpe, Thorpe Minot. The Hill guys—the boys who lived on Hayden Hill, the richest part of Stony Bay. No one I knew well. A . . . a party.

And Cass.

I swallowed. "What time?"

He reached into the pocket of his parka and pulled out a blue Sharpie. Uncapping it with his teeth, he took my hand, his thumb dancing lightly over the inside of my wrist. He turned my palm closer. "How far, again, is it from your house to your dad's restaurant?"

"Three miles," I said faintly, feeling all the hairs on my arm stand on end.

He made an x on the base of my wrist, traced up to the line of my index finger, made another x, and then slid his hand down my palm, making three x's below my thumb. "An approximation," he said. Then wrote "Gwen's" by the first x, "Castle's" by the next. And "Shore Road" by the three x's. Then "Eight o'clock Saturday ni—"

"Ha!" my cousin laughs. He grabs my wrist and pulls me under, before hauling me above the water again.

I splutter and wipe my hair out of my face. "Nic! What the hell!"

"Thought I might find you here. What are you doing, crazy? You were headed straight for Seal Rock. Head-first."

I have inadvertently gulped in a mouthful of brackish water and am coughing. "I—"

He thumps me hard on the back, dislodging another series of coughs. I dive back under, come up, flicking back my hair, then notice that he's freckled with large spatters of white paint. Jackson Pollack Nic.

"What?" he asks as I frown at him.

I twitch my finger from his bespattered face to his speck-led shoulders. He looks down. "Oh. Yeah. We were doing old man Gillespie's garage ceiling. Then I went to check out the island job. Didn't have time to clean up." He scrubs his hand through his mop of sandy hair, much of which is also coated with paint. "Maybe I should have?" he offers. "Is this not a professional look for a job interview?"

I'm treading water, trying not to let myself be dragged away by the rushing creek current.

"How'd that go?"

"Aw . . . you know." Nic cups his hands in the water, splashes it on his face, slapping his cheeks. "It was what's-his-face, the island president. In his shorts with the blue embroidered whales and his effing pink shirt. He acted like it was all competitive. But I know from Aunt Luce that no one wants that painting and repair job. Too much aggravation. Almost as bad as yard boy. We've got it in the bag. Hoop's pissed."

"You've got a steady job all summer and Hooper's mad?"

Nic dunks under, bobs up. "He doesn't want to work for 'those summer snobs.' Painting, we could've headed around the state, maybe camped out on Block Island or something, whatever—gotten the hell off island, for Chrissake. Hoop'll come around, though. Anything's better than working for Uncle Mike."

Yeah. These past few years Nic has done anything and everything to avoid working for Dad. Or, lately, even having dinner with him.

My cousin whacks me on the shoulder and starts doing a fast crawl to the rocky shore. I used to be able to beat Nic every time, but since swim team, and especially since he's been training for the academy, no contest. He's nearly drip-dried; shaking the last drops off his shaggy hair, by the time I clamber up next to him and throw myself down in the sand. He tosses himself down next to me.

We lie there for a while, squinting at the evening sun filtering through the trees, saying nothing. Finally he stands up, reaches out a white-splotched hand to pull me to my feet. He glances around the shore.

I know what he's searching for. A skipping stone for Vivie. I study the sand for a thin, flat rock, but Nic's eyes are better trained, longer attuned. He finds one—"Here's a keeper"— slips it into the pocket of his soggy shorts, jerks his head toward the sandy roadside. "Hoop let me take the truck home. Party on the beach tonight. We're going to start this summer off with a bang."

Great, both Cass *and* a party on the first real day of summer. Talk about Kryptonite.

Chapter Seven

After we stop at the bridge for my clothes, we head down High Road and pass the Field House, where the mowers are stored—and where the yard boy's summer apartment is, right over the garage. But for sure Cass wouldn't be staying there—he'd be going home to that sailing ship of a house. Just in case, I scrunch lower in my seat, the peeling vinyl scraping my thighs.

Nic shoots me a look, but says nothing. I sink farther down, yawning for extra authenticity. Soon I'll be skulking around my own island in a wig and a trench coat.

"So the bonfire's on Sandy Claw tonight," Nic says. "Bo Sanders. Manny and Pam and a few more. Hoop wants to hit it, but he doesn't wanna drive home, so Viv's picking us up."

"You can drop me off at the house."

"No way, cuz. You're coming. The recluse bit is getting old. You know you love these things."

And I do. I mean, I always have. Just . . .

"You're coming," Nic repeats firmly.

"Yes, sir, Master Chief Petty Officer, sir." I salute him.

"You mean Admiral, Ensign," he corrects, elbowing me in the side. "Show some respect for the uniform I don't have yet."

I laugh at him.

No one can say Nic is unambitious. Since career night fresh-man year, he's had One Big Dream. The Coast Guard Academy in New London, Connecticut. He's got pictures of it—their sailing team, their wrestling team, on the wall of the bedroom he shares with Grandpa Ben and Emory, the Coast Guard motto—WHO LIVES HERE REVERES HONOR, HONORS DUTY—scrawled over his bed in black Sharpie, he does the workout religiously, obsesses about his grade point average . . . basically a 180 from the laid-back Nic of old, the guy who could never find his homework binder and was always looking up with a startled "Huh?" when called on in class. It's the same raw focus he's had with Vivien since childhood. One can only hope that that discipline someday extends to picking up and washing his own clothes.

"Seriously, Gwen. If I have to drag you. I can bench nearly my body weight now." He cracks his knuckles at me threateningly, then shoots me his sidelong, cocky grin.

I elbow him back. "For real? Does Coach know? How long till you can bench *him?*"

"Only a matter of time," Nic says smugly.

I burst out laughing. Coach is huge. "You really need to work on your inferiority complex, Nico."

"Just calling it like it is, cuz." Nic's smile broadens. It's quiet for a second. Then his face sobers. "I want that captain spot so bad I can taste it. It's gotta go to me, Gwen."

"Instead of Cass or Spence, who always get what they want?" A note Nic hits a lot. He was by far the star swimmer before they transferred in last September.

Nic shrugs.

I bump his shoulder with my own. "You leave them both behind every time, Admiral."

We ditch Hoop's truck in his pine-needle-covered driveway and reach our house on foot just as Vivien pulls up in her mom's Toyota Corolla. She beeps at us, waving Nic over. He leans through the window, kisses her nose, then her lips, hands slipping down to gather her closer. I look away, squeeze the dampness out of the fraying hem of my shorts.

Viv. The first serious Nic Cruz Goal I can remember.

We were eleven and twelve. I decoded the scribbly cursive in his I WILL notebook, this goal journal he kept hidden under his mattress—not a safe spot when your cousin is hunting for *Playboys*, wanting to bribe the hell out of you. But the I WILL journal proved even more useful than porn, most times.

Kiss Vivien.

I figured Hoop had dared him. Despite the wedding ceremony when we were five, I didn't think of them as a couple. It was thethreeofus. But there it was, spelled out in red pen right in the middle of his other goals: *Be next Michael Phelps. Own Porsche. Climb Everest. Find out about Roswell. Make a million dollars. Buy Beineke house for Aunt Luce. Kiss Vivien.*

For some reason, that one I didn't tease him about.

Then a few months later the three of us were sitting on the pier at Abenaki, enjoying the post–Labor Day emptiness of the beach. Nic reached into his pockets, pulled out a bunch of flat rocks.

"Pick me a winner," he'd said to Vivie. She'd cocked her head at him, a little crinkle between her eyebrows, then made a big show of finding the perfect skipper, handing it to him with a flourish.

"One kiss," he'd said softly, "for every skip."

The stone skated over the water five times, and my cousin claimed his reward from my best friend while I sat there still and silent as the pile of rocks, thinking, *I guess Hoop didn't dare him.*

"Gwen's trying to bag out on us, Vee." Nic's voice breaks into my thoughts.

Vivie shakes her head firmly. "Miss the first bonfire of the season?" she calls through the open window. "Not an option!" She reaches over, holds up a supermarket bag, shakes it at me. "I got the gear for s'mores!"

Nic has already climbed into the front passenger seat. He ducks forward, flipping it so I can climb in the back. "C'mon, cuz."

I sigh and tell them to hold up while I change my soggy clothes. When I get inside, Mom's got the phone to her ear, frowning. She holds a finger to her lips, jerking her head at the couch. Grandpa's fast asleep, head tipped back, mouth open. Emory is curled like a cashew nut, his head in his lap, snoring softly.

"Yes, I understand. Yuh-huh. Extensive cleaning. Yes. Top to bottom. Of course. By four o'clock tomorrow? Oh, well, that *is* a Saturday and—uh-huh. Okay." Mom sighs, rustling the pages of the book on her lap. "Allrighty then."

When I come back out in a baggy shirt and an even older pair of shorts, Mom's off the phone and buried in her latest bodice buster. She carefully marks her spot with a finger. "You're going out?"

I shrug. "Beach with the guys. What was that? Someone already giving you hell?"

Mom sighs again. "It's those Robinsons."

I'd already turned toward the door, but stop in my tracks.

"They're back?"

"Renting the Tucker house again for the next two weeks. Some wedding in town—cousins of theirs. Want the house to *sparkle*. By tomorrow." She rubs her thumbs over her temples. "Here for only a few weeks every few summers, and I swear, they're more trouble than half the regulars put together."

"Can you pull that off? By tomorrow?"

She shrugs. "No choice, really. I'll manage." Mom's theme song. Her glance drops to her book once again and she smiles at me wickedly. "I'll think about it later. I'm pretty sure this Navy Seal is about to find out that the terrorist he's been sent to capture is his ex-wife—and she's pregnant with his triplets . . . *and* married to his brother."

When I slide into the backseat of the car, there is the necessary interval of waiting while Nic and Vivien make out. I hum under my breath, trying to ignore the kissing noises and rustle of clothes. After a couple of minutes, I lean forward, tap each of their shoulders. "I'm right here," I whisper.

Nic looks back, wiping Vivien's shiny peach lip gloss off, winks at me. Vivien just smiles in the rearview mirror, eyes bright. Then she reads my face. "What's wrong?"

"The Robinsons are coming back," I say flatly, digging in my pocket for the mascara I grabbed from the bathroom.

She blows out a breath, ruffling the little strands of hair stealing out of her pigtails. "When?"

"Tomorrow."

"Shit," Vivie says, turning the key in the ignition, squealing backward with a jolt. Nic and I brace ourselves, his hand against the dashboard, me with my feet flattened against the back of the driver's seat. Viv jerks the car forward and revs the motor like she's in the Indy 500. She flunked her driving test three times.

"Yeah," I mutter.

Nic's leaned back now, his elbow resting on the sill of the open window. "Don't worry about it," he says.

I swallow, shrug, scratching at a mosquito bite on my thigh. Vivien roars into the driveway of Hooper's house, narrowly missing the mailbox, and leans heavily on the horn, blasting so loudly I expect it to blow leaves off the nearby trees. Without looking, Nic reaches over, lifts her hand, and kisses it. "I think you've made your point."

Hoop bounds down the steps, his hair sticking up in all directions. As usual he looks like he dressed in the dark—plaid shirt, ratty striped shorts. He whacks Nic on the back, then slides in next to me, too close. "Yo Gwenners!" he says, nudging me with a pointy shoulder.

"Hey, Hoop, whoa, can I have some space?"

"Sure, sure." He slides a fraction of an inch farther away, then smiles at me goofily. We peel down the hill, headed for the less ritzy of the Seashell beaches. The summer people stick to Abenaki, which is shielded from the open sea, has gentler waves and a less rocky beach. That's where they moor their boats. But Sandy Claw is where the local kids go, the place for illegal fireworks and loud music from someone's car speakers. In fact, the sound of the music as we drive close is so loud

Vivien has to shout to be heard. "This catering thing, tomorrow? It's got a black-and-white theme. The uniforms work fine for us, Gwen, but Nico, you'll need a dinner jacket."

Nic groans. "Tell me no tux. Please, Vee. I lose half the cash I make renting the damn thing."

"If I have to wear a monkey suit, I'm out," Hoop says. "Turns off the ladies."

Vivien's eyes widen at me in the rearview mirror, comically large. Five-foot three-inch, clothing-challenged Hoop, the chick magnet. Maybe if he'd stop calling them "the ladies."

Sandy Claw's already crowded when we get there, kids we've grown up with milling around the bonfire and the shore.

Hoop springs out of the car and heads for the cooler, brushing aside the cans of Coke and orange soda with single-minded purpose, rummaging for the beer. Vivien hauls a plaid picnic blanket from the back of the truck. She hands it to Nic, giving him her glowing, mischievous smile. After laying out the blanket, they immediately begin doing their thing. It's a testament to . . . something about Nic and Vivie that no one even bats an eye at them macking all over each other. Nic calls to me as they lie down, "Grab me a brew, cuz?"

"To drink or should I pour it on you?" I call back. He ignores me, all wrapped up—literally—in Vivien.

Pam D'Ofrio walks over next to me, says only, "Really keeping it PG tonight, aren't they?" in her flat, deadpan voice.

We're joined by Manny Morales, Marco's—the head maintenance guy's—son.

We talk for a few minutes about summer jobs—Manny's doing dishes at this place called Breakfast Ahoy, Pam's working at Esquidaro's Eats, one of Castle's rival restaurants.

"It beats babysitting," Pam says. "Last year I sat for the Carter twins. They were four and so crazy their mom insisted I put them on those leash things when I took them out. My first day, we were walking to the playground and they wrapped their leashes around a telephone pole, tied me up like a spider with a fly and ran off. Took me ten minutes to undo the knots. Little SOBs."

"Didja quit?" Manny asked.

Pam shakes her head. "No guarantee what I quit for wouldn't have been even worse."

Manny asks, "You gonna rat me out to my dad if I snag a beer?" He's sixteen and Marco's strict.

We shake our heads.

He comes back, settling down heavily next to us against the waterlogged old tree trunk that's been on the beach forever. Nic and Vivien carry on like our own private floor show.

"Must be nice," Pam says. "Being comfortable doing that. In public." She shakes her head. "Can't imagine." Pam has been with Shaunee, her girlfriend, since eighth grade.

Manny drains half the bottle, wipes his lips with the back of his hand. "At least they're putting a ring on it," he says, lifting his elbow at Nic and Vivien.

"*What?*" I ask.

"Getting hitched, right?"

I scoot back in the sand, staring at him. "What?" I say again. Then laugh. "No way. Why would you think that?"

"My brother Angelo works at Starelli's Jewelers, in the mall. Nic and Vivien were in this weekend, checking out engagement rings." Manny scratches the back of his neck, looks uncomfortable, like he just said more than he should have.

I peek over at Vivien and Nic. He's smoothing her hair back and giving her these nibbling kisses along her jawline.

It can't be true. Vivien's incapable of keeping anything to herself about Nic (*way* more than I want to know about my cousin). And Nic, while he doesn't tell me everything . . . he'd never keep a thing that big from me. Ever.

Manny's pushing at the sand with his feet, avoiding my eyes, and I realize I should have said something in return, but I can't even find words.

Getting married?

That's *crazy*.

I mean, I imagine they probably will eventually. *Eventually.* Vivien is seventeen. Nic just turned eighteen last month. . . .

Mom and Dad were seventeen and eighteen when they got married. But look how that turned out. And that was years ago. A whole different time. Nic and Viv . . . now?

"Not *that* crazy. It happens," Pam comments quietly. I didn't realize I'd spoken out loud. "Dom married Stace right out of SBH."

Yeah, and Stacy took their one-year-old and moved to Florida two years ago.

What about senior year? What about the Coast Guard?

Is Vivien pregnant? No, impossible, she's on the Pill and Nic is hyper-responsible.

I lie back on the blanket, rest my arm across my eyes, listen to the general blur of conversation. It's still warm, but the angle of the sun has that flat, end-of day slant. When I peer through the canopy of my arm, I can see that Vivien has temporarily disentangled herself and is toasting a marshmallow, carefully turning it to the perfect puff of brown on each side, just the way Nic likes it. At cookouts this summer, I know he'll nearly burn her hot dog—Viv likes it charcoal-briquet style—and load it down with ketchup, mustard, mayo, relish. After the Fourth of July parade on Seashell, when everyone eats Hoodsie Cups, she'll snag two but eat the chocolate half of both, swapping with Nic so he gets both vanillas.

Now he's watching her lazily, sifting through the sand next to him, probably in search of another flat skipping stone.

But . . . an engagement ring?

Hooper is attempting to get Ginny Rodriguez to give him the time of day by asking her to bet on whether he can drink five beers in ten minutes without barfing.

Manny scratches the back of his neck again, red-faced and uncomfortable. The flush could be the beer, but he seems to know he put his foot in it. "Gwenners," he starts, then looks up and jumps to his feet. "Dude. You came."

I shield my eyes and peer over at the newcomer.

Great.

I mean come *on*. Three times in one day!

"Sure I did," Cass says easily, lifting a hand to greet Pam. He gives me a quick glance, then looks down, lashes shielding his eyes. "I'm an island guy now, right?"

"You are not," I practically growl, "an island guy."

Manny straightens, startled. Pam's eyebrows rise and she looks back and forth between us.

"Course he is, Gwenners. He's working for my dad. He's

an honorary Jose, aren't you, dude? Nab something from the cooler and take a load off. The first days are killers."

"Ah, it'll be okay," Cass says, "once I figure out the whole horizontal thing."

That's it. I feel suddenly exhausted. Cass. Nic, Viv, engagement ring. The Robinsons. The lobsters. I clamber to my feet, feeling as though I weigh about a thousand pounds—and, let's face it, probably looking like it in my baggy, so-attractive clothes. I walk over to Nic and Viv, nudge Nic sharply with my toe, jerk my thumb toward the pier. "Let's head out."

Like Pam and Manny, Nic does a quick double take at my tone, checking Vivien for translation. She glances over at Cass, wrinkles her nose, then stands up, pulling Nic with her. We walk to the edge of the pier, dangle our legs over. Well, Nic and I do. Vivien slides her legs over Nic's, entwines her hand in his. I open my mouth to ask, then think: *If they haven't told me, they don't want me to know,* and shut it again.

"Check that out," Vivien says in a hushed voice, pointing out across the water. It's low tide, shoals of rippling sand peeking up out of the sea-glass-green water, ancient-looking gray-brown rocks, the sun burning low and pale orange in the sky. "This is the most beautiful place in the world, isn't it? I never want to leave. Everything I love is right here." She rests her head on Nic's shoulder.

I look at our legs lined up together. Viv's skinny and already tan, Nic's well-muscled and sturdy, and mine, long and strong.

Nic scrounges in his pocket for the skipping stones from earlier, hands me one, nods at the ocean. I squint, slant the stone to what seems the perfect angle, fling it out. One. Two.

Three . . . sort of a sinking four. Nic edges Vivien off his lap, cocks his head to the side and throws.

Six.

"Still the champion." He hauls Vivien to her feet, swoops her in for six kisses.

"It's not as though Gwen is after what you are," Vivien points out, a little breathless after kiss number four.

No, it isn't. But . . . God, I wish, for the millionth time, that I could be like her and Nic, so sure of what they have, what they want. That I didn't always feel jangly, restless, primed to jump off a bridge and let the current carry me away. I glance over my shoulder at the distant blond figure standing by the bonfire.

Especially tonight.

Chapter Eight

Dark's just starting to glow into light the next morning when I bike down to the beach. I can barely make out the figure standing at the end of the pier, hands on hips, surveying the water. Only that familiar stance tells me it's Dad. As I get closer, I see his tackle box open, a big bag of frozen squid beside him. He called last night, told me to meet him at Sandy Claw early.

I'd expected him to get on me for bailing on him at Castle's this summer. But when I'd said on the phone "Hey Dad, I'm sorry that I—" he'd cut me off.

"You gotta do what you gotta do, Gwen. But, since you're not gonna be around every day, I want to do this. I've got something for you." Now he looks up from the hook he's baiting as I scramble over the rocks. Noting the cooler I'm carrying, he gives me the flicker of a smile.

"What'd you bring me, Guinevere?"

He takes the loaf of zucchini bread with a grunt of satisfaction, motioning to me to pour coffee from the thermos. I stayed up late last night, following the directions in Vovó's stained old copy of *The Joy of Cooking*, and turning that engagement ring over and over in my head. When she's worried, Vivien gives herself pedicures and facials. Nic lifts weights. I bake. So, Vivien ends

69

up looking more glamorous. Nic gets fitter. And I just get fat.

"Damn good thing you can cook. Not like your mom. A woman who can't cook . . ." He trails off, clearly unable to think of a terrible enough comparison.

"Is like a fish without a bicycle." I was on debate team last year and we used that quote from Gloria Steinem as a topic.

"What does that mean?" Dad asks absently, wiping his lips with the back of his hand. I guess you could say he's handsome. Not stop-you-dead-in-your-tracks gorgeous, but good-looking enough that I can squint and understand what Mom was thinking. He's still fit and muscular in his mid-thirties, his hair thick. Nothing soft about Dad. He wears flannel shirts, year-round, sleeves rolled up to reveal the ropy muscles of his arms. He's got high cheekbones and full lips, which both Emory and I inherited. "Did you bring cream cheese?" he asks.

"No, I did not, because cream cheese on zucchini bread is disgusting." I hand him a tub of butter and a plastic knife.

"Sorry I haven't seen much of you lately, pal. I've been doing the grunt work, gettin' set up for the summer crowd. Sysco trucks coming and going to restock—they *never* tell you what time, keep you hanging all damn day—and I've got the new summer bunch for training—you know what that's like." Even though it's been twenty years since Dad moved here from Massachusetts, his *er*'s are still *a*'s and his *ar*'s are *ah*'s. In fact, his accent gets stronger every year.

I refill the cup of coffee he's already gulped down and pour one for myself.

"Start cuttin' up the bait," he directs, mouth full, handing me a box cutter and jerking his chin at the bucket of squid.

It's still early June and not all that warm in the mornings yet. I feel as though my fingers are freezing to the slippery squid as I try to slice them—harder to do on the jagged rock than it would be on a flat surface. The tide is high, so the air's not as briny yet, there's a fresh breeze coming off the water, and the waves slap gently against the rocks. The dark blue sky overhead is fading fainter in the east.

"Good coffee."

"Thanks."

"Gwen."

"Yes?"

"You're making the pieces too big. The fish'll just run off with the hook like that."

"Sorry, Dad."

More silence as he polishes off half the zucchini loaf and I deal with freezing cold slimy bait.

"Dad," I finally say. "You were eighteen when you and Mom got married, right?"

"Barely," he says. "Here, let me bait your hook."

"Would you say that was . . . too young?"

He gives me a sharp look from under his thick brows. "Wicked young. We had no business getting hitched. But . . . well . . ." He clears his throat. "You were on the way and—why are you asking me this? You're not in any kind of trouble, are you?"

"No! Of course not. Jeez. I'm on the Pill."

He winces, and I realize I should have said I'd never even held hands with a boy, not reassured him about my effective birth control. Whoops.

"It was a medical thing. For my complexion and because my period was—"

Dad holds up a hand, hunching his shoulders in pain. "Stop! As for me and Luce, we were kids. Had no freaking clue what we were getting into." He holds out his coffee cup. "Got more?"

I splash hot black liquid into his cup, the plastic top of the thermos, then ask something I've always wondered about. "Do you regret it? Marrying Mom? Like, if you had a do-over, would you?"

Dad takes a sip of coffee, screws up his face as though it's burned his tongue, blows out a breath. "I'm no good at this garbage"—the way he says it sounds like *gahbage*—"imagining things fell out some different way than they did. Waste of time. That's your ma's territory, with all her foolish books. If you mean, do I regret you, no." He hands me my pole, reaches into his back pocket, pulls out a wad of bills. "Your back pay."

I take it from him, count it out, then hand him back half. Our tradition. He'll put it into his pocket, then take it to the bank for my college fund when he deposits Castle's income. Dad's big on the fact that it matters that I see the money before half of it is gone. I'll give most of the rest to Mom.

"You can have first cast, kiddo."

I hoist the pole to my shoulder, fling it out, watching the fragile transparent line shimmer in the air as the hook dips into the waves.

"Decent," Dad says. "Put a little more arm into it next time."

He grins at me. For a moment, I feel this surge of affection for him and I want, the way I wanted yesterday with Mom, to tell him the whole story . . . the boys and Nic and Vivien and the ring and . . .

But we've never talked like that. So, instead, I reel my line in, hopeful for an instant as it snags hard on something, until I realize it's just a clump of kelp.

"Pal, look." Dad clears his throat, squinting as he stares out at the far horizon. "I'm gonna give you something my folks didn't give me when I was your age."

Not a car. Not a trust fund. Dad's parents were, as Mom puts it, "unfit to have pets, much less kids."

"What is it, Dad?"

"You can bait that hook and hand me my pole. What I'm going to give you, Gwen, is the truth."

Here's where, in one of Mom's books, or the classic movies Grandpa Ben likes, it would turn out that Dad was actually royal but estranged from his family. That I was the next heir to . . . My imagination gives out at this point from sheer futility.

Dad casts, a perfect arc, line shimmering, glimmering out into the sea. "What're you waiting for, Gwen? Get going!"

So I shove slimy squid onto another hook and cast out myself. I know I do it well. Strange how you can be good at something that doesn't mean anything to you at all. But it's always mattered to Dad. The times we spend fishing are some of our best, most peaceful. When he's on the water, all Dad's rough edges smooth out, like he's sea-glass.

"You got your mom's brains, and her looks. Sweet Mother of God, she was a beauty. Stopped your heart, seeing her." He rubs his chest, looks out at the water, and then goes on. "You got those and my guts. You're a hard worker and you don't belly-ache about every little thing." He pauses, wipes his fingers off on his faded shorts. "But the only chance you have of getting

73

anywhere with any of that is to get the hell off this island."

"I love Seashell," I say, automatically. True and not true. I tip my face up as the first fingers of the sun stretch across the water. My feet in their worn flip-flops are cold, the chill of the rocks seeping through the thin rubber soles.

"Yeah, *love*," Dad says. "That'll get you nowhere fast. Look. I'm not going to sit here moaning about the mistakes I've made. What's done's done. But you've still got time. Chances. You can have . . ." He stops, his attention snagged by a distant sailboat. Dad checks out sailboats—the big beautiful ones like this Herreshoff gliding by, ivory sails bellying in the wind— the way some of the guys at school check out cleavage.

"Can have what, Dad?"

He throws back a gulp of coffee, grimaces again. "*More*."

I'm not sure where he's going with all this. Dad's not really one for self-reflection. He concentrates on casting out his line, jaw tense.

After a few minutes he continues. "Here on Seashell, it's always going to be us against them, and let's face it—it's gonna be them in the end, because 'them' gets to choose what happens to 'us.' Get off island, Gwen. Find your place in the world. You got a ticket in your hand already with the old lady losing her marbles."

My line sways, spider-webbing in the water. Dad catches me by the elbow with one hand, and then carefully reels in my line, calloused warm hand over mine. "She's loaded and she's losin' it. You're gonna be there every day. Her family isn't. Make the most of that."

"What are you talking about?"

"She's redoing her will this summer. I heard her nurse, Joy, talking about it on line at Castle's. Her son wants to take over power of attorney, so she's tying up the legal stuff . . ."

"Dad, that has nothing to do with me." Is he really suggesting what I think he's suggesting? I feel like throwing up, and it's not the combination of frozen squid and empty stomach. I look at Dad's ducked head, incredulous.

"For God's sake, the damn fish took the bait right off the line without me even feeling a tug. Bastard. Put some more on, pal. What I'm saying is you've got the goods to go places. Do it for me. Do it for your ma. Just be real smart, is all I'm telling you. Pamper that old lady within an inch of her life. Her family's off in the city, she's on her own. Better you wind up with a nice little chunk a change than them, the way I see it."

"Dad . . . are you saying . . ."

"I'm telling you to keep your eyes open for opportunity. Mrs. E.'s not noticing stuff around her house the way she used to—and she never was one of those ones that knew exactly how many silver crab claw crackers she had, not like some of the fruitcakes your mom cleans for."

I close my eyes, picturing Mrs. Ellington's porch, the engraved silver of the tea service, the polished antiques, the leather-bound, gold-embossed books in the bookshelves. Her family legacy.

This is *my* legacy? Does Dad actually believe that the only way I'm likely to have anything is to grab somebody else's? What happened to all his lectures about hard work and the people who got ahead were the ones who sucked it up and put their nose to the grindstone, and . . .

"Dad?"

I can't seem to come up with anything more to say. He stares out at the water, at the distant horizon, eyes somber. I keep chopping bait, sliding it on the hook, bending and casting out. I remember Mrs. Ellington watching that separation of sea and sky during our interview, Nic, Viv, and I doing the same last night, and for the first time I realize that none of us are seeing the same thing. That all our horizons end in different places.

"So, I need you to fill in for me at lunchtime today. This won't be a usual thing. But I just had to fire this kid—too much of a moron and always showing up late and high. I'm short-handed for this afternoon. We're gonna get slammed. Can you pinch hit? I'll pay you overtime, even though it's not a holiday. C'mon, pal."

"I have a rehearsal dinner with Vivien and Almeida's tonight. Plus watching Em all day. And Mrs. Ellington starts Monday. I can't work all the time." Visions of any summer lazing are quickly fading to black in my head.

"If you play it smart, like I said, you won't have to." He brushes zucchini bread crumbs off his faded olive green shorts, crumples the now-empty foil wrapper and sticks it back in the cooler. "But today, I need you. The first few weeks I'm figuring out who the bad apples are. And you're my good egg."

"Dad. About what you said. I mean, about Mrs. Ellington—"

"Just think about it, Guinevere, smart advice from your old man." Dad takes the pole from me, securing the hook. "Embroider it on a pillow. Spray-paint it on your wall. Just never forget it: Don't be a sucker. Screw them before they screw you."

Chapter Nine

Back home, I push open the screen door to the familiar sound of Nic running through his Coastie fitness routine—the little grunt he always makes when he picks up a weight, the clatter and puffed exhale when he sets one down. I hardly wanted to get out of bed to meet Dad, but here's Nico—who I happen to know was out until three in the morning with Vivien—ensuring his physical fitness.

"You are not a normal teenage boy," I say as I enter the living room, which is like climbing into a gigantic wet sneaker. Em's curled on the couch, nestled in a blanket with Hideout the hermit crab in his arms and Fabio drooling on his leg, dividing his attention between watching Nic sweat and some Elmo video.

"No." Panting, Nic rolls to his side, lets the weights he's been bench-pressing crash to the ground. "I'm better, stronger, faster."

"Smellier," I say. "Where's Mom?"

"Robinsons'," he grunts, picking up the weight again, his damp, sandy brown hair sticking to his forehead.

Oh, right. Making their house sparkle. On a Saturday. *God, Mom. Doctors are on call, not you.*

I sit down next to Emory, ruffling his hair. He smells sticky and sweet, no doubt from the bowl of Cap'n Crunch he's got resting on his lap. He snuggles his head against my shoulder, shoving Hideout under my nose.

"Say good morning to Hideout."

"Morning, Hideout." I catch a whiff of spaghetti sauce— Emory sneaks him bites during meals.

For a few minutes, Em and I both watch Nic like he's theater, while I turn over in my head various casual, subtle ways to bring up the ring. I inhale, bite my lip, blow out a breath a few times. Nic's too focused on his weight curls to notice that I look like one of the bluefish Dad caught as it flopped around on the rocks.

How would this even work? Would it be a long engagement? Like—they'd marry when he got out of the Coast Guard Academy? Or are they planning to do it *now*? I'm picturing Viv moving into the bedroom Nic shares with Grandpa Ben and Emory. Or Mom and me having to move out of the room we share and sleep together on Myrtle to give them privacy (though that's never seemed too high on their list of requirements). Or Nic and Vivien resurrecting the battered old tent we used to pitch in the yard all summer as their love nest. I can't see them moving in with Viv's mom and stepdad. Al usually glares at Nic like someone from the Old Testament, and Mrs. Almeida pitches a fit when she even catches them holding hands.

It's so ridiculously implausible in the light of day. Because it's all the same—Nic's focused scowl on the uplift, relaxing into pained relief as he sets the weight down, his faded, torn, "lucky" camouflage green workout shirt, sleeves torn off—

everything. Manny must have been talking through his beer brain.

"Do I look like I've gained weight to you?" Nic asks abruptly, my staring at him with a crinkled forehead finally getting through.

"Yup, those shorts make your butt look huge."

He frowns at me. "I'm serious. I've been eating over at Viv's all the time since school got out and her mom's desserts . . . If I bulk up too much, my swim timing will suck, and those guys will take their edge and—"

"Nico, you're fine."

He blows out a breath, lowering the weight and panting.

"Can you hold my ankles while I do crunches?"

I drop to the floor, loop my fingers around his sweaty, hairy ankles. I've been doing this for him for years, and the familiarity of it makes me brave again.

"Nico, Manny said— Are you and Vivien—"

"D'you think I should shave my legs?" he interrupts, panting.

"For prom?"

"For speed."

"I don't think your pelt slows you down too much, cuz. Nobody else on the team does it."

There's a sharp, military-sounding rap on the door. I get up and open it to find Coach Reilly awkwardly holding a plastic bag. He's so out of context that I blink. I've never seen him on the island. Cass, now Coach. It's a Stony Bay invasion. He thrusts the bag at me as though it's a bomb with a ticking time clock, then glances around the room, his brows pulling toward each other. "Your ma here?"

79

I glance into the bag to find it full of romance novels with titles like *The Desirable Duke* and *The Sheik Who Shagged Me*. I so don't want to think Coach reads these.

"My neighbor was gonna chuck 'em. I know Lucia goes for this kind of thing. So . . . she's not home?"

I shake my head, try not to squint at him. Dad calls Mom "Luce," only "Lucia" when they're arguing. But the way Coach says the word, it sounds . . . different. I didn't think he thought of her as "Lucia"—as anything but my mom, Nic's aunt. I'm beginning to think I know absolutely nothing about what's going on with anyone.

"Come on in." I open the door wider.

He shoulders his way into the room. "Hey, Nic the Brick." Nic, who's at the top of a weight curl, grunts a hello.

Emory gives Coach Reilly a distracted wave. Coach ruffles his hair, asks, "When you going to run track for me, Big Blue?"

Em holds out his arms, says, "Whoosh, faster than a loco-motive. Speeding."

"Just what SB High needs, buddy," Coach says, sitting down heavily on one of the kitchen stools and unzipping his SBH jacket. He looks even more flushed than usual.

"Can I get you some water?" *Or a defibrillator?*

"Naah. Gwen, gonna cut to the chase. Got a kid on the swim team who's in a jam. Screwed up in English and flunked that big final. Two-thirds of his grade shot to hell. The teacher will let him retake at the end of the summer. But he needs a tutor. I know you saved Pieretti's butt with Lit 1 last fall. If Cass doesn't maintain a good average, he's off the team. We need him.

I figured since he's right here on the island this summer, it would be easy for you guys to find the time."

Of course I knew instantly it was Cass. Not because I think of him as a bad student, but somehow the minute I heard Coach say "swim team," I knew. Cass is getting to be like that one rock on the beach that you stub your toe on every time.

"I don't think I'm the best person to help him," I say. "Pam D'Ofrio tutors. And she's on island too."

I hear a sound like a cat choking up a hairball. It's Nic, clearing his throat.

"You okay, Brick?" Coach asks.

Nic coughs again in that same incredibly fake way, then wheezes out. "Need a cough drop. (*Hack, hack.*) Gwen—can you show me where you keep yours?"

He jerks his head toward Mom's and my bedroom with these big pleading eyes. Mystified, somewhat irritated, I follow him.

The minute we're inside, he grabs my forearm. "Do it. Man up and do it."

I lean back against the door. "Why? If Cass gets booted, your shot at captain is in the bag."

Nic grimaces. "No way do I want to win like that. Get it handed to me. Besides, Somers ups my game. I do my best when I'm trying to outdo someone. I need that edge." He's been looking at me intently. Now his eyes fall to Mom's ruffled pink-and-brown bedspread.

"Look, I know things are maybe a little"—he rubs his perspiring jawline without looking at me—"whatever. With you and Somers. I mean, pretty damn clear last night, whatever the hell *that* was. But do this. For us. I need Coach to write me a rec for the academy. He went there. That's huge. I need it."

"You honestly think he wouldn't rec you if I don't tutor Cassidy? You've been on his team since freshman year. Cass and Spence just got on last year."

"Probably. But I don't know for sure. I need sure. The CGA is one of the hardest damn institutions in the country to get into. Every boost counts," Nic says, stretching his arms over his head, revealing armpit hair that may actually be piling several minutes onto his swim time. "C'mon, cuz."

I fix him with my own intimidating stare. "You will owe me forever for this. I own your soul."

"My ass, maybe. Not my soul. God, this is just tutoring, Gwen. I'm not asking you to screw the guy."

My face must change color, because Nic starts stammering. "I didn't mean . . . I meant . . . I wasn't . . . That didn't come out like . . ."

I point a finger at him. "Your soul," I repeat. "Vivien can have your sorry ass."

"Deal," Nick says swiftly. "My sorry soul is all yours."

When we get back, Coach has sat down next to Emory, and is looking at the pictures in the Superman comic book Em is leafing through, his arm around Em's shoulders. I skid to a halt, swallowing, and realize I'm not sure when I last saw Dad do that.

Making one last attempt to extract myself from this situation, I ask casually, "Have you mentioned this idea to Cassidy? Because he might not be up for it." I hear Nic hoist one of his weights again and wonder if he's going to bop me on the head with it.

Coach spreads his hands. "He'll be up for what he needs to be up for. This is important as hell. We have a shot at state coming up but only with Somers. On your end, adding tutoring during the summer looks damn good to colleges. You know Somers can afford to pay top dollar."

Family, money, looking good to colleges. My Achilles' heels. Assuming you can have three of those.

"Help me out here, Gwen. Take one for the team."

Even without the Nic pressure, it would be nearly impossible to say no to Coach. He's a good guy. Everyone knows he was crazy about his wife, who cheered at every meeting, brought hot chocolate for the boys on the bus, and who died last fall.

I take a deep breath. How bad can this be? Obviously, based on yesterday, I already knew I was going to be seeing more of Cass this summer than I'd planned. This is purely professional. I didn't quit timing the swim team after what happened in March, after all. I just managed to avoid any personal conversation. I can do the same with this. "I'm in."

Coach claps me on the back hard enough to knock the wind out of me and says he'll speak to Cass about it. "You two can work it out next time you run into each other." He punches his hand into the pocket of his jacket, jingling what sounds like loose change. "Gwen? Keep it on the down low. No need to let the world know he's had any struggle. Once or twice a week should cut it. He's a smart kid. He'll do whatever he needs to do to get where he wants to go."

Yeah. I know.

83

Even though I thought I'd escaped, here I am at Castle's once again, trying to get out of wearing my little hat with the crown around it.

"Whatcha think of this week's specials?" Dad asks, nodding at the blackboard.

I've parked Emory at a picnic table in the shade and set out finger paints, a situation that could turn critical at any moment.

"Stuffed peppers," I read out loud from the top of the black-board. "Maple-basted bluefish?"

"Well?" Dad asks, tipping back on his heels, squinting at the board. "I figure two new specials a day—or every coupla days, just to keep 'em guessing."

"Dad . . . People come to Castle's for . . . beach food . . . sum-mer food. Burgers. Hot dogs. Lobster rolls. They're not going to want to stop off after spending the day at the beach and have maple-basted bluefish. Ever. Where'd you get that, anyway?"

"Food Network," he says absently, rubbing his chin with his thumb. "We gotta do something. Last time I drove by that damn Doane's, there was a line all the way down the pier."

"They sell ice cream and penny candy. There's always a line. I'm not sure maple-basted bluefish is playing to the same crowd."

Emory tugs at me with one hand, holding up the other, coated in red paint, like Lady Macbeth. I pull him over to the little outdoor sink at the back and rinse him—and me—while Dad follows, continuing. "Nah, think about it, kid. The sea-son's here, we get the college kids, the renters. The renters'

84

kids. They're doing the marijuana. They get the munchies. They come here—they see the specials. We sell out."

"Dad . . . if kids get the munchies, they want cheese fries or brownies. Not maple-basted bluefish." No one wants maple-basted bluefish. Blech.

His gaze sharpens on me. "How do you know this, Guinevere Angelina Castle?"

Um, I'm a teenager? I go to high school? "Health class."

Dad shakes his head. "Don't you dare go down that dead-end road, mess with your brain."

"Don't worry, Dad. I stick to cocaine."

He scowls. "Well, knock it off. That stuff's wicked expensive. And pull up your shirt—there." He jerks his head at my neckline. It's not even low. I tug it up anyway. Dad tosses me my purple apron, even better coverage, and tells me to man the side booth. "And put on your hat."

Within ten minutes, we're totally overwhelmed. Nedda, who must have the patience of all the saints, because she's worked here for three years, is slaving over the grill. A busload of tourists headed to Foxwoods is taking up two-thirds of our parking lot and three-quarters of our burger supply. A skinny new guy named Harold is languidly manning the fry basket. I've got Emory parked at a back table now, with a grilled cheese.

"Gwen, table six, fast. We're running behind," Dad barks. "I'll handle the orders, you hustle 'em out there. We get more tips if a pretty girl does the running."

Dad rarely dishes out compliments, so they always hit hard when he does. I'm blushing a little as I gather up the tray of burgers and birch beers and head out to six. Which . . . naturally . . . is Cass. And someone who looks a lot like him. Not his dad. Dark-haired, but with the same lean-muscled look and piercing blue eyes.

Cass has his back to me, hands braced on the table. "We've been through this a million times, Billy. What more do you want from me?"

"Some sign that you'll listen to your own brain instead of Channing's. We all know how well that worked out at Hodges, squirt."

I suppress a smile at the nickname.

"That was a year ago, Bill—and it was just a joke. That place takes itself way too seriously."

"A joke that got you out on your ass. Still pretty damn embarrassing for Jake too, since *he works there*. Spence's dad might have finessed it so expulsion didn't show up on *his* record, but it's on yours, little brother. For keeps."

Cass is now digging a thumbnail into the wood of the picnic table. The backs of his ears are flushed. I'm standing there with their food, blatantly eavesdropping. I always kind of wondered why he and Spence came to SBH last fall as juniors. Prepped-out Hodges is where Stony Bay kids go when price is no object.

"Look, you're smarter than this, squirt. I'd hang it up if I felt like you'd learned your lesson, but you haven't. This garbage with your grades looks like more of the same screwing up to me. To everyone. I love Spence, but he'll always come out smelling like a rose. You won't."

"You're my brother, Bill, not—"

"Dad and Mom would tell you the same thing."

86

"They have. Constantly. You know Mom, she loves to over-explore. Look, I'm paying my dues—working on the island, mowing freaking football fields' worth of lawns. I did a dumbass thing, got a few lousy grades. Let's move on, for Chrissake," Cass says, standing abruptly. "Shouldn't the food be here by now?"

He whirls around and almost directly into me. One of the drinks splashes tsunami-style into the plate of fries and onto my apron.

"I—was just bringing you this." I start mopping at the fries, but they're hopeless. Then I brush at my shirt, totally frazzled. "I'll get you some more. No problem. It'll only take a minute."

"Is that ours?" his brother calls out.

"I'll take it," Cass says, reaching for the tray. "You don't have to wait on me."

"It's my job," I say. He's got his hands on the tray, and mine are there too in a kind of flashback to our near-wrestle over the lobsters. And my peacoat, last spring. I drop my hands, wipe off my palms, shove the soggy napkins into my apron pocket.

He stands there balancing the tray in one hand, looking out at the cow pasture that's directly behind Castle's, jaw clenched. "You heard all that, right?"

I shrug. "It's okay. I mean, nothing to do with me."

He examines my face, then grins. "I call bullshit. You want to know."

"Ha. Don't kid yourself. I couldn't care less what you did then." My turn to look off at the cows, try to absorb their barn-yard zen. "Or now."

He sets down the tray, slants a hip against the table. His

brother's gotten up and is heading for the service window, no doubt to complain about the ditz who ruined their fries.

"Ever been inside Hodges—aside from the pool area?"

"Other than the girls' locker room, no."

"Pretentious as hell for small-town Connecticut." He shrugs. "Not to mention that you had to call the teachers 'master' and 'mistress' whatever. Should be called 'Stodges' instead of 'Hodges.'" He tugs at his collar as though the mere memory is choking him.

I'm smiling despite my determination to project complete indifference.

Cass cocks his head at me, folding his arms. "Oh, never mind. Why am I telling you this? You don't care."

"Do *not* do that. Now you have to tell me."

He rocks back on his heels, smiles. "Careful, Guinevere. You might forget you hate me."

"I—"

I look over to see if Dad has noticed my dawdling, but he's apparently in some sort of near altercation with a vendor, who is holding a huge cardboard barrel of ice cream. Automatically, I check the table where Emory was drawing, but he's not there. Oh God.

The parking lot.

The road.

I whirl around.

Then I feel a soft brush past me, and my little brother steps in front of Cass, head titled. He's so small, even though he's eight, that reaching up to Cass's chest is a big deal. He touches

88

it lightly, moves his finger across it in a slow, snake-like motion. I have no idea what he's doing.

"Superman," he says proudly, like he's seen through Cass's disguise. He traces the shape again—it's an *S*, I realize—and beams at both of us.

Cass looks down, game face on, but not freaked out. I hope.

"Hi, Superman," Emory repeats, invisibly drawing the shield thing around the *S*.

I don't know why he's doing this. Cass has neither dark hair nor a cape waving in the wind. Maybe the blue of his shirt or the way he stands with his shoulders back, chin lifted.

Now Dad looks over. "Sorry," he calls to Cass and his brother, who's returning with a fresh order of fries, then to me: "Gwen, don't let your little brother pester the customers, for God's sake."

"It's fine," Cass calls. His brother sets the fries down on the table and immediately Em's reaching for them.

"Superman," he repeats, popping one in his mouth and chewing cheekily.

"Em, no!" I struggle as I usually do when people meet him for the first time, whether to explain or just let them take Em as Em.

"My brother is—"

Cass cuts me off. "We bumped into each other on the beach yesterday. He was with your grandfather. I gave them a lift up the hill. They seemed tired."

I blink. "Before or after your rescue attempt with the lobsters?"

"Before." Cass winks at Emory, who is eating another fry.

"The Man of Steel never rests. Or maybe that's Jose the yard boy. I get my alter egos confused."

"Hi there," his brother says to me, with a short wave. "Bill Somers."

"This is Gwen Castle, Billy. She's the one I was saying should tutor me for that English makeup."

Wait. This was his *idea? Not Coach's?*

"Good to meet you. And—don't pull your punches with squirt here. He deserves it."

Cass's ears turn red. He shoots Bill a swift death-glare.

"Gwen!" Dad calls. "Get your little brother back over here. You don't have time for screwing around."

Bill tells me it was a pleasure, Cass has retreated into his bland, neutral look, and Emory's made a major dent in their fries. I stammer out an apology, take Em's greasy hand, and turn to go, only to run into the solid wall of Dad. He's got yet another new plate of French fries, not having missed a thing.

"Sorry about this. These're on the house too," he says. Then, stern, to me: "Get back where I can keep an eye on you, kid. *Emory's* the one who is supposed to need a babysitter."

God, Dad. I feel my face burning. But Cass is looking down at the ground, not at me, nudging at the pebbles with the toe of his sneaker, all neutral face. Dad's bristly and defensive, Bill faintly amused. Only Emory is completely at ease. He sidles up to Cass, traces the shield design once again, sweeps his finger in an *S*. "Superman," he says.

"I wish," Cass mutters.

Chapter Ten

The first thing I see when I get home, sticky with spilled soda and French fry grease, are Nic's big bare feet sticking over the edge of Myrtle. Vivien is crouched over them in dark purple bikini bottoms and a low-cut black tank.

Good God. It's four in the afternoon and they're in our living room. On the couch under the wedding picture of my no-doubt-virginal grandmother. Not exactly the time or place for . . . having a foot fetish? Please tell me my cousin has clothes on. I clear my throat.

Vivie glances up, smiles, completely unembarrassed, then bends back over Nic's toes.

And blows on them.

"Uh, guys?!" I say. "Maybe you could . . . take it somewhere else. Officially dying here."

Nic sits up—thank God, dressed. "I'm doing penance," he explains. "Making up for my sins."

My glance shoots to the crucifix, my grandmother's sweet, serious face.

"Uh . . ." I haven't moved from the doorway. Viv sits back on her heels, squints at Nic's foot, and then picks up a bottle of—"Oh my God, you guys, really!" I practically shout—clear nail polish and begins applying it to Nic's other foot.

Nic looks at my face and bursts out laughing. "You look so incredibly freaked out," he manages, then starts laughing again.

"Nico, hold still!" Vivie slaps at his leg.

"Gwen, Gwen, listen. Viv and I were schlepping a bunch of fish chowder over to the Senior Lunch at St. Anselm's, and Speed Demon here is doing her thing—"

"I was only going fifty."

"In a thirty-mile-an-hour zone, Vee." He nudges his toes lightly into her stomach, turns back to me, more serious now but still smiling. "She's wigging out because we're late and she doesn't want Al to get all over her—but I can hear the chowder sloshing and if my little felon here racks up any more tickets she'll be answering to the law, never mind Al."

Viv wrinkles her nose, sticks her tongue out at him. "You totally exaggerate how bad my driving is."

"Uh, no, I don't. You're a maniac. And I like having you in one piece. So she's barreling along and then we get to this stoplight and the light turns green and the truck in front of us isn't moving. So Vee leans out the window and says, 'What are you waiting for, asshole?' and flips the driver off."

"God, Viv," I interrupt. "Don't *do* that. We've told you like a billion times. You never know when you might run into some psychopath."

"Exactly. 'Cause this guy gets out of the car and he's like eight feet tall, three hundred pounds, tattoos, leather vest, chains, and he is effing furious. He comes over to the window and gets in Viv's face and says, 'Gonna repeat that?'"

"And I, like, burst into tears," Viv says. "I'm picturing him killing Nic and then God knows what he'd do to me. My life is flashing before my eyes."

"So I know I need to talk this guy down because I sure as hell can't *take* him down."

"But it's the *way* you did it, Nic. He gets all chummy and buddy-buddy with this jerk." Viv's voice deepens. "'So sorry, man. My honey here is a little touchy today. Normally she's sweet as pie but she gets kinda high-strung at that time of the month, you know what I'm saying?' And then this Neanderthal is clapping Nico on the back all-man-to-man and saying yeah, he has a wife and four daughters and he's thinking of getting an RV that he can park in the driveway because their cycles are all the same and on and on and on—"

I'm laughing now, and so is Nic again. "Well, he did save you," I point out.

"Yeah, but then they spent ten minutes telling women-are-cray-zee stories, which, I'll have you know, Nic completely made up. He's telling the guy that I once threw a pizza at him because he got the wrong toppings. That I threw his ball cap in a wood chipper because I was jealous of the time he was spending watching Sox games."

"But again, I did save you," Nic says, reaching for her hand.

"By making me sound like an out-of-control crazy hormonal bitch," Viv says. "So having to get a pedicure is his penance for being Captain Macho. And so is wearing flip-flops next week so Hooper and Marco and Tony can admire his pretty tootsies."

"They do look *dreamy*, Nico," I say. "And anyway, if she were really mad at you, she would've gone for pink."

Vivie winks at me—and then pulls a bottle of Day-Glo fuchsia polish out of her purse. "That was just the undercoat," she says.

"Aw." Nic ruffles her hair. "You're so cute when you're all riled up, honeybun."

"Watch it, or you'll get a *manicure* too."

He leans over and kisses her . . . and kisses her . . . and kisses her. On and on and on. I might as well be in the next county.

Still, it's good to know that this exists—true love—in my world. And not just in Mom's books.

Al Almeida is telling us what he expects of his catering crew tonight in a hushed, urgent tone, shifting his eyes to each of us in turn. The group of us is in a respectful circle outside the turreted canvas tent set up for the rehearsal dinner on Hayden Hill, the highest point of Stony Bay, windblown, exclusive, overlooking the water but from far, far away. We soberly observe him, appropriately dressed in our black-and-white outfits, peasants at the gates of the palace. Al's intimidating, actually, with beetle-y brows and military-short hair. "All right—listen up." He checks his watch. One of his watches. He always wears one on each wrist.

"Showtime is in ten minutes. Seven o'clock. We've got a ton of littlenecks. Sorta skimpy on the oysters and the jumbo shrimp, but we've got extra-large for backup. You"—he points at me, Vivien, Melissa Rodriguez, and Pam D'Ofrio—"keep that raw bar stocked and ready. Empty spaces look cheap, and they don't want cheap." He pauses, lowers his voice further, and adds, "The bride's family's loaded, groom's is running on fumes and Mayflower ancestors. Something to prove there." He glares at Vivien, who has taken Nic's hand and is absently kissing his palm. "You, young lady—pay attention. This will be up to you when all's said and done." Viv drops Nic's hand and stands at attention, mock-saluting her stepdad. She throws me a quick glance, flipping her braid and nodding down at her left hand, where her middle finger is discreetly extended. Viv gets along with Al, but oh, how she hates his lectures.

"You"—Al points to Nic—"keep the water glasses stocked and the ashtrays empty. Dominic—keep the wineglasses full. Two-thirds. Not completely. Don't trade places." He glares at Nic and Dom, who is Pam's older brother. "You're twenty-two, Dominic; you're underage, Nic. We don't need any legal hassles."

He turns back to Vivien, Pam, and me. "Keep those apps coming. We want them to fill up on the passed hors d'oeuvres before we bring out the lobster. Got it?"

We nod.

Al jerks his chin in satisfaction. "Go get 'em, team."

He always adds this at the end, as though he's suddenly morphed into Coach Reilly.

I've helped cater for Almeida's for years and in all that time, I've never seen anybody I knew well at any of their events. Stony Bay is a small town, but the people I know don't have events catered. Unless you count takeout from Castle's.

Tonight my luck runs out.

I've finished passing out the garlic toast with Boursin and sundried tomatoes—only one lone straggler left—and am going back for another trayful, looking around for Vivien so I can complain about the man who just spent ten minutes staring down my shirt while demolishing the tray, when, for the second time today, I bump right into someone. "Shoot, oops," the guy says, at the exact moment I say, "Sorry, I wasn't looking where I was—"

Then I stop dead. Because it's Alex Robinson, tall, dark, and elegant as he was last summer. Despite how things ended, I get goose bumps. But Alex . . . he's looking at me with absolutely no acknowledgment on his face, like I'm some random side dish he didn't order and is wondering how to send back. Is it possible he doesn't recognize me? How many half-Portuguese girls did he hook up with last summer?

"Oh. Uh. Hi." Alex wipes at the slosh of ice water I've spilled on his blue-and-white striped seersucker jacket. "It's, uh, Gwen, right?"

That's a bit much. I debate saying "No, Suzanne." Instead, I widen my eyes. "Do we know each other?"

Alex blinks at me, a preppie owl. "Er . . ."

I school my face to look patient and baffled.

His eyes dart around, finally settling back on me. He clears his throat. "Look, I know it's Gwen. Your . . . your mother was cleaning our house today. I thought maybe you'd come along with her."

I open my eyes still wider. "Really? You missed me? Aw, that's so sweet! I *would* have come, honest, but I had to stay home with Alex, Jr. He can walk now, and he's just getting into *every*thing, the little rascal!" I channel Mom for a look of weary maternal pride.

He pales. "Now . . . wait . . . I—"

I'm enjoying this, because I am a mean and spiteful person.

"Were you like that too, Alex? What a chip off the old block our little cutie is." I let one hand drift to my stomach and smile, Madonna-like.

Alex blinks, then shakes his head. "Ha-ha. I'd forgotten your sense of humor. If—er—*that* had happened, it would have just, uh, been born." His eyes flick to my cleavage. Two guesses what he does remember. "How, uh, have you been, really?"

I balance the tray on my hip, brush away a strand of hair the light breeze has blown against my lips. "Fine. You?"

"Terrific," he says. "Great. A good year at Choate. Headed to Princeton in the fall. My dad went there, so that's . . . all . . . good." His gaze once again drops to my chest, as though it exerts some sort of magnetic pull.

"Hmm" is the only thing I can think to say.

After Alex ended things last fall, when I imagined seeing him again, I always looked fantastic and he groveled at my feet. I was never wearing my ill-fitting Almeida's Arrangements T-shirt—complete with mermaid extending a plate of stuffed quahogs—sweating, and with my unruly hair escaping its ponytail. I did *not* imagine how hard it would be to think of anything to say to him. Maybe I should have remembered how little actual talking we did.

"So." Alex's gaze roams down again, then off toward the raw bar. "I just, ah, thought I'd go try the—um—shrimp."

"Sure," I respond. "Why not? You've already sampled all *I've* got to offer." This is too much, I know, but as usual, once I start talking, I can't stop myself. The kiss-off text he sent me still makes me pissed, even nearly a year later.

"Now, look," Alex says, "I—I—" His eyes dart around the

tent again. "I have to . . . I think I hear someone calling me."

He wheels away from me, walks off—practically sprints.

"That was enlightening," says a voice in my ear.

I turn and stare into laughing ocean-blue eyes. "Wouldn't it have been more efficient to castrate him?" Cass continues, filching the last piece of Boursin toast.

"I considered it." I pick up the butter knife on my tray and wag it at him. "But I didn't think this was up to the job."

"Sounds like Alex wasn't either," Cass says. "Maybe somebody beat you to the castrating." Then he reddens, like he just realized we're talking about Alex's penis, which I have clearly gotten to know.

When he blushes like that—now it's spreading from his ears all over his cheekbones—I remember the Cass of that summer on the island. His hair is so many shades of blond now—gold and amber and yellow and dark blond at the roots—but the season he spent on Seashell, he was a towhead with fair, unfreckled skin. It was one of those crazy-weather summers, sheets of rain for days on end, high winds. Instead of the usual activities run by the island "camp counselor" that Seashell used to hire—kayak lessons, bike races, scavenger hunts—they had kids' movies in the Club House every Saturday night to keep everyone under fifteen busy and distracted. The first time I met Cass, he opened the door for me as we were walking in. Then he turned bright pink.

"His castration would be no loss to anyone, trust me," I say, and then want to clap my hand over my mouth. Cass may have mentioned Alex's equipment, but I had to go rate his performance? *God.* This is not a subject that should be raised between us.

"I know that kid." Cass squints at Alex's retreating back. "We were at tennis camp together two years ago. His forehand sucks. Which tells you something right there."

I burst out laughing, then *do* clap a hand over my mouth. "So . . . tutoring," I say, trying to straighten out my face. "How many classes, exactly, did you screw up?"

Okay, that was a bit rude. I'm feeling off balance. Cass smells like lemons—I think he's wearing aftershave. I've never seen him formally dressed. Now he's wearing a tailored blue blazer, sky-blue shirt that brings out his eyes, yellow tie.

I may have been brainwashed by Grandpa Ben's old movies, set in eras when the clothes made the man. I'm so used to Nic's stinky rumpled wife-beaters, Dad's aged plaid flannels, Hooper's dubious pattern combos. Dressed-up Cass is like a creature from another planet. One I want to colonize. *Oh, God, please stop.*

Al Almeida walks by with a platter of lobsters, steam rising, and I finally get a grip.

I shift my eyes back to Cass. "The shellfish here? Taken care of," I say, just to say something. "No need to ride to the rescue, Jose."

"You're welcome for that, by the way, Maria. I'm sure you meant to thank me this afternoon."

"Can I remind you that I didn't *ask* for your help?"

Cass's teasing smile fades. "I know. I'm . . . ah, I'm asking for yours, though. That tutoring? It's . . . it's important. I know it's probably the last thing you want . . ."

I shrug.

"I can pay. I mean, you know that. I flaked out this spring—

just wasn't . . . concentrating. So I basically about flunked out of English lit . . . Spence can screw around and still pull in the grades. He said only a moron could flunk ELA." Cass shuts his mouth abruptly as if he's said too much.

I could reassure him. I could tell him it's no problem. Or that he's not a moron. Instead I say, "Why do you put up with that guy?"

Cass's jaw sets, a muscle jumping. "He can be a prick, but he's a good friend to me." There's a note of challenge in his voice, a glove he's throwing down that I am definitely not picking up. When I say nothing, he adds, "Right. So will you . . . ?" He breaks off, raising his eyebrows.

And now here's Nic bearing down on us, glaring. "Gwenners, Al's all over Vee because he says you're slacking off—the whole 'how are you going to run the show if you can't keep your staff in line' deal. You need to get back to work."

It's been a given for a long time that Almeida's would go to Vivien, since her stepdad has no kids of his own. Still, I hadn't exactly seen myself as "her staff." I get a chilling image of what it would be like to still be wearing my quahog shirt at sixty, no longer the equal, nowhere close, of my own best friend.

"My fault," Cass puts in. "I was keeping her, figuring out a summer schedule. For tutoring."

"Yeah." Nic's tone is sub-zero, a direct contrast to the angry heat that, for some reason, is burning off him. "Wouldn't want you to let that slide and end up off the team. Not when we're so close to state, right, Somers?" Then he turns to me, letting Cass stew in the cloud of testosterone he's emitting. "Vee needs you."

Cass leans back a little, studies Nic's face. "How about you?

Getting much swim time? Hear you're working for Seashell Maintenance too. Gonna be able to get your hours in?"

"I'll manage," Nic says, still frosty. He's standing up straighter, as if to emphasize his two-inch height advantage. "Got the ocean right at hand, twenty-four/seven, after all."

Cass stares out at the distance, his eyes dreamy, as though he can see the water from here. "I was thinking about that. How we should probably do some training over the summer, especially now that they're not running the swim camp at SB—get some of the guys out, keep the team vibe going, get ourselves some wind and water challenges."

In the distance, I can see Al waving his hands in despair, jerking his head toward the denuded raw bar.

"We'd better go," I say, giving Cass a smile so quick it's more like a grimace.

"Wait." He touches my shoulder as I turn to go. "Call me. Or you could come to the Field House—to figure out the timing. For tutoring, I mean."

Nic now has me by the other elbow and is hauling me away. "You are *not* going to the Field House apartment with that guy," he hisses, practically shaking me by the arm.

I yank myself free. "What's with you?" I ask, suddenly worried Nic has been taking steroids or something. "You were the one all hot to have me tutor him!"

"Yeah, well, while you two were in your little football huddle over here, I was pouring water at his family's table, and some lady was asking Mr. Somers about Cass getting the captain spot on the team this year, saying he was a shoo-in."

Nic's face is stormy, almost threatening.

"So what? You'll get it, Nico. Cool down."

"No, listen," Nic continues, flexing his fingers. "Look . . . I feel weird telling you this, but . . . I get to the next table and it's Spence Channing, buddy-buddy with Alex Robinson. Talking about you. Alex says you were 'a fun time.' A *fun time*? That assclown. Spence just laughs and says you're a *swim team tradition*. He's on my fucking team and he's disrespecting my cousin. I mean, I'm on the bus, I hear how they talk about girls—all 'I'd tap that' and 'she's hot, but-her-face'—but this is *you*, Gwen. Who the hell does he think he is? Who the hell does he think you are?"

I swallow. My face heats, freezes, then gets hot again. Spence knows who I am. Better than I'd like.

"Then I have to refill his goddamn water glass, not punch his face in . . ." Nic's hand curls into a fist and he glares across the room, then looks back at me. "Aw, cuz. I'm sorry. I shouldn't have said anything. I wasn't thinking, too pissed off, I—"

"No big deal, Nico. I have a ways to go before I become a tradition. Plus, I'm going to have a hard time with Hank Klein, unless he breaks up with Scott Varga. But, you know me, I thrive on a challenge."

"Don't, Gwen," Nic says quietly. "Not with me."

I'm silent as we push through the half-plastic, half-cloth curtain that shields the main tent from the makeshift kitchen/prep area.

"About time, Guinevere!" Al says, thrusting another tray of shrimp and cocktail sauce at me. I take it, pull back the curtain and scan the tent, searching for the navy stripes of Alex's seersucker jacket.

It's sort of like *Where's Waldo* . . . there are a lot of blue-and-white striped jackets. Finally I locate him, still sitting next to Spence. But now he's talking to some redheaded chick on his left and Spence has on his half-amused, half-bored face. Which is his go-to expression, the world-weary aristocrat. He only looks happy when he's swimming, training, or hanging out with Cass and the rest of his crew.

He perks up when I appear at his elbow. "Castle! Am I glad to see you. A favor? The bartender's a little elusive. Snag a bottle of champagne for us here?"

Brushing a piece of his shiny, very straight dark hair out of his eyes, he gives me his practiced slow smile, the trademark once-over. Spence is good-looking, no lie. But there's something too sharp. Like you could paper-cut yourself on him without him even noticing.

I take a deep breath, tightening my grip on the tray. "Not my job, Channing. I just do the setup and pass the food. Plus, you're underage."

"It's a wedding rehearsal dinner. All rules are suspended. *All* of them. I just walked by my uncle Red in the backseat of his car with one of the bridesmaids." He lowers his voice to a loud whisper. "Don't tell Aunt Claire."

Since I have no idea who Aunt Claire or Uncle Red are, this is unlikely. But it throws me off for a second before I say, "I'm not here to wait on you. I'm here to tell you you've got the wrong word."

An emotion—in this case, puzzlement—actually crosses his face. "Come again?"

"If I were a swim team 'tradition,' Spencer, I would be something that happened *repeatedly*."

Another emotion, a brief flash of embarrassment. "I didn't mean for you to hear about that."

"Maybe next time you should pay more attention to who's pouring your ice water. Did you really think Nic wouldn't pass that one on? He may be your teammate, but he's my cousin. Blood trumps chlorine."

Alex has picked up on my raised voice and peeks over, takes in the situation, turns away, clearly distancing himself from any potential "scene." He hated scenes, probably why he broke up with me by text.

"I think the word you were going for is *mascot*. You should work on your vocab, or your SATs are going to tank."

I walk away to the sound of Spence's startled laughter.

When Vivie and Nic drop me outside our house, I hold my hand up in farewell, climb two steps, and plunk down wearily on the porch. The back of one of my shoes is jabbing into my heel like a blade saw.

The sky is hazy June-night beautiful, with the moon cutting sharp into the dark, but the stars are nothing but pinpricks. The night breeze is shifting, stirring through the woods, over the water, bringing in the silty, sandy smell of low-tide.

I look down the High Road. The quartz embedded in the tar glitters in the moonlight. Seashell has no streetlamps. This late at night, barely any windows are still lit in the long line of houses along the road. The Field House is five down from ours. I wonder if Cass stayed late at the party. I didn't see him as we packed up the van to leave. Partly because I tried really hard not to look. Will he spend the night in town in his sailing-ship house, or here on Seashell? I rub my hands up and down my arms, abruptly chilly in the night breeze, and wonder why I'm suddenly thinking about Cass Somers so much. Gah. Part of the whole point of this summer was to forget him.

I let myself in through the rattly porch door with the broken latch—the one Nic keeps saying he'll fix—and the house is quiet, peaceful, so different from all the sound and drama in the tent.

Mom's dozed off on the couch, her brow crinkled, still clutching a brightly colored paperback. Leaning over, I pull it out, dog-ear the page she's on (which I can't help but notice begins with "Begorrah, ye she-witch, I've half a mind to put ye over my knee"), then pull the quilt off the bottom and cover her up. I should wake her, coax her to sleep in her own bed, rather than in the dubious comfort of Myrtle's exhausted orange plaid arms. But tonight, I want a room with only me and my thoughts.

I can hear the soft rumble of Grandpa Ben's snores coming from the room he shares with Nic and Emory. I wish I could peel away the whole evening—last night too—like I do my sticky clothes, erase it in the outdoor shower the way I scrub off the smell of smoke and shrimp.

Chapter Eleven

"I was hoping it would just be us," Viv mutters, after Grandpa Ben has squeezed between the front seats for a second time to adjust the radio to FBAC, *"Your Station for the Best in Nostalgia."*

Grandpa's drumming his fingers on the window, singing loudly to "The Way You Look Tonight," with Emory gamely echoing him, "The way your smile just BEAMS . . . The way you haunt my DREAMS." Both of them are beaming themselves, identical big-toothed grins. I try to shake off guilty resentment that they're tagging along.

Yesterday was the longest day in history. I need girl-time with Viv. So I baked brownies early this morning with that sole purpose. My plan was to ply her with sweets at Abenaki Beach and get to the bottom of the ring thing. Viv will spill—I just need to get her alone.

But just as she was about to gun her mom's car, Grandpa bounded down the steps with Emory, a large cooler (which I knew from bitter experience would hold a variety of highly idiosyncratic Grandpa Ben items), and a new(ish) metal detector slung jauntily over his shoulder.

"I feel lucky!" he announces now as we rocket down the hill to Abenaki, seemingly unperturbed by Vivien's violent swerve to avoid an abandoned Razor scooter lying in the middle of the road, as though it had been tossed there by the tide. "Today, we make our fortune." He brandishes the detector out the window.

Vivie and I sit on the short, silvery wooden pier, looking out at the ocean. It's scattered with sailboats, spinnakers billowing. Grandpa Ben hunts for treasure on the wide sandy beach. Em sits cross-legged, totally preoccupied with a bucket of water and a shovel. I love this about him—that when he concentrates on one thing, the rest of the world fades away.

He's wearing, as always, a Coast Guard–approved life jacket. Despite that, I keep clutching at the back of his T-shirt, or the elastic of his shorts when he bends over too far or tries to peer over the rim of the pier. I've had so many nightmares involving the top of his head disappearing beneath the whirling waves.

Particularly ominous today, the sky is gun-metal gray and the water correspondingly dark. Not the best for sunbathing, which is why we're on the warm wood of the pier rather than the chilly sand. The occasional sun shooting out around the clouds is heated, but there's a breeze whipping straight off the water and right into us.

Emory upends his shovel full of icy water onto my leg, making me gasp. "Em, no!"

He smiles at me, scoops, pours out another chilly trickle.

Viv stretches drowsily, her skin already lightly golden against the graying wood of the pier, her small spattering of freckles looking as though someone flicked a paintbrush over her nose. Nic calls it her "constellation" and is always pretending to discover new shapes in it, tracing them with a finger.

"Nic was so tense after catering. I had to drive him out to the bird sanctuary to . . . calm him down." She points her toes, stretching further, then scoops her fingers around her instep, lengthening the stretch with a balletic grace.

"Uh-huh. My cousin, the ornithologist. I'm sure the binoculars got a *lot* of use."

"Well . . . it *is* secluded there." Her slightly wicked private smile overtakes the sweet and innocent one she uses in public. "Just Nic, me, and that crime-scene tape they use to keep us from disturbing the piping plovers' mating season."

"You, Nic, and the plovers doing the dance as old as time." I start giggling. She lets go of her foot and gives my hip a gentle shove.

"It's not like we can snuggle up in the bedroom Nic shares with Grandpa Ben and Emory." She looks down at the tossing gray-green water, worrying her bottom lip, waxy with cherry ChapStick. The only thing Nic ever complains about with Viv is her addiction to that and sticky, flavored lip gloss. "I was probably more stressed than Nic, anyway."

"Any reason why?" Without looking at her, I dip my finger in Em's bucket, trace a circular shape on a wood slat, press my thumb down in a diamond shape, a subliminal suggestion.

She takes a deep breath, opens her mouth as though she's going to say something, then closes it again. "Nothing big," she says finally. "Just . . . you know . . . Al . . . being all up in my face about forgetting to make sure everybody's water glasses were full and so on."

That makes me think of Spence's dickish "team tradition" comment. "Did Nic tell you—"

"Nic always tells me to just blow him off," Viv says. "And he's right. So my stepfather is the poster child for Type A. Doesn't mean I have to be the same. Even if I *am* taking over the biz when Al and Mom retire."

"Yeah, about that," I say. "You're not an indentured servant in medieval times. You don't *have* to be the heir to the throne at Almeida's." Dipping my finger into the bucket again, I write my name in cursive. Emory watches me, then writes curves and loops himself, but they don't spell anything.

Viv shakes her head, her brow smoothing out again. "Aah, Gwenners, you know me. Not a brainiac like you. I couldn't care less about college. Seems like a waste of time, considering the grades I get. It's good to know where I'm going to be instead of flailing around looking for my place in the world. I'm lucky." She sounds so cheerful at the prospect of spending the rest of her life putting together Dockside Delight picnic baskets and clam boils. That's the thing about Viv—whenever Nic and I tip into glass half-empty, she can nudge us back to half-full—and the waiter will be along any minute to fill it to the brim. "Plus, I rock at management. Look at me with Nic."

"Yeah, you've totally whipped that guy into shape. At least ten percent of the time he's on time. Sometimes even wearing a clean shirt."

"I like him without the shirt," Viv says.

"Keep your twisted perversions to yourself."

She laughs, sits up, and pulls the cooler closer, flipping open the lid. "Don't try to pretend you don't share that one, babe. I've watched you at meets, and whatever else you might say about Cassidy Somers, you can't deny his assets there. That? The boy does well."

I flush. Viv's instantly contrite. "Sorry. I know you don't want to talk about him. Think about him. Or whatever."

"Just because you and my cousin have mated for life doesn't mean I have to," I say.

Viv raises her eyebrows. "I was just talking about noticing when someone was cute. You're the one going straight from shirtlessness to mating. Interesting."

"Stop it. Don't go making me and Cass into you and Nic. Clearly, that's not what's going on here."

"And that would be . . . ?" she asks, burrowing into the cooler, then making a face. "Goat cheese? Not in the mood. *Is* there a mood for goat cheese?"

I take the cooler from her, rustle around to find the foil-wrapped brownies, pass them to her. She puts her hand on her heart, mock sighing with relief.

"Maybe I'm just not the kind of girl who—"

Viv shakes her head at me. "Shit. Stop. I hate it when you do that. It's not like you're Spencer Channing with his five girls in the hot tub at once."

"Is that story even true? Because when you think about it, it sounds like a ton of work. You'd have to feed them and talk to them and find a way to entertain the girls who're waiting while you're busy with one or two—"

"Right—so they don't leave or . . . or molest the pool boy out of sheer boredom," Vivie continues, smiling.

"Yeah, you're getting tired . . ." I add.

"It's more work than you expected," she sighs, brushing chocolate off her fingers.

"Makes a great rumor . . ." I say. "Not much fun in action."

She looks down at her hands, her face going serious. "Speaking of action . . . Gwen . . . do you think Nic really wants the Coast Guard? Or it's just . . . an escape fantasy? Like touring around the state painting houses this summer, when he's really better off working steady right here. Have you seen the things those Coasties do? They're freaking Navy Seals. If he gets into the academy, that'll be Nicky . . . all that stuff with helicopters and tow ropes. Why not just take a sensible job, like at Almeida's?"

I try to imagine Nic going into the flower-arranging and food service business, for real. It's so much easier to picture him dangling fifty feet above the churning ocean during a hurricane.

I'm distracted by something far out to sea. Moving. Bobbing. A seal?

We don't see them often around here. The water's too choppy—cold and unpredictable even at the height of summer, and there aren't enough rocks. Straightening up and squinting harder, I follow the motion. Whatever it is disappears under the water with a flick of surf. A cormorant? No, no long neck.

I nudge Vivien, who has rested her cheek on her knees and closed her eyes. "What's that?"

"Oh God, not a shark!"

Three summers ago, a great white was seen off the coast of Seashell and Vivie, traumatized by Shark Week on Discovery Channel when she was little, has lived in terror of becoming the star of the next episode of *Mauled!* ever since.

Whatever it is bobs back up again.

"No fin," I report. "Besides, it's moving up and down, not gliding menacingly forward, ready to leap onto the dock and have you for dinner."

"Don't even joke about that." Vivien shields her eyes with her fingers. "Not a shark. Just some crazy person who doesn't mind being shark *bait*."

We watch in silence as the head rounds the breakwater, coming our way. Now I can see brown shoulders glisten in the sun, arms pumping rhythmically. A man. Or a boy.

"Today's Nic's and my two-month anniversary," Vivien says absently, still staring at the water.

"Two months? Try twelve years. I was the one who married the two of you when you were five."

One glimpse of Vivien's downcast eyes and the slight smile playing at her lips and I get it. *Right. Two months since they've been doing it.*

"Nic's taking me to the White House restaurant. What do you think I should wear?" Vivien answers herself: "My navy sundress. I know Nic likes it. He couldn't keep his hands off me last time I wore it."

The swimmer has reached the dock and as I watch, he disappears while climbing the ladder, then, at the top, plants his hands flat on the slats, and swings his legs to the side, the way Olympic gymnasts vault over the horse. Then he stands up, shaking his hair out of his eyes.

"Hey—yet again—Gwen. Hi, Vivien. What's up, Emory?" Cass peers down at Em, then over at me.

Emory smiles at him before returning his attention to his bucket of water, now mostly empty. He leans over toward the ocean and I snatch at his life jacket.

Vivien straightens, hugging her knees to her chest, scanning Cass's face, then mine.

"Need a refill?" He reaches for the bucket but holds his hand away from it slightly, waiting for Emory to decide.

Em tilts his head and then scrapes the bucket across the dock toward Cass. I gaze at the horizon, at a band of cormorants drying their wings on the breakwater. After ducking the bucket full again, Cass stands over me, little drops of water glinting in the sun across his chest, then dripping from his hair and the bottom of his suit onto me. He points to Emory's life jacket. "He's still learning to swim?"

"He doesn't know how. At all," I say shortly.

"Never had lessons?"

"He had some water therapy when he was really little—at the Y—it freaked him out. Nic and I have both tried doing it here but it never took. I—" I cut off before I can tell him Emory's entire life story.

"I bet I can do it. Teach him," Cass says casually. "I worked at this camp, Lend a Hand, as an assistant counselor last year. That was my job, helping the"—he makes air quotes—"'reluctant swimmers.'"

I squint at his face. "Think you'll have time for that? They keep the yard boy hopping around here. Old Mrs. Partridge alone is a full-time job."

Cass grins, dimples grooving deep. I suppress a strange urge to dip my fingers into them. "She called me over at the end of the day Friday to tell me I'd done her yard all wrong. Again. That I was supposed to do it 'vertically.' But you were there, right? That *isn't* what she said."

"She'll switch directions on you every time. That's what Mrs. Partridge does with whoever's the current Jose. You'll get used to it."

"The current Jose." Cass turns the phrase over. "I'm not sure I'm down with being 'the current Jose.' Sounds like the flavor of the month." He flips his wet hair out of his eyes again, scattering drops on me, then lowers his voice. "I've only put in two days, still getting my rhythm going here, learning the ropes . . . you know. But this place has gotten . . . a little crazy, hasn't it?"

"It always was, Cass." I shield my eyes and peek up at him through the fence of my fingers.

"That's not the way I remember it. I mean, sure, there were always people like Mrs. Partridge, I guess. Yelling at us to get off their lawn and not pop wheelies on the speed bumps."

"Not people *like* her. Her. She's a Seashell trad—" I stop, swallow. "She's been here forever."

"Really? I don't remember her at all. She doesn't seem to know me either."

Clear as day, I can see Cass, age eight, leaping off this same pier on so many summer afternoons with the sky dark like the one today—skinny shoulder blades, gangly legs, fluffy flyaway hair, skinned elbows, barnacle-scraped knees. Not exactly what's standing here now. All that tan skin.

"You've changed a bit."

Emory chooses this moment to dump more cold water down my swimsuit.

Cass's lips twitch, he ducks his head like he wants to say something but rules it out. "For real, though . . . Part of my job is to rake the beach. Every other day," he continues. "Get the rocks and seaweed off during low tide. Nuts, since it all rolls back in with high tide."

"Oh, I know!" I say. "Crazy, right? I wonder what it's like to be so rich you expect nature to cooperate with you. That you can just hire someone to fix it."

As soon as I say this I feel stupid. *Remember who you're talking to, Gwen. The crown prince of Somers Sails.*

"Look, why don't we just try a starter lesson? See if it plays at all?"

Emory dumps some water on Cass's leg. It slides smoothly down the muscles of his calf. I close my eyes, open them to see Cass watching my face intently.

"You mean in exchange for the tutoring?" I hurry to ask.

"No," he says. "That would be a whole separate deal."

"What tutoring?" Vivien intercedes, firing me a "you didn't tell me this!" look. Which I return in spades. In my case, we're talking a few summer evenings. In hers, a lifetime commitment.

"Gwen agreed to help me get back on track in English." He reaches for Em's again-empty bucket, heading down the steps for a refill. Which means his voice is muffled as he adds, "You can't put it off forever, Gwen. We need to figure out logistics."

He comes back up, hands the bucket to my brother, then stands there for a second, looking at me. "As in your place or mine?"

A horn blasts from the parking lot. Vivien's eyebrows shoot up.

"Gotta go. Let me know where, okay?" He slides by me, pulls a red towel I hadn't noticed before off the slats of the pier. He cracks the towel into the wind, wraps it around his waist, then tosses over his shoulder: "Decide about the swim lessons. I may be no genius in Lit 2, but *that* I can do."

Okay, I watch him go. The whole length of the pier and then into the beach parking lot, where Spence Channing's convertible is idling like a big silver shark. How long has he been there?

A long low whistle and Vivien is fanning her face, then mine. "Whew. Is it hot here or is it just me?"

"There's going to be a whole season of this." I open the cooler, peer into it and finally fish out a granola bar for Emory, rather than . . . a can of sardines or a cantaloupe. "What the hell will I do?"

"That Avoid Him At All Costs plan of yours? I'm not sure he signed off on it." Vivien tilts her head, staring into the parking lot as the car backs up and surges forward, too fast, of course, because it's Spence and rules don't apply to him. "Maybe you should give him another chance?"

"You were the one who told me to watch out!"

"I know." She hunches her shoulders, shivering a little as another chilly breeze comes off the water. "It's just maybe . . . maybe you're watching out for the wrong things."

Chapter Twelve

Mom catches Nic and me before we head out the door Monday morning. "Did Mrs. E. talk about how often she's going to pay, Gwen? It would help a lot if I knew if it was every week or every two. And what about you, Nico? Marco and Tony still pay by the job? And did Almeida's give you some at the end of the night, or . . ."

Nic and I look at each other. A barrage of money questions first thing in the morning can't be a good thing.

"Like always, Aunt Luce. They bill the houses and then the owners send the checks. But Almeida's paid." He heads back into his room, returning with a roll of bills neatly wrapped in an elastic band. "Yours is in here too, Gwenners."

I reach out my hand, but Mom's faster. She takes the bills and begins leafing through them, her lips moving as she silently adds the denominations. Finally, she gives a satisfied nod, divides the money carefully in thirds, returning some to Nic, some to me, slipping the rest into her purse.

"Anything wrong, Mom?"

She blinks rapidly, which, if she were a poker player, would be her tell. "Nothing," she says finally.

"Sure, Aunt Luce?" Nic asks, tapping each of his shoulders

in turn. "Broad shoulders. Ready to listen. Man of the house and all that."

Mom ruffles his hair. "No worries, Nico."

Once she leaves, Nic and I have only to exchange a glance. "Damn, what now?" he says.

I shake my head. "If she starts taking in laundry, we'll know something's up."

Taking in extra is what happened last winter when the hot water heater melted down, the Bronco needed brake work, and Emory needed an orthotic lift in one of his shoes because one leg is slightly shorter than the other. Grandpa Ben also began spending a lot more time at bingo nights, honing his card shark skills.

"Shit." Nic rubs his forehead. "I don't want to think about this. I just want to think about food and sex and swimming and sex and lifting and sex."

"You're so well-rounded." I whack him on the shoulder with a box of Cheerios.

"I'm not supposed to be well-rounded," he says, through a mouthful of last night's leftover pasta. "Neither are you. And cuz . . . you can't tell me you don't think about it."

"I don't think about it," I answer resolutely, concentrating very hard on pouring milk into my cereal.

Nic snorts.

We look up as the screen door squeaks open to see Dad standing there. He looks pissed off and for a second I'm afraid he overheard our conversation. Not a story he needs to know.

But then he drops his aged khaki laundry duffel inside the

door, kicking it to the side wall with one foot. "Screen door's still broken," he mutters, scowling.

Nic fixes Dad with a stare, then returns his attention to the steady movement of his fork.

"Top step to the porch is rotting out too," Dad says. "Fix it, Nicolas. Like I told you last time. Ben could put a foot through that. Or Emory, the state it's in. A man takes care of his family."

"Or he just bails on everyone," Nic mumbles without looking up from texting on his cell. Grandpa Ben, coming in, fresh from the outdoor shower, sprig of lavender in hand to put under Vovó's picture, gives Nic a warning glance, shakes his head. Dad is slightly deaf in one ear, but not immune to tone.

"What was that?" he asks, plunging his index finger into his ear. "What did you just say to me?"

"I said I'll get to it, Uncle Mike." Nic forks up the last of the pasta.

"Told you about it last month, Nico." Dad grabs his bag again, dumps his laundry out on the kitchen floor near the washing machine in the closet. "A man tends to his own."

My cousin scrapes back his chair, rolls his shoulders back, stretching, then clangs the plate into the sink. "Going to work. Then Vee's. I'll be back late." He directs his eyes only to me and Grandpa.

"Too hard on the boy, Mike," Grandpa says in the silence that follows the clap of the screen door.

"He's not a boy anymore. He should be thinking first about pulling his weight, not lifting those." Dad points to Nic's dumbbells. "Where's Luce?"

"Where is she always?" Managing to look dignified despite

the towel wrap, Grandpa heads for the refrigerator. He takes out a grapefruit, setting it on the cutting board. "Working."

Brows lowering, Dad looks at him sharply, but Ben's face is innocent as the cherubs painted on the ceiling at St. Anthony's.

Dad says, "You get a hammer and some wood glue, I can fix that door right now."

"Why aren't you after *me* to fix it, Dad? The ability to hammer a nail isn't just for Y chromosomes."

"Like I said, it's the job of the man of the house."

Grandpa draws himself up straighter, clears his throat.

"The *young* man of the house. You've fixed your fair share of doors, Ben. No one's taking that away from you." Dad reaches for the hammer I've pulled from the tool kit in the kitchen closet.

He gets the door fixed in about twenty seconds, all the better to slam it slightly when he leaves a few minutes later.

What was that about? I'm not even sure who provoked who more. Grandpa Ben reaches over and pats me on the shoulder. "*Seja gentil,* Guinevere. By Nico's age, Mike owned a business, was about to be a father, *pai.*"

His dark brown eyes look old, watery, full of too much sorrow. "Then with two little babies. He didn't have much chance for horsing around."

I know every child of divorced parents is supposed to secretly hope their parents fall back in love and reunite. But I never have. Dad's leaving removed a buzzing tension from the house, like a downed wire that might be harmless but could suddenly shock you senseless if you tripped over it. Grandpa

Ben, Mom, Nic, me, Em . . . we're peaceful together. *É fácil ser gentil*. Easy to be kind.

The Ellington house is eerily quiet when I arrive. I knock on the door, tentatively call "Hello!" but am met by nothing but silence. Do I just march in?

After several minutes of knocking, I kick off my shoes, head into the kitchen. The teakettle's whistling on the stove, there are breakfast dishes on the table, a chair pushed back. But no sign of Mrs. E.

She's not on the porch. Not in the living room or any of the downstairs rooms. Now I'm starting to panic. It's my first day and I've already lost my employer. Did she go off to the beach alone? I'm right on time . . . wouldn't she be expecting me?

Then I hear a crash from upstairs, along with a groan.

I take the steps two at a time, panic rushing up as fast as I do, calling Mrs. E.'s name.

"In here, dear," she calls from a room at the back corner of the house, following that up with what sounds like a muffled curse.

I dash into the room to find her sprawled on the floor in front of a huge open closet door, covered with dresses and skirts and shirts. Seeing me, she lifts a hand in greeting and gives an embarrassed shrug.

"Guinevere, I must say, I am not enjoying being incapacitated! I was reaching for my beach hat with my cane, overbalanced, and took half the closet down with me. Just trying to get a hat. How I shall contrive to change into my bathing suit, I cannot imagine. And the ladies will be here any minute."

I take her hand and try to pull her to her feet, but she's too wobbly for that to work. Finally, I have to put a hand under each arm, haul her upright.

"Dear me," she mutters, swaying, "this is pure bother. I'm so sorry, dear Gwen. How undignified!"

I assure her it's fine and, limping, she makes her way slowly to a green-and-white sofa in the corner of the room. I walk behind her, which is awkward because she keeps stopping, so I bump into her back three times in the short distance. Luckily, she gives a low chuckle instead of getting angry or falling over again and breaking her hip. Reaching the couch, she sits down heavily, grimacing and rotating her ankle, shoving aside a big green leather case. It's flipped open to reveal what looks like our junk drawer at home crossed with *Pirates of the Caribbean*—a crazy tumble of diamond rings, pearl necklaces, gold chains, silver bracelets, coral pins, an emerald necklace. I can't help noticing this enormous diamond, so large, square, gleamingly clear that it reminds me of an ice cube. That thing could choke a pony. I would be afraid even to touch it. What would it be like to be so used to priceless things that you don't set them carefully against the velvet, just toss them in like we do to the jumble of pens that don't work, takeout flyers, flashlights, Grandpa Ben's old pipes, discarded plastic action figures of Emory's?

Mrs. E. gives another little groan, rubbing her ankle with a grimace.

"Should I get some ice—for your ankle? Or something to rest it on? Are you okay?"

She reaches out to pat my cheek. "My dignity is slightly sprained, but I shall recover. My wardrobe is in far more need of assistance than I—" She jabs her cane in the direction of the spill of clothing. "If you would be so kind?"

Rehanging the closet is like traveling through time—there are sequined dresses and wild seventies prints, sheaths Audrey Hepburn could have worn to Tiffany's, full-skirted, tight-waisted outfits, bell-bottomed pants. Mrs. E. has evidently never parted with a single outfit. I have a flash of an image of her trying them on in front of the mirror like an aging little girl playing dress-up. When I finally rehang the last of them, I turn around to find her completely nude.

Before I can stop myself, I let out a little screech. Mrs. E., who was bending over, picking something up off the floor, sways and nearly falls. I rush over to steady her, and then don't know where to grab hold. Luckily, she catches herself on the arm of the couch as I wave my hands ineffectually behind her.

"Gwen, dear," she says serenely, stretching out her wrist, from which a black bathing suit is dangling. "I fear I am going to require your assistance here."

This is not how I imagined my first day at work. Flipping burgers, sprinkling jimmies, and frying shrimp is looking really good. Or weed-whacking. Or simply hijacking one of the lawn mowers and getting the hell off island.

"Close your eyes, dear," Mrs. E. says briskly, possibly seeing me visibly brace myself. Her own eyes look sad.

I squeeze them shut, then immediately realize I actually

have to see what I'm doing in order to pull black spandex onto an octogenarian with a broken foot and a cane.

So, okay, I'm not that comfortable with my own body. Who would be when their best friend is Vivie the Cheerleader? When their school job is timing for a bunch of buff boys in Speedos? When your mom marks time by saying things like, "That was before I was such a blimp"?

But this takes body consciousness to a whole new level.

I'm bending over, yanking the suit over her soft, blue-veined calves, when she makes a little sound.

"Am I hurting you?" Oh God. I should have stayed at Castle's, should have scrubbed toilets with Mom, should have. . . .

"No, no, dear girl, it's just that after a certain age, one barely recognizes oneself. Especially in a state of undress. It's rather like the portrait of Dorian Gray, if he were female and wore a swimming suit."

"Yoo-hoo!" calls a voice from downstairs.

"That will be the ladies," Mrs. Ellington says, a bit breathlessly, as I tug the swimsuit over her hips. "Go let them in. I believe I can manage from here."

I open the door to find Big Mrs. McCloud, as she's always called on Seashell (her daughter-in-law is Little Mrs. McCloud), Avis King, Mrs. Cole, as always clutching her tiny terrier Phelps like a purse, and, surprisingly, Beth McHenry, who used to work with Mom cleaning houses until she retired. They're all wearing straw hats, sunglasses, and bathing suits. Among the ladies, there are no cover-ups, no sarongs, just brightly flowered suits with skirts, freckled skin that's seen a lot of sun, wrinkles, and what Mom would call "jiggly bits." I didn't imagine my day would involve so many octogenarians in swimwear, but it's kind of nice to see it all displayed so proudly. I usually wrap a towel around my waist when I'm in my suit in public. Avis King, who is built like an iceberg—small head, ever widening body—marches in first.

"Where's Rose?" she growls, sounding like Harvey Fierstein with bronchitis. "Don't tell me she's still asleep! It's high tide and perfect weather." She looks me up and down critically. "Lucia's gal, am I right? You're the one hired to be her keeper this summer. Ridiculous waste of money, I say."

Keeper?

"Hello, Gwen!" Beth McHenry says, smiling at me, then furrowing her brows at Avis King. "Lordy, Avis. Rose did get a concussion just a week ago. Henry's only being careful."

"Pish. Just because Rose has a few memory lapses and a bum foot!" Mrs. McCloud pronounces. "Twice last week I hunted for my reading glasses when they were on my head, and put my car keys away in a box of saltines. No one's hiring *me* a watchdog."

"I'd like to see them try," Mrs. Cole murmurs in her sweet voice.

"Typical of Henry Ellington, though. Just like his father. Won't come take care of the situation himself, hires other people to do it." Avis King shakes her head. "How can you possibly know you've got good help unless you look them straight in the eye and interview them yourself? Any fool knows that."

Help? My shorts and gray T-shirt suddenly morph into one of those black dresses with the ruffly white aprons servants wear in Grandpa Ben's movies. I resist the urge to bob a curtsy.

Then I hear the slow thump and drag of Mrs. Ellington descending the stairs and hurry to reach her, but before I can, she appears in the doorway, smiling at her friends. "Shall we move on, girls, before the tide turns? Come, Gwen!"

After the beach, the ladies scatter, Mrs. E. lunches and naps. Then asks me to read her a book, and hands me—I swear to God—something called *The Shameless Sultan*.

Yup. Whatever else it may be, calm, quiet, well-ordered, lucrative . . . apparently the Ellington house is not going to be a refuge from the overdeveloped muscles and half-naked torsos that decorate most of the books at home.

But at least I don't have to read aloud to Mom.

"'Then he took her, as a man can only take a woman he yearns for, pines for, throbs to possess,'" I read softly.

"Speak up, dear girl. I can't hear a word you're saying."

Oh God. I'm nearly shouting the words now—over the sound of the lawn mower rumbling from the front lawn. At any moment Cass could come around the corner to find me pining and throbbing.

I read the next sentence in a slightly louder voice, then halt again as the mower cuts off.

Mrs. Ellington waves her hand at me impatiently. "Gracious! Don't stop now!"

That sounds frighteningly like a line from the book. I doggedly continue. "'With every movement of his skilled hands, he took her higher, hotter, harder—'"

"Just with his hands?" Mrs. E. muses. "I was under the impression more was involved. Do continue."

Was that the sound of the carport side door opening and closing? No, I'm getting paranoid.

"'Waves of rapture such as Arabella had never dreamed existed swept through her ravished body as the Sultan moved, ever more skillfully, laving her supple curves with his talented—'"

Someone clears their throat loudly.

Mrs. E. looks over at the porch door with her expectant smile, which widens even further at the sight of the figure standing there. "My dear boy! I didn't know you were coming."

"No," a male voice says, "apparently not."

Chapter Thirteen

I've closed my eyes, waiting/hoping to literally die of embarrassment. But the deep, rumbling voice does not belong to Cass.

Instead it's a middle-aged man wearing a pale blue V-neck cashmere sweater, creased khaki pants. He walks farther onto the porch with an air of ease and authority. Do I have to explain what I was reading, or do I just pretend it's all good, la-la-la?

I have no idea who this even is until he looks me over with Mrs. Ellington's piercing brown eyes.

Henry Ellington. Whom I barely remember and who just caught me reading virtual porn to his elderly mom.

He reaches down to hug Mrs. E. "I had a meeting in Hartford this morning. I've only got a few minutes before heading back to the city for another one, but I wanted to check on you."

"Poor boy—you work too hard." She pats his cheek. "Even when you're on vacation here. I cannot imagine how anyone can think of numbers and balance sheets and the stock market with the ocean only a few feet away."

"That may be why I hardly ever vacation."

I stand up, slide *The Shameless Sultan* discreetly, cover side down, onto the table next to the glider, and edge toward the screen door. "Mrs. Ellington—I'll give you two some time to . . . um . . . catch up. I'll just go—"

Henry immediately straightens up and holds out a hand. "Guinevere?"

"It's just Gwen."

"Gwen, then." He sweeps his arm to one of the wicker chairs. "Please, sit, make yourself comfortable. You look like your mother—I'm sure you hear that all the time. A fine woman."

I smooth my hands on my shorts, which suddenly seem *really* short, especially when I see him glance quickly at my legs, then away.

"Mother," he says suddenly. "Would you be so kind as to give me a private moment with Gwen?"

I blink, but Mrs. Ellington doesn't seem remotely surprised. "Certainly, dear heart," she says, reaching for her cane. "I'll be in the parlor."

Listening to the slow scrape and thump of her receding, I sense I'm losing an ally. Henry looks at me somberly from under lowered brows.

"Um . . . the book . . . Your mom picked it out. I wouldn't have chosen it myself. I don't read that kind of thing. Well, not a lot, anyway. I mean, sometimes you just need . . . that is . . . Not that there's anything wrong with that kind of book, I mean, they're actually really empowering to women and—"

He cuts me off with a raised hand and the ghost of a smile. "I'm well aware of Mother's taste in literature, believe me. You don't need to worry about *that*."

His tone's flat. I try to interpret his last sentence. What *do* I need to worry about?

He shifts back in the glider, looking out at Whale Rock. Lifting a hand to his forehead, he slides it down to pinch the bridge of his nose between his thumb and forefinger.

"We're all grateful—my sons and I—that you're available to look out for her. She's always been very capable. It's hard for her to accept that things change. Hard for all of us."

I can't tell if he's simply speaking thoughts out loud or wants some answer from me. "I'm happy to help," is all that comes to mind.

I wait for him to continue, but he doesn't; still gazes instead at the waves flipping over the top of Whale Rock—high tide—where a cormorant is angling its dusky wings to dry.

Eventually, I look out too—at the grass running down to the beach plum bushes, which part to make way for the sandy path to the water. Then there's Cass, kneeling, edging the weeds away by hand from the slated path, about ten yards from the porch. He's now wearing a—it can't really be pink?—shirt that sticks to his back in the heat. I watch the muscles in his back flexing.

After a few minutes of uncomfortable silence, Henry seems to pull himself back from some distant place, clearing his throat. "Well then, er, Guinevere, tell me a little about yourself."

Flashback to my conversation with Mrs. E. I get this awful, familiar tingle, like a sneeze coming on, but worse—a sense of terror about my impulse control. Like when it's incredibly still in church and your stomach rumbles loudly, or you just know you won't be able to suppress a burp. I dig my nails into my palm, look Henry in the eye, and desperately try to give appropriate answers to bland questions about school and career plans and whether I play a sport, without offering that my most notable achievement so far appears to have been becoming a swim team tradition.

The questions trail off. Henry looks at my legs again, then out at the water. Over by the bushes, Cass swipes his forearm across his forehead, then his palm against the back of his pants, leaving a smudge of dirt. I count one, two, three waves breaking over the top of Whale Rock.

Then Henry leans forward, touches his hand, rather hard, to my shoulder. "Now listen carefully," he says. Up till now he's been shifting around in his seat, kind of awkward and ill-at-ease. Now his eyes spear mine, all focus. "This is crucial. Mother needs her routine kept consistent. Always. I'd like to be able to *count* on knowing that you will give her breakfast at the same time every day, make sure she gets out in the fresh air, eats well, and takes a nap. It was in the evening that she had her fall, and she hadn't rested all day. She managed to get herself to the phone, but she was very confused. If one of the neighbors hadn't come by . . ." He rubs his chin. "Mother will just go and go and go. I need to make sure these naps happen like clockwork from one to three."

"I'll look out for that, Mr. Ellington. Um . . . sir." It actually isn't that different from Em . . . he too goes till he can't, gets overwhelmed and overtired. Although I doubt "Itsy Bitsy Spider" and the Winnie-the-Pooh song will do the trick for Mrs. E.

He flashes me his mother's smile, incongruous in a face that seems like it was born serious. "You appear to be a sensible girl. I imagine your life has made you practical."

I'm not sure what he means, so I have no idea how to

respond. Inside the house, Mrs. E.'s cane taps close, up to the screen. "May I come out now, dear boy?"

"A few more minutes. We're nearly finished," Henry calls. The tapping recedes. Catching my raised eyebrows, he says, "I didn't want to discuss Mother's fragility in front of her. She'd be embarrassed—and angry."

Back still to us, Cass stands up and stretches, revealing a strip of tanned skin at his waist. His shirt, definitely pale pink, clings to him. He shades his eyes and looks out at the water for a moment. Dreaming of diving in and swimming far out beyond Whale Rock? I know I am. Then he sinks to his knees again and continues weeding.

"One more thing you need to know." Henry's head is downcast; he's fiddling with a crested gold ring on his pinkie. "Everything in the house is itemized."

At first, this seems like some random comment.

Like, "We've had the picture of Dad appraised."

Some rich-person thing that doesn't mean anything to me.

Then I get it.

Everything is itemized, so don't slip any of our family treasures into your pocket.

"Every spoon. Every napkin ring. Every lobster cracker. Just so you know," he continues. "I thought you should be clear on that."

Cass rears up, flips his hair off his forehead, that swim-team gesture, then kneels back down.

Did Henry Ellington actually just say that?

Heat races through my body, my muscles tighten.

Take a deep breath, Gwen.

He seems to be waiting for me to say something.

Yassir, we poor folk can't be trusted with all your shiny stuff.

I shut my eyes. Not a big deal. It's nothing. Forget it. God knows I ought to be used to Seashell. When I helped Mom clean Old Mrs. Partridge's house a few summers ago, Mrs. P. took me aside. "Maria, just so you know, I will be checking the level of all of the liquor bottles." But Henry should know better. Mom's so honest that when she finds change scattered on a desk or a bureau she has to dust, she writes a note saying she picked it up and dusted underneath it, then replaced it, then lists the exact amount. Even if it's four pennies.

It's just a job. Know your place, take the paycheck, and shut up. Other people's stories—issues, whatever—are their own.

But no matter how I try to tamp them down, hot embarrassment and anger scorch my chest. I want to tell him where he can shove his lobster pick. But then I hear the slow beat of Mrs. E.'s cane moving around the kitchen. The halting thump-slide of it and her injured foot. The little rattle of her pulling out china, still determinedly independent. I lick my suddenly dry lips. "I understand."

Henry gives me a slightly sheepish smile. "I'm glad you've got that straight. We're all grateful for your help." He reaches out a hand and, after a hesitation, I shake it. Giving me a card with phone numbers on it, he tells me the first is his office line and to let his secretary know it's "in regard to Mother" if there is any sort of problem. "My private cell number is the second one. Use that only in the case of dire emergencies."

I promise I won't call him for idle chatter (not exactly in those words). He brushes off his hands as though he, not

Cass, had been doing manual labor, gives one last glance out at the water. "It *is* beautiful here," he says softly. "Sometimes I think the only way I can bring myself ever to leave is by forgetting that."

The minute the screen door slams behind him, I sink onto the glider, look out at the dive-bombing seagulls, close my eyes and breathe in, trying to let the familiar rolling roar of the waves calm and focus me.

"What the hell was *that?* Jesus Christ, Gwen!" Cass is leaning a palm against one of the porch columns, jaw muscles tight.

I sit up, shifting gears from one embarrassing moment to the next, my cheeks going hot. Does this boy have to be present at every humiliation? Worse, does he have to be *part* of them? He *listened*. Just like he eavesdropped about Alex . . . and knew all about what went down with Spence. Not to mention what happened with Cass himself. I swallow. "I need the job." I'm saying it to myself as much as to him. My voice wavers. Cass's dark eyebrows pull together.

"He treated you like a servant. A dishonest servant. No one needs a job that much."

Though he's been working hard, sweat dampening his hair, grass sticking to his knees, a smudge of dirt across his forehead, where he must have brushed his hair away, he still looks so *good*. All the anger I couldn't show Henry floods in with a boiling rush.

"That's where you're wrong, Cass. *I* do. I do and so does pretty much everyone who works on Seashell. Including whatever island guy lost out on the yard boy job because your daddy bought it for you to teach you some Life Lesson."

He glares at me. "Let's leave my dad out of this. This is you. I can't believe you just sat there and took that crap from him."

"You haven't been on the island very long. Don't quite know your place yet. Taking crap is what we do here, *Jose*."

He rolls his eyes. "Yeah, yeah. Lots of entitlement. Got it. But it's not what *you* do. I can't claim to know you"—he pauses, has the grace to turn red, then forges on—"but I know you don't put up with crap. That made me sick."

"Maybe you should take your break now and lie down. I'm sure it'll pass."

"Dammit, Gwen!" Cass starts, but then Mrs. Ellington is at the screen door, making her slow way onto the porch with her cane, tap, slow tap, tap. Her eyebrows are raised.

"Is there a problem, dear boy? You look overheated."

Cass shoves his hair back again—leaving a bigger smudge of dirt, sighs. "It's nothing." Pause. "Ma'am."

Mrs. E. studies us, the faintest of smiles on her face. But in the end, all she says is, "Henry really did mean it when he said he could only stay for a few minutes. He's already rushed off. Poor dear. I would love some iced tea, Gwen. Why don't you get some for—" She pauses.

"Jose," I say, just as Cass reminds her of his actual name.

"Maybe Jose should carry around his own water bottle," I add, "like the rest of the maintenance crew. Then he wouldn't need waiting on."

"Jose dumped his water bottle on his head about two hours ago—it's ninety-five today, no sea breeze, in case you hadn't noticed, Maria."

Mrs. E. has settled herself on the glider where Henry had

135

been only a few minutes ago, regarding us, head cocked, the smile broader now. Her eyes are bright with interest. My nerves are still buzzing. At Henry—even though he's just looking out for his mother. At Mrs. E., watching us like characters in a soap opera. At Cass, with his pink shirt and his attitude. At some random guy who zooms by on a Jet Ski, its buzz-saw sound cutting through the lap of the water. While I'm at it, at Nic, who ate the last of the Cap'n Crunch last night, which resulted in an early morning Emory meltdown, which could be soothed only by Dora the Explorer, definitely the most irritating cartoon character on the planet.

"All men need to be waited on," Mrs. Ellington cuts into my thoughts. "Helpless creatures, the lot of them."

"Nah, we have our uses," Cass says. All the heat evaporates from his voice when he speaks with her. "Killing spiders, opening stuck jar lids—"

Caught between wanting to punch him and just laughing, I roll my eyes to heaven. I hate the way he flips the charm on— that he knows, damn well, just how effective it is.

"—starting unnecessary wars, that sort of thing."

She gives her deep belly laugh. "Warming our bed at night. I do miss that. The captain was like a blast furnace."

Cass's eyes widen a little, but he says only, "I can get the iced tea myself. If that's okay with you, ma'am."

"Certainly not—Gwen, please get him some tea, and some for the two of us, of course."

I stomp into the kitchen and throw ice cubes into glasses as if tossing grenades. Which reminds me of Dad rattling pans at Castle's when he's pissed off. A thought that makes me even more angry because I seem to be headed steadily down that highway of rage with no exit ramps.

"She said I should come help you slice the lemons."

Cass is standing in the doorway, one elbow braced against the jamb. Considering how ticked he was only a few minutes ago, he looks entirely too calm and sure of himself.

"Oh? That another useful man-skill? Opening jars, slaying lobsters, slicing lemons. Well, thank God for the Y chromosome then, because we helpless womenfolk would surely perish without you."

The corner of Cass's mouth quirks up. "Technically, yeah, you would. That's connected to the whole bed-warming thing, I believe."

The last thing I want in my thoughts or my memories or my mind in any way at this moment is any association whatsoever with Cass's bed. Of course, that means it's right there, like a photograph. His bed, broad, dark wood dolphins carved into the four corners—those old-fashioned dolphins that look less like Flipper and more like gargoyles, riding smiling on the waves that curve to make up the top and the sides of the bed.

The heat of anger seems to be slipping into another feeling altogether. I'm flushing and trying to will that away. I look out the window over the kitchen sink, up at the faint water stain that looks like a beagle above the refrigerator, anywhere but at him. The deep blue eyes that are locked on my face. His faint smell of warm dirt and grass and salt and his sticky T-shirt.

"Why pink?"

"Huh?" He blinks.

"Your shirt. Why is it pink? Is that some 'I'm comfortable with my masculinity' announcement? Because it's the sort of thing that could get an island kid beat up."

"No statement. Unless my statement is that washing a red towel with your white shirts and your boxers and bleach is a dumbass move." Cass's eyes drop to my lips, and then take their own tour of Anywhere Else in the Room—down at the floor, out the side window as Marco speeds by, clanking garbage cans in the back of the truck, at the laminated sheet of hurricane prep instructions stuck to the side of the refrigerator.

Then back to my lips.

Now I'm just looking back at him, and the air in the kitchen is still and close. Ninety-five and no breeze. And the humidity has to be high today, because I can feel a trickle of sweat edge down between my shoulder blades down the line of my spine and I wonder if a hurricane might actually be coming, because the air has that kind of flat charged feel and *what am I, a meteorologist?*

My fingers twitch to reach over and brush the dirt and a lone blade of grass off his forehead. I can practically feel the heat and the dampness of his skin. I can't read his face or his eyes, but I'm searching them. Cass takes a deep breath, wipes his upper lip with the back of his hand, his gaze steady on me.

"I'm positively parched!" Mrs. Ellington calls. "If I don't have my tea soon, you shall return to find nothing but my desiccated bones lying out here."

"*That* would certainly piss off Henry Ellington." I hurry over to the fridge, pulling out a lemon and practically lob it at Cass, who catches it without even looking at it, still studying me. Unreadable but intent.

Chapter Fourteen

I'm lying on my bed, staring at the slow beat of the ceiling fan, which makes loud whooshing and clattering sounds but never seems to do anything for the temperature. Mom and I call it "placebo fan."

My thoughts flick around.

Do I really want this job? Between Henry and the bathing suit and *The Sultan*?

Don't think about that. You need this job.

And Cass. That look.

I roll over, trying to find a cool spot in my narrow bed.

Spence. Alex. *Swim team tradition.*

Mom counting out the money and Grandpa being a little more stooped and Emory . . .

Whatever's going on between Dad and Nic.

Viv and Nic.

I'm itchy and jangly, so tired of watching the numbers on the clock shift that, no matter how late it is, I can't just lie there anymore.

"Hungry, Gwen?" Mom asks when I head out to the living room. She's curled up on Myrtle, reading a book whose cover features an unnaturally buff man wearing a kilt, an eager expression, and nothing else. "I can heat something up," she offers.

"Just insomnia," I say. "Carry on."

"It *is* getting to the good part. Lachlan McGregor and his sworn enemy, the McTavish, have just realized Lachlan's stable boy is a *her* who's been binding her breasts . . ." Mom's already picked up the book again, vanishing into it as I watch.

"And now they're aaaaall in therapy," I say. Fabio rouses himself from his dead dog imitation by the wood stove, staggers over to the couch, and attempts to fling himself onto Mom's stomach. He falls down, looks around with an "I meant to do that" face and then slinks under the couch.

To my surprise, Nic, who I thought was off with Vivien and the plovers, is lying down on the porch, staring at the sky. He's got one arm folded behind his head, the way he always used to when we would lie out at night, little kids, Fourth of July, watching the fireworks from town bursting over Seashell. Then I notice the cigarette glowing between the folded fingers of his other hand.

I snatch it away—"What the hell, Nic?"—and throw it onto the gravel, where it glows bright as a firefly for a few seconds. Viv's real dad died of lung cancer at thirty-six.

He sighs. "C'mon! You know I don't smoke. I just bummed one off Hoop because he said cigarettes help him focus."

"Hoop's an idiot. You know this." I sit down next to him, wrapping my arms around my legs.

He stands abruptly. "Let's go jumping. I had a beer and I'm tired as hell and I don't want to think. You look pretty wired too. Bridge or pier?"

A little rush snakes through my blood.

Replaced by a quick guilt.

"Where's Viv?" I ask. Nic and I hide from her how often we do stuff like this. It mystifies her. *What, life isn't scary and dangerous enough?"* she says. And to be honest, I wonder what it is in us that needs the rush. But I don't court the danger, like Vivie thinks. I just hook up with it from time to time.

"She's making a truckload of cupcakes for some baby shower. Strawberry on strawberry. Waaaay too pink for me." He shudders. "Get your suit, cuz."

"Uncle Mike stay for breakfast?" Nic asks as we drive to the bridge in Mom's Bronco. "Or did he just come by to drop off his laundry for his ex-wife to do, and make his only nephew feel like shit."

"Nic . . ." I sigh.

He shakes his head. "Why's he got to get on my ass so much?"

I massage my forehead with the palm of my hand, that itchy tense feeling multiplying. Nic reaches out, pulls my head toward his chest with the crook of an elbow, ruffling my hair with his knuckles. "Forget it. Not your problem. I told you I didn't want to talk about anything heavy and there I go. Let's just jump."

But a few minutes later:

"I heard from my mom today," he says as we clamber up the wide wooden rails, worn and silvery with age. We've done this so often, we know which loose ones to skip over, which strong ones to rely on, planting hand over leg on the copper-nail-studded boards.

"Anything new?"

I know there won't be. My aunt Gulia is caught in an endless loop of bad boyfriends and bad jobs and bad choices. Her whole life is like my last March.

He shrugs, takes a deep breath, gives a yell, and flings himself out into the air above the rushing water. I wait for his head to bob back up.

"You're stalling!" Nic calls up. "Going soft?"

It is a rush, that moment when you're suspended in the air, and then rocket deep into the cold water. When I splash back to the surface, the adrenaline is tingling through me, more of a cool thrill than the water. I'm laughing as I come to the surface, and so's Nic.

"Aunt Gulia and Dad being a grouch in one day. No wonder you're tense."

"Hey, at least she didn't ask for money this time. Grouch? I'd say Uncle Mike was more of a dick. But then, so was I." He shoots me a wicked grin. "At least Vee knows how to take care of that."

I put my hands over my ears. "La-la-la!"

"It's funny how you're such a prude about that when you—" Nic stops, his voice cutting off like Cass's mower earlier today. The water suddenly seems colder. "When I what?"

"Gwen . . ." he starts, then trails off, ducking his head under the water as if trying to clear it. When he resurfaces, I'm ready.

"Just say it, Nic."

"Spence Channing? For real? What were you thinking? I thought he was just . . . blowing smoke. Like that rumor about him doing five girls in a hot tub. I mean, come on, who does

142

that? Entitled prick. But I never thought—" He shakes wet hair off his forehead. "That Alex guy, okay, typical douche giving you a snow job. But *Channing*?"

"Don't get all self-righteous on me, Nico."

"Gwen . . . I didn't mean it like that. You know I don't judge."

"You had a little slip there."

He sighs. "I know. It's just . . . Let's get out."

We swim for shore, climb back up to the Bronco, pull towels out of the trunk. Then Nic turns to me, pinching his thumb and index finger together. "We're this close to screwing up and getting stuck, Gwen. You know? I worry about it with me. That I'll be pissed off and not thinking and do something that ruins everything. I don't want to worry about it with you too. You're . . . you're too smart for that. But one little slip, and there you are . . . stuck in this place with some baby or some STD or some crummy reputation. I don't want—"

"I already have the crummy reputation, Nic." *And you're the one looking at engagement rings at age eighteen and not telling me.* But the accusation tangles into a lump in my throat. I can't ask. Not after he's had to deal with both his mom and my dad today.

"Not really. 'Cause I never heard a thing until Hoop was going on about it. He thought I already knew."

"Yeah, I pretty much thought everyone knew." My voice catches on *everyone*.

Nic looks at me. I look away.

"Well, not me," he says. "Probably not a lot of people. And it's not like I'm going to pass it on. I just don't really get where your head was. I told you not to go to that party."

"I'm the swim team mascot, remember? I *like* to party."

He swears under his breath, hunches his shoulders, twitches them like he's shaking something off. Nic shutting down.

I dive out into the water, shut my eyes, swim away from him, off to Seal Rock. It's firm and familiar under my hands. Still faintly warm from the sun. I climb up, rest my cheek on my folded knees, and look out, far out, to the edge of the ocean.

Nic's right. I should never have gone to Spence's party. When your host is famous for hot tub orgies, you sort of know what to expect. But I wasn't going to *hide* after what happened with Cass. I wasn't going to let those Hill guys, those swim team guys, think I was good enough to record their times in the pool, good enough for a one-night stand, but not good enough to socialize with. Nic and Viv were at the White House Inn. The only hotel on Seashell—which Nic had to have saved for ages to afford. I'd spent the afternoon lingerie shopping at Victoria's Secret with Viv, after helping Nic call in an order for the flowers and the gift basket to be left in their suite. I teetered along the cobblestone path in my unaccustomed heels next to Hoop, who was cracking his knuckles as though expecting a wrestling match at the door. As we paused on the walkway, Emma Christianson brushed by us—tall, blond, angular, high-cheekboned, the image of money and poise, and I lost my nerve.

"Are we actually invited? We're not walking into some scene where they'll beat us up or anything, are we?"

Hoop rolled his eyes. "Daaaaamn, Gwenners. You know how these parties are. Spence invited hell near everybody from school—he's gotta save face since Somers threw that big one earlier. They're so crazy competitive. Dumbasses. Come on, I'm going to get me a beer and some serious action. Don't worry, you look fiiiiiine."

I'd borrowed a dress from Viv, who is considerably smaller than me—everywhere. So it was super-tight. And red. And low-cut.

I was used to parties with only a keg, or just six-packs bobbling around in melting ice in a dingy tub. This one had an entire bar—black-and-white and mirrored in a dizzying way—set up with four blenders churning out margaritas and some sort of pink drink. Spence, in a black T-shirt with a purple lei draped over it, was dumping the last of a bottle of rum into one of the blenders. He watched as we walked in and flashed me his perfect smile, the one that rarely reached his eyes—but it did now. "Whoa-ho, it's the princess of Castle's. Whaddya know. Didn't think you'd show for this one, Gwen."

Pouring a tall glass of the pink stuff, he reached over, wedged one of those little umbrellas in it, pressed it into my hand.

"I was just going to go for a Coke. Not much of a drinker," I said.

"Yeah, she's a freakin' lightweight," Hoop confirmed. Then he gave me a friendly pat—on my butt—and slid away, shoulders bobbing to the music.

"Yet here you are." Spence's eyebrows lifted.

What I'd told Spence was true. Still, I immediately took a nervous slug of whatever the drink was, nearly choking on a chunk of ice. Spence just sat there while I coughed, sputtered, and eventually got control of myself. I put my glass down and hiked the top of my dress up. He smiled more broadly and gave me a practiced once-over, as though tracing the path of the blush I could feel rising.

They must offer a secret course for these guys on Hayden Hill: Putting Girls Off Balance 101. Well, to hell with it. I turned on my heel and headed toward the door I'd seen Hoop vanish through. Time for me to stick with my own kind.

Hoop had collapsed bonelessly on the couch and was animatedly recounting to some girl I didn't know the story of a marlin he'd once landed off the coast of the island. I recognized the story. It was Nic's marlin.

I drifted from room to room, trying to look as though I knew the house and exactly where I was headed in it. There was a hallway with a series of marble busts, a huge oval mirror, some tall shiny black standing vases with waxy white lilies. Then a room set up to look like it was outdoors, even though it wasn't, which contained several cockatoos in cages that reeked as though the newspaper hadn't been changed in a while. One of the cockatoos hopped up and down as I entered, screeching, "Live bait! Live bait!" I twisted the gold-plated handle of the French doors and headed out onto the terrace. Even Spence's birds disconcerted me.

It was a huge terrace, like a whole outdoor version of the house. I could dimly make out a figure at the curved end, looking out over all of Stony Bay. I knew who it was just by the way he was leaning on his elbows, by the glint of the hair on his down-tucked head. I wanted so badly to walk up behind him that my right foot nearly tingled, and I was suddenly afraid it would take control, dragging me into a place I knew better than to go. How on earth could I still feel that way? *Nice work,*

Sundance. This swirl of hurt and shame and loss and confusion tightened in my stomach. I bumped back into the terrace-y room, to be greeted by the same creepy cockatoo shrieking, "There's gold in them thar hills!" I swallowed down the last of my drink, now warm and full of strawberry seeds.

"You didn't shut the door all the way." Spence was leaning against the wall by the door. He gestured at the French doors behind me. "The birds need the temperature carefully regulated. Very important to my mother. But then, she's in Marbella right now, and what she doesn't know won't hurt her. So, Gwen Castle, what are you looking for, in here all by yourself? Got to be a reason you came to this party."

His eyes were the weirdest yellow-green color, slightly tilted up at the corners. Cat eyes. They'd always seemed to skip over me before, but now they were fixed steadily on my face. When I said nothing in response—since I had no real answer—he raised a thumb slowly to his lips and chewed on his nail, completely without self-consciousness, despite the fact that, now that I was looking, I noticed that all his other nails were bitten to the quick. Then he nodded like he'd come to a decision.

"You need another strawberry daiquiri." Slipping his arm around my waist, his fingers resting lightly on my hip, he towed me out the door.

"I really don't *need*—"

"Come on, Gwen Castle. You haven't had enough. Not yet. Besides, you've always struck me as a girl who gets an awful lot of 'not enough.' That won't happen tonight."

We took a different route to the bar than I'd taken before, down a long hallway with red-and-gold flocked wallpaper, hung with dark oil paintings of sea captains who looked as though they were sneering, and uptight round-faced women, presumably their wives.

"Your ancestors?" I asked Spence, searching their faces for his familiar smirk.

"Bought at estate sales. It's all for show, Castle, right? All about the look of the thing."

A side door opened and an elderly man emerged, wearing a paisley dressing gown like someone in one of Grandpa Ben's movies. His thinning hair was ruffled up around his pink ears and he was rubbing one eye like Emory when he's tired.

"What's all this noise?" he asked Spence.

"Party, Dads. Remember?"

This was Spence's dad? He was like eighty—*had* to be his grandfather.

The man frowned. "I agreed to this?" he asked vaguely.

"You bought the booze," Spence responded.

The man nodded wearily and disappeared back through the door he'd come out of. He didn't shut it completely, and Spence reached out and gave it a shove with the flat of his hand until there was an audible click.

Then he cut his eyes at me, as though waiting for me to say something.

"Your father doesn't mind you partying?"

"Dads? Nah. He doesn't care. Though, strictly speaking, it was just his credit card that bought the goods, not the man himself." He shrugged, gave a little laugh. "What? Don't look at me like that, Castle."

I had no idea how I was looking at him, although I suspect

it was with pity. Our house could practically fit in his foyer, but it never felt sad and empty like that, despite the distant party sounds. "I—"

"I'm sure you have crazy relatives locked in your attic too. What family isn't dysfunctional, right? Come on, let's get you what you need."

He poured me another daiquiri and one for himself, then led me back down the hallway. And I followed. That's the thing, I trailed right after him into this big study, where he waved me to a big puffy couch, all swirly embroidered flowers on a white linen background, then sank into an equally puffy chair across from it, studying me over the rim of his glass. "You really are pretty as hell, Castle. Much hotter when you don't wear the baggy clothes. Don't stress about what happened with Sundance. How could he help himself? Besides, it's just sex. No big deal."

That's exactly what it hadn't felt like. Not *just* sex. Not no big deal. Not at all. Not to me.

But this was the last thing I was going to let Spence know. I gulped my drink, shook my head, laughed in what I hoped was a carefree and dismissive way. "I've already forgotten the whole thing. Water under the dam." Was that right? Bridge? Dam? I should put this drink down now.

He whistled. "Don't tell Cassidy that. Not in those words, anyway. We guys are touchy. Good to know there are no hard feelings, though."

"I'm not planning on any heart-to-hearts with Cass Somers."

"C'mon, Gwen. He's a good guy. Don't be mad at him." He examined my face more closely, then whistled again, longer and lower. "O-ho. You're not mad. You're hurt. Damn, I'm sorry." He sounded as though he meant it, and to my horror, tears sprang to my eyes.

"Oh man. I didn't think . . . You always seemed so . . . Don't do this, okay?" Spence set his drink on the coffee table, swept my glass out of my hands, one smooth motion. Then did the most unexpected thing. He leaned forward to kiss the tears away, lifting my hair away from my face, tucking it behind my ears, whispering against my cheek. "Sobbing girls are my weakness. They slay me, every time. Shh. Secret. Word gets out and every girl at school will know how to get to me."

"No more five chicks in the hot tub, then," I said shakily.

"Six," he murmured, still smoothing back my hair. There was a smudge of black on his lower lip from my mascara. "But who's counting? You have dreamboat eyes, you know that?"

"Did you use that lame line on all six?"

"Nah. Didn't bother. None of them were looking for a deep and meaningful relationship. Neither, of course, am I. And tonight, I'm betting you aren't either. Right?"

He was right. I wasn't. Not that night. Viv and Nic and the hotel—Cass—flashed into my head and then zoomed out as Spence bent toward me, moving forward to my lips this time.

On the drive home from the bridge, Nic keeps glancing over at me, shoulder muscles tense.

"Look," he says finally. "I shouldn't have brought it up. I just . . . I mean, you're pretty, you're cool, and you've never really dated, and . . ." He drums his thumbs on the steering wheel, his mouth open like he hopes the right words will

150

just magically fly into it. Finally: "Did that ass Alex break your heart?"

"Please. Alex got nowhere near my heart. I thought he did back then, but it was nothing. He just hurt my feelings, the putz."

"Then did Channing . . . ?" He trails off, clearly finding the thought completely impossible.

Hunching back in my seat, I kick my feet up on the glove compartment

"C'mon, Gwen. Talk. Tell me."

I shake my head. "No, thanks."

Nic reaches over and tries to pull my head to his shoulder but I'm stiff, edging him away. "I'm good," I say. "Let's just drive."

Chapter Fifteen

But "just driving" is almost worse than trying to explain that party to my baffled cousin, because it reminds me of the worst, most painful part of that night. Which I don't want to think about. But I can't stop.

When I woke up, I had no idea where I was—only that everything about it felt bad. I was wedged in an uncomfortable position against a wall, my dress twisted up behind my shoulder blades. My mouth was sticky-sweet and my head heavy and fogged. Someone next to me was snoring.

I lay there categorizing the feelings. 1) I was not at home. 2) I didn't like where I was. 3) I was not alone. Then the soft snoring sound next to me and the long foot looped around mine, the distinctive smell of expensive, musky aftershave and the sickly sweet taste of strawberry pulled it together.

I was at Spence Channing's party. In a bed with Spence Channing. And yeah, I'd chosen all this.

Unhooking his ankle from my own, I inched slowly—slll-ooooowly—down to the bottom of the bed and then blinked at the dim floor, the ladder stretching up, the shelf of mattress above me.

This was a bunk bed.

Spence muttered and groped for my waist for a second, but then rolled onto his stomach and snored louder.

I was in a bunk bed with a boy who drank strawberry daiquiris. For some reason, probably because I was still a little buzzed, that seemed like one of the most surreal parts. I was in a bunk bed where the sheets were decorated with nautical flags. With a boy who at some point in the night had gotten up and put on paisley pajama bottoms. While across town, my best friends were in a hotel room that probably smelled like roses . . .

Don't think about that.

I needed to get out of this room.

After bumping my head on the hard corner of a bureau, I finally reached the door, groped for the handle, and let myself out, blinking, into the hallway. The light was dim, but still hurt my eyes. There was a guy—Chris Markos?—slumped against the wall in a half-sitting, half-lying position. Out cold.

Judging from the people scattered on couches and chairs and the floor—all crashed—this was one of those parties that would be described as "epic." There was Matt Salnitas on the couch with Kym Woo—who I knew was dating his brother. Maybe there were enough dramas going on that no one would notice mine. Unlike the last party I'd gone to. *Don't think about that. Just find Hoop and get out of here.* I peered out the window to the corner of the driveway where he'd parked his truck and my heart sank. No truck.

"C'moooon, man . . . just drive me," said a voice from the kitchen. "It's not even outta your way."

"Jimbo. We've been through this." The voice in response sounded tired. "I've got your back. *And* your car keys—till morning."

Walking into the fluorescently lit kitchen, I instantly whipped my hand in front of my eyes. Seated at stools at the counter were Jimmy Pieretti and Cass. Jimmy had a big bowl of unshelled peanuts in front of him and he was waving one at Cass for emphasis.

"I need to do something, Sundance. I need to impress this girl."

"Trust me. Serenading her from her yard at three in the morning is not what you're looking for. Hi, Gwen."

In the brightness of the room—and the muddiness of my head—Cass was looking like the poster boy for WASPiness. White T-shirt, faded khakis, tousled blond hair. All he needed was a golden retriever at his knee and a grandfather handing him an heirloom watch to complete the picture.

Jimmy, by contrast, looked like I felt—a bit grubby and rough around the edges. "Gwen! Hi, Gwen! Let's ask Gwen about this! She can solve my romantic issues."

Cass's eyes met mine for a second. Though his were neutral, I could translate the thought there loud and clear: *Yeah, 'cause Gwen here is so wise with hers.*

But how could he possibly know? He was outside when Spence led me down the hallway to his bedroom, from the poufy parlor sofa to the bunk bed.

But he did. I could see it in his eyes, the tension of his knuckles clenched white around the countertop.

"Alexis Kincaid, Gwen—man, it's like she doesn't even see

me. I need to get her attention. Because we are soul mates, Gwen Castle, and this is a thing she should *get*. So I'm thinking I sing to her. Outside her window. A ballad or something. 'Cause girls get off on that, right? That and the thing where you run through the airport to stop them before they get on the plane, but neither of us are going anywhere, so that won't work. So. Singing. What do you think, Gwen?"

"*I* think I'm not driving you to Alexis's house so her dad can call the police on you again." Cass slid off his stool and poured two glasses of water, clinking ice into them. "Take these." He shot them across the marble countertop, one glass landing perfectly centered in front of me, the next Jimmy.

My brain was thick with wool and the sharp beginning coils of self-disgust. I did not want my pieces picked up by Cass.

I slid into a stool next to Jimmy, put my face in my hands.

"Come on, Gwen. Tell Sundance here to drive me to Alexis's. This party's over for me. Actually, it never began because my dream girl never showed. Please, Gwen."

I pulled my hands away from my cheeks, found blotchy smudges of mascara on the tips of my fingers. Instead of pleading for Jimmy, I said, "Can you take me home, Cass?"

His lips compressed and he flicked his gaze up to the ceiling, as if he could see Spence's room from here. But all he said was: "Sure. We can save Jim here from himself on the way."

Boys never need any time to get going. It's Mom who has to hunt for her purse and then make sure she has her car keys and her freezer pack stocked with diet soda. It's Vivie who has to run back for one last swipe of lip gloss, redo her hair, mirror check. Cass just pulled car keys out of his pocket, jingling them in his palm, grabbed his parka, Jimmy took a slug of water, and we were good to go.

I trailed after them to Cass's car, which turned out to be a red BMW. Ancient, though—that boxy square shape of old cars—and the paint had lost its sheen and faded to Campbell's tomato soup orange-red. Jimmy, groaning, forced himself into the backseat, even though I argued with him.

"No. No. Gwen Castle. I'm a gentleman. Please tell Alexis Kincaid the next time you see her. C'mon Cass, just one little drive by? What's the harm in that?"

"It's called stalking." The back of Cass's hand brushed by my bare calf as he shifted the car into reverse. And, God help me, I felt a tingle. A freaking shiver even though I was even now in the process of the walk—or drive—of shame. My second in the last month. After two separate guys. What in the name of God was wrong with me?

"It's called love," Jimmy argued.

"No way, Jimbo. He's like a dog with a bone with this when he's had a few," Cass said to me, under his breath. "Totally normal under most circumstances."

Cass's profile faced forward, not the slightest bit bent in my direction, straight nose, strong chin, his hair silver-frosted by the moonlight and flashing bright in the reflection of the headlights. I curled my legs under myself, shifted uncomfortably on the seat, stared at the strip of duct tape on his coat, wondered why he didn't just buy a new coat. Mom, Nic, Dad, Grandpa, me . . . we had to push things beyond their life spans, rejigger them to get as much wear as possible. But not the Hill guys.

They could just use and toss, replace. Right? We got to Main Street, circled the roundabout, headed down the most historic part of town, past all the houses, orderly and tucked in upright little rows and clean-looking. All those houses that looked like they were full of careful tidy people who always made good choices. That coil of shame sharpened, tunneled a little deeper into my chest.

Cass pulled into a circular driveway and Jimmy started to climb out, mumbling, "I'm already regretting everything I did and most of what I said tonight. Do you maybe have amnesia sometimes, Gwen? Could you have amnesia about this? If I ask nicely?"

"I will if you will, Jim," I said. In the light of the open door I saw Cass flash me a quick glance, frowning, but Jimmy didn't look back, wedging himself out of the car.

The door crashed behind him and suddenly the air in the car seemed to evaporate, suffocated out the window. Gone. Cass felt too close, the whole space too crowded, like I couldn't move my arm without nudging against his, or shift my leg without it sweeping past his, or have a thought without it being about him. But his profile was remote and distant, eyes on the road, hands set on the steering wheel, responsibly at ten and two. Then he pulled one off, fisted it, let it go. Clench. Unclench.

Silence settled around us like a hot wet blanket. But what was I supposed to say?

"Full moon on the water. Make a wish," I muttered finally, just to say something. Mom always said that, pointing out the pretty. Suddenly I so much wanted my mom to put her arms around me and fix everything, the way she could when I was five.

"What?"

"Full moon on the water. Make a wish."

He shook his head slightly, shrugged, jaw tight. I swallowed, pulled the hem of my dress down farther over my thighs. Then we were crunching up on the crushed clamshells of my driveway. *The Castle Estate*, I thought grimly.

He shifted into park, took a deep breath as if he was going to speak . . . I waited.

"Welcome home," he said finally.

Silence. I wiped one of my eyes, rubbed my finger dry on my dress, leaving a black smudge against the scarlet fabric.

Cass reached over, flipped open the glove compartment, handed me a stack of rough brown napkins from Dunkin' Donuts. Home away from home for the swim team with their early meets. Of course he would keep them neatly piled in the glove compartment, not shoved in haphazard, the way Nic or I would do in the Bronco. He put his hands back on the wheel, rubbed his thumbs back and forth on it, staring at them as if they were moving independently. "Are you okay? Did anything . . . bad happen to you?"

Nothing I didn't bring on myself, I thought. Then I realized he was asking if I was . . . forced or something. I shook my head. "There was none of that. Nothing but my usual gift for doing stupid things with the wrong people." I wiped my eyes, shoved a brown napkin into my coat pocket.

Cass winced. "Point taken. If you're going to do stupid things, Spence is a great choice. You had to know that."

"He's *your* friend."

"Well, yeah. Because I don't have to date him."

"This was not exactly a date."

"Yeah, what was this? Another little kick in the heart?"

"What do you care about my heart, Cass?"

He opened his mouth, shut it again. Folded his arms and stared stonily out the window. Rigid. Faintly judgmental. Which brought a pull of anger out of my coil of shame. What right did he have, anyway?

"Big deal, anyway, Cass. It was just sex." I snapped my fingers. "You're certainly familiar with that concept. Thanks for bringing me home." I searched around for the car handle and pushed it open, but before I knew it, Cass was standing outside it, reaching out his hand for me.

"What are you doing?"

He looked at me as though I was either crazy or not very bright. "Walking you to the door."

"You don't have to do that. I'm . . . really not the kind of girl who gets walked to the door."

"Jesus Christ, Gwen!" he said, then shook his head and pulled on my hand. "Just let me get you safely in."

"I can make it from here."

"I'm walking you to the door," he told me, leading me up the worn wooden steps. "Not taking the chance that you're going to go throw yourself off the pier or something. Because, forgive me for noticing, you seem a little impulsive tonight."

"That's one word for it."

"Gwen . . . I . . . Would you . . . I mean . . ." He stopped on our doormat, beside Nic's sneakers and one discarded rubber fishing boot of Grandpa Ben's, apparently running out of words. "I'd like to . . ." He shut his eyes, as if in pain.

I waited, but after a second he just said, "Never mind. The hell with it."

And turned, crunching back across the clamshells to the car.

Did I use Spence? Did he use me? I don't know. In the end, did it even matter? We'd just been bodies. Arms, legs, faces, breath. *Just sex*. No big deal.

Still.

Explaining that night was never going to be easy. Not then, to Cass. Not tonight, to Nic. Not ever, to myself.

Chapter Sixteen

Cass is apparently fighting with a bush when I pass him the next day on my way home. He's got hedge clippers and is whacking away, making a big dent in the side of one of Mrs. Cole's arborvitaes. It's completely lopsided now. As I watch, he stops, takes a few steps back, then starts making a dent on the other side. The bush, which used to resemble an O, now looks like the number 8. After a few more unfortunate trims it looks like a B.

I can't help it. I stop, cup my hands around my mouth, and call, "You should quit while you're ahead—it's only getting worse."

He turns off the hedge clippers, "What?"

I repeat myself, louder, because Phelps, Mrs. Cole's terrier, is yapping away inside the house, scritching his claws frantically on the screen door. Cass sighs. "I know. I keep thinking I'll fix it and . . . I don't want this woman to come out and have a heart attack. She seems a little high-strung. Screamed when I knocked on the door to ask where the outdoor plug was."

I study him. He seems to have shaken off our weirdness from yesterday, and the whole Henry Ellington . . . thing.

He takes a few steps back again, tilting his head, scrubbing his hand over the hair at the back of his neck. "D'you think she'd notice if I dug this up and replaced it with another bush? That may be my only hope."

"Got a spare arborvitae up your sleeve?" At least today he actually has sleeves, as in a shirt, thank God. I open the gate and walk in. "Maybe if you just trimmed down that top part and made the other side a little flatter?"

He revs up the hedge clippers, begins trimming on the wrong side. I wave my hands in a stop motion. Cass flips the off button again. "What now?"

"Not *that* side! You're making it worse again. Just hand it to me."

"No way. This is *my* job."

"Yes, and boiling the lobsters was my job. You had no problem barging in there."

"Christ almighty. Can we move on from the lobsters, Gwen? You honestly have this much of an issue with accepting help?"

"I'm pretty sure the issue at the moment is *you* not being able to accept help. Just give me the clippers."

"Fine," Cass says. "Enjoy." He hands the clippers to me, pulling his hands back quickly and shoving them in his pockets. Then he studies my face. "Actually, you do seem to be enjoying yourself. Too much. You *are* planning to use those on the hedge, right? Not on me?"

"Hmmm. That hadn't occurred to me." I turn the hedge clippers on and look him over speculatively. He bends down, wrenches the plug out of the wall.

"Hey! I was trying to help."

"I didn't like the look on your face. It made me worry for

the existence of my future children. I haven't forgotten that butter knife that was the only thing standing between you and Alex Robinson singing soprano."

"I just never thought I'd see you be inept at anything. Haven't you done this before?"

"Hey, I'm not inept. I'm just not . . . ept yet. And since you're so curious, no, mowing our lawn is my only landscaping experience."

"Did Marco and Tony know this when they hired you? *Why* did they hire you?"

"I don't know. My dad talked to them first, and when I came in they just asked if I minded hard work and being outdoors most of the day. I figured I'd be mowing. Period. Maybe some weeding. I didn't think I'd be planting and trimming and tying bushes to fences and I sure as hell didn't think I'd be raking the beach."

I've plugged in the hedge clippers again and now I turn them on and start in on the top of the hedge. "You can always quit," I shout over the whir.

"I don't quit. Ever," he shouts back. "I think you're making it worse."

I lop off a few more branches, then run the clippers down, making the bumpy side as flat as the other. Then I stand back.

It definitely looks better. I move over to the matching arbor-vitae on the other side of the steps and start working on that to make it look the same.

"Now you're just showing off," Cass calls. "I can do the rest."

"No way, Jose. Clearly you can't be trusted."

This sentence drops between us like a brick shattering on the pavement.

Again I get a flash of his white-knight rescue from Spence's party. Granted, a cranky white knight, but still . . .

Jaw tight, Cass walks over to the Seashell truck, pulls a plastic bin out of the back, and starts scooping the severed branches into it. I buzz the sides of the other tree flat.

"*There* you are, *garota bonita!*" Grandpa Ben calls. He's trudging along up the road with his mesh bag full of squirming blue crabs, holding Emory's hand and dragging the unenthusiastic Fabio by his leash. Em is in his bathing suit, clutching a sandy-looking Hideout and looking sleepy. "I bring you your brother. Lucia is working tonight and I have the bingo."

"Superman! Hello, Superman! It Superman," Emory tells Grandpa, his face lighting up.

"Hey there, Superboy," Cass says easily. My brother runs over and immediately throws his arms around Cass's leg. And kisses him. On the knee. Cass seems to freeze for an instant, then pats Em's bony little back.

"Hey buddy. Hello, Mr. Cruz."

"Superman," Emory repeats. Clearly, for him, all that needs saying. He gives Cass his shiniest smile and plunks down in the grass, nuzzling Hideout against his neck.

"I will not lie, *querida*. He's been cranky. *Está com pouco de bug* today. We got ice cream, but no. No help." Grandpa Ben pulls his watch out of his pants pocket. It's not a pocket watch, but he keeps it there, out of habit, afraid, from his fishing days, that it would snag on something. "I need to go now. I get there late, Paco stacks the deck."

"Where's Nic?" I've babysat for the last four nights that Mom has worked late. So, Nic's turn.

"The swimming," Grandpa Ben says. "Be good for your sister, *coelho*."

Emory ignores him, focused on Cass coiling up the extension cord.

"Which beach?" Cass calls. "I'm pretty much done here."

"Sandy Claw."

"Huh." Cass finishes wrapping and loops the cord between his shoulder and his elbow, which shows off his biceps nicely. I think he's even fitter than before—already. Bring on the Yard Boy Workout. "Maybe I'll get on down there and give him a run for his money. What do you think, Gwen? Want to come check out my form?"

He flashes the dimples at me.

Oh dear Lord.

I wrinkle my nose, toss my hair back. "I couldn't care less about your form."

"Right," Cass says. "I can tell."

I examine his face sharply, but his tone is completely innocent.

Maybe it's the total contrast between the terse, tense Cass on that March night, when I had no way to read him, no compass at all, and the sunny, smiling one now. Maybe I'm just light-headed from the heat . . . But I give him the tiniest of smiles. And get a full-on grin in return.

I tell myself it's okay to feed Em fast when we get home, use those nasty frozen dinners Mom relies on, Emory doesn't mind, and Grandpa and I despise, dumping crinkled French fries out on a baking pan, letting Em consider ketchup a vegetable. I assure my conscience I'm not hurrying through the shower, or Emory through his bath, for any reason at all.

If there were an Olympics for kidding yourself, I'd take home the gold.

Then Em doesn't *want* to go to the beach. He's sleepy, wants to be lazy, cuddle. He settles himself on Myrtle, Fabio collapsed and drooling heavily on his thigh. He points at the screen. "Clicker."

"Fresh air," I say firmly.

"Clicker. Pooh Bear. Dora."

"Jingle shells. Boat shells. Hermit crabs," I counter.

Emory's lower lip juts out. "Seen today already," he says.

"Superman?" I coax, finally.

Chapter Seventeen

I don't have much hope that Nic or Cass will still be there when I get to the beach. Em wouldn't walk, so I had to plunk him, Hideout, and Fabio into our old Radio Flyer wagon and drag it down the hillside. Not really drag, more like run ahead of it, because it picks up speed as we descend, and Fabio remembers being a puppy and hops out, nipping at my heels and yelping all the way down.

My cousin and Cass are apparently facing off at the end of the pier, ready to dive again. Viv is sitting on one of the wooden pilings, counting down on Nic's watch as Em and Fabio and I walk out.

"To the breakwater again?" Cass asks, breathing hard, hands on his bent knees.

"The far one this time," Nic answers. He swipes his arm across his forehead, then shakes his head, sending droplets of water flying. He squints and points at the second wall of rocks, blue-black, jagged edged, barely visible above the waves. Cass nods, shortly.

Viv shields her eyes, evidently on shark watch.

"Want me to count off?" I call. "On five, four—" And Nic dives before I say "three." Cass shoots a *what-the-hell* look back at me, then he's in. We watch Nic's arms flashing. Viv's shouting, "Go Nico, go Nico!" Fabio leaps around, yipping, happy to be part of the action. I feel this impulse to cheer for Cass. Against my own cousin? Blood may be thicker than chlorine, but hormones seem to scramble the equation.

"Go!" I shout loudly, not quite sure for who. "Go!" I shout it again, drowning out my thoughts. Drowning out another memory of the summer Cass spent at Seashell, the first year we were all old enough to swim out to the breakwater alone. Of him, little-boy skinny, standing on the rocks, pumping his fist in triumph, slapping Nic's back, high-fiving me, and then doing his ear-blushing thing, missing his two front teeth.

Nic *is* ahead, thanks to his unfair advantage.

Then there's another splash, a sharp bark from Fabio, and I whirl around. Em's not there. Em is not there and I didn't put his life jacket on. For the first time ever, I forgot. I wasn't holding on to his hand or leg or a fold of his shirt, which I do even when I *have* put a life jacket on. I'm hurling myself off the pier in an instant, Viv's screams echoing in my ears.

It's high tide.

High tide. Emory's in his Superman pajamas, which are darkish blue, the color of water. I'm swishing my arms around wildly, grabbing for his fingers, his hair, his big toe, anything. Coming up for a choking breath, then plunging down again, clawing through the cold depths. Then I touch warm skin, his leg, oh thank God, yank him toward me, his head bumping up against my shoulder, hauling us to the surface with an inhale that sounds like a sob. He's coughing . . . he's coughing, so he's breathing, but he immediately starts to cry. I'm towing him toward the steps that lead from the deep water to the pier, gasping into his hair.

Then I feel someone beside me.

"You got him," Cass says, warm hand around my waist. "He's safe. You got him. Breathe. Both of you." Emory howls louder and I can hear Viv gabbling, "Oh my God oh my God." This is my fault. I looked away at the wrong time. I didn't put a life jacket on him. Cass has his hand on my back now, steering us up the steps.

Viv is waiting with a towel and I wrap Em in it and gather him into my lap. "Em, talk!" I order. "Say something."

"Hideout!" Emory bursts into even stormier tears. "*My* Hideout. He wanted to see the water. He drownded."

Cass turns to me for clarification.

"Stuffed animal," I say, combing my fingers over Em's scalp, feeling for bumps. He keeps crying, shoving my hand away.

"What color?" Cass peers into the water. "Brown? Black? Blue?"

"Red."

"Perfect." He dives back in, so cleanly there isn't even a ripple.

Nic has reached the steps now and hurries up, eyes worried. "Dude, you cool?"

"Hideout!" wails Emory. Vivien, Nic, and I debate taking him to the ER just to have him checked. Teary-eyed Vivien and I are in favor, Nic tells us we're overreacting.

"Remember the time you fell off Uncle Mike's boat when you were, like four? You were *fine*. Same thing."

"But it's Emory," I say. Em was born so early, at twenty-eight weeks, a fragile two pounds. Then when he was four he had viral meningitis and a fever of 106. Whenever he gets a cold in winter it always, inevitably turns into bronchitis. Pretty much everything that could go wrong does go wrong. I'm clutching him so tightly that he stops sobbing to say, "Ow. Be nice."

"Here you go, buddy." Cass has climbed up the ladder from the water to the pier thrusting out a bedraggled, waterlogged stuffed hermit crab.

Em's tears turn off, his lips part, then wing into a smile. "Saved him. Superman saved Hideout." He snatches the crab from Cass, hugs it, squeezing out a bucketload of water, fingers its head for bumps, kisses it, then scootches over and puts his hand on Cass's cheek, petting him the way Mom does to Em himself.

Cass clears his throat, shuffles one foot on the wet wooden slats of the pier. "No problem, man. He might need a little CPR—and a dryer—but he'll be fine."

"Thanks, Somers. Quick thinking." Nic nods at him, chin lifted, arms crossed.

"Not as quick as your footwork on the dive," Cass says coolly. Nic's jaw tightens.

"Badly played, man," Cass continues. "Very un-CGA."

Nic's face shades stormy. He looks quickly at Viv, then me, then down at the pier.

"Three-second advantage," he scoffs at last, like *Whatever*.

"Yeah. Exactly." Cass shakes his hair out of his eyes, which seem a slightly more wintery sea blue than usual.

"Jeez, enough with the pissing contest," I say. "Let's get Em home." Nic takes him out of my arms and looks at me, face impassive. I give his back a little nudge toward shore, almost a shove. He nods, a motion so small it's almost undetectable, walks off. Vivien trails, wringing out Hideout, occasionally glancing back over her shoulder at us, standing so close we're each dripping water on each other. She cocks her head at me, then hurries after Nic and Em.

I touch Cass's arm quickly. "Thank you."

"No big deal." Then he turns to me with a straight face. "But, hey, was that a stuffed *hermit crab*?"

I laugh, and it feels so good, unknotting the tension that's been snarled in my stomach for days. "I know—it's like a bunch of toymakers were in a boardroom somewhere, snapping their fingers, and said, 'I know! A crustacean line! Just what every kid wants.' But Em loves him. So really . . . thanks."

"You did the more important save, Gwen. Keep this up and I might have to forfeit my superhero cape. Or talk to Coach about that Lifeguard of the Year award you earned back in March."

The Polar Bear Plunge.

For a beat, it just lies there, like a glove thrown down. Smack. Then I meet his eyes. I don't know what mine are saying, but after a moment, he looks away, up to the sky, then down at me, lips parted. I follow his gaze to my chest, where of course my too-tight tank top is completely plastered. White. Practically transparent.

That's what this is about?

I snap my fingers. "My face is up here."

Cass reaches for his towel, now an interesting shade of mottled pink, wraps it tightly around his waist. "Um, sorry. Are you cold, by any chance, Gwen?" An infinitesimal smile, just enough to bring out one dimple, pulls at the corner of his mouth.

I groan. "You have no idea what a pain these are. Since I was twelve I've gotten this! Like I'm boobs attached to a faceless girl. Sometimes I just want to take 'em off and hand them to whoever can't be bothered to see the rest of me and say, 'Here. I think this is what you're really after.'"

Cass flips his hair back. "And we were doing so well there for a second. I didn't mean to objectify you or disrespect your personhood. You look"—he throws his hand toward me—"like you look. Sue me for noticing." He meets my eyes. "By the way—just let me give your little brother a few lessons. Otherwise, you're going to have a heart attack worrying, or an ulcer blaming yourself for not being on guard twenty-four/ seven. And let's make tutoring happen. At this point you're just making bullshit excuses. I need this, okay? I need to stay on the team."

"Why is that so important to you?" I ask. "It's not like you're applying to the Coast Guard. You'll get into whatever college you want."

He shakes his head. Looks at me. "You have no idea what I want. None." His voice has abruptly gotten hard.

I take a deep breath, shut my eyes, exhale. "You're right. I don't. I don't know what you want. You did a good thing and I'm being a jerk."

I'm relieved to see both dimples groove deep. "Whoa. Is that an actual apology? I forgive you. If you forgive me for standing in front of a girl like you and letting my eyes wander. My mom would be pissed with me."

I have only the haziest of memories of Cass's mom from

that one summer. Adults you don't know well all seem blend together when you're little—someone big who talks about things you don't understand that don't sound interesting. No memory at all whether she was tall or short, blond or dark. Or even kind or not. I try to picture her at meets and I can't. I can just see Cass's dad cheering.

"She's a therapist," he adds. "Specializes in empowering girls and women. She's written books about it. *How the Patriarchy Silences the Female Voice.* That was her best seller. Oh, and *Men, Why Do We Bother?*"

"Ouch," I say. "Really?"

"Yep. Mom doesn't like to leave any feeling undelved . . ." He wrinkles his nose, squinting. "Is that a word?"

"Close enough," I say. Try harder to remember Cass's mom. Picture her in hemp clothing with wild hair, fingers tented. Then with hair drawn back into a stern bun, power suit on. Neither seems right.

"Sometimes family dinners are like therapy sessions. I feel like we should all be lying around on couches while my mom over-explores our psyches. 'How does having pizza again make you fee-el, Cass? I think we need to examine your broccoli issues, Bill.'"

I'm still stuck on *Men, Why Do We Bother?* I don't want Cass to have some uptight, disapproving family. It doesn't fit with my image of his dad from that summer, from my memories of feeling comfortable running into their house, never bothering to kick off my shoes outside the door. "And she wound up with three sons," I say.

"Yup, I was the one last try for a girl. I would have been Cassandra . . . you know, after the girl no one listened to in the *Iliad*. Who died."

"Instead you got named after the cool guy in an iconic classic movie."

"Yeah, well, he got offed in the end too."

"Well, my mom named me after the world's most famously unfaithful woman."

Cass flinches, then looks out to sea. "I'd better get home. I've got this—family thing tonight—and you'd better go dry off. I'll put together a program for Emory."

He strides down the pier without looking back. I scan the parking lot, half expecting to see Spence's car idling there like the other day. It's not. But it might as well be, because Spence was right there between us.

Again.

And we were doing so well there for a second.

Chapter Eighteen

Mom plops heavily down on the couch as Nic and I describe what happened with Em, both of us trying to take a bigger share of the blame as though it's the last slice of pie.

"This was all me, Aunt Luce. I was stupid-focused—didn't even get that he didn't have a life jacket—"

"No, Mom, it was my fault. I was"—*distracted by Cass in his swim trunks and this weird truce we keep zigzagging in out out of*—"not paying attention when I should have—"

"It shouldn't always have to be Gwen, Aunt Luce. I dropped the ball completely, 'cause I—" Nic's face turns red.

"I was the one who was on the dock with Emory—I was the one who brought him there. With no life jacket."

Finally, as we both stutter to a halt, Mom sighs, her eyes taking in Em, already nodding to sleep on the corner of the couch, long eyelashes fluttering, still clutching Hideout. She brushes her hand under her eyes, then ruffles Nic's hair, cups my chin. "I ask too much of you two, I know. I look at you both, good kids, and I want you to have everything I ever wanted and didn't get. But we can't let Emory slip through the cracks. We have to keep him safe. He can't do that for himself."

Grandpa Ben, who is punching tobacco into the pipe he

hardly ever smokes, a rare sign of extreme agitation, points the barrel of the pipe at me, then Nic, in turn. "Our *coelho* needs the swimming lessons. We will get the young yard boy. He talked to me about it the other day."

Nic bristles. "*I* can teach him. Why do we have to bring in Cassidy Somers?"

"You tried, Nico." Mom pats his knee. "So did Grandpa. And Gwen. Sometimes these things are better when it's not family doing the teaching."

"Yeah, remember when Dad tried to teach me to drive?" I shudder.

"It would have been better if it wasn't Mrs. Partridge's fence you hit," Mom says. "She still brings it up every single time I clean her house, the old battle-ax."

Grandpa holds the lighter to the bowl of his pipe, takes deep breaths in and out. At last he settles his pipe in the corner of his mouth and says, "We talk to the yard boy. You"—he points to me—"you ask him tonight. He is here on the island, yes?"

"At the Field House," Nic says. "I'll tell him."

"No, I need you to drive me to Mass," Grandpa Ben says. "My *coelho* had a lucky escape today. Thanks must be said. Guinevere can work it out with the yard boy." His brow crinkles. "Perhaps we can pay him in fish?"

I wince at the mental image of me slapping a dead mackerel into Cass's arms at the end of a lesson. "We'll work something out," I say. "And, guys, his name is Cassidy. Not Jose. Not the yard boy. Why is that so hard for everyone to remember? Also, he's not *that* young. He's our age. I mean, I think he's a little older than me but it's not like he's ten. I mean, obviously. Look at him. And you should remember him anyway, because he spent the summer here once—that crazy one, with the weather, and . . . and . . . remember? Not to mention the fact that he's on Nic's swim team, for God's sake."

Grandpa, Nic, and Mom are all staring as though I've sprouted an additional head. Green, with pink polka dots.

"This the polite one with the abs?" Mom asks.

Grandpa says, "You know how hard it is for us to get to meets. And all boys look the same with those little caps and those bathing suits *muito pequeno*."

They do not.

Emory is still sleeping when I leave, so I haul along Fabio as a handy excuse to make my visit brief. Cass is not going to want our aged, flatulent, over-excitable dog hanging out for long. A quick business transaction, that's all this needs to be.

But when I knock on the door of the Field House apartment, it's not Cass who opens it. It's Spence. He's looking particularly toothpaste-ad perfect. It helps that he's in tennis whites.

"Helloooo," he drawls, propping the door open with the heel of his foot and doing his full-body survey maneuver. Must be a reflex. From what I've heard, Spence never does any-thing—any*one*—twice. "Fancy meeting you here."

Fabio licks his leg, then nudges against him lovingly, wait-ing for a pet behind the ears. Spence bends down and scritches him, and Fabio immediately rolls over on his back. *Traitor*.

"Just had something to ask Cass. He home?"

"Making like Sleeping Beauty." Spence jerks his thumb toward a closed door. "I thought I'd get a game out of him, but he crashed. Said he just needed a power nap, but it's been an hour now. Come on in."

I tell him I'll come back another time. Spence, not even bothering to argue, just dismissing this, opens the door wider. "I won't bite. Unless you ask *very* nicely. C'mon. It sucks that he's a working stiff this summer. He's tired all the time and not up for anything decent. Or, more to the point, indecent."

"Poor guy," I say sarcastically. Then Fabio is charging into the room, all eighty-five pounds of him dragging me behind, launching himself onto the couch in one of his ill-timed bursts of youthful energy. I need to get him, and me, out of here, now. Fabio has been known to "mark his territory" on strange couches.

"Way to make an entrance, Castle. Yeah, it stinks, my boy being all blue-collar." Spence sounds completely sincere, oblivious to the irony of complaining about the evils of having a summer job to a person who obviously also has one. "I'd never do that. Weeding, mowing. Lousy way to spend three short golden months of no school. I'd tell the old man to shove it. But you know our Cass. *He* does what he's told."

Yeah, especially by you.

"He's not 'our' Cass." I look around the room. Nasty. Avocado-green appliances, heinous bright yellow walls, faux cherry-wood cabinets with the veneer peeling back to reveal the sticky plywood underneath, fake brick linoleum that's cracking and curling up at all the corners. Seashell has its tennis courts resurfaced annually and spent a fortune to have some former golf pro analyze the course. And then give private lessons. The yard boy's apartment is apparently not on the punch list.

"As you wish, princess. Popcorn? I'm starving, and Sundance has nothing else to offer us." He clangs open the microwave door, shoves the bag in, slams it shut. "This job is sucking the life out of him. Worse than damn school. Personally, *I've* got no intention of doing anything worthwhile this season. I've spent the past two at Middlebury language school or Choate tennis camp. This can be a sea change. My summer to get tan and lazy, fat and happy."

I toy with the idea of making a cutting remark about his lack of ambition, but, honestly, that all sounds nice if you can swing it. Except the fat part. Which I can probably manage on my own.

"I've rarely been tan," Spence continues over the whirring cycle of the microwave. "Hardly ever lazy. Never fat." He pulls the bag out, sucks his fingers, cursing under his breath.

"You forgot happy."

He shrugs, a dark look crossing his face.

Fabio is still entranced by the couch, which has a big pile of laundry tumbled on it. Many pink items. It occurs to me that this is the first time Spence and me have been alone since that party.

I need something to do with my hands, so I pick up a T-shirt and fold it, then another, match up a pair of socks, roll them into a ball.

I hear this exhalation of breath, like a snort, from Spence

and look up to find him watching me. "How domestic. What a nice little wife you'll make."

I drop the second pair of socks. What am I doing, morphing into Mom? I flush, but when I check Spence's face again, he's just smiling at me, extending the bag of popcorn.

"Something cool to go with?" he offers. "A six of Heineken was my housewarming gift for Cass. You're *fun* when you're loaded."

"The swim team tradition, yeah, I know, Spence," I say. "Like you've said."

"I apologized for that, Castle. Just being a dick. What I do best. Well, second best." He waggles his eyebrows at me.

I resist the urge to stick out my tongue at him, settling for shaking my head.

"How's your brother?"

That he would ask, which seems unlike him and also implies that Cass talked about Emory, throws me.

"He's fine," I say shortly. "That's why I'm here. I want to take Cass up on his offer to teach him to swim. So you can just . . . pass that on, and I'll get going and—"

"Cass nearly drowned when he was six," Spence says. "Rip tide at the beach. We were there with my dad, who was . . . But whatever, I got the lifeguard and saved him." He looks at his watch. "Hell, it's nearly seven now and I've got to be at the club at eight. I'm gonna wake him up."

He heads toward the closed door. I hurry after him. "No, don't. I'll come back."

But Spence keeps going and I follow him right into the bedroom. Which is painted the same eyesore green-yellow as the main room, but has walls covered with hand-drawn maps, signed in a clear, careful hand: *CRS*.

Cass is lying on his stomach, arms wrapped around his pillow like he's hugging someone close. His hair's all rumpled and his mouth a little open. The sheet comes to his waist, his back is bare, and I hope to God he is wearing some pink boxers under there. I start backing to the door, just as Fabio charges into the room and lands on the bed, and Cass's butt, with the kind of flying leap he hasn't been able to manage at home for about four years.

Spence bursts out laughing and Cass jerks his head up, big-eyed. Then he sees me, and Spence, and they widen even more.

It is also the first time the *three* of us have been in any close proximity since that party.

"What's going on?"

"Dude, definitely your color." Spence points to the pillow-case, which is also pink.

"What's going on?" Cass repeats, looking back and forth between us. He pulls the sheet more tightly around himself and there are no creases or folds and I don't think there is anything under there besides Cass. Fabio licks his shoulder, that embarrassingly intent dog-licking thing.

"Nothing. I was just leaving." I grab the end of the leash and pull, but Fabio plants his legs more firmly and slobbers on the back of Cass's neck. Spence laughs, goes over, and gives my treacherous dog a gentle shove onto the floor.

"No need to rush outta here," he says. "Chill, Castle. We could probably all use a beer. I know *I'm* getting one."

He heads out of the room, leaving me alone with a probably

181

naked Cass and Fabio, who chooses this moment to mark his territory.

On the bottom of the bedpost.

Like it's a fire hydrant.

Or a lamppost. Outdoors. Far away. Where I wish I was.

I cover my eyes, groan, hear the sheet rustle and Cass say, "What the—oh!"

"I'll get a sponge. Take care of that. No problem. He just likes to pee on things he finds, um, interesting. It's a bad habit—he's old and he has no manners. Or you know, bladder control. I'm so sorry. Can I die right now?"

Cass's laughter drowns out the last few words of my sentence.

"Don't," he says, after a moment. "A corpse on my floor would be way worse than this."

My fingers are still shielding my face. "I'm sorry my dog has no . . . self-control," I repeat.

"Well, it would be bad form if *I* did that. But it's pretty normal for a dog," Cass says. "You ever gonna put your hands down?"

"I'll have to if I'm going to clean that up." I turn away, pulling at Fabio, who mercifully yields and follows me as I bump into the doorjamb, then pull the door shut behind me.

"Here," Spence says, trying to hand me a beer.

"Last thing I need." I push the frosted bottle away and look around for paper towels. But there are none, because Cass is seventeen and Nic would never think to buy any either. No dishtowels, of course not. What now? In one of Mom's (or Mrs. E.'s) novels, the heroine would daintily raise her skirt and tear off a bit of her petticoat. But this would never happen to one of Mom's heroines because this is the sort of thing that only happens to me.

Spence scratches his head, takes a pull of beer. "Aren't you all supposed to be the wild island kids? Doesn't anybody get hammered around here? Ol' Nic Cruz is like a Boy Scout or something. And your friend Vivien—I've never even seen her at a party."

"She and Nic pretty much like their parties private," I say. "It's not as if you and Cass are draining the kegs all the time either."

In the end, I settle for toilet paper, knock firmly on the bedroom door. Spence, apparently losing interest in the whole drama, turns on some basketball on the small TV.

"C'mon in."

Cass has his back to me, pulling on well-worn jeans, buttoning the fly. How well they hug should be the last thing on my mind right about now. And yet. God.

I mop up and then keep scrubbing the nearly dry floor because I am now so embarrassed I don't know what to say. He's also quiet and I can't see his face and that makes me even more nervous, so I do that thing I do and blurt out the first thing that comes to mind.

"Were you wearing anything under there?"

Chapter Nineteen

"Okay!" Viv calls, pulling over to the side of the road as I'm walking home from the Field House of Humiliation as the sun is finally sinking into the sea. She's leaning over to whip open the passenger-side door. "Enough's enough. Get in the car."

"Is this a kidnapping?"

"Yes. In. Now."

I jingle Fabio's leash. "You sure?" Vivie knows all about Fab's bad habits.

"I think he's into marking wood and fabric. Not vinyl. And besides, I just delivered twenty pounds of spicy mussels in garlic broth and chorizo in this car *after* getting stuck at the bridge for forty minutes beforehand. Fabio can't make the stench much worse. Get in now before I have to get forceful."

I slide in, studying her sideways. "Do you have a weapon?"

The brakes squeal as Viv backs up, too fast, then charges forward, even faster. "My weapon's my driving, and we both know it. I'm going to drive around with you until you tell me what the hell is going on between you and Cassidy Somers. I thought he was going to throw you down on the pier."

"It's not like that. Jeez, Vivie, slow down."

"Gwen, it *is* like that. That guy looks at you as if he'd like to spread you on toast."

I start laughing. "Toast? What?"

Vivien chuckles. "Okay. That was random. But I work in catering—we think in food. You know what I mean, though." She shoots me a squinty-eyed look. "Because you're doing it right back at him, baby."

"Well, he jumped in the ocean to rescue a stuffed animal. Most guys would have shrugged. I was grateful. He was being nice." I kick my feet up on the dashboard and the faulty lock on the glove compartment flips it open. At least eight speeding and overdue parking tickets tumble out onto the already cluttered passenger seat floor.

Vivien shakes her head, short, tight wound pigtails whipping against her cheeks. "Nico keeps telling me and telling me he's going to fix that thing."

"You'd be better off fixing the tickets, pal."

She shifts in her seat, staring me down. "Yeah, no changing the subject. *Nice?* First off, that wouldn't be the first word I'd pick for the way you guys look at each other. Also, you're deciding not to hate him now? When did that happen?" She lowers her voice to a dramatic pitch. "And exactly how? Details, Gwenners. You're totally breaking the friend code."

I see the opening I've been waiting for and pounce. "Maybe you better recite that code for me one more time."

"I must be informed of any and all events in your life as they happen. Most particularly, we must dissect and analyze every single one of them to pieces. Especially when we're talking about your love life. How else am I supposed to know when to come over with a bunch of Ben and Jerry's and when to take you lingerie shopping?"

"Ugh," I say. "Count me out of that one. I'd rather face a firing squad than the mirrors in Victoria's Secret."

"I hate it when you down yourself, Gwen. You're changing the subject *and* missing the point. I'm your best friend. I must know *all*."

I fold my arms. "Must you, now?"

"Totally."

"Is that supposed to be mutual?"

"Of course. Since when haven't I told you every little thing about me and Nic? He's still pissed off that I told you about that thing he does with his thumbs."

"Gah, I could have done without knowing that. Jesus, Vivie . . ." I play with a stray thread at the bottom of my cut-offs. "Ring shopping?"

Pink slowly floods her cheeks, then moves down to the base of her throat. "I was wanting to talk to you about that."

"Well, why didn't you? I'm right here! We see each other every day! You couldn't have said, 'Hey Gwen, pass me another brownie and FYI I'm engaged to your teenaged cousin'?"

Viv shifts lanes without signaling, prompting a violent round of honking from the car behind her. "I . . . thought you'd think it was weird."

"Well, it *is* weird. But what's weirder was you not saying anything! And Nic not saying anything!"

"What about *you* not saying anything? How long have you known, anyway?"

"Forever. Like two weeks."

Shouldering the car off to the side of the road, Viv turns to me. "Look. I'm sorry. Nic and I just decided to keep it on deep down low. God knows if Al heard he'd freak the hell out. So would my mom. I'd be in . . . I don't know . . . a convent in no time."

"You didn't trust me to keep the secret?" I ask more quietly.

Her expression changes, hardens somehow. "No. I know you can keep secrets. Seems to be your specialty, matter of fact."

What?

"I don't know *myself* what's going on with Cass!" I blurt out. "How can I tell you about it when I don't even know what to tell myself?"

"I'm supposed to help you figure that out," Viv says. "That's in the friend code too. But I wasn't talking about Cass. I was talking"—she takes a deep breath, squares her shoulders—"I was talking about Spencer Channing. When were you going to tell me about *Spence Channing*, Gwen? *Ever?*"

I slide down in the car seat. I can't even look at her, my best friend in the world. This is somehow worse than Nic knowing. I clap my palms to my cheeks to cool my face down. "Viv . . . you've always had Nic. Always. You've always been solid together. Always. After what happened with Cass . . . not to mention me being so stupid about Alex and my dad finding us. I thought you'd . . ." I clear my throat, but can't find any more words.

"You thought I'd . . . ?" Vivien reaches out to pull my hands down, turning my chin so she can look me in the eye.

"Think I was a slut. And if you thought that . . ." I pick at a

187

piece of flaking vinyl. Vivien just keeps looking at me, until I finally say, "Then maybe it would be true."

She bumps her head back against the headrest.

"Which is stupid, I know, but whatever," I say.

"God, Gwen! Really? Come on! I would never think like that about you. I've had a lot more sex than you have. Am I a slut?"

"But it's not like you and Nic. It's not True Love. It's . . . just sex."

She looks at me for a long time, eyes troubled. Then asks, "Are you sure? Does Cass know that? Did Spence?"

I ignore the part about Cass. "*Just sex* is what Spence does! All he does. He was the one who came *up* with that attractive phrase."

She makes a face. "That's weird. Makes it sound like he doesn't even like it. And he's supposed to be this huge player. Was he, um, good?"

"What? I don't know. I don't remember too well," I confess.

She makes a face. "That sounds like a no to me. How about Cass?"

I shrug. "I feel weird talking about this. Like I'm scoring them. 'And the ten goes to . . . while the other two get considerably lower marks.' Now I *really* feel like a slut. Plus there was Jim Oberman, freshman year."

"Oh, stop." She whacks me on the shoulder. "No one even remembers that. Plus, all you did was make out with Jim. And it was pretty much all him. He was a loser who had to amp it up to sound like more. The thing is . . . It's just . . . I've only had Nic. No basis for comparison. I just wonder . . . a little . . . sometimes. I mean. Hardly ever. But, you know."

My jaw practically drops. I never thought Vivien even *saw* anybody but Nic. I don't think *he* sees any girl but her. I've never even heard him call anyone else pretty. Except me, which doesn't count.

"About any guy in particular?" I ask carefully. Then I think *Oh God, what if it's Cass?* I mean, how could it not be? Look at him. But that would be beyond awkward.

"No!" she says hastily, flushing. "Of course not! Why would you think that?"

"Because it's hard to wonder about some abstract guy. Unless he's like a celebrity or something."

"Well, yeah, that's sort of a requirement if you have a pulse," Vivien says. "But no one I know. At all. Forget I mentioned it . . . And, shit, don't tell Nic." Her voice is suddenly urgent. "Promise me you won't." She reaches out and grabs my sleeve. "Swear, Gwen. Never ever let Nic know."

"I don't think he'd be jealous, Viv. He knows your heart's his. Always has been. Always will be."

"That's right," she says firmly. "Completely. Always." But there's a little waver in her voice and she doesn't look me in the eye.

Chapter Twenty

This could be bad. Very bad.

Dad's house is on the water. I mean . . . *on* the water. It's on the marshy, open-to-the-ocean side of Seashell, near Nic's and my jumping bridge. You walk from the road through a patch of woods and then out across some double planks to his house, which is on wooden pilings, so it's six or seven feet over the marsh to get to the tiny porch and his little ramshackle red house with buoys hanging outside, and fishing rods always stacked by the door.

"Hurricane bait," Dad calls it, but kind of with love. He got it cheap from this island guy who was moving to Florida, just at the right time, when he and Mom were splitting up, the year after Em was born.

Tonight, when I take Em for our weekly dinner with Dad, I put his life jacket on, just to cross that tiny three-slab-long stretch of sun-dappled water. Even Emory thinks this is crazy. He keeps shoving at the straps, saying "Gwennie, off."

I'm pretty sure, to him, the whole falling off the dock thing was much worse for Hideout.

I can smell pancakes as we come up the path. Dad always does the breakfast for dinner thing. He gets sick of actual lunch and dinner, after churning them out at Castle's all day and night. I'm carrying Emory, who may not have a fear of the water but seems to hate setting foot on the ground now.

"How's the old lady?" Dad calls as we come in. "And what the hell is your brother doing in that thing?"

There it is.

I miserably explain about the fall. Mom and Grandpa didn't blame me aloud . . . but this is much worse than not fixing a broken door. Dad's not exactly one to hold back on the criticism.

Kneeling down, Dad unbuckles the life jacket, then hands Emory a plate of scrambled eggs with ketchup frosting.

"Hideout fell in. Superman save him," Em summarizes cheerfully, settling down at the card table where we eat.

"Yeah, fine." Dad clears his throat. I left out the Cass part of the story, so he no doubt thinks that's just another one of Em's dreams. "Guinevere." He stands, looks at me. "You screwed up, but you didn't lose your head. Still, the kid doesn't need a life jacket on dry land. You'll get him all worried."

This time I do tell him about Cass and the lessons. "Somers . . ." Dad says doubtfully, rubbing his hand against his stubbled chin. "Like Aidan Somers? The boat-building guy?"

"His son." I turn to the cabinet, pull out more plates, haul out the syrup, start moving it all to the table.

"Rich kid," Dad says flatly. "Don't know about *that*. Besides, why isn't your cousin doing this, Mr. Big Swimmer?"

"Nico already tried to teach him, Dad, and wanted to try again. Grandpa said no, he said it was easier to learn from someone who isn't family."

Dad grunts. "That's hogwash. I taught Nic to change a tire, pitch a tent, drive. He learned all that just fine."

"Well," I venture. "You're not technically related to Nic. I mean—he's mom's nephew, but—"

"Technically?" Dad says, dumping more eggs onto a plate and tossing the pan into the sink with a muffled sizzle. "I took that kid under my roof when he was a month old, changed his diapers, took him to the ER when he broke his arm, paid for his whole life. That makes me family, the way I see it."

He hands me the big serving plate of pancakes, eggs shoved to the side, mutters "Technically!" again, and sits down at the table, immediately picking up his fork.

"What's your interest in all this?" he asks, scraping his chair in with a loud squawk.

"Wha—?" I'm blushing again, picturing Cass asleep on his stomach, the smooth, taut lines of the muscles in his back, the look on his face when I blurted that question, his eyes flashing wide and ears going bright pink. Little boy Cass that summer, cheeks puffed, blowing a dandelion wish for me when I told him my secret about Vovó.

I stack pancakes on Em's plate, adding butter and syrup. Cutting them up neatly and precisely, tasting a forkful to make sure it's not too hot. Avoiding Dad's eyes.

"How well do you know this guy?" he finally asks against my silence, whacking the bottom of the ketchup bottle to dislodge the last dregs.

Better than I should. Not at all. I knew him the summer we were eight. We go to school together.

"He's on the swim team with Nic."

Dad's impatient. "How well do *you* know him?" he repeats.

There's a warm, silty breeze blowing in from over the salt marsh, but I have goose bumps. Does Dad know? *What* does Dad know? We're best off when I'm his pal, like when I was a kid. He stopped hugging me the year I turned twelve and suddenly looked much less like a kid than I still was. Every once in a while, he'll look at some outfit of mine and say something like, "Pull your shirt up . . . there," gesturing at my chest without looking at me. That time with Alex on the beach . . . he hardly knew what to say. Started with "Nice girls don't—" and then went mute. He hasn't mentioned it since. But it's not forgotten. I can see it in his eyes.

"Gwen?" Dad's voice is sharp now.

"Be nice to Gwennie," Emory urges. He leans on one fist, trailing a square of pancake through a lake of syrup. He has a milk mustache.

"Look, I'm not asking for the kid's résumé. He's the yard boy. I'm sure Marco and Tony checked him out. But if I'm going to trust him with my son in the water, I want to know he's responsible."

Well, not with hedge clippers, that's for sure. And not with . . . not with . . . I can't think of an answer that isn't totally inappropriate. My life lately seems to be an endless series of mortifying encounters. I push my pancakes around on my plate.

"Simple question, simple answer." Dad's snapping his fingers at me. "Gwen! You're zoning out like your ma."

"He's responsible," I say, glancing up.

"All I need to know. I'll take your word for it, he's a good egg. Finish your pancakes. I made a ton because I thought Nic would be coming. What's the excuse this time?"

Nic has skipped the last three dinners. His reason tonight was vague: "Tell Uncle Mike I have something really important I have to do. *Really* important."

Pretty obvious why he'd want to bag out this time, but Nic is usually more gifted with justifications.

More engagement ring shopping? A marriage license? A blood test? A doctor's appointment?

Viv and I have broken the ice. But every time I open my mouth with Nic I close it again without saying a word, this weird twist in my gut. He's practically my brother and he can't tell me? How come he and Viv can both confront me about Spence, but I can't do the same to them?

Snapping fingers. It's Dad again. "Where *are* you tonight, Gwen?" He narrows his eyes at me. "What's wrong? What's going on with Nic?"

Em's forkful of eggs and ketchup hovers halfway to his mouth. He peeps back and forth between us, big brown eyes alarmed.

I parrot Nic's lame excuse, that same spiral in my stomach. I want to say, *I don't know, I don't know, and I don't know why I don't know. And just talk to him and find out and fix whatever it is. Please just fix it*, but what comes out is, "Yeah, what *is* going on with you and Nic, Dad? Why are you being such an asshole to him?"

Silence. Dad frowns over his plate, dicing pancakes with precision, his knife scraping loud.

"Asssshole." Emory samples the new word, drawing out the *s* sound, one of the ones he struggles with.

"Just our luck. He got that one down perfectly. Nice work, Gwen." Dad forks a few more pancakes onto my plate.

"Now you're being one to me. I mean it. What's the deal with you two?"

"Your cousin needs to grow up."

"He's got another year in high school, Dad." *I hope.*

"When I was his age—" Dad begins.

"Yeah, yeah, I know. You had shitty luck and—"

"Stop talking like that in front of your brother," Dad thunders. Em shrinks back in his seat, reaching out a maple-sticky hand for me. I grab on to it, squeeze. Dad grumbles, he doesn't roar. What *is* this?

"What I mean is, is that what you want for me and Nic? Just what you had? What about all that stuff you said at Sandy Claw?"

"Eat your pancakes," Dad huffs, shoving a forkful into his mouth. "At least, without your cousin here there's enough to go around. That kid eats like there's no tomorrow. I swear, half the money I give your mom goes down his throat."

"You're mad at him for having an appetite now? What in God's name?"

Dad has the game face Mom never will, but I see guilt flash across it. "You don't understand," he says.

"No. I don't. Help me out. What's your deal here?"

He reaches for the plastic gallon of milk, sloshes more into his glass. "It never gets better, kid. Bills, bills, bills. Your little brother's got asthma. He's got physical therapy. He's got speech therapy. He's got occupational therapy. Insurance covers some, but the damn bills just keep on coming."

"I know, Dad. But what does that have to do with Nic? He didn't cause any of that."

Dad clears his throat, looks over at my little brother; abruptly stands and flicks on the television, shoving in a DVD. Em looks at him uncertainly for a moment, but then he curls up in Dad's big recliner, cuddles Hideout against his cheek, soaks in Rudolph the Red-Nosed Reindeer. Any day can be Christmas for Emory. Dad sits back at the table, leaning toward me to say quietly, "I bust my butt all the time and every dollar that comes in flows back out like I've got a hole in my pocket. I don't play the numbers, I don't smoke or spend it at the bar. I'm careful with the cash, Gwen. And it still doesn't matter a damn."

"So cutting Nic loose will help?"

"You know I won't do that. Gimme a break. I look out for what's mine. Like I do with Em. Even if the kid is nothing like me."

The words hover in the air.

Dad shovels another forkful of food into his mouth.

I feel sick.

Emory has Dad's brown eyes. He has his crooked big toe. Dad's smile, though he uses it much more often. Anyone, anyone, would look at them and know they were father and son. But Dad left. He doesn't see the day-to-day. He doesn't see Em tilt his head against Grandpa Ben's shoulder, huskily singing Gershwin lyrics as they watch another Fred-and-Ginger movie. He doesn't see Emory hurry to the refrigerator to pick out Mom's bagged lunch when he sees her pulling on her sneakers in the morning. He doesn't see Emory carefully align his fingers to respond to Nic's high fives, his face glowing with big-boy worship. He hears how hard it is for Em to talk, the draggy slowness in his voice. He sees that his face is sometimes blank of everything, and even we who love him best can only guess what's happening inside. He sees everything that makes him different and nothing that makes him Emory. I feel sick, yeah, but I also feel sorry, so sorry for my father.

"My family . . . we're not the Brady Bunch, but everyone's always been all there, if you get what I'm saying."

I think I may throw up. "Emory's all there."

"C'mon, Gwen. Your aunt Gules is a nutcase, but she's not . . ." He's been sitting straight but now seems to deflate a little. "Not like your brother. No one we know is like your brother. I just don't know how the hell this happened."

"Do you know how many things have to go right to make a perfect baby, Dad?" I hold out my hands, settle each finger into the next, slotting them both together. "It all has to—"

His hand closes on mine, rough from work, freckled from the sun. "No, I don't. I don't know that sort of thing. I don't want you to know either, for Chrissake. Just stay away from all that. I only know your brother is never going to get better. There's always going to be something. Ben's getting on. Your mother takes crap care of herself. Every time I turn around Nic is working on his body or out messing around with Vivien. With plans to light out for God knows how many years after that. That leaves you and me, pal."

"Everybody helps with Em," I say—although lately it's mostly been Grandpa and me—and my voice is choky, hardly recognizable. "What's different now?"

"Castle's. I gotta start doing breakfasts. Put in more outside tables. All costs money. I don't have extra."

My knuckles are white around my fork. "Nic's extra? Or would that be Emory?" I look over at my little brother, his hair sticking up in front because there's a bit of syrup in it, kicking his foot in time to "We're a Couple of Misfits."

Dad scrapes back his chair, shifts over to stroke the back of my brother's neck. Em tips his neck back, leans his head against Dad's open palm.

Dad stares at me over his shoulder. "No, he's not extra. Screw my life."

Chapter Twenty-one

I am a huge cliché.

I am a teenage girl at the mall.

I am a teenage girl at the mall trying on bathing suits.

I am a teenage girl at the mall trying on bathing suits even though she has a perfectly good one from last year that fits fine.

Worst of all, I am a teenage girl at the mall trying on bathing suits even though she has a perfectly good one from last year that fits fine and hating how she looks in every single one.

It doesn't help that I am also a teenage girl who baked two batches of sugar cookies and a pan of congo bars last night as a chaser for dinner with Dad. I'm trying not to think about how few leftovers there were this morning. Nic must have scarfed some when he got in late, right?

Aren't these stores supposed to *want* to make us look good? Then what's up with the cheapo overhead lighting that high-lights every single flaw and creates a few extras for good measure?

Cliché #5: I am a teenage girl with body issues.

Which get worse in bathing suits. (#6)

And I'm doing this for a boy. (#7)

Well, not because he asked or anything. Not that he had

time to do anything but blush after I blurted, *"Were you wearing anything under there?"* and then did a bat-out-of-hell from his apartment. But Spence must have passed on the reason for my epically awkward visit to the Field House, because this morning Grandpa Ben came in from his early morning walk.

"I met the young yard boy getting to work. He had trouble starting the mower, so I showed him the tricks. He said he would tutor Emory in the swimming today at three."

Did he say anything else? Did he mention me? Did he . . . Yes, right, absolutely. He lined up the tutoring, then said, "By the way, Mr. Cruz, I think you should know that I have reason to suspect your granddaughter was picturing me naked."

I've got a perfectly adequate bathing suit but it's a one-piece and black and bears a distinct resemblance to Mrs. E.'s beachwear. I suspect dressing exactly like an octogenarian is a fashion don't when you're seventeen. On the beach. With a gorgeous boy.

Who's simply giving swimming lessons to your brother.

Out of the goodness of his heart.

I wheedled the use of Dad's truck out of him, saying I needed it to take Emory to speech. Though, really, it was more that I felt he owed me one after last night's bleak lecture, stark as black-and-white headlines on a newspaper. Your brother = your future. No amount of sugar, butter, and flour can quite get the taste of that out of my mouth. Then Grandpa wanted to come along because there's almost always a few yard sales happening on Saturdays in Maplecrest.

Which brings me to the non-clichéd part of all this.

"Guinevere! Your brother has lost his patience with this store and I am losing it with him. Have you gotten what you need?"

Yes, my grandfather is right outside the changing rooms. Also . . . my little brother.

"Not yet!" I call.

I can hear Grandpa move away, trying to dicker down the price of a cast-iron frying pan. "You cannot mean to charge so much for this. It's brand-new. It hasn't been seasoned yet. It will take years of cooking in it and wiping down with the olive oil to be worth the price you are asking."

Then I hear him calling, alarmed, for Emory, who I know must be doing his I'm-bored-in-this-store routine, hiding in the center of those circular racks of clothes until Grandpa spots his feet.

I've tried on four tankinis. I think I read once in one of Vivien's magazines that, like, ninety percent of the guys on the planet hate tankinis. Which can't be right. I mean, I'm certain men herding goats in Shimanovsk don't care one way or another. And if they include the men who want every part of a woman except her eyes covered, that's unfairly skewing the percentages and—

I reexamine the pile. No, and no, and Jesus God, let me forget how *that* one looked.

"Almost done," I call feebly.

Forget it. I'll just wear the black one-piece. It's not like it's a date. I mean, he told me about it through my grandfather.

I wonder how long it took him to stop blushing. When I left, throwing some excuse about Fabio over my shoulder, I heard him come out from his bedroom and Spence ask, "What happened to your *face?*"

Outside there's a commotion and a "You can't come in here!" and Grandpa Ben saying "*Acalme-se,*" and thrusting this bikini in through the side of the curtain.

A bikini.

Vivien wears bikinis. Viv even wears string bikinis. She looks great in them because she has exactly that sort of body . . . all lanky and coltish and boyish-but-not. She says she doesn't look good because she hasn't got enough on top, but she has to know she pretty much does, or she would stick to What the Well-Dressed Senior Citizen Will Wear, like me.

"*Apenas experimente, querida,*" Grandpa calls. "Just try it."

I don't know if it's because of the color, which is this mossy green, which sounds nasty, but spring moss, brighter than olive, but still deep and rich. Or because I can hear the sales-woman outside getting more and more agitated and I'm afraid she's about to call security. Or because . . . well, I don't know why, but I try it on.

It's not a string bikini. It's not an itsy-bitsy bikini. It's sort of retro, but not in a really obvious way.

In it, I don't look like Vivien in her bikinis. I don't look like one of those swimsuit models posing knee deep in the Carib-bean with this shocked expression like, "Hey, who put all this water here?" I don't look "nice." I look, in fact, like The Other Woman in one of Grandpa Ben's movies. The one who saunters into the room to the low wail of an alto saxophone. I look like a Bad Girl.

For the first time, that seems like a Good Thing.

Of course, that was hours ago and I left my courage in the dressing room of T.J.Maxx.

I bought the bikini.

But here I am on the beach wearing a long T-shirt of Mom's (Mom's! At least I've bumped down a generation or two, but still!) while Cass gives Emory his first lesson.

And basically ignores me completely.

Which is fine. He's here for Em.

He gave me this nod when we first got to the beach and I slid Emory off my back.

A nod.

A nod is sort of like acknowledging that there's someone present with a pulse. It's the next best thing to nothing at all. Boys do not nod at girls they have any feelings for.

Wait—

Do I even want Cass to have feelings for me? Please, come on. How can I possibly . . . after everything?

He's here for Em.

I nod back. *So there, Cass. I see your impersonal greeting and return it. Just don't check my pulse.*

Because . . . because even though I should be used to Cass on the island and Cass in the water, and his sooty eyelashes and curling smile and his dimples and his body . . .

Jesus God.

I close my eyes for a second. Take a deep breath.

Cass squats down next to my brother. "So, Emory. You like cars?"

Never good with direct questions, Em simply seems confused. He looks up at me for clarification. Cass bends and reaches into the backpack by his foot, pulls out a handful of Matchbox cars and extends his palm.

"Cars," Em says happily, stroking the hood of one with a careful finger

Cass hands him one. "The rest are going to be diving into the water, since it's such a warm day. So what I'm going to need you to do is come on in and find them."

My brother's forehead crinkles and his eyes flick to mine. I nod. Cass reaches for his hand. "Here, I'll show you." Em cheerfully lets go of my fingers and glides his hand into Cass's.

"What are you doing?" I ask nervously. I have this vision of Cass throwing the cars off the pier and directing Emory to dive in after them.

"Just getting him used to me, and the water," he says over his shoulder. "It's okay. This is what I did at camp. I know this." Em looks skinny and pale next to his wide shoulder, tanned skin.

I follow him, unsure. Am I supposed to hang back and let Cass do his thing, or look out for Emory? In the end, habit triumphs and I stick close.

There are only a few people on the beach, some of the Hoblitzell family, people I don't know who must be renters. As usual, I can see a few eyes flick to Emory and then skip away with that *something's not right with him* expression. It doesn't happen often . . . he's a little boy and people are mostly kind. But the saleslady at T.J.'s yesterday kept talking to me or Grandpa when Emory was touching stuff. "Get him to understand that he's not allowed to do that." I wanted to slap her.

At the tideline, Cass halts and Em echoes him, digging his toes into the wet sand. For about five minutes, Cass does nothing, just lets the waves wash over their feet. Then he reaches forward, placing one of the cars a little way out in the water. "Can you get down now on all fours and reach this?" All his attention is on the little boy, as though he's forgotten I'm there. It reminds me of the way he is at swim meets, turned inward, concentrating completely on the task at hand.

Maybe that's it. It's not weird between us. He's concentrating.

Which is what I want. It's not as though I'd like Cass focused on me while Em sinks below the waves. Exactly the way *I* did with him.

For forty-five minutes the game continues. Each car is a little farther out in the water. Cass lies on his stomach. "Can you do like me?"

Emory obeys without question or hesitation. I'm worrying because the slight waves are slapping closer to his face and Em hates that—always yells when we scrub his face in the bathtub.

"Okay now. Last rescue. You do it one-handed. You hold your nose like this to keep the water out and reach far. If you get a little wet, just squeeze your nose tighter and keep reaching. But you have to close your eyes while I put out the last thing."

Em's eyelashes flutter shut, his fingers pinching his nose. Cass drops something into the water about ten inches out and *smack*, a wave slaps right across my brother's lowered face. I jump up from where I'd been sitting, wait for the howl of outrage and terror. But all I see is a flash of red and blue clutched tightly in Emory's hand, held aloft triumphantly, and the smile on his face.

"Way to go, buddy. You saved Superman." Cass straightens up, then raises his hand for a high five. Em knows those from Nic, so he presses his hand against Cass's, then scrambles over to me, waving his treasure.

It's one of those plastic Superman action figures with a red cape and the blue tights, a little worn, some of the paint scraped off the manly square features. But Em doesn't care. He carefully traces the S on the chest, his lips parted in awe, as though this is a miniaturized live version of his hero.

"How 'bout another try in a few days? Maybe we could do this twice a week. It's better if the gap between lessons isn't too big," Cass tells me, putting an elbow behind his head and stretching, like he's getting the kinks out.

Em has extended Superman's arms and is flying him through the air, his face lit with joy.

"That'd be great! Fantastic."

I sound way too enthusiastic. "I mean . . . Fine. It would be fine. Emory would like that."

It's all about Emory, after all.

Silence.

More silence.

Cass bends down and starts carefully restoring the Matchbox cars to his backpack, drying them first with the (yes, pinkish) towel around his neck

"Okay then," I say. "I should get him home. He's probably tired."

Cass makes one of those noises like "Mmmph."

"Thanks for the lesson, Cass."

"No problem."

"?"

"—"

"It's really hot today."

"Yep." Sound of bag zipping.

"How was the water?"

"Ask Emory."

"I'm asking you."

"Subjective question," Cass says, standing up, one-shouldering the backpack, and finally venturing beyond monosyllables. "Mom and Jake are like me. We can swim in anything, no matter how cold. Bill and my dad are wimps. They wait till, like, the beginning of June." He says this last with complete disgust.

"No Polar Bear Plunges for them, huh?"

Ack, shouldn't have mentioned that. But . . . jackpot. Eye contact. Completely untranslatable eye contact, but hey.

I do the elbow-behind-head stretch thing he did earlier. Two can play at the "I-just-need-to stretch-my-muscles" game. But Cass is not looking at me, plowing his foot through the sand.

Emory pulls on the bottom of my shirt. "Cookieth," he suggests. "Cookie. Then Dora Explora. Then bath. Then story. More story. Pooh Song. Then bed."

Guess I've got my itinerary laid out for me.

Nic's hardly been home one single evening since school let out. Mom's picked up an office building in town that she cleans two nights a week. Grandpa Ben has the bingo and Mass and the St. Anthony of Padua Social Club.

I take off my shirt.

Cass doesn't fall over like Danny Zuko when Sandy appears in head-to-toe spandex at the end of *Grease*. Thank God, right, because I've always hated that scene. Great message: *When all else fails, show some skin and reduce the boys to slobbering, quivering messes.*

He doesn't even seem to notice. Just stands there, very still, jaw clenched, looking out at the water.

Okay, I didn't want it to be all about my body or even mostly about my body, but *hello*.

I shake my hair over my face. "Okay, Em, let's hit the road." I bend down to let him clamber onto my back and perform his trademark chokehold on my trachea. Which is handy because it means I don't have to say an additional "good-bye and thank you" to Indifferent Boy. Or wonder why my throat hurts.

Emory's mesmerized by *Peter Pan*. I'm wondering what's up with Tinker Bell and her jealousy issues. It's not like anything was ever going to work out between them. She's three inches tall and he's committed to never hitting puberty.

Speaking of never, why is there never anything to eat in our house except Nic's Whey Protein Isolate Dietary Supplement powder ("Guaranteed to Bulk You Up"), Mom's freezer-burned Stouffer's lasagna, Grandpa's fish, shellfish, linguica, and pile of farmer's market vegetables, and Em's favorite foods—ketchup, Cap'n Crunch, eggs, frozen French fries, bananas, pasta, more ketchup?

Why don't I have any representation in the cabinets and refrigerator? There isn't even any sugar or flour . . . and absolutely nothing left over from my baking spree.

Mostly, I acknowledge, because I really don't care. I love food, but shopping for it is one chore that Mom and Grandpa and Nic do that I am happy to hand over to them.

But that means there's nothing to drown my sorrows in. I mean, sure, I like vegetables, but who sits on the couch in their robe and eats half a dozen pickling cucumbers and a tomato?

Grandpa chuckles at the rapt expression on Emory's face as Peter Pan duels with Captain Hook. He scrapes the bottom of his grapefruit clean and prepares to fill it with Raisin Bran.

"Girls talk too much," Peter complains on screen.

"You think so, Peter? Maybe that's because boys never explain," I say back. "So we have to talk because they're too busy being idiots who give us the silent treatment."

Grandpa shoots me an amused look. Then he grins in that same "those young people and their silly antics" way Mrs. Ellington did.

I stomp into my room, throw myself face-first on my bed. Which really isn't built for that particular cliché and shudders under me, letting out a squawk. Next thing you know I'll be sliding down the wall of our shower, sobbing and singing depressing pop songs into my shampoo bottle.

I scrub my face with my hands. Maybe Spence Channing has the right idea. Maybe "just sex" is the safest way to go. Because these . . . feelings . . . hurt. I thought . . . I don't know what I thought, but I *felt* like something had changed. That Cass and I had finally moved beyond . . . well, just *beyond*. Whether it was smart or not.

And it probably wasn't smart.

No, it definitely wasn't.

Not when I don't even know which Cass is true.

My first mistake after the Polar Bear Plunge was coming in Mom's Bronco. The Bronco is old—like only a year younger than me. The rear hatch is battered from where we got stuck in the deep sand once and had to be pushed out by a bulldozer. There's something wonky about the underbody, so when you drive there's this rattling sound as though major car parts are about to drop off. When I pulled into the Somerses' driveway that night, it was filled with pretty little sporty cars—the Bronco loomed over them the way I tower over most of the girls at SBH.

Some of them were still getting out of the cute cars and sauntering delicately across the gravel of the driveway. Bringing me to my second mistake.

Clothes.

I didn't think, I didn't "plan my outfit." I knew I should. Viv kept pulling clothes out of my closet and holding them up to me, frowning, saying things like, "Did you even try this one on before you bought it? Mall run!" But doing that seemed so deliberate, like we were preparing . . . staging for . . . I'm not sure what, but I couldn't face it. So I was just in jeans and a black V-neck (okay, low V).

I also opened the door of the Bronco without shutting off the music, so, since I was distracted while driving over and didn't turn off Emory's CD, it blared *"Baby Beluga in the deep blue seeeeeeea."* I hastily flipped the key in the ignition and shoved it in my pocket. From farther up the path, I heard muffled laughter, which probably had nothing to do with me, but I still wanted to turn and run.

I held my wrist up, looked at the neat blocky boy handwriting, the carefully drawn map. "Saturday. 8:00. Plover Point."

And I headed in.

Unlike most parties I'd gone to, the music was not at top volume. There was some sort of hidden sound system, but it was muted, background music.

Everything was so clean, though. And white. Cream-colored couches, ivory walls, pale straw rugs . . . pristine. For Cass's sake I hoped this wouldn't turn into some drunken bacchanal, because those rugs would be almost impossible to get vomit out of, not to mention red wine if there was any and—

And I was thinking like the daughter of a cleaning woman.

Just for tonight I wanted to put that aside. I wished I'd shopped for an outfit. I wished Viv and Nic had come, instead of laughing not-so-mysteriously and saying they had "other plans."

Then I saw Cass, who was standing at the kitchen island, taking people's car keys and putting them in a wicker basket. He was wearing a buttery yellow oxford shirt untucked over his jeans. When he saw me, his face split into his most open, unpracticed smile, the one that grooved his dimples deep and crinkled the corners of those blue eyes. He leaned forward, elbows on the counter.

"You came. I didn't think you would."

I fanned out my hands, presenting myself, game show-hostess style, suddenly more at ease.

He took me in, head to toe, then said in a mild tone at odds with the intensity of his glance:

211

"You're trustworthy, right? I don't need to snag your keys?"

"Totally reliable," I said, looking around. I knew most of the kids at the party—from the hallways and the cafeteria anyway. But in this elegant atmosphere they seemed alien creatures transported from some A-list universe. Boys I'd never seen in anything but jeans and T-shirts were wearing black or dark blue button-down shirts, and the girls were in all that was tight and clingy—and yet classy. A line I'd never managed to walk successfully.

I shivered, twisting my hair into a coil at the back of my neck.

"You okay, Gwen? Not still cold from your historic rescue, are you?"

"No. Completely recovered." I tossed my hair over my shoulder, succeeding in whacking Tristan Ellis in the face with it.

"Hey, watch it," he said, palms raised as though I'd chased him with a machete.

I gave myself a mental shake. "This is so . . . glamorous," I murmured to Cass.

"Give it about twenty minutes to fall apart. Let me take your coat."

I didn't want to hand over my tired navy peacoat, which, I now noticed, had bristly golden fur all over it from Fabio. So I stepped away from his outstretched hand, clearing my throat. "To be honest, I didn't know this was going to be so dressy. Maybe I should go."

His voice, already deep, went huskier. "Gwen. Stay. You're not intimidated by—" He glanced around the room, then pointed to some kid who was squirting shaving cream on the face of someone who had apparently already passed out. "*That*, are you?"

The shaving cream guy shouted "Boo!" and the other kid woke up with a jolt, his hands flying to his face. There was the quick *zzzzt* of a camera phone as someone took a picture.

"No. Of course not!" But I took another cautious step away.

He moved forward again, reaching for my sleeve, gesturing for me to unbutton the coat. I shook my head. He pulled again on the sleeve so that we were sort of playing peacoat tug-of-war.

"This coat seems very important to you. Is there something I should know? You *are* wearing a shirt under it, right?"

"I am," I said, unbuttoning.

"Damn."

I hated it when guys talked about me with my top off. Even guys like Dad's age did it—and once one of Grandpa's friends, who didn't know I knew some Portuguese. Then Grandpa said some words to him I *didn't* know and he apologized for about half an hour. But the thing is . . . I didn't hate it when Cass joked about it. There was no ick factor. Just this buzz of warmth and cold skating over me. Then, something more recognizable. Panic.

"I'm not the one who's always shirtless!"

Cass looked pointedly down at his shirt.

"I seem to be fine now. I don't remember ever coming to SBH topless either. Is my memory going? Or are you talking about while swimming? Because, last time I looked, all the other guys on the team weren't wearing shirts either. Why am *I* the one breaking the Gwen Castle dress code?"

Oh God. I might as well have borrowed his Sharpie and written *"You're the one I look at!"* on my forehead. I needed a muzzle. Or a drink. No, that would have an anti-muzzle effect. Plus, I'm not good with that and I'd wake up with shaving cream all over my face.

I didn't know why I'd felt so comfortable with him in the car and was such a basket case now. Because we weren't alone? Shouldn't I be *more* nervous about being alone? Shouldn't I be wishing more people would crowd into the kitchen so that I wouldn't grab him and push him up against the Sub-Zero and—

I spotted Pam D'Ofrio across the room, waved as though I hadn't seen her in five hundred years rather than five hours, thrust my coat at Cass, and headed off.

He let me go, but every time I turned around, I met his eyes, as if he'd been waiting for me to look. After about twenty minutes, he came over, took my hand. "I'm going to show Gwen the house, Pam."

He led me through, pointing out rooms, a long curving staircase, down a paneled hallway. "Jake's old room. This was Bill's, but he's married now with a daughter, so he doesn't come to stay very often. Mine's down this way."

I expected him to take me to his room. Of course I did. So I wasn't surprised when he opened the door, flipped on the lights. The first thing I was struck by was how relatively clean it was. Bed unmade, maybe a half-dry towel or two tossed around, but no piles of smelly abandoned clothes. The next by how perfect it was—pale blue walls, darker blue sheets, a dark blue coverlet with dark green stripes, curtains to match. There was a big, well-stocked aquarium, blue lights flickering.

On the wall was a mirror that looked like the portal of a

ship. The bed was big, made of oak, with old-fashioned dolphins carved into the sides, and the walls were covered with maps. Some were framed, and looked like something a little kid would draw, on construction paper, with x leading to pirate treasure. Some were just on big sheets of white thick paper. Almost all of them were hand-drawn.

Cass, who'd been silent while I studied my surroundings, finally spoke up. "Just so you know, I had almost nothing to do with this room. My mother hired some decorator while I was away at camp two years ago and he went all 'carrying the nautical theme through the house' . . . There was also a wooden marlin on the wall and a statue of some guy in a yellow raincoat with a pipe. I ditched those because it was like sleeping at Red Lobster. I kept expecting to wake up and have somebody ask me whether I wanted tartar sauce with that." Cass was talking a little fast. He took a deep breath and glanced at me.

"So no crusty old Sailor Man watching over you in your sleep?"

"Buxom mermaid, maybe. Old sea salt, no way."

I'd come up close to one of the maps now, close enough to see that it was the coastline nearby, the mouth of the river, the bridge to Seashell. In the corner, tiny, were the initials CRS.

"This is all your work? You drew this?'

"Most of them. I like maps." Cass shrugged. He'd sat down on the bed now, elbows on knees, hands dropped between them. Casual pose, but he kept flexing and unflexing one hand.

I was waiting, at this moment, for The Pass. I wasn't as experienced as everyone believed, but let's face it. I was in his room. He was on the bed. But he was just sitting there, staring at his hand. Now we were both doing it. *See Cass's hand flex. See Cass's hand unflex.* Maybe I'd totally misread him. Maybe he was gay? But then I looked over and saw his eyes. Alert, intense, full of something that made my throat catch. Nope. Not gay. Besides, there was that kiss . . .

Another quick look in his eyes, and I had to turn away again, try to get back the thread of what we were talking about . . .

This was ludicrous. I spent most of my time around boys. The island guys. Dad, Nic, Emory, Grandpa. The swim team. The largely male staff at Castle's during the summer. I wasn't some convent-educated virgin who fainted at the sight of facial hair.

I cleared my throat, sat down on the bed next to him, tossed my hair back again, this time without endangering anyone. "So . . . what is it about maps? I mean—why do you like them?"

"Uh. Well, I'm not really good at putting this into words. I guess no one's ever asked." He paused, looked up at the ceiling as though the answer might be there. "I like the way you can represent the terrain of something curved or bumpy on a flat surface. I like the way you can chart all these different directions, so you can look at all the possibilities, from every angle. I like to just get in the car and pick an area, see if I can map it . . ." He shook his head, looked down. "It's just kind of my weird thing, what I do when I need to think."

I glanced down at the map on my hand. So did Cass.

"You didn't wash it off," he said, smiling.

"It's been a day and a half. You used a Sharpie. I'm not going to never wash this hand again or anything. Like you were the Pope or something."

"I'm definitely not the Pope," Cass said. Now he rested farther back on the bed, on his elbows, and looked up at me through his long lashes, very still. I edged a little closer.

He smelled so good, like beach towels, a pool in the sun. Sharply clean.

I was *smelling* him now? Also, I had not tried very hard to get the Sharpie off my hand. What was happening to me?

Before I did something else creepy and random, the door opened abruptly and Trevor Sharpe stuck his head in. We both startled back. "Sundance, where's the second keg? Please tell me there is one. We're seriously low on ice. Tell me there's more of that too. Channing says we really need to change up the lame music. It's killing the vibe, man."

Cass shook his head, sighed. "The keg's in the garage. Ice too. Tell Spence to do whatever the hell he wants about the music."

Trevor muttered something I didn't hear that made Cass say "Shut *up*," in a surprisingly angry voice.

When the door shut, he flopped back on the bed, laced his knuckles behind his head. "I didn't really think this party through. I wasn't too keen on multiple kegs, but . . . Do you want the rest of the tour or—do you want to tell me what weird thing *you* do? After all, I showed you mine."

His breath caught, as though he hadn't expected to say *that*. He disentangled one hand, pulled at his collar, then jiggled his foot back and forth.

"Well, um, for starters, I have an unnatural attachment to my peacoat. We're very close."

"Good to know. So it was a big deal that you allowed me to take it off you."

"Huge. A milestone."

"That so?" His voice dropped lower, so I leaned forward to hear him better. I mean, of course that was why I did it. "And besides that?"

A loud chorus of "What shall we do with a drunken sailor?" erupted from downstairs, then a hammering on the door. "Sundance! One down already! Mitchell threw up on the rug in that gray room."

"Clean it up," he called without looking away from me.

"No way, man. Your house."

I almost offered to go clean it. Really.

Then Cass's cell phone rang and he answered it, lowering his voice and turning slightly away from me. "Yeah. Yeah. I've got it handled. This is a bad time, but it's all under control."

If his buddies were going to use his cell to get his attention, it was only a matter of time until they barged in again. I stood up, twirled my hair into a knot, let it go loose.

"Any more?" Cass pressed. "The peacoat can't be *it*."

Abruptly I pictured the words on the girls' bathroom wall after Connie Blythe caught her boyfriend pushing me up against the lockers to kiss me freshman year. But Cass wouldn't have heard of that—this was his first year at SBH. "Oh, I have no secrets. *Everyone* knows about me."

That came out in a way I didn't intend, sadder, more ashamed, and Cass gave me a sharp glance, then stood up quickly. "Hey . . . d'you want to head out to the beach? Take a walk?"

The beach. Okay. That was good. The beach was my home, my safe place, evened the playing field. Which I desperately needed leveled, because as we walked through the house again,

I kept, despite how pointless it was, cataloging all the differences between Cass Somers's life and my own. At our house, we have stacked blue plastic milk crates to hold Mom's love books and Nic's training manuals and Em's brightly colored children's books and my . . . whatever. This house had glass-fronted cases with low lights and leather-bound editions. Our paint is dinged, and where we have wallpaper, it's faded and peeling. They'd had an interior decorator and a "theme."

But the beach, with the sand and the familiar sigh of the ocean, the beach was an equalizer.

It was a full moon shining across the water. Freezing. Hardly any stars. Cass exhaled a puff of white, chuckling silently as we crunched over leftover snow. When I looked back, I could see several intertwined silhouettes on the porch. Evidently the music hadn't *completely* killed the vibe.

Cass was walking purposefully. It suddenly made me falter. Maybe there was a guest house. Maybe that's where this had been intended to go all along. He was silent and the sound of nothing but our footsteps clomping along was making me nervous. Each step seemed to say a different thing, like when you pull the petals of a daisy. "He really likes me, No he doesn't, This isn't about a hookup, Yes it is."

"Do you know," he said softly, "the first maps were all of the sky, not earth? The ones on cave walls? I always thought that was cool."

"Why were they?" I ask. "Do you know?"

"Not for sure. I've made up explanations—like that back then they thought the earth was too big to map, but they thought they could see the whole sky—didn't know it was reversed."

It isn't about a hookup, I thought. It can't be. That's not a line. That's nothing like something Alex would say. Or Jim Oberman.

"Sorry about that back there. Like I said, I underestimated the party thing. I just had one . . . so you would . . . um, come."

I stopped dead. "You did not!"

He shrugged, smiled, his ears going pink. Or maybe that was just the cold.

"You couldn't have just asked me on a date?"

"I didn't think you did those."

What was *that* supposed to mean? I'd landed hard on the "He likes me not" foot. "What? You think I just put out? Is that what the kiss in the car was about?"

Cass took a step backward. "No! I mean, yes, I do like you, but I didn't just . . . that is, yeah, I've thought about that, I mean you . . ."

My temper was now rising fast enough to banish the cold. "Do you have any idea what you're saying? 'Cause I have none. You've thought about *what*?"

"Oh for God's sake!" Cass said, kicking away a piece of ice with his foot. "What do you want me to say? You. I've thought about you."

Me? Or sex with me? Or both? "Why don't we just go back to the party? Since I don't *do* dates."

He huffed out a breath of exasperation, white in the dark air. "Because whatever you want to believe—or hear—I really like you. You. Come on, Gwen. Let's just keep walking." He reached out his hand, palm up, holding it steady, letting me measure the sincerity in his eyes.

I took his hand. His fingers curled around mine and he tucked both our hands into his parka pocket. We walked for a while in silence. After a few minutes, Cass said, "You're shaking again. I seem to keep leading you into hypothermia."

By this point, what with all the high emotion, I had absolutely no idea where we were. When I looked around, I saw to my surprise that we'd walked a full circle around the house, and wound up standing right near my truck. Was it a sign? Should I leave now?

"Gwen . . . I just want everyone to go away. Except you. I don't know why I thought all this was a good idea. Safety in numbers or something. Do you think we could just get in your car, get away for a bit before we have to face the keg-heads again?"

It seemed like a simple question.

The house was throbbing with loud people and even louder music. The night air was still, breeze soft and silty from the river, peaceful. I couldn't read Cass's expression, but I wanted to. I wanted to stay outside with him and talk the way we had in his room. "We could just warm up a little," I said, nodding my head at the Bronco.

He opened the door for me. The front driver's one, not the backseat door, waving his hand to gesture me in, in a gentlemanly way. Then he came around to the passenger side, sliding himself in. I flipped the key in the ignition, turned on the heat, swiftly muted Raffi talking about his Bananaphone.

"So . . ." I started, wondering where to go from here, whether I should tell him some private and personal thing about myself in exchange for knowing about his maps. I went

221

for: "Does this ability to map things mean you never get lost?"

"I get lost," he said firmly. "Like now. I can't tell what you're thinking. About me."

But then maybe he could, because his eyes widened and he bent toward me, so slowly I almost didn't realize he was moving. Or was it me?

Then his lips were on mine. One cold hand rubbed the back of my neck and the other slid slowly down the curve of my side, coming to rest just above the waistband of my jeans. I made a sound, which should have been shock, or protest, not a hum of pleasure.

But that's what it was, because Cass Somers was the virtuoso of kissing, the master, compelling and accepting in equal measure. Like before, he didn't rush immediately into deep kissing, just a soft firm pressure, then sliding to kiss my cheek, slipping back, hovering, waiting for me to fall into him.

And I did.

Before I knew it, I was running my hands all over his back, and his fingertips were slipping up my sides to my bra. It had a front clasp and his hands went *right there*, unerring. Then he moved them aside, muttered, "Sorry," against the side of my mouth. "I . . . I . . . God, Gwen."

"Mmf," I responded logically, slanting his chin to angle his jaw toward me, pulling his lips to mine again.

Don't talk. If he talked, I'd think, and stop those fingers, which were edging my bra straps down and off, smoothing a slow caress back up my forearms, trailing goose bumps in their wake.

Cass broke the kiss. His eyes were bright sea blue, pupils

222

wide and black. I stared at him, stunned, consciousness slowly returning, which he must have seen in my face because he pulled back.

He cleared his throat. "Stop?"

Shaking my head emphatically was wrong. A mistake. Certainly, so was me flipping up the arm rest and moving closer. Which resulted in Cass pulling me right into his lap.

I took my hands out of his hair (warm at the roots, frost cold at the tips) and reached down. What was I doing? I was doing exactly what Cass was, and my fingers folded on his as he pulled the lever to recline the seat and BOOM I was lying on him and his hands were all over my back, then swirling my hair aside so he could put his open mouth on my neck.

Oh my God. Cass Somers had lightning-fast reflexes and some magic potion coming out of every pore that dissolved self-control, caution, rational thought.

It was all gone and the only thing I could think was that it was the best trade I ever made.

I was the one who practically crawled into his lap. I was the one whose hands slid first up under his shirt to all that smooth skin. After a few more minutes, he was the one who stilled my fingers with his own. "Gwen. Wait." He shook his head, took deep breaths. "Slow down . . . We'd better . . ."

He sat, tugging me up with him, and said, "Let's go back to the house. I'm not thinking clearly."

I should not have said, "So . . . don't. Think clearly."

But I did say that.

He looked at me, startled, a little blankness and a little—what was it?—in those blue, blue eyes. I didn't take the time to define it. I shrugged off my shirt, pushed myself farther onto his lap and reached down for the button of his jeans.

"Gwen—"

"Shh."

"I don't—"

"But I do."

And we did.

In the Bronco, afterward, we lay entangled on the passenger's seat. Cass stretched a long arm down to the ground for his discarded parka, picked it up one-handed and draped it over us. I rested my cheek against his chest and listened to the echo of his galloping heartbeat. He slid his finger up and down from my knee to my thigh, a dreamy slow motion. I didn't feel self-conscious or like I wanted to get away fast, the way I had with Alex. For the first time all those phrases I'd heard but never believed—"it felt right" and "you just know"—made sense.

He shifted his hand to my spine, ran slowly up the line of it, smiling a little, as though he enjoyed every bump and hollow. He took another deep breath, then ducked his head to kiss my forehead. "Thank you."

I didn't think that was strange, then. It melted me even more. It seemed so Cass, born to be polite, acting as though I'd given him a gift, rather than that we'd opened one together.

I pulled his face close, nudging his cheek with mine.

"You always smell like chlorine, even when you've been out of the pool for ages," I whispered.

"Probably in my pores. I swim every day."

"Even when the season's over?"

"Every day." He started twining one of my curls around his finger, letting it slip out, wrapping it again. In a strange way this seemed as intimate and personal as what we'd just done, that he still wanted to touch me, after. "Uh—we have an indoor pool . . . so . . ."

"I feel gypped on the tour. I didn't see the pool."

"Didn't really think it was a great idea to point it out—in case anyone was following us. Before you know it, half the high school would have been in there with their clothes on. Or off."

I looked down at myself, pulled the parka up a little more, suddenly remembering how little I was wearing.

"Don't do that," Cass whispered. He readjusted the parka down, stroked my back with his index finger.

I buried my nose in the hollow of his throat, inhaling the chorine, the hint of salty sweat.

Then, for some reason, maybe the clean scent of him, the image of that spotless house abandoned to the rest of the partygoers, while we stayed in this bubble, came into my head.

"Are your guests going to be in there ransacking and pillaging your home while I'm out here waylaying the host?"

His chest shook under me. "There may be a bit of ransacking. Probably a massive treasure hunt for Dad's liquor cabinet. And, for the record, *I* waylaid *you*." Despite the joke, he sounded a little worried, so I sat up.

"We'd better go in."

Semi-uncomfortable moment while I hunted for my bra,

and he ducked his head, looking away as he tucked in, zipped his jeans. But not bad awkward, sort of nice awkward, especially when he reached over to pull my peacoat closed, knotting the tie at the waist, then took my hand and opened the door. "After you."

"You are so polite, it's terminal," I said. "You should see someone about this. You're a seventeen-year-old guy. You need to do more grunting and pointing."

"Truth? I'm feeling sorta speechless right now."

By this time we were walking up the driveway, the sound of our feet crisping on the icy gravel. Then it happened. We must have tripped the motion detector and floodlights came on, illuminating us bright as day. Or someone flipped a switch. I never knew which. But anyway, suddenly we were bathed in dazzling white-blue light and pummeled by the sound of clapping, cheering, hooting. "Way to go, Sundance!" shouted a voice I couldn't identify, and there was laughter.

And then a voice I did recognize gave a long, low whistle, and Spence called, "I know I told you where to go to lose your V card, Somers. But I didn't think you'd cash it in so fast. Nice work."

I stumbled on the icy driveway, wobbly heel flipping, turning incredulously to Cass, while in the background there was a chorus of *Ooooo*'s and *Were you gentle with him, Gwen*'s. He was blushing so fiercely it prickled my own face with heat. And suddenly "Thank you" took on a whole new meaning. I pulled my hand from his, shaking my head, backing away, waiting for him to deny it. But instead he looked at me, then down at the ground, broad shoulders hunched. I saw it in his eyes.

Guilt.

And everything that had felt warm and good and happy crumbled.

I walked away. What else could I do?

Behind me, I heard Cass say, "Shut up," but I just kept walking.

Walking. Which is what I should do now, walk away from confusing teenage boys. Let the sea breeze blow them—him— right out of my head. I hoist myself off my abused twin bed. I hadn't bothered to change out of my bikini after Em's swim lesson. So on goes Mom's shirt and a pair of Nic's workout shorts—from the clean folded pile on Myrtle, not the redolent heap moldering in the corner of the room.

Grandpa's wearing his plaid robe. Which means he's staying in. Which means I can go out without Em. At last, a free night. I'll go find Vivie. I peer out the window at her driveway. Both her mom's car and the Almeida van are there. She's got to be home.

Whistling for Fabio, I jingle the leash. The old guy barely raises his head from the floor long enough to give me a "you've got to be kidding, I'm on my deathbed here" look, then collapses back down.

I shake the leash again. Then he notices the leftover linguica on Emory's plate and—alleluia—it's a miracle. He's still chewing in that sideways way dogs have when I get to the porch. Skid to a halt.

Cass is coming up the steps, hands shoved in the pockets of his tan hoodie, blond hair blowing.

He stops dead when he sees me.

I'm frozen, the door half open.

Cass is here at my door.

What is he doing here at my door?

Did I conjure him up out of that memory?

"Just come for a sail with me," he says abruptly. Then adds, "Uh. Please."

Behind me, I hear Grandpa Ben warning Peter about the crocodile: *"Olhe para o crocodilo, menino."*

Emory's piping voice: *"Crocodilo menino!"*

Maybe I've forgotten English too. "Come for a what? In what?"

He points at the water visible over the tree tops, where you can see the tiniest of white triangles and a few broad horizontally striped spinnakers gleaming in the warm slanted light. The sun is lowering, but there's about an hour before it sets for good.

"One of those little things out there. But mine's at the dock," he says, moving his index finger back and forth between us. "You. Me." Fabio licks Cass's barefoot toes. He's bending down to nudge Fab behind the ears. "Not you, bud. No offense."

"Because his bladder can't be trusted?" I finally find my voice and a coherent thought.

"Because I only have two life jackets."

Chapter Twenty-two

Luckily for both of us, Cass does not turn out to be a Boat Bully—what Nic, Viv, and I call those guys who get on a boat of any size and suddenly start barking orders, throwing around nautical terms, and acting all Captain Bligh.

He doesn't say much of anything except "It's chilly out there. Got a sweatshirt?" until we get onto the dock, and even then, it's mostly technical. He tells me to bend on the jib, which I do after some brief direction.

Am I going to be stuck out on the water with the silent stranger or the charming Cass? And why am I even here, when before he could barely speak to me?

Over on one side of the beach, there's a grill smoldering, and Dom and Pam and a few of the other island kids are gearing up for a cookout. I could go over, sit down, fit right in.

But the island gang doesn't seem to notice us. Cass ignores them as well. His nose is sunburned and I have this urge to put my index finger on the peeling bridge. When he ducks his head, busy with the mainsail, I can see that the top of his hair is bleached white blond, almost as fair as when he was eight.

He works quickly, efficiently, still without saying anything.

I catch him looking up at me through his lashes a few times, though, smiling just a little, and the silence begins to seem more tranquil than tense. I'm compelled to break it anyway. "Your boat?"

"Uh-huh."

"You bring it out from town?" Did he have time to do that? Did he shower? I lean discreetly closer to try to tell. Should *I* have showered? I passed my time wallowing in self-pity rather than body wash. He looks very clean. But then, Cass always looks that way.

He shakes his head, tosses me a life jacket. Fastens his own. Squints his eyes against the sun as he looks out at the water.

"You have a mooring? Here?" Moorings on Seashell are strictly controlled, and there have been incidences of actual fistfights over who gets which spot. Or any spot.

"Dad," Cass offers, in a neutral tone. "Ready?"

I've been around boats most of my life. But mostly motorboats, which have sounds and smells and movements all their own. You always get a whiff of gasoline when you back up to head out, see a slick of it rainbowing on the surface of the water, then the surge forward and the bang, bang, bang up and down of the bow if it's choppy. When I raise the jib and Cass the mainsail, it's so noisy, lots of clanging and the sail flapping around. Then the wind catches and they billow out, the hull kicks up and forward, spray flying in our faces, and we head toward the open water. I'm unprepared for how silent, how serene, it is then. There's almost no sound at all except the scavenger seagulls dive-bombing and the thrum of a prop-plane high, high up, heading out to the distant islands.

Cass asks if I know about ducking my head under the boom when the boat comes about, and I do. He shows me by example how to hook my shoes and lean back.

The water is thick with boats of all kinds, huge showy Chris-Crafts and Sailfishes skimming along the water. Far away there's some sort of ferry headed somewhere and what looks like a tanker far out on the horizon.

"Do we have a destination?" I ask.

"Here," Cass says, as though we aren't whizzing through the water, as though we were just in one spot. "Unless you'd like to go somewhere else. Another direction."

The wind is whipping now, blowing my hair into my eyes, across my lips. I pull it back, twist and knot it at the back of my neck. Cass looks at me, riveted, as though I've performed some rabbit out of the hat trick. But all he says is, "Ready about." One turn, and we're flying along. It's like being one of Nic's stones skimming over the surface of the ocean without ever landing hard enough to sink. Out here, the water is a deep bottle green, foamed by whitecaps, and I want to reach out and touch it, dive in, even. This is better than jumping . . . more exhilarating, more breath-stealing, more of a release, just . . . *more*.

I'm smiling so hard my cheeks are starting to hurt. I check Cass's face. He's intent on the water, the tiller, all focus and game face. I need to tone it down. He was so weird before. And he's still not talking.

But then, he clears his throat and says, "Thanks. For coming. Sorry I was"—he nods back in the direction of shore—"a douche on land."

"Yeah," I say, "what was going on there?" Then add hurriedly, "If it's about the lessons, you don't have to do them. We'll understand. I mean, even just that one was great and it'll probably come more easily now. He just needed to get over being afraid."

"It takes longer than an hour to get over being afraid. It's not that at all. I was just . . . thinking about stuff. Nothing about you two. A family thing."

I remember him using that same phrase after The Great Hideout Save.

"Should I ask if you want to talk about it?"

The jib flaps a little and he tightens the line, almost unconsciously, without even having to look, then clenches and unclenches his hand, looking down for a second before quickly returning his attention to the crowded waters around us. "That conversation with my brother you, uh—"

"Eavesdropped on?"

He flashes me a smile. "Yeah, just like I did with ol' Alex at the rehearsal dinner. But yeah, that talk is one I get a lot at home."

"I got that impression. You going to tell me what your Big Sin was now?"

He moves the tiller to the left, getting us out of the line of fire of a Boston Whaler with a bunch of girls in bikinis in it. "I got a million of them."

"Mostly alongside Spence?" I say, then regret it, expecting him to snap something about us having that in common, those Spence sins, or just shut down completely.

But he says, "Yeah. We started together at Hodges in kindergarten. It wasn't so bad then, but the older you get, the more it su—the worse it is. I mean—the rules, and what they think is important and just all this—shi—garbage. He hates that as much as I do and cares less about pretending he doesn't. So we started messing around—" He hesitates.

"Define messing around."

Cass shoots me a smile. "Not like *that*, obviously. Just stuff—like—there's this big statue of the guy who founded Hodges—marble, in a toga, with a wreath—"

"Hodges was founded in Ancient Rome?"

"Asinine, right? So, sophomore year, Spence and I would, you know, put a bra on it or a beer in its hand or whatever. We did that for a few weeks, and then they caught us."

"Don't tell me they kicked you out for that. You'd have to do way worse to get booted from SBH. The last kid who was expelled set all the choir robes on fire while sneaking a cigarette in the chorus closet."

"Yeah, and from what I hear about that one, he was smashed and it wasn't exactly a Marlboro he was smoking. That guy managed to pull off all three strikes and you're out in one day. Chan and me . . . not that efficient. So, yeah, disrespecting our illustrious founder"—he makes air quotes around those two words—"strike one. Then we borrowed the groundskeeper's golf cart and almost drove it into this little pond they had."

"Small-time, Somers." I lean back, folding my arms across my chest. Until I realize how stupid that probably looks with a life jacket on. And that I'm totally borrowing his gesture. Isn't mirroring a mating signal in the animal kingdom? Soon I'll be rolling over and exposing my soft underbelly.

"Now I'm supposed to impress you with How Bad I Am,

Gwen? Is that what it takes? Okay, so the dining hall looks like . . ." He drags on his earlobe, searching for words. "Hogwarts. No, worse, like where Henry VIII would go to eat a whole deer leg or whatever. Or Nottingham Castle. So, Spence and I figured we ought to up the authenticity of the whole medieval thing. We borrowed a key from the custodian—snuck in at night with a couple bales of hay and these big wolfhounds that Spence's dad had. And a chicken or two. This pot-bellied pig. Long story short, the headmaster was not as much of a fan of historical accuracy as you'd think. That was that. Strike three."

I'm laughing. "I hate to tell you this, but you're going to have to work a lot harder to go to hell. Or even jail."

But he's unsmiling, clenching that fist again.

"Oh God. I'm sorry. I just don't think that's so bad. Honestly, if they had a sense of humor. I mean, I'm sure your family is very funny, I mean, not like funny-strange but like they—"

"I get what you mean. And they do have senses of humor. But, uh, not about getting expelled. From a school that your dad and your brothers and your mother and grandmother all went to. Not to mention that my brother Jake is on staff there, a coach. None too cool to have your loser little brother booted."

Loser? Cass?

"Ouch. I'm sorry." I rest my hand on his, the one on the tiller, leave it there for a second, feel this shiver—each nerve ending, one after another, vibrating with awareness—spread up my arm. I yank my fingers away, busy them in twisting my hair back into a knot again.

"But I'm not. I'm *not* sorry." His voice rises, like he's drowning out someone else's voice, not just the waves. "That's the thing. Getting out of there was . . . right. It was not the place for me. SBH is—I like Coach better, the team is better, the classes are fine . . . I'm happy to be where I am."

"Your family's still mad? After all this time?"

I have this image of Cass's dad bringing a bunch of us—summer kids, island kids, whoever wanted to come—out in their Boston Whaler that summer. He'd take a pack of us tubing or waterskiing, things we island kids never got to do. Keep going out all day to make sure everyone who wanted a chance got one. He let us take turns being in the bow, holding on tight as it rose up and slapped down, soaking us with spray. And once, when I stepped on a fishhook at the end of the pier, he carried me all the way back on his shoulders to the house they were renting so he could clip it off with pliers and ease it out, telling me these horrible knock-knock jokes to distract me.

"They're not mad," Cass says. " 'Disappointed.' "

In the universal language of parents, "disappointed" is nearly always worse than "mad."

"After a year?" I ask. I should change the subject. The knuckles of Cass's fist are white. Clench. Unclench.

"After yesterday. My grandmother and my mom went and talked to the headmaster a few days ago. He said he regretted kicking me out, since he knew I would never have done that stuff myself, that it was all Spence's bad influence. Which it wasn't. But he said if I apologized and admitted I wasn't the one who came up with it, I could get back in. Which would be great for my transcript and probably get me into a better college and . . . you know the drill."

His voice has deepened, mockingly, on the last sentence. Clearly a lecture he's heard often.

And I do—I know the drill. I know it exactly. Realizing I do, that I get it, is like cold, hard ocean spray in the face—a shock, but then sort of soothing. Sure, no one's imagining me winding up at some Ivy—but it's that same sense of what's next. I look at Cass now, at his hair blowing all those shades of blond, at his eyes, focused, determined, the stubborn set of his mouth. And this is the hardest, weirdest part of not being that barefoot girl and that towheaded boy running down the sand to the water, all legs and elbows and unself-conscious. Suddenly, you edge your way to the end of your second ten years and BOOM. Your choices matter. Not chocolate or vanilla, bridge or pier, Sandy Claw or Abenaki. It's your whole life. We're suddenly *this close*, like Nic said, to the wrong move. Or the right one. It matters now.

His blue eyes are grim. I slip my hand over his now fisted one again. He turns his head sharply, closer to mine.

Then the Boston Whaler full of bikini-clad girls sweeps a wide horseshoe, zooms past us one more time. One of the girls is waving the top of a bright orange bikini in the air, sun gleaming on her wet skin. No sweatshirt for her. Or life jacket.

The waves slosh into the boat, surf slapping us in the face and we rock back and forth crazily.

"Friends of yours, Cass?"

I have this sudden awful fear that they are. Former classmates, fellow Bath and Tennis Club buddies, whatever. The people he really belongs with. To.

"Nope. Yours?"

"Despite the island girl rep, no. We usually save our topless antics for land."

"We'd better head in, then," Cass deadpans. I whack him on the shoulder as though he's Nic, and he grins back at me with an expression that is . . . definitely not my cousin's way of looking at me. And a slow smile that builds. I feel that race of electricity slip-slide over my skin again, and meet his eyes full on, the way we did in Mrs. Ellington's kitchen. And that March night.

He tightens the line on the mainsail without looking away from me, waiting for my eyes to fall. But I keep watching him, noticing, in the small confines of the sailboat and the strange stillness of this moment, things I hadn't seen before. A tiny white scar that cuts through the left corner of his dark left eyebrow. Faint flecks of green in the deep blue of his eyes. The little pulse beating at the base of his throat. I don't know how long it is that we just look. When I finally turn away, everything on the water seems just the same. Except my sense that something has shifted.

Shutting my eyes, I tip my face up to the sun and the wind, then open them to find that we've lost the gust and the boat is still, except for rocking a bit in the wake of some huge power-boat that just sped by, full of guys wearing aviator sunglasses.

"So, this island girl thing. What's that?"

"C'mon, Cass. Don't play dumb."

"I'm the one needing remedial English help, Gwen, I am dumb."

I turn to him incredulously. He stares back at me. His eyes

seem to see all the way into me, and pull something else out.

"The last thing you are is dumb, Cass. I mean . . . here on island . . . we're the . . . well, you know how there are townies and non-townies in Stony Bay?"

"I guess," he says vaguely, as if he really doesn't know.

"Well, island kids are the townies and then some. Especially if we're girls. We're like summer amenities."

"What's that supposed to mean?" Cass jerks up on one elbow, eyebrows lowered.

"That we're picnic baskets. Useful, even kind of nice to have when it's hot and you're hungry. But who wants a picnic when summer's over?"

Cass clearly doesn't know what to say to that. Or there's actually some sort of wind and water crisis that involves intense concentration and not looking at me at all. Lots of rope hauling and a few orders barked at me in some sort of sailor lingo I don't understand, which he translates after a beat or two of my silent incomprehension.

"So you *are* a Boat Bully after all," I say.

"Huh? Can you take the tiller for a sec—yeah, like that." His warm hand steadies mine, heat settling in, then lets go.

"You're one of those guys who gets all nautical and bossy on the water."

"I am not. I just know what I'm doing here. Just keep holding that steady. I'll get the wind back soon."

Since I don't know sailing, I have no idea whether he actually needs to pull and loosen and adjust all these things or if it's just a way to tune out. But then he looks at me, smiles, and the sparkle of the water is reflected from his eyes. "Don't worry."

I find myself answering, "I'm not worried."

And I'm not. I'm not worried. I'm not awkward. I'm not self-conscious. I'm not anything except here. It feels like forever since I've been "here" without being "there" and "there too" and "what about there." But none of those exist. Just me, Cass, and the blue ocean.

He starts to say something, but whatever it is gets drowned out by the roar of an enormous Chris-Craft surging by, leaving a tidal wave of foaming wake behind it.

We toss back and forth against the sides for a second before Cass decides it's probably a life-saving decision to get out of the line of oddly thick traffic on the high seas. I don't think I've ever seen so many sails and spinnakers and wakes. Is there a race? Or is everyone as reluctant to have their time on the water end as I am?

We sail in silence until the sunset turns the sky streaky Italian ice colors: raspberry, lemon, tangerine—all against blue cotton candy. Then we head home and dock the boat. I climb out, hand him my life jacket.

"I'd walk you home, but I'd better get this back out to the mooring before dark."

I say I understand. Though I actually want him to walk me home. In the dark.

"Tomorrow night at six," Cass says.

"Is?"

"Tutoring. You can't put it off forever, Gwen." He holds out one hand, its back facing me, and ticks things off on his fingers. "You told me how Old Mrs. P. Likes Things Done. I boiled your lobsters—"

"I thought we'd agreed not to bring that up again."

"I'm making a point," Cass says. "You helped me with the hedge. I took you sailing." He's ticked off four fingers now.

"You gave Emory a lesson . . ."

"That's not in the equation. We're even now. I know you like to be one up, Guinevere Castle. So time for you to tutor me and find out just how stupid I am."

"I've never thought you were—"

He holds up one finger. "I really do have to go," he says. "Tomorrow. At six. Your house."

"Why not the Field House?" Why am I now *wanting* to be alone with him?

"Besides the fact that it's messy, disgusting, and smells like dog piss?" Cass asks. "Your grandfather told me all about the job he had as a teenager sharpening knives. I don't know Portuguese, so I can't be totally sure what he said next . . . but I got the idea he'd be dropping by with some sharp ones if we were alone in my apartment. Six. Your house."

Chapter Twenty-three

My brother can*not* stop talking about the swimming lessons. As Grandpa is putting him to bed he tells and retells the story: "I was brave. Went in the water. Superman helped, but I was bravest." The next morning he wakes me up, shoving his suit at me, bending down to remove his PJ bottoms. "More lesson today."

I groan. "No, bunny rabbit."

He fixes me with an exasperated stare. Then nudges Hideout at my stomach, saying fiercely, "Hideout bite you."

When I roll over, pull the pillow over my head, he moves on to Mom, then Nic, then Grandpa Ben. When none of us agree that it's a lesson day he just puts on the suit and sits by the door, legs folded, Hideout in his lap.

I worry about it to Vivien. "This was not such a hot idea. He's like obsessed with Cass."

"Must run in the family." She tips her head to scrutinize the daisy she's just painted on my big toe.

"You're hilarious. I'm being serious, this could be bad. What happens when Cass gets bored and moves on? Where does that leave Em? Waiting for Superman."

She snorts. "Give me your other foot. God, Gwen, what do

you do to your soles? They're like leather, and the summer's barely begun. It's too soon to have summer feet."

"Mine are permanent. I'm scared for Emory, Vivie. Pay attention."

She scrabbles in her big aluminum folding nail case for a pumice stone, frowns over two, selects the rougher. "I know you are. I hear you. You're afraid Cassidy Somers is going to show up for Emory. Dazzle him. Then let him down. Hmm. I wonder where that fear comes from." She drops the pumice, setting her palms together, tapping her fingers, movie-therapist style.

"Thank you, Dr. Freud. Ouch. Don't take *all* the skin off, Viv. Jesus. It's not farfetched. He let me down. Why won't he do the same to Emory? Maybe letting people down is what Cassidy Somers does."

"Maybe expecting good to end badly is what Gwen Castle does. Sweetie, it's different. You guys are nearly adults. You had sex without knowing each other. That never ends well—" She holds up a hand to forestall my inevitable comment. "I know, I know, what would I know? But I *do*. Things may be solid with me and Nico, but that doesn't mean I'm blind and deaf to high school drama. I know about Ben Montoya and his never-ending soap opera with Katie Clark, who won't put out, so he sleeps with girls who do, then ditches them for Katie, making everyone, including himself, miserable. I know about Thorpe, who's in love with Chris Fosse, who is straight and never going to love him back, so he had that fling with the college boy from White Bay, who fell for him, and now Thorpe is all guilty and conflicted."

"Wow, I totally missed out on *that* scandal."

"Oh, very dramatic. Supposedly the college kid like serenaded Thorpe outside his window, and then Thorpe had to come out to his parents, who apparently were the *last* people on the planet to know where Thorpe stood."

"Where was I when this happened?"

"Pining over Cassidy Somers. Or maybe Spence Channing," Vivien says, reaching for the foot lotion, eyes cast down into her box.

"God. Never Spence." I groan.

She gives me a sharp look over her glasses. (Vivien is really farsighted and has to wear these little granny glasses to do her intricate toe designs.) In the silence that follows, I realize exactly what I've revealed by what I left out. I rub my forehead. "The thing is, Viv—"

"What I'm saying," she continues smoothly, "is that you are in a sex situation with Cass. That gets cloudy. There's none of that with Emory. No hormones, no drama. He's just a kid who needs help. Cass knows how. Why would he screw that up?"

"Was. I *was* in a sex situation with Cass. Not now."

"Uh-huh," Vivien says. "Of course not. Because we all choose who we choose. With our brains and nothing else. You're right, Gwen."

Chapter Twenty-four

"Positive you don't need some permit for this?" Mom asks, watching me line up pencils at the kitchen table.

"Mom, it's not daycare. It's teaching."

She regards me dubiously as I rip open a stack of yellow lined-paper notepads.

"This is the polite boy, with the abs?"

"We've been through this. Yes. Nic's teammate. I'm helping him pass an English test. No abs involved."

Mom's hovering. She never hovers. She has to know what's up with Nic and Vivien, but I've never seen her show it by word or glance—not when Nic comes in at the crack of dawn after "dinner at Viv's," not when Vivie and Nic vanish into the bedroom when Grandpa Ben is out and I've got Em. Why do *I* get the suspicious eyes?

I guess because I've never brought a boy home. "Nic's teammate" sounded nice and distant and official . . . but kind of like a lie. Not the real story. Like every other way I define Cass. Mom, who never gives me sharp looks, keeps studying my face. I consciously try not to blush.

She realigns the placemats on the table. Nic, Grandpa, Em,

Mom, me . . . one two three four five. Mom frowns, readjusts number five.

"Mom. It's tutoring. Not a date. What are you worrying about?"

"Nothing, Gwen. Just making sure."

After a series of firm knocks, Cass shifts back on his heels outside the door, wearing dark jeans and a button-down cobalt-blue shirt. His face is faintly flushed and freshly shaved—there's a tiny cut near his chin. Still damp, his hair appears to have been recently combed. Basically, he comes across as though he's taken trouble with his looks.

Not good. I might have changed four times, but he has no way of knowing that. There's no concealing his tidiness—he looks like someone who might have a bouquet of flowers hidden behind his back.

"You didn't need to dress up," I tell him immediately.

Glancing down at his shirt, he raises his eyebrows. "This was the only thing that was clean. And not pink."

"Oh. Well. Come in."

He strides in, looking around curiously at our combined kitchen/living room/workout room/playroom. His face is expressionless. All the soaring ceilings and expensive lighting and artwork at his house, all those rooms . . . and look at us. Sagging Myrtle and worn, peeling wallpaper and a few of Emory's creations taped up, along with a photograph of Rita Hayworth that Grandpa Ben is way too fond of, and some of Nic's exercise routines posted in sequential order high along the wall. Also Vovó's solemn portrait/shrine and a pin-the-tail on the donkey game that we put up for Em's birthday and haven't taken down because it helps him with fine motor skills.

"I like this. A lot of personality."

"Isn't that what guys say about ugly girls?" I snap.

"Is this a bad time or are you just randomly pissed off?" He scrubs his hand through his hair, and it flops back into disarrayed perfection once he's done.

"I'm not randomly pissed off. I'm—"

Randomly pissed off.

I'd been fine two minutes ago. Now I'm totally uptight. *Not a date. Just tutoring.*

Cass has moved around me to the table where I'd laid out the yellow lined pad and pencils, opening up his backpack, the same one he had on the beach with Emory. That softens me immediately. He slaps a copy of *Tess of the D'Urbervilles* down on the table and grins up at me, looking through his lashes. Long lashes. Why do boys get those when girls are supposed to need them?

"So, we sit here?" He pulls out a chair, piles into it, rests his elbows on the table, looks up at me again.

"Uh, yeah. Here's fine. My room is kind of small and it—"

Is my bedroom. Has a bed.

Just then, Mom comes out of our room, stopping dead, as though she hadn't been expecting anyone.

Cass leaps to his feet, extending a hand. "Hello, Mrs. Castle. I'm Cass—Cassidy Somers. Gwen's agreed to give me some Lit 2 help."

Mom stares at his hand for a moment as though she has no idea what to do with it, much as I do when Cass makes one of his super-polite moves. Then she gingerly extends hers and Cass shakes it. As they do, I get a whiff of some sort of lemony-spicy scent.

Aftershave?

Cass is wearing aftershave.

Ha. He did put in an effort. *Now,* this gives me a little thrill, when seconds ago I was upset by the thought. I'm becoming more bipolar by the minute. Maybe because the aftershave is fighting with the perfume I put on, from a bottle Vivien gave me four years ago. Which has probably expired and is emitting toxic fumes and scrambling my brain.

"Well, yes, then." Mom takes possession of her hand once again. "I'll just—get back— Would you kids like a snack or anything?"

Like what, Mom? Milk and cookies? Frozen Lean Cuisine?

"Nah, thank you, I just ate," Cass says. "Thanks for letting us do this here, Mrs. Castle."

He really is insanely polite. He sounds like a teenager from a fifties sitcom. *"Golly gee, Mrs. Castle, you sure are swell."*

"Our pleasure," Mom returns, rising to the occasion. "Make yourself at home, Cassidy. I'll just get back to work. You two won't even know I'm here."

Work? Now?

She goes to the kitchen closet, pulls out the vacuum cleaner, attaching the filter. Then she turns it on and assaults Myrtle the couch, who I imagine is wearing an expression of upholstered surprise. We've pretty much given up on doing anything to

247

maintain Myrtle. The vacuum cleaner sound roars through the room like a jet plane.

Cass seems to be suppressing a smile. He taps the cover of *Tess*, calls over the roar, "I guess we should get started. I have some questions."

"Fire away," I yell. Mom is laying into the part beneath the cushions in a kind of frenzy. I can hear these clanking sounds as things that belong nowhere near a vacuum cleaner get sucked up anyway.

This has to be her way of being a chaperone, but honestly, what does she think is happening here? We're going to leap on each other in a frenzy of lust after talking Thomas Hardy— always such an aphrodisiac—brush aside the pad and pencils and Do It on the table?

Now I'm remembering Cass tipping his forehead against mine, perspiration sticking us together, his hand cupped around the back of my neck, one of mine flattened against his racing heart.

I clear my throat and focus on his paperback copy of *Tess of the d'Urbervilles*. It's easy to see he barely read it. The spine is uncracked, there are no notes or turned down pages or underlinings.

"Yeah," Cass shouts, upping his volume slightly as the vacuum cleaner starts to cough out a Fabio hairball. "This is the book I didn't even get a third of the way through. I hated every single character in it." He hunches over a little bit, picking at a tiny gap in the corner of the cover, making it larger.

"Everyone does," I tell him. "It's like the Classic No One Loves."

"Honestly? But we still have to read it."

"Yup."

"Why? They're just people behaving badly."

"People behaving badly is, like, most of literature, Cass."

He squints at me. "I guess. And life. Maybe."

"Maybe," I concede. *What are we saying here?*

"That Angel Clare dude is a complete prick."

Mom's now moved on to the rug, and has sucked up something that's rattling around frantically. Talking is like trying to be heard standing on a jetty in a hurricane.

Angel who? Oh, right, Angel Clare. The hero of *Tess*, which I reread last night just to be in practice even though it's number one on my list of Books I'd Like to Throw Off the Pier. "I thought you didn't read the entire book."

"SparkNotes," he admits, again with that embarrassed expression.

"Hey, we've all done it. Just to supplement, of course."

He shrugs, with a smile. Mom jams the nozzle of the vacuum cleaner under his feet. He lifts them up obediently. I duck my head under the table.

"Mom. Do you *have* to do this now?"

She flips the deafening vacuum cleaner off, says quietly, "Sorry. You know how I am. Can't stand a mess."

"Try to survive this one until we're done," I whisper.

"Sorry, honey," she responds in a normal voice Cass is sure to hear. "Didn't realize you two wanted to be alone."

"We don't— Ow!" Attempting to raise my head, I've smacked it on the underside of the table.

"You okay?" Cass reaches out to touch my hair, succeeding in covering my hand as I'm rubbing the spot. He tight-

249

ens his grip for an instant, then pulls his hand away. "Should I get ice?"

"No, I'm fine." Not really. I'm imagining the deepening shades of red I'm cycling through, trying to recall their names from art class sophomore year: scarlet, crimson, vermilion, burgundy. "Let's just keep going."

Mom coils up the vacuum cleaner cord, looping it hand to elbow, hand to elbow, carefully not looking over at us, as though we have, in fact, started going at it on the kitchen table.

Now the kitchen door slams. "Mommy!" Em soars across the room to her. He's followed by a sweaty-looking Nic. Who smells particularly ripe.

"Nico! You stink like old gym socks!" Mom says. "Take your shirt off, outside, please, and get into that shower."

Nic, however, has spotted Cass. His expression hardens into one of unnatural grimness. "I was running up the Ocean hill carrying Em," he says. "Seemed like good training. Now I'm going to lift, though, so the shower will have to wait."

The combined odors of Cass's subtle aftershave and the disgusting reek of Nic are overpowering. I wonder if Cass will keel over and I'll have to perform CPR. This speculation should not feel so much like a fantasy.

Cass is biting his full lower lip now, looking down at *Tess*. I can't tell from his downturned face whether he's amused or completely horrified by the three-ring circus that is my family.

"Hi!" Emory's face lights up completely. "Superman. Hi!" He points triumphantly at Cass, like *ta-da!*

"Hey there, Superboy," Cass says easily. My brother immediately comes over and throws his arms around Cass's neck. And kisses him. On the neck.

Cass pats Em's back. "Hey buddy." His voice is muffled by Emory's hair.

"Superman," Emory repeats.

Cass adjusts so that Emory has room to sit on his chair, but Em's having none of that and climbs into his lap, occupying it firmly, like Fabio in his "here I stay" mode on my bed.

Time to intervene.

"Em, you need to give Superman some room. He has to—"

"It's fine, Gwen." Cass cuts me off. "Want to keep going? You were about to explain why Angel Clare wasn't a di—uh—jerk. I'm all ears."

"Well, of course he's a jerk! I mean, come *on*. She tells him she was basically raped and he can't forgive her because she's 'not the woman he thought she was' even though I'm sure *he'd* been around. That's without even mentioning the scene where he sleepwalks afterward, carries her to the cemetery and puts her in a coffin."

"*This* is why I read romance novels," Mom says, abandoning all pretense of not eavesdropping. "None of that nonsense there."

Cass rubs his nose. "Seriously? I didn't get to that one. Must not've been in SparkNotes."

I wave my hand, exasperated. "It's supposed to symbolize that the person he loved is really dead to him now, and—"

"But it's just basically twisted—" Cass interrupts. The door to Nic's room slams open. He's wearing a wife-beater, takes a few menacing steps into the room, then lifts the forty-pound weight and starts doing bicep curls with a belligerent expression. Very Stanley Kowalski. Hullo, Nic was the one who begged me to take *on* this tutoring thing.

Cass lifts an eyebrow at Nic. "Cruz, hey."

"Bro," Nic returns, practically snarling. He swings the weight to the other arm. More curling. More glowering. Cass's eyebrow remains in an elevated position. How does he do that?

"Shiny." Emory smoothes Cass's hair, pushing it behind one ear. I notice now that it's longer than usual, and has a little wave to it. It *is* shiny. I practically have to sit on my hand to avoid reaching over and brushing back the other side.

I need to do something to break the tension. "Sure you don't want a snack?" I ask, forgetting how lame that offer seemed when Mom made it.

"Nah. I'm fine. Thanks, though." His eyes meet mine and linger a few moments before returning to the paperback edition of *Tess*. Who I'm starting to hate even more than before. *Look back at me. What was that you were thinking?*

Mom has settled herself on the couch with a book that, naturally, has one of the more aggressively sexual covers. Most of hers are not quite so bad, but this one has a guy with his shirt off, one thumb hooked into his overly tight white, practically painted-on pants, crooking his index finger out at the viewer. *Come and get me, baby.*

Nic's set down the first weight with a thunk; picked up an even larger one. Em's now resting his head on Cass's shoulder. His lashes float down, snap up, drift down again. He's falling asleep.

It all just keeps getting better and better.

I start to say something, though I'm not sure what it could possibly be, and in comes the missing piece in the whole situation, Grandpa Ben, carrying a large plastic bag in which there is an enormous dead fish, judging by the size of the tail fins sticking stiffly out the top. He's got another bag full of kale greens and root vegetables and is grinning from ear to ear, prominent front teeth accounted for.

"Look what Marco caught—right off the pier at Sandy Claw. He got three even bigger than this monster." His voice drops. "Above the legal limit, but who's counting? Can you believe it? We eat well tonight!" He stops, noticing Cass. "Ah, the young yard boy. *Como vai, meu filho?*" His delighted smile spreads even farther across his face as he looks back and forth between me and Cass. "*Você tem uma namorada?*"

Cass said he didn't know Portuguese. Please God, let that be true. My grandfather did *not* just ask him if he had a girlfriend. If Cass got that, I'm going to go over and knock myself out with one of Nic's weights. The fifty-pound one should do nicely.

But his blue eyes are simply questioning, searching me for translation.

"He wants to know how you are, and if you like, um, fish."

"I do," Cass tells him, "thank you. And I'm fine."

Emory's now definitely asleep. Drooling on Cass's last clean shirt.

"You will stay to dinner!" Grandpa Ben orders, one finger extended, a Portuguese tyrant. "*Você vai jantar conosco!*" He pulls a sprig of lavender out of the vegetable bag, tucks it into the vase beneath Vovó's picture. Blows it a kiss. Then marches majestically to the kitchen counter, calling, "Yes? Yes?" over his shoulder.

"I'd love to," Cass calls after him. "I'm starving!"

This time there is no mistaking the laughter in his eyes, or the way his glance lowers quickly to my lips, then returns, innocently, to meet my eyes.

I give up, bury my face in my hands.

"I'm having a great time," Cass says, very softly, so quietly perhaps my big-eared mother and nosy cousin can't hear. "All good."

Is it? All *I* know is that I can't seem to stop—this—or slow it down. Or remember exactly why that's what I want.

Here's what happens before dinner. Nic finally gives it up and goes to shower, shouldering past Cass's chair, unnecessarily close, waist wrapped in a towel, muscles bulging. Implication: Mine are bigger than yours, minor-league swimmer boy, and I can mess you up if necessary. Cass does not look intimidated.

Mom asks Cass to carry Emory to the couch. Em wakes up halfway, perhaps because Cass has him awkwardly slung over his back, head hanging. He starts to melt down until Cass agrees to read his current favorite book, which involves a "dear wee little fairy who lived under a petunia leaf." Seven times, until Mom takes pity on either Cass or me and shuffles Emory off to take a bubble bath.

Grandpa Ben, in some sort of Old World display of machismo, reincarnating himself as a knife salesman (did he really ever do that? I haven't heard one single story about it up till now), decides he needs to whack the head off the fish with one blow, and chop up all the vegetables with some sort of enormous butcher knife. Cass and I try to slog through more *Tess* but keep getting interrupted by loud thwacks and Portuguese curses from the kitchen counter.

Nic comes back in and he and Cass have another manly conversation in which they both use monosyllables and say basically nothing.

"Hey, man."

"Dude."

As the fish is cooking, Grandpa Ben comes over to the table and sits down across from us, grinning broadly once again. I shut my eyes, waiting for him to interrogate Cass about his suitability as a husband, but instead, he gives a startled, concerned exclamation.

"Coitadinho! Olhe para os seus dedos! Olhe a sua mão!" And I open my eyes to find him pulling the note-taking pencil out of Cass's fingers, calling for my mother. "Look at this, Lucia!"

Mom folds her hand on her mouth. "Oh my."

"What is it?" I ask, a little frantically. Cass's ears turn red, the flush rapidly spreading across his cheekbones.

"Your poor hands, honey. How long have they looked like this?"

"It's nothing," he says in a muffled voice, trying to pull his arm back from Ben. "They were much worse before."

"What are you cleaning these with?" Grandpa demands. Cass has curled both hands into fists and buried them under the table.

"Uh. Hydrogen peroxide. Please. It's nothing."

Grandpa Ben smacks himself theatrically on the forehead. "No no no! That seals in the infection, *na infecção*. That's how you get the poisoning of the blood."

"What's going on here?" I ask, grabbing for Cass's right hand, expecting to see it oozing blood from every pore. I didn't notice anything odd about them during the swimming lesson. Or on the boat.

"Nothing," he mutters. "No big deal. Blisters, Gwen. I'm not used to mowing more than one lawn a week."

I turn his hand over, gently pry his fingers open and suck in a breath. His palm is a mass of blisters, new and old, popped and unpopped, some of them blood blisters. It hurts to look at it.

Grandpa Ben barks a few Portuguese phrases at Mom.

"Don't worry about it," Cass continues, urgently. "I just pop 'em and wait for them to seal over. It's not a big deal. The other hand isn't nearly as bad."

"No!" Grandpa Ben booms as Mom returns from the sink with a bowl full of steaming soapy water. "That is what you do *not* do. You let them pop on their own, heal under the gloves. Otherwise, you get the *infecção*. Are you wearing the gloves?"

Cass flinches, either because Ben is insistently lowering his hands into the hot water or because he feels incredibly self-conscious about all this attention. Or both. "Uh. No."

"Is your father raising an idiot?" thunders Grandpa Ben. *Nice, Grandpa.*

"Do you have to scrub so hard?" I ask.

"Do you want your boy to get sick with the high fever?" Grandpa Ben doesn't stop scrubbing away.

"Of course not," I say swiftly, not even bothering to argue with the "your boy."

"Does it hurt a lot?"

"Only my pride. 'S fine." Cass's voice is noticeably more cheerful than it was a moment ago.

Grandpa Ben finally stops his triage and barks another order at Mom, who returns a minute later with a clean towel and gently dabs at Cass's hands.

"We'll wrap them up for now," she says. "Just until they dry out. Then leave them uncovered overnight with some antibiotic cream. In the morning, wash them with soap, let them air dry, tape 'em up. Wear work gloves, the canvas kind."

"He doesn't have any work gloves," Ben growls. "Idiot. In the morning I will go to the Garrett's Hardware and get him a pair of decent ones."

After all this drama, dinner is anticlimactic. There's a lot of clinking of spoons and requests to pass things. I resist the urge to cut up Cass's food for him, as his bandaged hands make him closely resemble a mummy or a terrible burn victim.

"Walk him back to the Field House, you! He won't be able to turn the key in the lock," Grandpa Ben orders.

He's *suggesting* I go to Cass's apartment alone now? What happened to the knife salesman?

"It's true, honey. Those hands must be so sore. I wonder how you've been able to do anything at all, Cassidy. You must be made of tough stuff."

Cass shrugs, clearly embarrassed.

Tough stuff, Mom? Really?

All her vigilance and caution have apparently faded away

in the light of Cass's hands. Mom loves a victim. Even a self-inflicted one.

Or maybe it's his charm, not his hands. Because that can make anyone's caution fade away.

Certainly mine.

It's a cloudy, moonless night, hard to see on the unlit High Road. I stumble and Cass's palm catches me immediately under the elbow.

"Ow."

"Don't do that!" I say. "Your hands are hurting." I yank my elbow away.

"Blisters, not shrapnel. It doesn't feel any worse than it has for a while. Really. It's not—"

"If you say it's not a big deal again I *will* hit you."

Cass starts to laugh, then laughs harder, until he has to stop on the darkened road. I can vaguely make out the flash of his eyes and his teeth, but not much else. "You send more mixed messages than any girl on the freaking planet," he says when he finally catches his breath. "You need to come with a goddamn YouTube instructional video."

"I do not. I'm very clear."

More laughter. Now he's practically wheezing. It's hard to listen to someone laughing so hard without starting to smile yourself. "I've *never* given you mixed messages. The messages just changed. That's all."

"And changed again, and again, and again."

"I'm not like that." My voice thickens. Am I really some kind of confusing tease like the ditzy heiresses in Grandpa

Ben's movies? The ones you want to smack sense into? I'm not. Right?

"Watch out, the lawn mower's right there," he says, hauling me expertly around it with a little arm swing, like a dance move. Then he's opening the door. No key.

"You didn't lock it."

"Course not. What are they going to steal? I don't see Old Mrs. Partridge sneaking in to grab my gym shorts and a can of tuna."

"But the whole reason I'm walking you home is so you don't have to fumble with the key!"

"I wasn't the one who came up with that excuse," he reminds me, "but I was damned if I wasn't going to go with it." He reaches in to flick on the switch and the light slants out into the night, casting him in shadow, glinting off his hair, blinding my eyes.

"G'night, Gwen."

As I hit the bottom of the stairs, he calls, "The *whole* reason?"

Chapter Twenty-five

Dad's rapping at the screen door with his knuckles. "C'mon, Gwen. You too, Nico. You don't get a choice this time. I need ya."

Nic unfolds himself from the couch, dropping his *Men's Health* fitness magazine with a decided plunk, looks at me, shrugs.

Both of us have done this for years. All the years since he left. Dad shows up, tells us he needs help, and we trail along, without knowing quite what we'll end up doing—scraping barnacles off the bottom of his boat, picking up supplies for Castle's at Walmart because the Sysco delivery is late . . . playing mini golf at Stony Bay Smacks and Snacks.

But we haven't had a mystery trip once this summer, and I wonder now if it's because of the standoff between Nic and Dad.

We slide into the front cab of Dad's truck—me in the middle, Nic, huge feet propped on the glove compartment, slouched down. Dad frowns as the engine sputters for a second before kicking in. He swerves impatiently around a bunch of summer kids gathered in a cluster by the Seashell gates, then peels down the road.

"Gonna give us a clue, destination-wise?" Nic asks after a while.

"Clamming," Dad says. "Stuffed quahogs are the special this week, and you know they taste better when we dig 'em up than defrost 'em. Esquidero's is running a quahog week too, bastards, and I'm damned if they're going to screw me out of my special."

"Nothing else?" Nic's voice has an edge to it now.

"I need a reason to see you guys?" Dad asks, barely pausing at a stop sign. "Neither of you are working at Castle's this summer. You skip out on dinner, Nico. Every time, lately."

Nic begins drumming his thumb against his knee. Shifts the station on the radio from some angry talk show guy ranting to mellow rock.

Dad shifts it back.

I can't help feeling like there's more to this than clams. Am I here to be a buffer? An ally?

"What's up with you and the Almeida girl these days?" Dad asks Nic abruptly as we pull off to the side of the road by the causeway. The clamming is better here, the water always shallower than at either of the island beaches.

Nic's head jerks in surprise. Dad is always hands-off in the relationship-discussion area. That's Mom's turf. "What do you mean?"

"What I said. You two still—"

"Yeah," Nic interrupts. "Why?"

"You being smart?" *Smaht.* Dad's accent is always stronger when he's angry or uncomfortable.

"About what, Uncle Mike?"

Dad glowers at him. Nic glares back for a second. I want to knock their hard heads together.

Nic relents. "Yeah. Always. Both of us. Why?"

"My job to ask."

"Since when?" Nic seems to know how belligerent that sounds. He clears his throat, and adds, "We're good. You don't need to worry about any grandnieces and -nephews any time soon."

Dad grunts. He and Nic have identical flushes of color on the backs of their necks. "Good, then."

"Can we do the group hug now?" I ask. "This is just so sweet. I know I feel a lot closer to both of you since you've poured your hearts out this way."

Nic jabs me in the rib with an elbow, but he's smiling slightly. Dad looks like he's considering grinning, then decides against it. "Get the rakes." He jerks his head toward the truck bed.

Rakes resting over our shoulders, buckets in hands, we wade out into the water.

Nic bumps his rake against my calf. "What was that?" he asks, voice low. "No glove, no love, from Uncle Mike?"

I shrug.

"He's never said a word to me about it before, not ever, not once. Not when I actually could have used it," Nic continues. "Why now?"

"Maybe he thinks it's time he did."

But if Dad picked this as a family bonding moment, his technique needs work.

We fan out in the water, working separately, not talking.

Anyone who knows anything about clamming knows it's sandy, gritty, backbreaking work. In cold weather, your fingers nearly freeze as you scrabble in the grainy sand searching for the quahog shells. In summer, the back of your neck burns since you're stooped over for hours. It's not getting out in the open ocean, like fishing. It's not even standing on a pier casting out and the excitement of a tug on your line.

Still, I've always loved clamming. When I was little, I liked the muddy sand fights with Nic, the competitions Grandpa Ben would judge: who got the most clams, the biggest, the smallest, the weirdest shaped. I loved the meal Grandpa Ben would make afterwards, clam chowder with fresh summer corn and tomatoes on the side, or spaghetti with clam sauce rich with garlic and parsley. I still love those, but there's just something about mucking around in the water, concentrating on what you can find and feel with your fingers, thinking about things without letting them weigh you down.

Today it isn't working, though.

The whole *reason?*

My fingers sift automatically. I slap a horsefly off my arm.

Pulling up one more big quahog, nearly the size of my outspread hand, I toss it into the wire basket, then take a deep breath and put my silty palm to my heart, inadvertently leaving a print on my white tank top.

The basket's nearly full.

I squelch my way to shore, wiping sweat off my forehead and no doubt leaving more sand. My hair clings to the back of my neck, sticky with sand and salty water.

"What's up with the kid?" Dad says from behind me. I

hadn't heard him come closer. "Aidan Somers's boy?"

"He's teaching Em to swim. His name is Cass, Dad. He's not just his father's son." I see a tiny pocket open in the sand, the smallest blowhole, plunge my hand in, close my hand around the hard shell.

"That one's too puny. Uniform size, pal, you know that." He squints at me. "I knew him. Aidan Somers. Did. Years ago. The boy looks like him."

"I guess," I say cautiously. Where is this going?

"Worked at the shipyard at Somers Sails. Summer I was seventeen."

I straighten up, wipe my hand on my shorts. I never heard Dad ever had a job outside of Castle's, where his own father started. And ended.

Nic comes up next to me, cocking his head at Dad, then shooting me a quick, astonished look.

"Best summer of my life," Dad adds. "Those boats. God." He tips his head back, closes his eyes, face softening. "My job was crewing, getting them to whoever paid the big bucks to own 'em."

"I didn't know you could even sail," Nic breaks in, at the same moment I say, "Why don't you have a sailboat of your own, Dad?"

He leans back. "The kinda boats I could afford . . . Messing around in an O'Day—compared to the ones at Somers's? No contest. Sailed a Sparkman and Stevens down to Charleston with Aidan Somers. That boat . . ." He has a faraway look in his eye—Dad, who is not a dreamer. "Felt as though it never touched the water at all. Closest I've ever gotten to . . . heaven.

All came together. I was good, good at it too. Somers—Aidan—offered me a job."

Nic and I have both stopped rooting around in the sand and are standing there, listening like it's a fairy tale. Mom and Grandpa Ben are the storytellers. Not Dad. Ever focused. Not looking back.

"And—?" Nic asks.

"Your bucket's only half full, Nic," Dad says. "Keep at it, both of you. And? And nothing. Pop died, Luce turned up pregnant, Gulia couldn't deal with her kid. I had no business taking off sailing. End of story."

I exhale, not realizing I'd been holding my breath.

Dad and Nic take Dad's boat out, motoring across Stony Bay Harbor to wash the quahogs and put them on ice. Consolation prize, Dad sends me home with a bucketful of clams. I'm wearing a pair of Nic's gym shorts because I didn't want to get my own too disgusting (and let's face it, his always are). The way my feet drag more and more slowly up the hill is not just because the clams seem to be reproducing in the basket, making it heavier, but I swear, my feet are increasing in density too.

By the time I get to the top to take the turn by the Field House, there's a river of perspiration pouring down my back. Cass's tomato-soup-red BMW is parked outside the Field House, no sign of him.

But then there's a low rumble and a squeal of brakes and the silver Porsche pulls in, Spence at the wheel, the rest of the cockpit full of the Hill crew—Trevor Sharpe and Jimmy Pieretti and Thorpe Minot. They're all windblown and laughing. Spence is wearing a tangerine-colored shirt. He tips his elbow on the horn. "C'mon, Somers! Get your working-class ass out here!"

They're a millennial update of *The Great Gatsby* . . . casual, careless, confident. The Field House apartment door opens and Cass comes out . . . one of them.

I'd gotten used to seeing him around Seashell, fitting in. His hair messed up by the wind and from him running his hands through it, his T-shirts sweaty, rumpled, the wrong color. But now he's all Hill Boy—dark blue shirt that's probably designer, judging by how it sculpts his torso so perfectly, pants that actually have a freaking crease in them. I doubt he ironed them himself. Nothing wrinkled, nothing out of place.

"Look how well he cleans up!" Thorpe calls, laughing. "C'mon, Sundance, let's get out and get you to forget your troubles."

What troubles?

"Look what IIIII've got." Jimmy waves a dark brown glass bottle of some expensive-looking beer. "Plenty more where that came from."

Cass is laughing. He shakes his hair off his forehead in his "I'm just out of the pool" way, which at this moment seems as though he's shaking off not water but the dust of this crummy island. He slides over the back passenger door, shoving Jimmy to the side with a hip, still smiling. He doesn't look over toward me, doesn't see me.

I have the weirdest feeling of loss. As though while Cass was on the island he was becoming a little bit ours, a little bit of an island boy. But it looks as though, after all, he really belongs across the bridge.

Chapter Twenty-six

"'Her body was like that undiscovered country that he had long yearned for and never found. And so he took her, planting his flag in her uncharted regions, as only a man can take a woman he yearns for, pines for, throbs to possess,'" I read to my rapt audience.

Mrs. E. is not alone in her taste for romance novels.

The reading circle has expanded to include tiny Mrs. Cole and Phelps, Big Mrs. McCloud, and Avis King. I can hardly be accused of corrupting minors, since Mrs. Cole is the youngest at seventy-something, but I feel uncomfortable anyway. Maybe because my mom loaned me the book. Or because during one of the pirate's more exotic seductions of the pregnant princess, Avis King made me reread a paragraph three times while she and the others tried to decide if the pirate's feats were physically possible. And really, *his flag?*

Jump-starting this discussion, Avis King, growling in her pack-a-day voice: "He'd have to be extremely physically fit."

Mrs. Cole, high-pitched and defensive: "I'm sure pirates were. All that sacking and pillaging."

Avis King: "Clarissa, you're all in a muddle, as usual. *Vikings* sacked and pillaged. Pirates spent a lot of time on the high seas on cramped boats without room to exercise."

"*This* pirate certainly gets a lot of exercise," Mrs. Ellington says approvingly. "I do like these modern romances. None of that foolish cutting away to the next scene just when things are getting good."

Big Mrs. McCloud, imperious as a queen: "Pirates all had bad teeth too. Scurvy."

Avis King: "Let's just move along, girls?"

But we can only continue a short way before there's more speculation. "The princess must be having a boy if she's interested in getting up to all that with the pirate in her condition.

"Oh Clarissa, that's a myth," says Avis King. "There was no difference at all in how I felt about Malcolm when I was expecting Susanna or William."

"I don't know . . ." Mrs. Cole muses. "I barely wanted to eat at the same table as Richard when I was with child with Linda, but with Douglas and Peter . . ." She stops, smiling reminiscently.

Mercifully, the ladies all ask for iced tea at this point. Mrs. Cole follows me into the kitchen. "This is hard," she says softly, in her whispery little-girl voice. I assume she means the pirate and the princess and concur.

"Well, it is kind of explicit, and that can be unnerving."

"Oh heavens"—she flaps her hand at me—"not that! Do you think I was born yesterday?"

Well *no*, which is part of what makes it awkward.

"No, it's that dear Rose has headed up all our summer traditions. Now she spends so much time sitting about. Doing nothing. Planning less. That's what I hate the most. The not planning. Like there's no future there," she confides, softly. "She's the oldest of us, but never seemed that way. I don't know what Henry Ellington's thinking, leaving her on her own so much. When my Richard broke his hip, our children and grandchildren were there all summer, waiting on him hand and foot. Drove him crazy, if you must know. But far better that than this . . . absence."

Just then the phone rings. As if summoned, it's Henry Ellington. "Gwen? How's my mother doing?"

The problem is, having discussed his mother with him a grand total of once, I don't know how much truth he wants. I say something about her appetite being good, and how she's gotten to the beach, and he cuts in with, "What about resting? Has she been getting her naps on schedule? Same time every day?"

Does it really matter about the time? She naps, but yes, we've occasionally come back later from the beach or gone for a drive to some farm stand in Maplecrest where they have these elusive white peaches Mrs. Ellington craves. I stammer that I try.

"I'm sure," he says, his voice softening. "I know Mother's will of iron. But do your best. I'll be coming down to see her today, as a matter of fact. But I'll probably get there while she's napping. Then I'd like to make dinner. Would you be offended if I sent you out to the market for us? It's my father's birthday and she's always sad. I thought I'd make her his favorite meal— that was their tradition."

Indeed, Mrs. E. is fretful and out of sorts by early afternoon. She agrees to go up to bed slightly early, then keeps calling me back to open a window, close a shade, bring her a cup of warm milk with nutmeg. She fusses that I put in too much honey, not enough nutmeg, the milk is too hot, there's a scalded skin on top. Finally, she lets me leave. I sit outside her door sliding my back down the wall, checking my texts from Viv and Nic, waiting for another summons, but all is quiet, so I inch slowly down the stairs, stepping over the fourth one that creaks like the crack of a rifle if you hit it the wrong way.

I'm lying in the front yard, shoulder straps pulled down for tan line elimination, reading the antics of the pirate and the princess, when I see Mom and her current cohorts coming out of the Tucker house across the street. Buckets and mops in hands signals that they're done. Which means that the Robinsons' stay on the island is done. *So long, Alex.* I get up to walk over. Spotting me, Mom gives a cheery wave, and then fans her hands over her face in a gesture of exasperation meant to convey that her existing cleaning team hasn't gotten any better. Angela Castle, who is Dad's cousin's daughter, is hauling the vacuum cleaner down the stairs, wearing a sour expression and a shirt cut down to her navel. According to Mom, Angela only consented to this job in hopes of winning the hand of some Seashell summer guy. "As if," Mom said, "we haven't all outgrown Cinderella. Yuh, that'll happen. Because nothing says sexy like mopping your floor."

Angela drags the equipment to the back of the Bronco, while Mom reaches into the Igloo cooler stationed there and extracts a Diet Coke.

Then, to me, under her breath, Mom says, "I hope we did okay. Those Robinsons are so particular. They always give it the white glove treatment after I leave and there's always something we left undone, so 'in all good conscience we couldn't pay you the full rate.' Good riddance, I say."

I think I hear Mrs. E. calling me, but all is still when I creep up the stairs and press my ear to her door. Just as I get back down, Henry Ellington comes in, wearing a beige cashmere cable-knit sweater tied around his neck, carrying a briefcase, and accompanied by a scholarly-looking man with thinning red hair, whom he introduces as Gavin Gage, "a business partner." Mr. Gage is one of those people who don't look at you when they shake your hand, glancing everywhere around the room instead.

Henry fishes a list of out of his pocket, written on the back of a bank deposit envelope, directs me to go to Fillerman's Fish Market after the grocery store because they have the "freshest salmon." Grandpa is always ragging on Fillerman's, saying they soak their fish in milk to get rid of the fishy smell from being sold too old. For a second, treacherously, as if Dad's words on Sandy Claw let loose a snake in my mind, I look at the one-hundred-dollar bill Henry has handed me and wonder how much of it I could keep if I hit up Grandpa or one of his cohorts for salmon instead. It'd be a service— the salmon would definitely be better.

"I'll bring you all the receipts," I say hastily, cutting off *that* train of thought.

"Of course." Henry loosens the sweater, draping it over the kitchen chair. "A shot of bourbon, Gavin? Gwen, take Mother's car." He slides me the keys, anchored by a carved wooden seagull.

I should not be intimidated by Mrs. Ellington's car, but even after our market drives and sightseeing tours, I still am.

The interior is cream-colored leather, the outside shiny ivory paint. It's like it's just left the showroom. I start to edge uneasily out of the driveway, tires crunching on clamshells. I feel as though I'm driving a gigantic marshmallow on wheels.

Just then the dark green Seashell Services truck wheels up, parking with a squeal. Tony gets out the front and Cass hops out the back, which is already heaped with hedge clippings. Tony shouts some words I can't hear, jerking his chin to the passenger seat of the truck, and Cass ducks in and emerges with a weed-whacker. Tony leans over, cupping his hand around Cass's ear to say something, jerking his head toward the Robinson/ Tucker house. Probably he's passing on the same information that Mom did. That they are demanding and high-maintenance. It strikes me how funny it is that Cass is no doubt as rich as the Robinsons, if not more so. But, in just about a month, Tony and Marco have accepted him as an island guy. They didn't see him last night, though, piling into the Porsche, careless, laughing, comfortable, every inch the aristocrat.

Cass waves the whacker, pumps it in the air, and Tony claps him on the back. Then they both burrow into the boxwood bushes, no doubt looking for electrical outlets. As I start to drive away, I allow my glance to stray to the rearview mirror, linger on Cass's backside. Tony's plumber butt is much less appealing.

He wasn't wearing gloves. Cass!

I hurry through the shopping list, frustrated because Henry has specified on the list that all these things need to be bought in particular places all over town. For God's sake. In addition to the fish at Fillerman's, there are rolls that can only be bought

272

at a bakery in White Bay, then all this other stuff from Stop & Shop. Then Garrett's Hardware for some kind of cedar plank for grilling the salmon. Which takes forever, because I can't find it, the store is a bit of a mess, and the cute redheaded guy behind the counter gets totally distracted when some chick walks in wearing cut-off shorts. Plus I find myself lingering in front of the work-glove display. Should I? No, that would be weird. Very weird. Then sorbet and meringues at Homelyke, and then the liquor store, where Henry wants Prosecco. I don't even know what that is, except that I'm not old enough to buy it, and Dom D'Ofrio, who works there, knows that all too well. I tell him it's for my boss and he just rolls his eyes. "Never heard *that* one before."

An hour and a half later, sweating, I loop the Cadillac back into the driveway, where Henry's Subaru is still blocking the circular drive. I'm hauling the various bags into the kitchen when I hear his distinctive voice from the front hall. "This, obviously, is an Audubon. Great-Grandfather Howard, my mother's side, invested heavily in art. We have several more at the Park Avenue house."

"A print," Gage's voice says firmly. "Have you had the others authenticated?"

"No, naturally I came to you with this first. How can this not be an original?"

There's a scraping sound, as though Mr. Gage is taking it off the wall. "Here. See. Henry, I assure you, you aren't the first generation in any family to find your finances in arrears. Just yesterday I was sent to White Bay to take a look at a Tiffany necklace that had supposedly been handed down in the family

273

since the 1840s. All the stones were paste. Useless. It happens more often than you'd think. By nature, my business is very discreet, so you don't hear a thing. I have a client in Westwood who had copies painted of all the fine art in the house. His parents had been famous collectors. Told his wife he was nervous about theft and was putting the paintings in storage and displaying the copies. Sold the originals to me."

"Sounds like a great marriage," Henry Ellington says drily. "The point is, what do we have here of any value?"

I got paper bags, not plastic, and am setting them down really gently, hoping they won't rustle and alert Henry to my presence, which I'm pretty sure is not wanted. I've had a lifetime of hearing "Other people's stories, Gwen. All we owe them is a clean house and a closed mouth." But it's hard to close your brain. What's going on?

"Henry, you know I'll do all I can for you. Some of the furniture is of worth. The Eldred Wheeler Nantucket tea table in the foyer would amount to about eight hundred dollars. So would the Walnut Burr table here in the dining room. The china cabinet Meissen vase on the fireplace mantel would be about three hundred. The most valuable asset I've seen is the Beechwood Fauteuil armchair in the sunroom. That would be just under two thousand."

Henry says, "Gavin," in a hoarse voice, then clears his throat. "None of that adds up to anything of significance, not to mention the fact that Mother would notice if the dining room table and her favorite chair disappeared. I'm sure you understand my position."

They're standing just on the other side of the kitchen door.

My heart is jack-hammering in my chest. I feel like I'm about to be caught, fired in disgrace, as though I *have* stolen all the valuable things in the house. I bend over carefully, pick up the three grocery bags I've already carried in and inch back out the kitchen screen door, so grateful it doesn't squeak like ours at home.

Then I stomp up the stairs, slam it open loudly, walk thunderously into the kitchen and call, "I'm finally back! Sorry, Mr. Ellington! There was—traffic on the bridge and um, Garrett's was out of the cedar plank, so I had to look around. Mrs. E. isn't up yet, is she?"

Tops of his cheekbones flushed, Henry swings open the kitchen door. "No, not at all, Gwen. Haven't heard a peep from her. She usually sleeps over two hours, doesn't she?"

I'm sure I too am totally red in the face. As I pile up the grocery bags, I knock over the cut glass vase of hydrangeas. It scatters across the table, nearly tumbling off, and the water drips onto the floor. I grab the roll of paper towels and clean up as Henry turns to the wet bar, asking Mr. Gage if he wants a refill. He doesn't, but Henry sure does. While he's rattling ice on the counter and breaking it into little pieces with this weird hammer thing, Mr. Gage says, "If I may look around a bit more? The upstairs?"

"The view *is* lovely from there," Henry says in a slightly too-loud, overcompensating voice, similar to the one I probably used a second ago. "But Mother is sleeping. Perhaps you can wait until she wakes up."

I'm stuffing the groceries into the refrigerator like the efficient, upright, honest servant I should be, rather than the shifty, eavesdropping one I've apparently become. My hands are shaking.

Then someone else's hand falls on my shoulder.

"Er. Guinevere."

I turn to meet Henry Ellington's eyes.

"Mother's told me what a hard worker you are. I appreciate your—" He clears his throat. "Tireless efforts on her behalf."

He reaches into his pocket, pulls something out, then flips it open on the kitchen table, bending over it to write.

A check.

"Rose Ellington is not easy," he says. "Used to certain standards. You meet them. I think you deserve this . . . a little extra."

He folds the check, extends it to me.

I'm frozen for a second, staring at it as if he's handing me something far more deadly than a piece of paper.

After a moment, as though that's what he had intended all along, Henry sets the check down on the kitchen table, on the dry, clear spot between where I spilled the water and where I put the groceries. As though it belongs there, as much as they do, as natural, as accidental, as those.

Chapter Twenty-seven

"He's robbing her blind," Vivie says. She hangs a hard left in the Almeida's van, throwing both Nic and me against the passenger doors. "He's divorced, right? He cheated with the underage babysitter and now her family's asking for hush money, his ex took him to the cleaners even though she was having it on with the doorman, he's broke because he's embezzling from his boss, and he's counting on Mommy to bail him out. Without her knowing."

"Wow. You got all that from what I just told you?"

"Drama Queen," Nic says.

"I'm not." Viv jerks the wheel, tires squealing, to turn onto Main Road. I land hard against the door.

"Why wouldn't he just ask her for the money?" I say, righting myself, kicking upright the bag of quahogs at my feet— we're doing a clam boil for St. John de Brito Church tonight.

"Those guys never *talk* to each other," Nic says. "I swear, we were painting the dining room at the Beinekes' today. Place was draped in sheets and stuff, and Hoop and I are doing the edging, but Mr. and Mrs. Beineke and their poor granddaughter are still eating in there. It's all 'Sophie, can you ask your grandmother to pass the butter' and 'Sophie, please tell your grandmother we are running low on salt,' even though the table's four feet by four feet and Grandma and Gramps can hear each other perfectly. They just let everything important stay unsaid."

"The question is, do *I* say anything?" I ask. "Or should I—"

"Left up here!" Nic interrupts, pointing right.

Viv turns left.

"No—that way!" Nic points right again.

Viv swears under her breath, making a U-turn that tosses Nic and me against the doors again.

"Do you think this is a handicap, Vee?" Nic asks. "Do you think the academy won't take me because I always have to make that little *L* thing with my hand?"

"Maybe you'll get a special scholarship," Vivien says, patting his shoulder, squinting at me in the rearview. "Gwenners, the thing is, you don't really know anything. You've worked for them for a few weeks. They've had a lifetime to complicate and screw up their relationship. Don't get involved."

Don't get involved. Don't think about it. *Nas histórias de outras pessoas.*

Thinking those thoughts is starting to seem like the snooze button on an old alarm clock, one I've hit so often, it just doesn't work anymore.

"Gracious, Gwen, where are you today?" Mrs. E. waves her hand in front of my face, calling me back to the here and now. On her porch, nearly at the end of the day. A day I've spent daydreaming about Cass and preoccupied about Henry, going through the motions with Mrs. E., who deserves better.

"Clarissa Cole tells me the yard boy, dear Cassidy, is teaching your brother to swim."

The island grapevine is evidently faster than a speeding bullet. Mrs. E. rests a hand, light as a leaf, on my arm. "Oh, uh, yeah—yes. He's got a lesson tomorrow."

"Would it be too much to ask if an old Beach Bat could come along?"

"To swim?"

"Merely to observe. I spend too much time in the company of the elderly, or"—she lowers her voice, although Joy-less the nurse has not yet arrived, having called to say she'll be late, and somehow making that sound like my fault—"the cranky. I've missed several days with the ladies on the beach—just feeling lazy, I'm afraid. It would be a pleasure to see how your dear boy handles this."

"He's not my dear boy, Mrs. E. We just go to school together."

She looks down, turning the thin gold bracelet on her wrist, but not before I catch the flash of girlish amusement. "So you say. Well, I was a young woman a very long time ago. I cannot, however, pretend that I haven't noticed that while the neighbors on either side have grass that is growing rather long and paths that are a bit overdue for weeding, my own yard has never been so assiduously tended."

Have to admit, I've noticed that too. And when he called to figure out a time for Em's next swim lesson, there was a certain amount of lingering on the phone.

Cass: "So I should go . . ." (Not hanging up) "Uh . . ."

Me: "Okay. I'll let you go." (Not hanging up) "Another family thing?"

Cass: (Sighing) "Yeah. Photo shoot."

Me: (Incredulous) "Your family thing is a photo shoot?"

Cass: "Stop laughing. Yes. We do the annual photo for my dad's company website, you know . . . It's a tradition . . . sort of an embarrassing one, but . . ."

Then all at once, I remembered that. Mr. Somers and the three boys. I couldn't see her, but Cass's mom must have been there too. Standing on the deck of their big sailboat tied off the Abenaki pier, white shirts, khaki pants, tan faces. Cass bending his knees to try to rock the boat, his brothers laughing, me starting to climb down the ladder to clamber aboard. Dad catching me and saying, "No, pal, you aren't family."

"You still do that?"

"Every year," he said. "I may be the black sheep, but apparently I photograph well."

His tone was light, but I heard something darker in it.

Silence.

I could hear him breathing. He could probably hear me swallow.

Me: "Cass . . ."

Cass: "I'm here."

Me: "Are you going to do it? What your family wants? Say it was all Spence, go back to Hodges?"

Cass: (Long sigh. I pictured him clenching his fist, unclenching.) "This should be easier than it is." (Pause) "Black and white. He's my best friend. But I'm . . . My brothers are . . . I mean . . ."

It's not like him to stammer. I pressed the phone closer to my cheek. "Yeah?"

Cass: "I'm not Bill, the financial whiz kid. I'm not Jake, the scholar/athlete."

Me: "Why should you be?"

Cass: "They want the best for me. My parents. My family."

At that point, Mom came into the room, sighing loudly as she took off her sneakers, flipping on the noisy fan. I told Cass to wait, took the phone outside, to the backyard, lay down in the grass on my back, staring at the deep blue sky. We had never talked like that to each other. His voice was so close, it was as though he was whispering in my ear.

Me: "I'm back. And the best thing for you is?"

Cass: "The whole deal. An Ivy. A good job. All that. I may not be as smart as my brothers, but I know that it . . . looks better . . . to graduate from Hodges."

Here's where I should have said that it didn't matter how it looked. But I couldn't lie to him. I knew what he meant. Instead, I asked, "Is that what matters? Looks? To you."

Another sigh. Then silence. Long silence.

I remember Cass's brother talking to him outside Castle's that day. Saying Spence would always land on his feet.

Me: "Wouldn't Spence be able to bounce back? He's pretty sturdy. And didn't his dad get the expulsion off his record?"

Cass: "Well, yeah. But if I sold him out, that would be on *my* record. In his head. In mine. I mean, who the hell would that make me?"

My next thought was unavoidable. *That you ask? That you worry? Not who I thought you were.*

Finally, Cass: "Okay, I really do need to go."

Me: "Yeah, me too. I'll hang up now."

(No hanging up)

Cass: "Maybe if we do it on the count of three."

"One. Two. Three."

I don't hang up. Neither does Cass.

Cass: (Laughing) "See you tomorrow, Gwen." (Pause) "Three."

Me: (Also laughing) "Right. Three."

Both phones: *Click.*

Mrs. E. insists that we drive her Cadillac to pick up Emory and then head to the beach for his lesson. Emory is clearly astonished being in a car that doesn't make loud squealing noises, like Mom's, and where the seats are overstuffed and comfortable, not torn up like Dad's truck. "Riding. A bubble," he says, mesmerized, stroking the smooth puffy white leather. "Like Glinda." His eyes are wide.

This time Cass has yet more Superman figures for Emory to rescue, and a fist-sized blue-and-green marble. He places that one pretty far out in the deepening water, and tells Em he has to put his entire face under to get it. Em hesitates. Cass waits.

I squeeze Mrs. E.'s hand. I've set up a beach chair for her and am sitting in the sand beside it.

"My Henry was afraid of the water as a little boy," she tells me quietly. "The captain was most impatient. He tried everything, saying he was a descendant of William Wallace and Wallaces were not afraid of anything—although I must say I doubt William Wallace could swim—and promising him treats and giving him spankings—that was an acceptable practice back then. But Henry would not go near the water."

Cass is lying down on his stomach next to Em, tan muscled back alongside small, pale, bony one. I can't see Emory's expression. I have to grip on to the armrest of the beach chair to stop myself from going to the water, pulling Emory out, saying this was a bad idea. Mom's words echo, that he's my responsibility, that he can't care for himself, that it will always be my job. I start to rise, but Mrs. E. presses down on my shoulder lightly. "No, dear heart. Give him a little time. I have faith. You must too."

I sit back. "So, how did Henry ever learn to swim?"

"Well, one day the captain took him to the end of the dock and dropped him in."

I'm completely horrified. "What did you do?"

"I wasn't there. I heard about it later. You must understand that some people were much tougher with children in those days. I would never have allowed it, but this sort of thing happened."

Cass has rolled over on his side in the water, propping himself on an elbow. He ducks his head sideways, completely under, then pops it back up, says something I can't hear to Emory. I hear the husky sound of Emory laughing, but he still doesn't lower his head.

"So what happened? Did he sink? Did someone dive in and save him?"

"No, he doggy-paddled his way to the pier. He was too terrified not to. But he didn't speak to his father for two weeks."

Can't say that I blame him. The captain sounds like a jerk

Slowly, slowly, Em ducks his head. I catch my breath, as if I could hold it for him. His hand reaches out, out, out and then his head splashes up at the same time his hand does, triumphantly holding the marble.

"Way to go, Superboy. You saved the planet!" Cass calls, and Em's grin stretches nearly from ear to ear.

"He's not your young man?" Mrs. E. leans over to ask, her lavender perfume scenting the salty air.

"No. Not mine." Cass is talking to Em, folding his fingers around the marble, pointing out to the end of the pier. Emory nods, seriously.

"Then I may ask him to be mine."

"Gwen, wait up!" Cass calls as I'm pulling out of the parking lot at the beach, Mrs. E. and Emory equally worn out and drowsy.

He's got his backpack slung over his shoulder and his hair is still dripping wet, scattering droplets onto his shirt. "I thought maybe I'd come by tonight."

Grandpa informed me this morning that he was the bingo host tonight, so no way. If things were awkward with my family, they would be even worse with Grandpa's friends raising and lowering their eyebrows and nudging one another over the fact that Ben Cruz's granddaughter is finally being seen with *um joven*. Even if she's just helping him with English.

"Not a good night for tutoring." I look down at his feet, rather than at his face. Man, he even has nice feet. Big, neatly clipped toenails, high arch. I'm checking out his *feet*? Jesus. He edges the sandy gravel of the parking lot with his toe.

"Yeah, well, not tutoring," Cass says. "I thought . . . maybe . . . I'd just come by."

I don't look over at Mrs. Ellington. Nor do I have to. Her *I told you so* is loud and clear.

"Like for another sail?" I squint dubiously at the sky, where thunderhead clouds are moving in.

"Or . . . a walk . . . or whatever?" Cass slides his hand to the back of his neck, pinching the muscles there, shakes his hair out of his eyes. "Maybe kayaking?"

I could point to the gathering clouds in their deepening shades of gray, or mention that the wind seems to be picking up. I could remember the poised, distant boy who climbed into the Porsche and say "no way." Instead I say, "Around six?"

Chapter Twenty-eight

"Hi, Mrs. Castle!"

I'm changing in my room (for only the second time—progress!) when I hear Cass's deep voice. Followed by Mom's uncertain one.

"Oh. Cassidy. Another tutoring session? Gwen's just showering. Come in! Do you want a snack? We have . . . leftover fish. I could heat it up. I'm sure Gwen will be out in just a minute. Here, come in, have a seat. How are your hands?"

I grimace. Obviously I come by my babbling genetically.

"Or are you here for Emory? How'd you say your hands were, honey?"

The smile in Cass's voice reaches through my closed door like sun slanting through a window. "They're fine. Better. No snack. Thanks. I'm not here for Emory. Or tutoring. I want to take Gwen out."

"*Our* Gwen?"

Shutting my eyes, I lean back against the door. *Nice, Mom.*

"Oh! Well. She's . . . in the . . . I'll just call her. Guinevere!" She shouts the last as though we live in a mansion and I'm hundreds of rooms away instead of about six yards.

I emerge from the bedroom, mascara on. My hair is wet

from the shower, dripping a damp circle on the back of my shirt. But he looks at me like . . . well, like none of that matters, and then, of course, it kinda doesn't.

"You don't want the fish?" Mom asks. "Because I could wrap it up. It wouldn't be a big deal at all. Must be hard to be living on your own without a home-cooked meal. I mean, you're a growing boy and I know all about teenage boys and their appetites."

She did *not* just say that. Note to self: Strangle Mom later.

"What?" Cass says, his eyes never leaving me. "Sorry, Mrs. Castle. I'm, uh, distracted. Today was long. Ready, Gwen?"

Flustered and flushed, Mom says, "You sure you don't want some cod?"

"No cod, Mom," I say tightly.

"I'm sure it's delicious, Mrs. Castle," says the prince of good manners.

Finally, fortunately silent, Mom watches us leave.

Cod?

God.

"Sorry about that—she gets—um . . . well . . . I mean, she's just not used to me going on a date. Not that that's what this is. I mean . . . *Should* I go back and get my copy of *Tess*? We've only done it once. Tutoring, I mean." I feel my face go hot. "How are your hands?"

He's laughing again. "Gwen. Forget my hands. Forget *Tess*. Let's just . . . go to the beach and . . . figure it out from there."

All these questions crowd into my mind. Figure *what* out? Why am I doing this again? Or is it different now? But for once, for once since that no-thinking night at Cass's party, I just push it all away. I focus on the pull of Cass's hand. Let myself be pulled. And say, "Okay."

As we head down the hill, the clouds that were gathering seem to have hesitated in the sky, moving no farther in. The breeze is sharp and fresh, only faintly salty. High tide.

Cass says, "I finished it. Last night. *Tess*. Still hate it. I mean . . . what was the point of all that? Everything was hopeless from the start. Everyone was trapped."

As his "tutor," I should argue and say that Tess's choices, and Angel's inability to forgive them, doomed them, that it wasn't really a foregone conclusion, things could have gone another way. But the reason I hate the book is just that—that from the start, everyone is hopeless, even the family horse, who you just know is going to drop dead at the worst possible moment. "You know what I hated most about that book?" I offer. "The line that made me want to pitch it off the pier?"

"I can think of a lot," Cass says.

"Tess moaning that 'my life looks as if it had been wasted for want of chances.' I mean, I know she's unlucky, but she feels so sorry for herself that you stop caring. Or I did at least."

"The one that got *me*," he says, his voice low, "the only one that did, and that wasn't sort of overdramatic, dumbass drama, was that paragraph about how you can just miss your chance."

"'In the ill-judged execution of the well-judged plan of things,'" I quote, "'the call seldom produces the comer, the man to love rarely coincides with the hour for loving.'"

"Yeah." He exhales. "That. Bad timing with what could've been a good thing."

Well.

That statement hangs there in the air like it's been written in smoke.

I clear my throat.

Cass kicks some gravel off the road. Then he laughs. "I can't believe you have it memorized." He glances at me, and I shrug, my cheeks blazing. "Actually, yeah," he says. "I can." He smiles down at the ground.

We're quiet again.

"I thought maybe I was wrong, just not getting this book," he adds finally. "Half the stuff I read doesn't stay in my head. Maybe more than half. I can't write a paper to save my life. The words—what I want to say—just get jumbled up when I try to put them down on paper."

"You know exactly what to do with Em, though," I point out, seizing on the change of topic like a life raft. We're nearly to the beach, walking so close together that I keep feeling his rough knuckles brush against my arm.

"It's no big deal, Gwen. Like I said, that's my thing. I might have started working at Lend a Hand—that camp—because of my transcript—and because Dad got me the job, like he's gotten me every other job—but I really got into it. Swimming's always been big for me. Figuring out how to make it work with different issues—that I can do. And Emory . . . he's easy. Not autistic, right?"

I shake my head. "We don't know what he is, but that's not it."

"Yeah, I could see he was different with the water. When you teach kids with autism, a lot of times there's this sensory stuff. You have to hold on to them really tight. And it's easier to get all the way into the water right away with them instead of going slowly, like Emory."

I slow, glance at him, fall in step again. "How do you know this?" A side of Cass I've never seen.

"When I'm interested, I get focused." He kicks a rock away from the road, hands in pockets, not looking at me.

I'm trying to decode his mood, which seems to keep shifting like the wind coming off the water, both of which now have a sort of electricity. There's a storm coming. I can feel it.

When we get to the beach, Cass reaches into his pocket and pulls out a loop of keys, unlocking the tiny boathouse, which smells both damp and warm, flecks of dust swirling in the air. The dark green kayak is buried under several others, so there's a lot of shifting around and rearranging and not very much conversation for a bit.

He hands me a double-handed paddle after we drag the boat down the rocky sand. "Want to steer?"

"I've never even been in a kayak before," I tell him.

"Bet you still want to steer," Cass says, grinning slightly as he trails his paddle into the water and heads into the inlet near Sandy Claw.

We snake around turn after turn in the salt marsh. I keep sticking my paddle in too far, flipping it out too fast, so sprays of water flip up, soaking Cass. The first few times he pretends not to notice, but by the fourth, he turns around, eyebrow lifted.

"Accident," I say hastily.

"Maybe we should just use one paddle. You're potentially more dangerous with this than the hedge clippers. Let's switch places."

Holding on to the side, as the kayak rocks precariously in the shallow water, I wedge myself around him. He settles back, then lowers his hand, gesturing me to sit. I sink down. There's water in the bottom of the boat and it seeps into my bikini bottom. Cass takes my paddle out and rests it on the kayak floor, lifts one of my hands, then another, situating my palms on the two-sided paddle, under his. "See, you can still have control. I know how you are about that." His voice is so close to my ear that his breath lifts the stray strands of hair that curl there. "Dig deep on one side, let the other drift on this turn up here."

I do as he tells me, and the kayak slowly turns, snagging briefly in the sea grass, then moving on.

We're only a few bends in the inlet from the beach when the clouds finally break and fat raindrops begin scattering around us, plopping into the water, splattering onto my shoulder. At first just a few and then the sky opens up and it's a deluge, as though someone is pouring a giant version of one of Emory's buckets onto the kayak. We both start paddling like crazy, but I'm trying to pull the paddle back and Cass is moving it forward, which stalls us till he again shifts his hand on mine, tightening his grip, says, "Like this," dipping the paddle in the right direction, so we're in sync at last.

Finally, we reach the beach and get out. Cass hauls and I shove and soon the kayak is at the door. He shouts, but I can't hear him above the rain. He hooks his toes under the kayak, flipping it upside down so it won't fill with water, then kicks the door open and pulls me inside the boathouse, yanking the door shut.

"I could have planned this a little better!" he shouts, over the barrage of rain pounding on the roof like drumsticks.

I could have pointed out that I knew it was going to rain.

Which I totally knew.

And ignored.

We're both drenched. His hair's plastered to his forehead and cool rivulets of water are snaking down my back. There are no lights in the boathouse; only two tiny windows and a dirty fly-specked skylight. Outside, all you can see is a gray wall of torrential water and, suddenly, a flicker of lightning.

"God's flicking the light switch," I say.

Cass shoves his hair out of his eyes and squints, assessing my craziness level. Which of course means I keep talking. "Grandpa Ben used to say that, when Nic and I were little and scared of storms and you know, hurricanes and stuff. Lightning was God flipping the switch and thunder was God bowling and . . ."

He's now cocking his head, smiling at me bemusedly, as though I really am speaking a foreign language.

I trail off.

"Um," I say. "Anyway. What are you thinking?"

"That I've gotten you wet and cold again." Cass lifts the bottom of his T-shirt, squeezing water out of the hem, then pulls it entirely off. Sort of like detonating a weapon in the tiny, warm, confined space.

I shiver, glancing around the boathouse for something to dry us.

There are a few old tarpaulins piled in one corner, but they look mildewy and rough and smell musty and are probably full of earwigs and brown recluse spiders. There's another flicker of lightning with a loud crack to follow, like a giant is splitting a huge stick over his knee. The rain seems to pause for an instant as though gathering strength, then an angry grumble of thunder rolls out.

"What d'you know?" Cass says, bending down and pulling something out from behind the Hoblitzells' dinghy, named *Miss Behavin'*. He tosses it toward me. A pink towel, which lands neatly at my feet.

I pick it up. "You can't get warm if you put the dry clothes on over wet ones," I quote, wondering if he'll remember saying that.

He grins at me. "As a wise man once said."

"Man?"

"You're questioning *man*? I was betting you'd go for *wise*."

"Which would be more insulting?"

He picks up another towel and sets his fingers and thumb at the back of my neck, urging my head down, then starts rubbing the towel through my hair to dry it.

He's just drying my hair. With a towel. This should not feel so . . . amazing.

"Insulting each other, Gwen? Is that what we're doing here?" His voice is low, so close to my ear.

I don't know what we're doing here.

Or maybe I do. He stops, dumps the towel to the ground, says gruffly, "I think you're good."

"Yes, totally." I back up, pull my soaking T-shirt up over my bikini, drop it to the floor with a squelch. Cass freezes. The atmosphere inside the boathouse suddenly feels more electrically charged than the storm outside.

We're only a few feet away from each other.

"You've got, um—" He makes this gesture with both thumbs under his eyes, which I can't interpret.

Another flash of lightning. A really loud rumble of thunder. For a second, since he's not moving, I wonder if I should act terrified of storms just for an excuse to throw myself at him, then I can't believe what a lame thought that is.

He reaches out his thumb, very slowly, and brushes it under one of my eyes. I close them both, and the thumb smoothes under the other one. Both of us take a deep breath in, as though we're about to speak, but words fail me. It's Cass who talks.

"Mascara . . . uh . . . here." Another graze of his thumb.

I step back, rub impatiently under both eyes with the pink towel. "Makeup. Ugh, I'm terrible with it. I mean, I can do it, but just the basics. Forget the eyelash curler, which is like some sort of medieval torture device anyway and . . . Maybe I should just give up completely on trying to be a girl."

"That would be a shame. Here, you're getting it all over. Let me."

"I should at least have gotten . . . the . . . water . . . proof kind." Now he has set his fingers on either side of my face, tangling in my wet hair, with the pads of his thumbs still pressing over my cheekbones.

"Water would help . . . clean this up," he says, his voice as quiet as mine. He nods toward the boathouse door. "I could go out and—"

Another crack of lightning, followed almost instantly by thunder. The storm is nearly directly overhead.

"Get struck by lightning? Uh, no," I say. I don't know what to do with my hands. I know what I *want* to do with them, but . . .

It's so dim now in the gray light coming in through the windows that I can feel more than I can see. I see the outline of Cass's head dip lower, then the faint rasp of stubble as his cheek brushes against mine, the roughness of the calluses on his hand as it slides over my hip.

Then he is absolutely still, motionless.

Very, very slowly, I lift my own hand, slide it up to rest on top of his and squeeze. His breath catches, but he still doesn't move. There's another flash of lightning. *One Mississippi. Two Mississippi.* The way to count out a storm. Another beat of silence, then I turn my face to the side and catch his mouth with mine. And I am finally, finally kissing Cass Somers again.

The hand I'm not touching slides down my back, gathering me closer, and he leans back so he's against the wall and I'm flat against him. His mouth is warm and tastes like rainwater and salty ocean both. I take my other hand and slip it into his hair, wet and slick, twist my fingers around a curl. He edges his legs apart, so I'm closer still. Then his fingers edge slowly up my back to where my bikini ties behind my neck, tracing the outline of the straps, nudging at the knot, slipping away again, tracing the line around to my front, then the dip of the bikini top, down, back up to the other side.

Slow. Tantalizing. I hear myself make this little sound of impatience in the back of my throat.

He moves his lips away from mine for a second, takes a deep breath, then hesitates.

Don't think, Cass.

I rest one hand on his jaw, reach the other hand back, yank at the bow at the back of my neck. I double-knotted it and it holds fast. I hear that impatient noise again, but this time it's him, not me. His hand covers mine, untangles, unknots.

Those long fingers moving so expertly, like on the lines of the sailboat.

I move back for a second to let the top fall to my waist but, plastered by water, it stays in place. Cass pulls me close again, wraps his palms around my waist, instead of making the move I expect. Want.

We've hardly paused for air and I'm completely breathless. I pull back, gasping as though surfacing after diving to the ocean floor.

We stare at each other, but it's too dark to see each other's faces. One breath. Another. Then he makes a little sound, like a hum, and lowers his forehead to my shoulder, circling his thumb around the front of me, dipping it into my belly button.

At which point, my stomach rumbles.

"Is that thunder?" he asks as the lightning flashes to illuminate his smile. "It sounded so close."

I cover my eyes. Then burst out laughing.

"Don't worry. We can take care of that." His thumb nudges teasingly into my stomach again. Then he steps back, moves over to the corner. I hear something fall over and clatter on the ground—an oar, probably, then the rustle of paper. But it's too dark to see what's going on, and, wait, why did he move away? We're plastered against each another in a dark enclosed space, damp skin against damp skin, and he . . . steps back? Isn't he supposed to be losing control? I yank at the ties of my bikini, retie them.

Cass is pulling his towel from the pile of life jackets he tossed it on. Flapping it out to lay it flat on the saw-dusty slats of the wood floor, as though we're on the beach. He picks something up and sets it on the towel, just as lightning illuminates two familiar white bags, both embellished with the black drawn figure of a mermaid, extending a plate of stuffed quahogs. Cass sits down cross-legged, then reaches up for my hand, lacing his fingers through mine and pulling gently.

"C'mon. I'm hungry too."

I drop down on my knees, sit back on my heels as he starts hauling things out of one of the bags. A long loaf of French bread, a big wedge of Brie cheese, strawberries, gourmet chocolate . . . I know the contents by heart. I've packed tons of these for delivery to day-trippers coming in off the boats.

"You brought a Dockside Delight?"

"It seemed like a better plan than the carton of raw eggs and the Gatorade, which were the only things I had in my fridge." He breaks a piece of the bread off and hands me the rest.

But instead of the warm feeling that was chasing itself all over me a few minutes ago, I'm suddenly chilled.

He had a picnic waiting. In the boathouse. Ahead of time.

"You planned this—" I say.

"Well, yeah, sure, partly—" Then, more warily, "That's bad? What did I do now?"

In flashes, like old photographs flicking from one moment to the next, I see the party.

The Bronco.

The boys and their knowing laughter.

The guilt in Cass's eyes.

Jim Oberman, freshman year, dragging me against the locker

to make his girlfriend jealous. Alex, just wanting to score an island girl. Spence. Just sex. Am I never going to be anything more than somebody's strategy, a destination marked off on a road map and then passed through for someplace better?

"You planned this," I repeat.

Cass sets down the bread, steeples his hands, and looks up at the skylight as though praying for patience. "Partly. Like I said. Not everything, because nothing ever goes quite the way you mean it to. Not for me, anyway. I wanted to take you out on the water. We both . . . relax there. By ourselves. So yeah, I planned that. I don't have a kayak, so I had to borrow one, which also involved premeditation."

"And having towels all ready in the boathouse?"

His tone is getting rougher now. "*Beach towels*. I thought we might go for a swim, after the kayak. Then have something to eat. On the beach. I didn't plan the storm, Gwen. Didn't look at the weather. And they're *towels*, not a sleeping bag and a jumbo box of condoms." His voice, which has risen, actually cracks. "That's not what this is about."

"Not at *all*?" I ask. Great. Now I sound disappointed.

The storm seems to be moving away, so no lightning to display his face. "Gwen. I'd be lying if I said that. And I'm not going to lie to you. Ever. But if I don't, are you going to kill me, freeze me out again? Or get up, walk out, leave us back where we were all spring? What's it take with you?"

"With *me*? I'm not the one who flips hot and cold constantly!"

"You're not, huh?" Cass says, getting to his feet. "From

where I'm standing, that's exactly what you do. I never know which Gwen I'm going to get. The one who acts like I'm something she stepped in or the one who—"

"Unzips your pants?" I ask.

He smacks his forehead with the heel of his hand. "Right. Because I couldn't possibly want anything more than to get some."

I stand. "It's just a setup, Cass," I say. "Like in March. A means to an end. That's what I am, what—what this is."

Fast reflexes. Before I know what's happening, Cass bends over, grabs the bag, and throws it against the wall. Splintering crash, bottles breaking, soda foaming. I take a step back. He jams his hands into the pockets of his suit, turns away from me. "Fine, Gwen. Gotcha. And you've got me figured out. Clue me in on this, then. Why do I bother with you? Why not just ram my head against a brick wall? It would be easier and less painful. Why are you so freaking—*burned*, that, that nothing I do counts! I'm not fucking Alex Robinson. I'm not that asshole senior with the psycho girlfriend Vivien told me about. I'm not . . . I'm not Spence. Can you get that? Like, ever? How come it's so clear to you when some made-up fictional characters are massively stupid and you can't see it at all when it's you and me?"

"Because you never tell me the truth! It's all charm, and la-la-la, and I'm Cass, I'll boil your lobsters, and I'll charm your pants off, but it's not what's *true*."

He takes a long, deep breath, pushing the heel of his hand against his forehead, as though taking his own temperature.

"You seriously need to get past those lobsters," he says, finally.

The storm is passing, darkness outside graying lighter, so I can see him slide his hand slowly down, cover his eyes, see the small shake of his head. He stands like that for a long time. When he drops his hand and opens his eyes, he keeps his head down.

"Gwen. I don't lie. I'm not a liar. I'm not a—a *user* or whatever you think. I'm me. And I thought you finally cared who that was. I thought that was what this summer was starting to be about." He raises his head.

"I don't know what this summer is about," I admit.

"Well, I do," he says, the slightest edge of bitterness in his voice. Then he turns fully to me, looks directly at me.

No, not bitterness. Hurt.

And I can practically see every weapon, any defenses he's had up, the distant look, the rich-boy poise, the shielding charm, slip from him, hear them all clatter to the floor.

He hangs his hands at his sides, lifts his eyes to mine again, and lets me read everything in his.

Hurt.

Honesty.

Hope.

The realization is quick, sharp, and shattering like that bag striking the wall.

I'm not the only one who can get hurt here.

Who *was* hurt here.

I can't fathom his face in the dark. But right now, in this moment, I don't need lightning to see.

He was right. I *should* come with a YouTube instructional

video. Or a complete boxed set. How the hell can I expect him to figure me out when I don't even get myself? And worse, I'm a total hypocrite—hurt and angry that he'd think about having sex with me, when I've gone there so many times in my own mind. I still don't understand what happened after the Bronco that night. Or even in it. No. But maybe . . . maybe there *is* an explanation, other than the one I've been so sure was the only truth.

Because nothing about Cass is, or ever has been, "no big deal."

It's very still. The rain has passed far into the distance, the high winds quieted down. Nothing to drown out my thoughts or the words I might say. Have to say.

"Guess we should go," Cass says, his voice remote again, as if he has decided this is just impossible.

I bend down, retrieve the rumpled bag full of broken glass, oozing root beer from a jagged tear in the soggy bottom. Wrap it up in a beach towel. Pick up the picnic pieces, cheese, bread, strawberries. Gather it all together. The cleaning woman's daughter.

But not only that.

"Cass." I swallow. "I—I can get past the lobsters."

"That's a start," he says, his voice cool.

"C-can I walk you home?" I ask. "So you don't have to turn the key in the lock?"

A long silence. "Is that the only reason?" he asks finally.

I take a deep breath. Another deep breath.

"Maybe not," I say at last, "the only one."

In the low tide, the waves are lapping lazily far down the beach. The only lingering signs of the storm are dimples in the sand from the pelting rain, and huge piles of kelp and rocks and boat shells littering the beach.

"Heavy lifting to come for the yard boy," I say, scrambling for casual.

Cass tips his head in acknowledgment.

I trip on something and nearly fall and he reaches out a hand to catch me, then lets it drop before he can touch me.

Slowly, infinitesimally, as though if I moved quickly I might scare him off, I reach out for his hand, tangle mine in it, fingers slipping between fingers, then hand locking on hand.

Silence while I try to find what to say.

But then:

"Thank you," Cass says simply. The way he did that night in the Bronco.

Good manners. It occurs to me that this is kindness. Not simply a habit, not only charm.

Then, as if he knows what I'm thinking, is reinforcing it, he moves close enough to me that I can feel his heat, warm skin. He tightens his hand on mine. But still, the walk uphill is long and silent.

When we reach the top, I turn to face him

"If . . . if . . . it wasn't about a jumbo pack of condoms. Or thinking I was easy. What was it, then?"

"We're going to talk now? Finally."

"Finally?" I breathe.

"Yes. We're not having *this* discussion in the middle of

the street, though. Come on." He tows me toward the dark hulk looming against the stars, the Field House. I hurry up the worn wooden steps, follow him into the hideous, haggy, yellow-walled apartment. Which seems all too exposed and open without any buffer between us. No party with room-fuls of people. No open Seashell road with a dozen possible witnesses. No Fabio. No Spence. Nothing but air and us.

We sit down on the couch. He takes a deep breath. Then another. He's nervous. He looks down at his hand. Clench, unclench.

"Just spit it out," I say. *Beautiful.* I sure do have a lyrical way with words.

He takes another deep breath. "I think I need some water."

"I think you're stalling. Please, Cass."

I wrap my hand around his forearm. He turns to face me. The sofa creaks. Definitely a relative of Myrtle's. Great how the furniture in my life talks more easily than I do.

"Let me help you out. Spence told you I was easy . . . so . . . He did, didn't he?"

"Truth? Yeah. That you had crumble lines."

"What the hell are crumble lines?"

"This garbage of Spence's. He likes to spout off all these theories about girls and how to get them."

"Because he's Mr. Notorious, I-Had-Five-Girls-in-My-Hot-Tub-at-Once."

"Three, for the record. Plus, one of them was his cousin who was just in there because she was in track and had run a marathon and her muscles were sore. What he says is to look for crumble lines—places where girls feel bad about themselves or whatever. Then you get them at the right moment and they do stuff they might not ordinarily do."

"That's the sickest theory I've ever heard," I say. *So right too*, I think, remembering that party and that side room. How it all had nothing to do with what I felt about Spence.

"Yup. And dead effective. How Spence plays his game. So, uh, he said you had a reputation."

I wince. He holds up a hand, stopping whatever I was about to jabber.

"So what, Gwen? I have a reputation in my own *family*. Not to mention at Hodges. It happens."

He shuts his eyes, pauses, then opens them and continues, his words coming out rough and hurried.

"I always told him to shut it when he brought you up with his crumble line crap. So yeah, he'd said that and yeah, I'd heard stuff. Locker room shit. But Gwen . . . I knew you. I mean, we knew each other. It was a long time ago, but . . . well. We did. I mean . . . That summer? We did know each other. We were always at the beach or on the boat or doing those crazy scavenger hunts. I didn't talk to you because of anything Spence said. I didn't, um, look at you and just see your body. I sure as hell didn't sleep with you because Spence told me to. That had nothing to do with anything but you and me. I asked you to the party because I *liked* you."

"Cass, why didn't you just ask me out . . . before that?"

"Because I couldn't read you anymore. I thought you'd say no. I'm no good at asking. And I hate doing stuff I'm no good at."

I stare at him. "Those are really stupid reasons."

"*Because Spence told me to* would be stupider," Cass says. "I thought maybe some opportunity would come up. When you waded into the water in your heroic rescue attempt, I figured you had to like me. Too."

He pauses, waiting for me to say something. Confirm something. But one thing is clear. Cass is much braver than me. I just look at him, silently urging him to continue.

"Like I said. I didn't think you did dates. That's what everyone said. When I asked. Because I did. Ask." He sighs, rubs the back of his neck, looks away from me. "So I invented the whole party thing. Which I realized afterward was a stupid-ass way of handling it. But, at the time, it was what I could do. I wanted to be with you. Any way I could."

"Cass—" I inch closer to him on the couch, edge my hand onto his knee. He covers it with his.

"Look, I want to get this out. So . . . so listen."

"I'm listening. I came to the party. And we . . ." I trail off, pull at a tiny elastic string at the side of my bikini bottom.

"For the record? Since we're telling the truth now? That was *not* all me. You . . . you can't sit there and act like, like, I took advantage of you. Because . . . because I may not have known . . . but you were *right there* with me. I know you were. I felt it. And I remember everything. Everything."

My skin prickles, awareness, total recall.

"I didn't plan on hooking up with you that night! That's the truth. You were the one who—" He stops dead.

"Pushed it, right?"

"No! No. That was both of us. But I didn't plan it. Going that far. If I had—if I had, I would have had protection, which, you may remember, I didn't. Which completely freaked me out afterward when you wouldn't even talk to me and just looked at me like I was scum."

"I'm on the Pill."

"How the hell would I have known that? You could have mentioned it."

"You didn't ask."

"We should have used a condom anyway. But I could hardly think, Gwen. One minute we were kissing and the next minute your shirt was off and that was it—no more thinking."

"You're helpless in the face of boobs?"

He studies my face for a moment, then, at the sight of my smile, breaks slowly into one of his own. Then sobers.

"Yours? Um, yeah. But that's not the point. The point is, what happened didn't have anything to do with what Spence said. Except that he screwed it all up for us. Well . . . he and the other guys. And me."

"And me," I whisper, almost hoping he doesn't hear me. But when I look up, his face is suddenly very close to mine. So he must have.

"Are we clear?" he asks gently, his eyes unflinching on mine.

"Clear," I say. Then look down.

And me.

I need to say it.

"Except . . . except for what I, um, did next." Praise God for that bathing suit thread. I pull on it, tangle my finger in it, loop it around and around, concentrating completely until Cass again covers my hand with his own, calluses brushing my knuckles. Then he's motionless. Expressionless. I'd rather not speak, or remember it at all, but—I have to say it. Tell him.

"Sleeping with Spence," I say.

His eyes, so straightforward and honest a second ago, go distant again. He picks at his thumbnail, jaw tight. When he finally says something, his voice is so soft I have to lean forward to hear it.

"Yeah . . . you . . . uh . . . what *was* that about?"

"Aside from me just being idiotic?" I sigh. "I was . . ." *Drunk. Scared. Hurt. Feeling out of place. Crumble lined.* All true, but . . . "Trying to hurt you."

He's had his head bent over that fascinating nail, but now he looks me in the eye, his voice flat and hard as his eyes. "Mission accomplished."

My stomach clenches.

I felt stupid about what happened with Alex. I ached about how things ended at Cass's party. I was ashamed about Spence. But in this moment, it's as though I have never truly experienced, or cared about, any of those emotions before, as though the volume has been cranked up on all of them to the Nth degree. I've been dumb with boys. Thoughtless, casual, stupid. But I was *mean* to Cass.

All this time I thought what stood between us was what he did to me. How I couldn't and shouldn't forgive it—him being *that* guy. When all along I was ignoring what I did back to him. How I didn't want to admit that I'd been *that* girl.

I feel my nose tickle, tears prick the back of my throat. My voice is thick. "I'm sorry. I'm so sorry."

It's quiet all around us. So hushed. I can hear my own heart. His head's ducked. I can see the flicker of his pulse in

307

the hollow of his throat, marking out the seconds of silence between us.

Then, slowly, he raises his head, takes his thumb, touches away my tears, smiling just a little, and I know this time it *is* a romantic gesture because my mascara is long gone.

"Me too," he says.

I take a deep breath, as though I'm about to leap off a bridge. That's exactly what this feels like—catching my breath, holding it, leaping, sinking down, trusting something will propel me back to the surface.

"So . . . I hurt you. You hurt me. Any chance we can get past that?"

Cass looks down for a moment, takes a breath. I hold mine. "Well . . ." he says slowly. "You'd have to promise . . ."

I nod.

Yes.

I do.

I promise.

". . . that you really are past the lobsters."

I smile. "Lobsters? What lobsters?"

Cass laughs.

I wait for him to lean forward, but instead he inclines back, raises an eyebrow at me.

My turn again.

After everything, still, it takes every single bit of courage I have to do what I do next. But I take it, use it, and tip forward to kiss first one dimple, then the other, then those smiling lips.

Chapter Twenty-nine

The sky's gone clear, washed with stars that glitter like mica. The night feels clean and peaceful. Cass is walking me home. Of course. We're both tired and yawning by now, quiet, but a whole different quiet than on the walk to the beach, or back to the Field House. Strange how silence can do so many different things.

We're close enough that I can feel the warmth radiating off his body, but not touching, not holding hands the way we had up the hill. I find myself waiting for that again, for him to take my hand. Something that simple. A bridge between us.

Instead, he tips his head to the deep bowl of the night, where the clouds have already scudded away. A tiny light glitters in the distance, flickers. Fireflies. Like stars around us.

"The first maps were of the sky," I quote.

"That's right," he says. "You remember that?"

Yes.

"That you had your theories on why. You thought they'd have been too busy escaping the mastodons, or whatever, to look up and want to draw what they saw."

"Maybe it reminded them there was more to life than mastodons?" Cass says.

I move a little closer, graze the back of my hand against him. But still, nothing.

More to life than what you are scared of. I reach out, this second time, no mixed messages, interlace my fingers with his.

I don't know if Cass knows that pulling off my shirt was easier for me to do than this . . . or apologizing about Spence.

But I think he might, because his fingers tighten on mine. Now we're crunching up my driveway. The lantern outside the door is tipped crazily to the side, one orangey bulb lit, flickering, the other burnt out. I can hear Nic's voice in my head, *"Gotta fix that."* And Dad getting on him for not having done it already.

Cass leans down, turning to me. I feel a buzzing in my ears. One ear, actually. He brushes his hand next to my cheek, into my hair, pulls.

"Ow!"

"Sorry." He opens his hand, smiles. "Firefly. You caught one."

The dark spot on his palm stays there a moment, then gleams and lifts into the sky. Then Cass pulls me slightly to my tiptoes, as though I'm much shorter than he is, as though I weigh nothing at all, and kisses me thoroughly. "G'night, Gwen. See you tomorrow."

It's Christmas.

Or it feels like it.

The instant my eyes snap open, I get that jolt of adrenaline, that tight thrill, the sense that this day can't help but be magical.

Except that waking up on December twenty-fifth on Seashell

generally means listening to the pipes bang as Mom showers, hearing Grandpa Ben explain once again to Emory why he has to wait until everyone else gets up to see what Santa brought, hearing Nic call out, "Gwen, I don't have to wrap this thing for you, do I? I mean, you'll unwrap it in two seconds anyway."

But now, warm summer smells blow through my window. Beach roses. The loamy sharp scent of red cedar mulch. Cut grass drying in the sun. I can hear Grandpa singing Sinatra from the small backyard garden. Mom echoing from the kitchen. "*Luck be a lady . . .*"

I stretch luxuriously. It feels like everything is new, even though I'm in the same clothes I fell into bed wearing last night, and here's Fabio, as usual hogging the mattress, legs outstretched, paws flopped, breathing bad dog-breath into my face. Still, it's like all the atoms in everything have been shaken and rearranged.

If I keep on this way, I'll be composing the kind of embarrassing poetry that appears in our school literary magazine.

But it's the first time I've had a "morning after" that felt delicious, not nauseating—even though it wasn't "after" anything but a lot of talking and some kissing.

Amazingly, Nic has left some hot water in the shower. I wash my hair, then spend a ridiculous amount of time rearranging it different ways, finally ending up with the same one as always. I yell at Mom because my dark green tank top is missing. She comes in, does that annoying Mom thing where she finds it in five seconds after I've been scrabbling through my drawers for ten minutes. Then she lays her hand on my forehead. "You all right, honey? You look feverish."

311

"I'm fine, Mom. Do you think I should wear this green one? Or the burgundy one? Or just white?"

My nerves are jumping, like sparklers that light, ignite, flare, fizzle. She's all serene. "I'm sure Mrs. Ellington won't care, honey."

I hold up one, then the next, then the next. "Which looks the best? Really, Mom—you need to *tell* me."

An "aha" expression flits across her face. But she says simply, "The green brings out the emerald in your eyes."

"My eyes are brown."

"Tourmaline with gold and emerald," Mom corrects, smiling at me.

I smile back, even though they really are just plain old brown.

I turn my back, pull on the green tank top. "You got through the storm okay?" she asks, beginning to refold the jumbled clothes in my drawer. "I didn't hear you come in. Musta been out pretty late."

"Um, yeah. We, uh . . . watched a movie. Made popcorn." *Kept our hands to ourselves.*

"That Cassidy is a nice boy," she offers mildly. "Such good manners. You don't see that much in kids your age."

This is one of the things about feeling this way. I want to grab on to every little bit of conversation about Cass and expand on it. "Yeah, he's always been very polite. He's so . . . so . . . Do you think I should wear the khaki shorts or the black skirt?"

"The black one is a little short, don't you think? Mrs. E. isn't as conservative as she could be, but you wouldn't want to push it. I thought he'd be full of himself. Kids who look

312

like that usually are. But he doesn't seem that way at all."

"He's not," I say briefly but dreamily. Embarrassing poetry, here I come.

I glance in the mirror over my dresser, put on lip gloss, remember Nic telling me guys hate it because it's sticky, wipe it off. Mom comes up behind me, puts her arms around my waist and rests her chin on my shoulder, staring into the mirror.

Dad's always saying how alike we look, and generally, I don't get it. I see nitpicky things like the gray scattered in Mom's hair, or the way my eyes tip up at the corners like Dad's, the crinkles at the corners of her eyes, the fact that she has a dust of freckles and I have none, that my skin is darker olive than hers. But today, the resemblance hits me as it never has before. I'm not sure why this is until I realize: It's the optimism in our smiles.

All good, but I don't know what to do with myself in the land of sunshine and butterflies. By the time I'm clattering down the steps in heeled sandals I never wear, my nerves are buzzing.

What if things are different in the light of day? How do I handle this, anyway? Do I run up to him when I see him mowing? Or is he going to want to keep things professional around the island?

Does this come easily to most people? Because I have no idea what the hell I'm doing here.

I listen for the sound of the lawn mower but can't hear anything. No handy arrow pointing to a yard to say "Cass is here."

Over-thinking. I'll just get to work. I pick up my pace, then nearly scream when a warm hand closes on my ankle.

"Sorry!" says Cass, sliding out from under the beach plum bush by the side of the Beinekes' house. "I was weeding. You didn't seem to see me." He slides back, stands up and beams at me.

Suppress goofy smile. "Um. Hi. Cass."

He brushes off his hands—still gloveless—and comes around to the gate, slipping through it. Today he's in shorts and a black T-shirt. "You can do better than that." He loops his arms around my waist and pulls me to him.

"Where are your gloves?"

"Better than that too." He drops a kiss on my collarbone. "Good to see you, Cass. I dreamed about you, Cass. . . . Feel free to improvise."

"Aren't you supposed to be wearing those work gloves? When you're working? Because otherwise your poor hands won't . . ."

Gah. I sound like Mom, or the school nurse.

I'm no good at this.

Luckily, Cass is good enough for both of us. "I missed you, Gwen. It's good to see you, Gwen. I dreamed about you, Gwen. Yeah, haven't gotten around to the gloves. More important things to focus on. Want me to tell you what they are?"

"Can I have a do-over?" I ask.

He nods. "Absolutely. Thought we got clear on that." He shifts his hands over my back. I want to tell him not to do that, it's got to hurt, but I'm not going to be the nurse anymore.

I trace the scar in his left eyebrow. "How'd you get this?"

"My brother Jake threw a ski pole at me in Aspen when I

was seven. In fairness, I was making kissing noises while he helped his girlfriend put her boots on. Back when he had girlfriends. You were saying?"

"I—I—" Give up. "I don't have any words today."

"Good enough."

Lots of kissing after this. Apparently too much, as a pair of 'tween boys walking by whistle, though one of them mutters, "Give her the tonsillectomy in private, man."

Laughing, Cass pulls back, his hands still locked around my waist. "I have a bad feeling the yard boy is going to be more useless than usual today."

"As long as you steer clear of the hedge clippers, it's okay, Jose. I can think of a few uses for you." I graze the corner of his mouth with my lips, nudging it open.

"Killing spiders," he mutters, kissing back wholeheartedly. "Opening jars."

"And so on," I whisper.

"Look," he says, pulling back after a while, for the first time seeming awkward. "I can't see you tonight. I have another . . . family thing."

"Oh, yeah, I understand," I say hurriedly. "No problem. I have to—"

He catches my hands and waits till I turn my face back so I'm looking at him.

"This got set up before you and I figured things out—a command performance kind of deal. I'd much rather be with you."

"Your grandmother?"

"And a few trustees from Hodges," he says. "Fun times."

Dad slams the screen door behind him that night, brandishing a crumpled piece of paper, laundry bag over his shoulder. "What exactly is this?" He drops the bag, flicks his hand against the paper. Irritation crackles off him as palpably as the smell of fryer grease. It's eleven o'clock at night, so Castle's must have just closed. Not his usual laundry drop-off time.

"What's it look like?" Mom asks, unperturbed, barely glancing up from her book. "It's a flyer for my business."

I click off the television, looking from one of them to the other.

"You clean houses. That's not a business."

"Well, it sure isn't a hobby, Mike. I clean houses and I want to clean more because We Need the Money. Like you keep saying. So I'm advertising." She plucks the paper from his hand, running her finger across it. "It came out good, didn't it?"

Dad clears his throat. When he starts speaking again, his voice slows, softens. "Luce. You know Seashell. They see these posted around, get the idea you're hard up for work, for cash, and next thing you know, the minute something disappears, some little gold bracelet from Great-Aunt Suzy, every finger will be pointing straight at you."

"Don't be silly." Fabio hurls himself onto the couch, gasping for breath from the effort, climbing into Mom's lap. She ruffles his ears and he snorts with pleasure, eyeing the melting ice cream in her bowl, ears perked. "My clients know me better than that. I've worked for most of the families on Seashell for more than twenty years."

Dad collapses next to her on Myrtle, rests elbows on his

thighs, bows his head into his hands. A streak of white skin gleams at the back of his neck above the sunburn he probably got last time he went out on the boat. "Doesn't matter. When the chips are down, you're not in the Rich Folks Club."

"Mike, you're such a pessimist. Have a little faith in human kindness." To my complete amazement, she ruffles Dad's hair, nudges him on the shoulder. I don't think I can ever remember seeing them touch, much less exchange an affectionate gesture. It actually gives me a lump in my throat, especially when Dad looks up, his hazel eyes big and pleading, a little lost, so like Emory's.

"You never get it, do you, Luce? You still think that the whole damn world is full of happy endings just waiting to come to you. Haven't you noticed Prince Charming hasn't showed up yet?"

Mom's voice is dry. "Yes, honey. *That* I've noticed."

Dad actually cracks a smile.

I'm almost afraid to breathe. My parents are having a minute of truce. An instant of genuine connection. For a moment (honestly, the first in my life) I can understand why they got married (besides the me-being-on-the-way thing).

There's a loud knock on the door. "Betcha that's him now," Mom says, smiling at Dad.

But it's Cass. He grins at me, then looks a little sheepish. "I know it's late," he starts.

"Almost midnight." Dad comes up behind me. "And who the hell are you?"

Cass introduces himself.

"Aidan Somers's son, right? Coach Somers your brother? Lobster roll, mayo on the side, double order of fries?"

317

Cass blinks, momentarily confused. "Uh . . . Yeah, that's Jake."

"Bit late for a swimming lesson." Dad surveys Cass, who is wearing a blue blazer, a tie, neatly creased khakis. "And you're not exactly dressed for one, kid."

"Don't be silly, Mike. He's come for Gwen," Mom says, sounding as though this is the most natural thing in the world.

"I wondered if she'd want to take a walk with me," Cass explains. "I know it's late," he repeats in the face of Dad's glare.

"I'd love to," I say instantly, grabbing his hand. "Let's go!"

"Wait just a second," Dad says. "How old are you, Cassidy?"

"Seventeen."

"I was seventeen once too," my father begins unpromisingly. "And I took a ton of girls to the beach late at night—"

"That's great, Dad. You can tell us all about it another time." I pull Cass out the door as Mom says, "A ton? That's a bit much, Mike. It was just me and that trashy Candy Herlihy."

"Are we ever going to leave my house without me having to apologize for my family?"

"Not necessary. I'm the one who showed up late." Cass yanks at his tie, loosening it, hauling it off, then shoves it in his jacket pocket, opens the door of the old BMW, which is parked in our driveway next to Dad's truck and the Bronco, pulls off the jacket and tosses it in. Then starts unbuckling his belt.

"Uh, strip in our driveway," I say, "and Dad's *definitely* going to think this is a booty call."

He laughs, tosses the belt in, followed by his shoes and socks, pulls his shirttails out, bumps the car door shut. "Just felt like I couldn't breathe in all that. I was headed home, saw your lights on . . . just wanted to see you."

He takes my hand again and we head down the road. I love nighttime on Seashell . . . all the silhouetted figures of the houses, the hush of the ocean. It feels like the only time the whole island belongs to me.

"How were the trustees?"

"Stuffy as hell. Like the atmosphere at the B and T." He takes a deep breath. "Not like this." Then he tugs me a little closer. "Or this." Ducking his head, he rubs his nose in my hair. I brace my hands on his shoulders, lean closer, feel warm skin under his crisp cool shirt.

He steps back. "Okay, island girl. Give me a tour? The Insider's Night Guide to Seashell?"

"We could just go to the Field House," I say, then wince.

"Not about a jumbo box of condoms, remember? Come on. You've got to have some secret places no one knows about."

In the Green Woods, through the tunnel of trees, the forest full of night sounds, by the witch hat stone. There's the low cry of an owl, loud over the distant rush of the water. Cass stops, hand on my arm.

"What?"

"Peaceful," he says. He shuts his eyes, drinking it in. "Barbershop quartet night at the B and T."

Almeida's has done functions at the Stony Bay Bath and Tennis Club. I know he's not kidding.

He stands there for a moment longer, then I whisper, "Come on, it's better by the water."

"It always is, Gwen."

The moon silvers the creek, the bridge above it, gleams on the rocks. The breeze moves over the marsh, sweet with sea grass, the old-wet-wood smell of the pilings. Cass sits down, leans back on his elbows, and looks at the sky, deep indigo and cloudless. I hesitate, breathing in the cool night air. After a few minutes, I walk a few feet away, unbutton, kick my shorts aside and wade into the rushing water, dipping underneath, surfacing to let the current, stronger and faster near the surface than below, seize me.

Then what's catching me are Cass's hands at my waist, his legs brushing mine, chin dipping into the curve of my shoulder.

Because the creek flows from the salt marshes into the ocean, the water's warm, half salty, half sweet. I taste it on his lips.

Like before, things move fast with us. Cass has quick reflexes, and I have curious, wandering, wondering hands. He pulled me out of the water, as certain of his destination—a circle of soft grass between the bushes at the top of the bank—as if he'd visited here before and kept the map in his head. *This is where we will go.* I lean back on one elbow, tipping my head to the side, as Cass's lips skate slowly up from my shoulder to my ear, so lightly, his lips are soft as a breath, but still enough to blow almost every thought away.

"My traitorous body."

That's one of those phrases that pops up all the time in Mom's and Mrs. E.'s books. A handy excuse for the heroines, like, "Gosh, I knew I should stop and be 'good,' but *my traitorous body . . .*"

I've felt like that before. Or like I was one place and my mind off in the distance somewhere. Observing. Or trying hard not to.

But not now.

My body doesn't feel as though it's betraying me, separate. I'm not drowning out thoughts and focusing on sensations. I trace the long line of Cass's jaw, dip a finger in a dimple, feel it groove deeper as he smiles. When I slide my hand up his side, brushing a drier path on the wet skin, the bump and groove of rib to rib, I feel him shiver, then the shake of him laughing a little.

"Ticklish?"

"Happy." He cups the back of my neck with one hand, nudges at the top of my neckline, edges it lower. But well before it tips into something more than making out, we both pull back, me bracing my hands on his chest, him moving back, breathing hard.

"Sorry. I—only meant to—" That flush edges from the tips of his ears over the rest of his face.

"I know. But let's stop here."

He pulls the straps of my tank top back into position, head ducked, gives a quick nod.

"Not, um, forever. But tonight . . ." I falter. "Because I want—"

Cass cocks his head at me.

I want. The beginning of that sentence feels as though it will lead me into tall grass where I might get stranded. I try again. "I don't want—"

"A jumbo box of condoms," Cass says.

321

"I'm not taking that off the table. I mean, not forever. Because I— Jesus. This is awkward. Feel free to chime in anytime."

"You get pissed off when I rescue you, Gwen."

"I get more pissed off when you're all calm when I'm—"

"Calm?" He sets his hands on my shoulders and gives me the smallest of shakes. "Hardly. 'Cause, no, I don't want to stop now. I mean"—glancing down at where our bodies are still against each other's—"clearly. But you're right to. *We're* right to."

"Right?" I'm not sure what he means.

"A do-over, do better, a redo. If this"—he twitches his finger back and forth between us—"goes, um, there, again—"

"When," I blurt. "When it goes there. Since we're telling the truth here."

He squeezes my shoulders, gives me a quick, hard kiss. "When. We're doing it in a place and at a time we both choose. Not in the car or on a couch in some other random hurried way."

"Not in a boat, not with a goat," I say, unable to help myself. He did sound like one of Emory's Dr. Seuss books.

"No and no," Cass says, laughing. "We're doing it in a bed. No goats."

"You WASPs are so conventional." I give his chest a shove.

"The first time," he amends. "After that, all bets are off. *And* we're doing it when we have more than just the one condom I've had in my wallet since I turned sixteen."

Not for the first time, I wonder why he didn't use that thing, or any other one, ages ago—what exactly he's been waiting for.

Leaning against the railing of our porch, I only wait for Cass's silhouette to be swallowed up by the night before hurrying down the steps again, in need of the rush, the peace, of jumping off the pier, swimming alone.

Swimming with Cass in the creek, bumping up against each other in the water, skin to skin, slip-sliding so close, then him ducking away, dodging me, was hardly calming.

God, isn't it supposed to be the guys who can't think straight? Whose bodies are screaming at their brains to just shut up because everything feels so *good*? Or is that another rumor someone started? Without thinking who it was going to hurt. Or just confuse.

The moon's full, leaving Abenaki bright as day, but without the clutter. Except that there's a lone car in the sandy beach parking lot, parked far over in the corner, nearly concealed by sea grass. But no silhouettes on the pier or the boat float.

I'm heading out on the pier when I hear it, slightly louder than the waves—this little groan, echoing in the dark. I freeze, look back over the beach, my skin prickling. See nothing but the usual tangles of seaweed and rock piles.

Must have imagined it.

But then comes the quiet rumble of a male voice, the higher pitch of a girl's. Him questioning, higher pitched at the end, her laughing, throaty. I find myself smiling. Some couple taking advantage of the atmosphere, the moonlight, the privacy, just as Cass and I did. I scan the beach, finally spotting a couple far away, beyond the bathhouse, all tangled up in each other on a towel.

The girl says something; there's a short burst of soft laughter. They're too far away to hear any distinct words and—

I squint to try to identify them for only a second before

realizing how creepy that is and edge back toward the pier.

Then a cloud shifts away from the moon, and the parked car is illuminated in a flash of silver.

Why on earth would Spence Channing be fooling around on a Seashell beach at midnight, when that house of his is like a damn hotel?

It occurs to me in this second that since he knew the exact body count in the hot tub, Cass was clearly at that party. What was he doing while his best friend was having "just sex"? Serving drinks?

How can two people be so different and still best friends?

Another—possibly awkward—question for another—less awkward—time. But not now. Now I take a running leap off the pier, soar, and sink into the cold, cleansing water.

I see the ash glow of a cigarette glimmering through the dark. My cousin's sitting on our porch steps, just an outline against the light from the kitchen door.

I walk up, snatch the cigarette from his unresisting fingers, toss it to flicker out among the clamshells. "I thought the smoking was a one-time thing, Nico."

"Yeah. Those one-time things." Nic straightens, cracking his knuckles behind his neck, and slams the screen door—snap top half, rattle bottom half—behind him as he goes inside. His voice drifts through the door. "They have a way of coming back around, right, cuz?"

"What's that supposed to mean?"

He reaches for the bowl of popcorn that's resting beside Myrtle, only to find that Fabio is nosing out the last of it. Our dog looks up at him, licking butter off his chops, and then, at the expression on Nic's face, slinks behind the couch, forgetting, as usual, to hide his tail.

"It means what's up with Somers? And you. Aunt Luce seemed to think something was going on."

"Nic. What's wrong with you? It's not like you tell me everything. Like when were you gonna—"

"You can't be married," he cuts in.

—tell me about the ring.

Wait. What? Are we talking about the same thing? "God, Cass hasn't proposed," I joke, not wanting to spook him. "We're just—" I don't know what we're "just." Or if "just" even works anymore.

"I didn't mean Somers. I meant me. CGA."

He leans back on Myrtle. I slide down next to him, bare back against the nubbly fabric, nudging his legs off to make room.

Nic rubs his bicep with a flat hand, jaw tight. He suddenly looks so much older than eighteen. "Hoop and I drove up there this morning. Had my tour. Gwen . . . I want it even more now. But I . . . what I didn't get before . . . You can't have any 'serious personal responsibilities.' That's what they said."

I squint at him, like bringing Nic into focus will bring everything else in too. "Who doesn't have serious personal responsibilities? I mean, hello. What, you have to be an orphan and a social misfit?"

"You can't have people you need to support." Nic scrubs his hands up and down his face. "Kinda problematic."

I pause for a second, then say, "Yeah, and it only becomes a bigger problem if you're ring shopping at eighteen, cuz."

Nic turns to me. "Wait—you know about that? We agreed not to tell anybody."

"Viv didn't fess up? Yeah, I know about it. You can't keep a secret for ten minutes on Seashell. Someone saw you two at the mall."

Nic sighs. "Vee's hated this whole academy thing from the start. You know that, right?"

Viv's worked hard to hide from Nic every hint of worry over his chosen career. Of course he guessed anyway, but . . . I trace my finger along the corner of Myrtle's frayed bottom cushion. Say nothing.

"She wants me to stay and . . . settle down. Here. On Seashell. Forever."

His voice cracks on the *forever*.

"You don't want that?"

My cousin looks at me, brown eyes blazing. "I'm eighteen. I don't know what the hell I want. Vivien—she's my anchor. I love her. Always have. But . . . how can I tell how I'll feel in four years? In eight, after I serve? I don't. I'm not even supposed to."

As if it's my own life flashing before my eyes—because so much of it is—I see a thousand moments of Nic and Viv. Him balancing her on his shoulders for water fights at Sandy Claw. Her teasing him about his terrible tent-pitching skills when we set up camp in the backyard, then laughing hysterically as it collapsed around them in a billow of rip-stop nylon. Him borrowing this hideous maroon tux with a ruffled shirt from Dom D'Ofrio and showing up in it to take Viv to prom, then, after her horrified reaction, pulling a classic black one out of the trunk of the car, along with her corsage. The three of us lying on the dock looking up at the moon, waxing and waning, glimmering across the water, their hands always linked over our heads, even when I was the one in the middle. He choreographed his and Vivien's first night together, like a master director, checking into the hotel early so he could scatter rose petals on the bed. When he finally lowered himself beside her, he whispered, "I want this to be perfect for you." He was incredibly embarrassed when he found out Vivie had repeated that to me, but how could she not?

"But . . . but you've always known. I mean, you two have been together forever. It's what you've always wanted. It was in the I WILL notebook."

"I knew you read that thing," Nic mutters. "Yeah, I mean . . . of course. Yeah, always. But I don't . . . want only that."

There's this weird tingling in my hand, and I realize I've been borrowing Cass's gesture again, my fist tight, my nails biting into the skin of my palm. Unclench. I take a deep breath, the way you do when you're about to say something important and game changing. Then realize I've got nothing. No big, wise revelation to turn this moment around, back into familiar territory where I know the stakes. Nic rubs his fingers across his eyes. He looks exhausted, hollowed out, like after a tough meet where SBH has lost, badly.

"So!" I say, at last, too enthusiastic, like I'm promoting a product, suggesting a cool way to spend a free Saturday. "Why get engaged now anyway, Nico? Why not just tell her it's CGA policy? Not your choice. Just life."

"I said exactly that. Tonight. You should have seen her face.

She got that panicky look, all blank faced and in-charge but blinking like she's about to cry, trying to act like it's all good."

I nod. I know that look from when Al hisses at her after a function, ticks off on his fingers what she got wrong.

Nic continues, words tumbling out as though they've been shut behind a dam that's broken now, water spilling everywhere, soaking everything. "Like she always does when we talk about what me getting into the academy means—the time I'm going to need to put in. Which is why I started with the ring in the first place. See, Viv . . . she knows exactly what she wants. Al and her mom are planning to retire in a few years. We can move into their house. They can take the RV, go cross-country. Her mom's been researching it forever, they, like, already have this folder full of maps and stuff, the whole thing planned out. Their life, our life . . . We can run Almeida's. Vee's not even into going to college. I thought it would be good to make a promise to her. So she wouldn't be scared. So she'd know I was always coming back to her. Like this . . . life raft. But now I am. Totally scared, I mean. Marco and Tony were working with us on Thursday, and they were laughing . . . *laughing* . . . about how Marco wanted to be in the Air Force, and Tony had this dream to be a pro wrestler and ha-ha-ha, we coulda been contenders. Like it was funny as hell that instead they were scraping barnacles off people's yachts and repainting their freaking bathrooms instead of doing what they'd planned."

I twist the hair at the nape of my neck, set it free, twirl it again, debating what to say, where even to start. "Well, Nico. Obviously I know nothing about successful relationships—"

He gives a brief bark of laughter.

"But . . . I'm pretty sure both people have to really want it for a marriage to have half a chance."

"I love Vee," he repeats. "I can't imagine loving anyone else . . ." He trails off, ducks his head, pulling up his knees, resting his forehead on them. He takes a deep, shaky breath, mutters something I can barely hear.

"Nic?"

"But," he says, and swallows, Adam's apple bobbing hard.

I rub the back of his neck. "But?"

"But before that guy from the Coast Guard came to talk at school, I never knew I wanted that . . . so . . . there may be other things out there just like that that I can't see yet." He says the last part fast, the words all jumbled together, sliding his hand through his hair, slipping his palm back down to cover his face again, like he doesn't want to look, doesn't want to see the truth. What's out there.

I don't either. And for a bit, the silence stretches on. Because I don't want this to be real, what's happening here. Our now that makes all our thens so distant and so past.

But.

Vivien loves Nic with her whole, unfiltered, warm heart.

But he is my cousin.

So I draw in a breath too, square my shoulders, set my hand on one of his. Tell him the truth he needs to hear, instead of the one I want to believe in. "Not 'may be other things,' Nico. Are."

He looks over at me, and to my shock, there are tears in his eyes. "I know. But I already feel like I'm cheating on her by wanting anything she doesn't."

I put my arm around his shoulder as he brushes his eyes

with the heel of his hand. For a second, he rests his head against me, tips it onto my shoulder, burrowing in for comfort just like Emory does. He smells like sweat and salt and sand, like family, like Seashell. The night is still, still, except for the familiar summer sounds, the shhh of the tide, the bzzz-whhr of the crickets, a dog barking a warning into the night, far, far away. Fabio, who has been snoring under the couch, snuffles, passes gas, and falls silent. Nic and I can clearly hear Emory's and Grandpa Ben's sleep noises. Grandpa Ben: "Snuffle snuffle snuffle . . . silence . . . snort." And Emory, who really does sound more like the snoring cliché: "RRRR . . . shhh . . . rrrr . . . shhh."

"What about Em?" Nic asks, swinging his long legs over mine, kicking his foot. "Where's he supposed to fit into the whole personal obligation thing?"

Yeah. Em. Dad telling me that if Nic left, I'd be the one picking up the slack with my brother. And when I go to college . . . what then? I rub my chest, pushing away the tightness there.

Because . . . can I even go to college now? Does that mean Em's my responsibility forever?

Well, of course he's my responsibility forever. Nic and I've talked about that, how we'll probably end up dividing care for him for the rest of our lives, but both of us thought it would be later on, much later on. And it probably will be—Mom's only thirty-six. But . . .

I love my brother more than I can find words to tell. But like my cousin, I want off-island. At least for a while. If I wind up, somehow, staying . . . I want it to be my choice.

"Cuz." Nic touches my cheek. "S'okay. For God's sake, don't

be the second girl I've made cry in three hours. I'll figure it out." He taps one of his temples, smiles at me. "I always do. And uh, speaking of figuring things out, anything you want to tell me about Somers?"

A much better place for my thoughts to go. I touch my lips, unthinking.

Nic gives me a slow once-over. "Oookay. Got it. No details. I only need to know one thing. He treat you right?"

"He's been a perfect gentleman."

"I'll bet," he mutters. His shoulders twitch as though he's shaking off any image of me and Cass together.

"I mean, he—we—"

"Big picture only, for God's sake. You happy, Gwen?"

"I am."

"That's all I need. I'm out." He slides off Myrtle, heading for the outdoor shower, then turns back. "If that changes, you know I'll kill him, right, cuz?"

Chapter Thirty

"Okay, buddy. The big one. You ready?"

I'm not.

Em has his toes curled over the edge of the raft, poised to jump. He's not wearing his life jacket, just has one of those overly bright, puffy foam swimming noodles looped under his armpits. His reflection looms over the water. Like me and Nic last night, swaying over the unknown.

But this is not me or Nic. This is Em.

Cass and I have already debated the wisdom of this three times during the walk down to the beach. Two more as we swam out to the raft, Emory's slight arms looped around Cass's neck, me pulling up the rear with the noodle and all my worries. We walked down the hill, debating, towing the wagon, Emory calm and collected, narrating the landmarks of the journey for Hideout, Fabio proudly aboard, head raised, like a dignitary at a motorcade.

Even when we hit the beach, I'm still arguing that Em's not ready yet to make that big leap, not without something that'll definitely, completely keep him above water—preferably something Coast Guard–approved. Cass saying he'll have something to hold him up, but it'll be in Em's own hands, his control, that that's important psychologically, repeating, "I know this stuff. Trust me, Gwen."

"I'm not sure Em gets *psychologically,* Cass. He doesn't think like that."

Saying my brother's limitations out loud feels like betraying him. We've always been careful not to, as if that story wasn't ours to discuss either, what he can't do, what he may never be able to do.

"Ready. Sssset," Em says, his brow crinkled in concentration, poised on the edge of the float. I grab the end of the noodle. Clearly not the solution. Cass gives me a raised eyebrow, peels my fingers gently from the yellow foam.

I look down at the water. So flat and green and clear I can see the ripples of the sand far below, crabs scuttling around, eel grass. I sigh. And stand back. Emory takes a deep breath, flips his hair back exactly the way Cass does, studies the water with Cass's focused frown. He's been studying more than just Cass's swim moves.

"Low tide. No surf," Cass says, close to my ear. "If you trust the water, it holds you up. We're both here. This'll be fine."

He counts down as Emory takes a deep breath, squints, concentrating hard on the water. "It's a bird. It's a plane. It's . . ."

My little brother has the noodle clamped tightly under his arms, ends sticking out on either side like wings, his eyes serious, focused on the horizon. He turns and flashes me a grin, a broader one at Cass, then shouts, "It . . . I . . . Superman!" He launches himself, rockets into the world with a squeal.

And he is fine. Bobbing up a second later, shaking the water out of his hair.

Giggling. He throws his arms out in a Victory V, which sends him sinking below the surface again. Then pops back up, still laughing, and starts heading for us.

I make a move toward the edge of the float, Cass catches my elbow. "He can do it himself."

He can. Em kicks in that overly splashy way little kids have, spiraling his arms back to the wooden ladder, anchoring it with his feet, clambering up. He splats the noodle onto the float, unself-conscious, confident. "I Superman," he repeats, the S sound coming out perfect, beaming, showing every one of his teeth.

Em jumped off and swam back to the raft at age eight— just like Nic, Viv, Cass, and me. The only milestone he's hit exactly on time.

Cass relaxes now, tension I didn't even read before suddenly gone, tan legs hooked over the pier, dangling toward the water, slanting back on his elbows. Emory does the same, kicking his feet, *splish, splash,* smiling from ear to ear.

I take in a long deep breath, as though I'm about to jump into the water myself. But instead, I look at my brother, lying flat on the float now, little-boy straight, arms against his sides, still grinning. I look at Cass, eyes tipped closed, drinking in the sunlight. It glimmers off his hair and the drops of water on his shoulders. From here, if you look far to your right, you can make out the shadow of Whale Rock, the long grass that leads up to the Ellingtons', the curve of Seashell around the bend of the island to where you can't see anymore.

Where you look. When you leap.

More to life than mastodons.

Chapter Thirty-one

"This is what comes after *Tess?*"

I rouse myself from the sleep I've fallen into on the glider during Mrs. E.'s nap to find Cass standing over me, holding one of her racy books. This particular cover features a man wearing an eye patch and all too little else, and a stupefied-looking woman in an extremely low-cut dress that he's clearly in the process of lowering farther. They are, of course, standing on a cliff. In a brewing thunderstorm.

"I'm not at all sure this is physically possible," he muses, squinting at the cover.

"Which part? Her breasts?" I sit up to scrutinize the book.

"No, I wasn't thinking of those, but now that you mention it . . . anyway . . . where's his hand?"

"Isn't this it?" I point.

"I thought that was her, er—"

"No, it's his hand. I'm sure."

"Then what's that?"

I peer at the book cover. When you examine it closely, she does indeed appear to have too few appendages and he too many.

"Stand up," Cass directs. "If I put one hand here on your

shoulder, and then you sort of collapse back, like she's doing—farther, Gwen—I'd need to have a hand right here on your back so you wouldn't fall off that cliff. But instead, his other hand is all over her tits . . . so why doesn't she hurtle to her death?"

"Tits, Cass? Ew."

"I know. There are no good words."

"Maybe she's a gymnast with superior muscle control."

"She'd have to be in Cirque de Soleil to manage this. See, if I take away this hand, you—"

I fall back on the glider with a rusty clang of springs.

"—wind up exactly where I want you."

I'm not someone who forgets where I am. But I have not spent any time lying on a gently swinging glider on a porch by the sea kissing a beautiful boy. *Don't think.* All my focus, every thought, narrows to this moment, the soft sounds we're both making, a few squeaks from the glider springs, the whole world faded to background music.

Until—"What in the name of God is going on here?" and Cass, scrambling, slides off me, landing on his butt and looking up at Henry Ellington with the same stunned expression I must wear.

Behind him is Gavin Gage, his face poised, neutral. Henry, however, is a thundercloud. An apocalyptic thundercloud turning darker and darker red. Cass moves in front of me. I shove my shirt back down. He starts to say, "This isn't what it—" then falters because that's one of the lamest lines ever, right up there with "It didn't mean anything" and "We can still be friends."

He switches to, "It's my fault."

336

"Where's my mother while all this is going on?"

I hop up next to Cass and hurriedly explain, face flaming, that it's okay, she's napping.

Which makes things worse.

"If this is your idea of what's acceptable while a helpless old woman is resting—in her own house—on my dime, you are very much mistaken." Then: "Who the hell are you?" to Cass.

"Uh—the yard boy."

"Not anymore," Henry returns succinctly. "Nor will *your* dubious idea of caretaking be needed from now on, Guinevere."

His mouth is screwed up in a line, he's ramrod straight. If he were a teacher in an old-fashioned book, he'd be hauling out a ruler to rap us across the knuckles.

Anger rises in me, steam in a kettle edging toward a boil.

"Henry, maybe we should all take a moment and calm down," Gavin Gage interjects unexpectedly. "Back when you and I were their age—"

"That's not the issue here," Henry barks. "Take whatever you brought with you and get out." His voice is softer now, but no less deadly. "You've abused my trust, and the trust of a helpless woman. There will be consequences beyond the loss of your jobs, I assure you."

I hate that he can do this. And he can. And with an impact far beyond this small island. My mind flicks fast. I think of our first "conversation"—*itemized*—his veiled threat. His muted discussion with Gavin Gage on the other side of the kitchen door. The way he folded that check and held it out to me, set it down on the counter like the ace of spades. And I can't do it—I can't keep my mouth shut, I—

"Listen," I start, "what makes you think you—"

Cass puts a warning hand on my arm.

I make a strangled sound, fall silent.

This isn't just about me now.

I need the money, yes. But Cass's dad got him the job. Getting fired would be one more screw-up, and I can tell just by the way he won't meet my eyes that this has already occurred to him.

"Gracious, Henry. Do be quiet!" calls Mrs. Ellington through the screen porch door. "If it's not bad enough you've woken *me* up, your bellowing is likely reaching all the way to Ada Partridge's house, and you know how she'll respond. It would be *most* embarrassing to have her call the police and have you arrested for creating a public disturbance."

Henry offers an explanation that is unflattering in the extreme to both Cass and me, in which the words *lewd, depraved,* and *wanton* appear more often than you'd think possible, since, maybe, *The Scarlet Letter*. Jesus, we were only kissing.

Instead of a shocked gasp at the end, Mrs. E. gives her low belly laugh. "That's what all the fuss was about? The dear children were simply—obeying my request."

Henry, Cass, and I all goggle at her. Gavin Gage sits down in one of the wicker chairs, crosses his ankles, amusement gleaming in his eyes. All he's missing is a box of popcorn and a soda.

Mrs. E. edges the porch door open with her cane and steps out. "You know I adore the theater," she observes serenely. "Sadly, I am no longer able to attend it in the city—such a great crush of people. It has been my dearest wish to see my favorite play, *Much Ado About Nothing*, performed once again. Your dear father took me to that once, when we were in London." She leans her cane against the weathered porch shingles, clasps her hands under her chin, tips her face to the side, magnanimous. "I still remember my favorite line. 'Lady, I will live in thy heart, die in thy lap, and be buried in thy eyes . . .' "

Cass's lips twitch. He ducks his head to hide it.

"I don't remember that they were all over each other like white on rice in that play," Henry says, sounding like a sulky child.

Mrs. E. waves a hand at him airily. "Shakespeare, dear boy. Very bawdy. Dear Guinevere and Cassidy were most reluctant but I urged them to be faithful to the text, and to rehearse assiduously."

Ridiculous from the start, this is now officially over-the-top. Henry glowers. Mrs. E. gives him her benevolent smile.

There's a long pause, and then Henry grudgingly allows that he must have misinterpreted what he saw. His mother graciously accepts his apology. Within minutes Cass and I have our jobs back.

Cass excuses himself to go back to work, but as I head to the kitchen to make tea, he pops his head in through the window. "Helpless old woman, my ass."

Chapter Thirty-two

Mrs. Ellington just saved my job—and Cass's. And for the next two hours, I betray her.

Gavin Gage's eyes don't glitter with avarice, or bulge with green dollar signs like in cartoons, but as I go through the whole tea-serving ritual with all the silver pieces, at which I am now a semi-pro, I notice his cool appraising glance every time I pick up a new item.

Mrs. Ellington chats away, asking Gavin about his family, recalling little details of his friendship with Henry, how they met at Exeter, were on the sailing team together, this French teacher, that lacrosse coach, etc., etc., and Gavin Gage answers politely and kindly, even reminisces about some trip they took as boys with the captain to Captiva.

The only comfort is that Henry Ellington is even more uncomfortable than me. He would so lose to Grandpa in a poker game. He keeps grimacing, shifting around in his seat, pulling at his collar. When Mrs. E. tries to engage him in polite social conversation, he's totally distracted, making her repeat her question. At one point he says abruptly, "I need some air."

And goes out to the porch.

Mrs. E. stares after him, then smoothes things over, saying that of course, Gavin, dear Henry did not mean to be rude. The poor boy works so hard. Gavin assures her he understands. It's all so far from what's going on under the surface that I want to scream.

Perched on our battered front steps that afternoon, Grandpa Ben performs his own ritual as methodically as Mrs. E. enacts her tea one. Emptying out his pipe. Tapping the fresh tobacco out of the pouch. Packing it in.

I told Grandpa everything. Or almost everything. Not about Henry walking in on Cass and me. But everything else, my voice hushed but sounding loud as a scream in my own ears. I expect Emory, crashed early on Myrtle, lulled to sleep by the soporific Dora, to bolt up, eyes wide. But he slumbers on, freeing Grandpa to smoke, which he hates to do around Em with his asthma. Grandpa says nothing for a long time, not until the pipe is lit and his already rheumy brown eyes are watering slightly in the smoke.

Then finally, "We do not know."

That's it?

"Well, exactly, Grandpa. But . . . but . . . it's clear Henry doesn't want his mother to know either. That can't be good."

"There are things you don't want Lucia to understand. Not all of them are the bad things."

I feel heat sting my face. "No—but those things aren't like . . . Those things are personal."

"Pers-o-nal." Grandpa draws the word out slowly, as if he can't remember what it means in English. That happens every now and then. More this year than last, more last year than the year before.

"Personal. Belonging to me," I translate.

Grandpa Ben tilts his head, as though he's still not clear, but then he reaches into his pocket, pulls out his worn dark leather wallet, nudges it open, hands me a picture.

Vovó.

Oh. Not that. My stomach hurts.

I think I know what Grandpa's doing.

I remember my Vovó, emaciated and pale near the end, but in this picture she's warm and strong, all curvy brown arms holding up a silver-flecked fish half as big as she is and laughing. The grandmother I remember, wholehearted and real, always smiling, not the solemn one formally posing on the wall, frozen in time.

I look at the photo for only an instant before I hand it back to him. I know what he's saying, without saying, and I don't want to hear it. Don't want to think about it. But I say it out loud anyway.

"Other people's stories."

He nods at me, a small smile. "You remember. *Sim. Histórias de outras pessoas . . .*" He trails off.

This is as close as we have ever come to talking about it. Another memory of that long-ago summer, nine years ago, the year Cass's family was on the island.

It was one of those New England years of weird weather. Hurricane season runs from June to November here, and it's usually a non-event. Something brews off the coast of Mexico, blows out to sea long before it hits us here. Marco and Tony watch the path on the Weather Channel, field the calls from summer people, stand ready to block shore-facing windows with plywood. We year-rounders don't worry so much, knowing our low-crouching houses are hunkered down to survive storms, outlast anything. But that year, Seashell was moody. Unpredictable. Currents and squalls from every different direction. There was a lot of heat lightning at night, rolling thunder that tumbled over the island like an angry warning, but came to nothing in the end.

Nic and I had the run of the island that summer. We were seven and eight. Marco and Tony hired us to catch blue crabs off the creek bridge to sell, hooking them with bent-out safety pins, piling our catch into Dad's emptied-out plastic ice cream buckets, but that was pretty much the only structured activity. We could climb onto the Somerses' boat and jet off when we wanted to. We could have sand fights with Vivie at the beach. Work on swimming out to the boat float, then the breakwater, our biggest goals. Dad was at Castle's 24/7 . . . he'd just extended the hours. Mom was newly pregnant, with Em, nauseated most of the time. If we left her a box of saltines and a stack of books, cheap and stained from the library or a yard sale, we could go off until sunset.

Vovó was nauseated too, but for a different reason. One I wasn't supposed to know about.

"It will only worry your mother," Dad explained to me firmly, looking sharply in the rearview mirror after we dropped Vovó off at the doctor's. "She's having a hard time as it is." *Hahd.*

343

Heavy on his accent. Which I knew meant he was worried.

"It will be fine," Grandpa said stoutly. "Your Vovó, Glaucia, she has been fighting germs her whole life."

But this needed more than Clorox and Comet, of course. Vovó got sicker, and the story for Mom was that she was working longer hours—that's why she wasn't coming by as much, looked a little thinner, and I stopped being worried and got scared.

So I told Mom. It felt like she started crying then and cried for the rest of the summer.

It was the angriest I've ever seen Grandpa. He threw a pan— he never did things like that—his eyes as wide with shock as my own when it hit the floor, eggs and linguica spattered everywhere. And yelled at me, all these words I'd never heard, strung together in ways I couldn't understand. Except for that phrase, because it wasn't the last time I heard it. *"Histórias de outras pessoas."* Other people's stories—Mom would say it later, when Nic and I scrambled to pass on some bit of Seashell gossip, some nugget of information to talk about at dinner. *Deixe que as histórias de outras pessoas sejam contadas por elas*—are their own to tell.

Grandpa reaches out for me now, nudges his knuckles beneath my chin. Once, twice. But I don't nod back. I feel a little sick. We've never brought that up. The whole topic, my part in it, ended when he threw the pan. Or later that evening when he bought me an ice-cream cone, cupped my chin in his hands and apologized, then said, "We will not speak of it again."

"Pfft," he says now, thrusting his hand rapidly through the air as though shooing away flies. "Enough. Enough of the long

344

face. Here, *querida*." He hunches back on his hips, reaching into his pocket, pulls out his customary roll of bills, held together with a rubber band—the wallet is only for pictures—extracts two fives and hands them to me. "Go out with the young yard boy. Be happy."

"What about the Rose of the Island?"

"To grow in the salt and the heat and the wind, very tough, island roses."

"You sound like a fortune cookie, Grandpa."

His eyes twinkle at me, and his broadest smile flashes. "Rose is strong, Guinevere. With other things not known for sure, I would rely on that. And here is your boy now."

Grandpa waves enthusiastically at Cass, strolling up with his hands in his pockets, as if flagging down a taxi that might pass him by. He makes a big production of ordering Cass to sit down on the steps, inspecting his blisters, then punching him on the shoulder with a wink. "Take the pretty girl and go now." As we walk away, he calls one last phrase after us. "Even though they look like that, *eu a deixo em suas mãos*." Heh-heh-heh.

What? *I trust her in your hands?*

Oh God. What happened to the knife salesman?

"You sure you don't know any Portuguese?" I ask.

"We really have to work on your greetings, Gwen. 'Hey there, babe' would be a lot better."

"I'm not going to call you babe. Ever. Answer my question."

"Nope. All I got was that he sounded happy. Phew. Thought he might have heard"—he jerks his head in the direction of the Ellington house—"the Henry Ellington story. Almost got you in big trouble there."

I'm so grateful that this story is mine right now that I turn, pull him close so quickly, I can hear a startled intake of breath, see a little spot he missed on his chin shaving, see that the base of his eyelashes are blond before they tip dark. "I'd say you're worth the risk."

"Forget what I said. Your greetings are great. Perfect."

I'm just about to touch my lips to his when I hear a loud "None of that funny business here!" and realize we're in front of Old Mrs. Partridge's yard. Where she's also standing, rooting through her mailbox impatiently.

I try to move back, but Cass's hand snakes behind me, holding me in place. "Good evening, Mrs. Partridge."

"Never mind that, Jose. None of this in a public street."

"Not the best spot for it," Cass allows. "But it's such a beautiful summer afternoon. And look at this girl, Mrs. Partridge."

"Look at this girl somewhere else," she says crossly. But there's just a shade of amusement in her voice and she leaves without further harassment.

I stare after her, amazed. "How did you do that?"

"She's only human. Seems kind of lonely," Cass says. "Now, where were we?"

Friday, early evening, we take the sailboat out again, anchor in Seldon's Cove and are lying, Cass's head on some seat cushions and a life jacket, mine on his chest, the thrum of his heartbeat in my ear. Since Seldon's is protected by two spits of land encircling it in a C, the motion of the water is gentler than in open water, as though we're being rocked in a giant cradle.

I close my eyes, see the sun glow orange-red through my

lids, feel Cass's thumb, the skin healing but still rough, trace up the side of my arm, sweep back down, then along the line of my other arm. I start to squirm, ticklish.

"Steady. I'm mapping you," he says, close to my ear, moving his touch to my jawline, then along my lips to the little groove above them.

"Useless fact," I say. "That's called a philtrum."

"Useful fact," Cass counters. "Maps came before written language." Now he's tracing the line of my chin. Under my ear, down, sweeping back. My chin? Not anywhere anyone has been interested in before. I'm resisting the urge to grab his hand and put it somewhere more risky.

"I've heard of math geeks, but map geek is new."

"Maps are the key to everything," he says absently. "Gotta find your direction." He clears his throat. "Hey, Gwen? I know that guy—the one who was at the house with Mrs. E.'s son. Spence's dad buys old paintings and stuff from him."

"Is he a sleazebucket?" I ask. "Because I think Henry Ellington might be."

The whole story, what I've seen, what I think I know, comes tumbling out—

Except. The check. Burning a hole in my pocket. A cliché I wish were true—that it would just ignite, drift out as ashes, blow away over the ocean, instead of lurking in the pocket of whatever I was wearing that day. Because I never did—I never threw it out.

"Would you tell? If you knew a secret that could hurt someone you cared about?"

Cass's brow furrows. For a second his fingers tighten on my chin.

"Ow," I say, surprised.

"God, sorry. Cramp. You mean, you mean if I were you? About this?"

"If Mrs. E. were your grandmother or something and you saw what was going on?"

He looks past me, out at the water for a moment as though reading the answer from the waves. "Hm. Tough one. It'd be a different situation then—family instead of someone you work for. 'Not my place' and all that crap."

"Uh-oh," I say, smiling at him. "You're admitting you *have* a place. Seashell's brainwashed you at last, Jose."

"This is my place." He settles his head more forcefully on the cushion, nestles my head more firmly onto him. "Right here."

As if I'm a destination he's reached, searched for. The X on a treasure map. "Cass . . . does this mean . . . Are we . . . ?"

My words are coming slowly, not just because of the lazy afternoon, the lullaby rock of the water, but because I have no idea which ones to use. I'm fumbling with how to put it, what to ask, hoping he'll somehow read my mind, fill in the blanks—

"What's Nic afraid of, Gwen?"

"Um, Nic? Not much. Why?"

"Because he's doing the same thing with swim practice you were doing about tutoring me. And I know in his case it's not fear of succumbing to my deadly charm. I keep texting him to set up a time when we, he and Spence and me, can get on with it. We need to practice as a team, the three of us. He keeps blowing me off. Spence too. But I can deal with Chan. I need you for Nic."

"It's really important to Nic. Getting the captain spot."

"That's why I don't get the blow-off. It's important to all of us. Nic has no monopoly."

"But he needs . . ." Here I falter, stumbling on the old lines. Nic needs it more. If he falls or fails, there's no safety net. But then there's Cass's brother Bill, saying how Cass has to work harder, how he won't come out of things smelling like a rose.

His voice roughens, less drowsy. "Speaking of what matters, in case you haven't figured it out—this does. Us. To me, anyway. Your cousin and I are not going to be blood brothers. My best friend may not be your favorite person. Fine. But no more reversals of fortune—not with you and me."

He says this last sentence so forcefully, I'm a little stunned. When I don't answer instantly he moves to sit up, looks me in the eye. "What?"

"So are we . . . ?" *Dating? A couple? Together?* "Seeing each other? It's not that you have to take me home to your family or—"

Cass groans. "Are all island girls this crazy, or did I luck out?"

I sigh. "Well, you know. Picnic baskets."

"Gwen. I mean this is in the nicest possible way. You will never be a picnic. Which is one of the things I lo—" He stops, takes a deep breath, starts again: "Can we just put the whole picnic basket thing away with the lobsters? For the record, to be clear, we're doing this right."

"The man with the maps."

He shakes his head, moving to his feet, tipping back against the railing of the boat so he can pull out the lining of first one of his pockets, then the other, then extend his open palms. "Map free. Know what that means? Need SparkNotes? You're my girlfriend, not my picnic basket, or any other screwed-up metaphor."

He says all of this firmly, his logical voice.

After a minute or two, he adds, "I mean . . . unless I'm *your* picnic basket."

I laugh. But he's not even smiling. He seems to be waiting for something. And I don't know what it is. Or exactly how to give it to him. Instead I say lightly, "I think of you more as a Dockside Delight." I slide over, lean into him, my hand tight against his heart, wishing that how I feel could just flow between us that way, without getting tangled up in words.

On the way home after sailing we don't say much. I'm yawning—a long day of being in the sun and the water—and so is he. We hold hands. It feels perfect.

It's only after I'm home, scrubbing off in the outdoor shower, that I realize he never did tell me what he thought the right thing to do was.

Chapter Thirty-three

Spence and Cass are on their way over to Sandy Claw, and Nic's already swimming drills. He's working on the one that helps your elbow-bending at the start of the pull, which involves swimming with his fingers closed into a fist. His eyes are tightly shut too, giving him this look of total absorption, complete intensity.

The sky's sharply blue, summer at its shiniest, sun glinting off the waves, horizon bright with spinnakers, schooners, every size of boat at home on an ocean big enough to contain them all. As I'm squinting out at Nic, Viv slides into place next to me, her dark hair wind-blown and loose today, none of her usual contained styles. Our legs swing side by side over the edge, like old times. "He never forgets," she says, touching the pile of flat stones next to the piling. "That Nic."

"He was looking around to claim his kisses before he got started."

She casts a quick look out at the water, then starts chipping at her nail, flicking at one of the little flowers painted on her ring finger. "Has Nic seemed . . . okay to you lately?"

I've never needed to be Switzerland, respecting boundaries

and borders with Nic and Viv. When we were younger, we all told one another everything. When they became a couple, there were different retellings, from Nic to me, from Viv, but it was all the same story. Now . . .

I didn't think, ever, that I'd have to scramble about which truth to tell. I never thought "other people's stories" would apply to the three of us. We *are* one another's stories.

"Tense," I finally say. "With you too? I thought maybe he was being weird with me, because of . . . well, because of me being with Cass. Has he talked about that with you?"

She shrugs, chews her lip. I recognize the look on her face, the "torn between loyalties" one.

"He's sort of macho-macho with Cass, giving him these 'don't lay a finger on my cousin' looks . . ." I say, trailing off so she'll talk.

"Yeah." Viv sighs. "He's pretty testosterone-heavy lately."

I wait for her to make a joke about not minding *that*, but instead she asks, "You don't think he's . . . on anything, do you?"

"On . . . you mean drugs? Like steroids? God no. This is Nic, he would never . . ."

I know that's not it. But . . . Nic's moodiness, his darkness, his obsession with weight lifting, the tension with Dad . . . No. He wouldn't.

Vivien doesn't look at me, her eyes fixed on the water, on Nic. He's now rolled over and is doing the backstroke, his form so perfect, it's almost mechanical, like the wind-up scuba Superman who swims doggedly in Em's baths.

"He would never," I repeat again. "You know that, right? You know him. Better than anyone."

I pull on her hand, bringing her gaze back to me. Then I realize it's like I'm asking her for reassurance when I should be the one giving it. I put my arm around her, give her a little shake. "Nico doesn't even take aspirin."

She's picked up one of the rocks, studies it, turning it over and over. Dark orange, worn smooth by countless waves, marked by holes. A brick. Probably from the steps of one of the houses on Sandy Claw, unwisely built on the beach, long ago swept out to sea in some forgotten hurricane. "You're right. Ugh. Don't pay attention to me. Al got the contract to some big political thing and was spazzing out all over me today. I kept calling Nic to talk and getting bounced to his voicemail. I thought maybe he was . . . I don't know. Doing the same thing with me that he does with your dad. Mike was calling him the other day when Nico was helping me pack up for a clambake and he kept checking his phone but not picking up. I'm just being paranoid."

"Yeah, Dad . . ." I shake my head. "Do you guys talk about that?"

Viv's pretty green eyes are sad. "Not much."

I reach out my pinkie, hook it around hers. "At least *we're* good. Right?"

She knots her pinkie with mine, pulls, still staring out at the water. "Yeah . . ."

"Viv. Look at me."

She turns immediately, gives a reasonably accurate version of her glowing smile. "We're golden."

I pick up one of the skipping stones, spiraling it over and over in my hand. The mica in it flashes bright in the sun. I slant it and skip it out to sea.

Once, twice . . . It goes all the way to seven, touching down lightly, glancing up, winging out hard, far, far, far, the farthest I've ever skipped.

Viv nudges me with her thin brown shoulder. "*You* gonna grant some kisses now? Come on, babe. I want to see how much you've picked up from Cass Somers."

I roll my eyes. "Ever think maybe *he's* learning from *me?*"

Someone clears his throat, and—fantastic—there are Cass and Spence. Cass has his game face on, and Spence a similarly untranslatable expression. How the hell did they walk this close on the dock without us hearing? Nic climbs up the ladder from the water, scattering droplets as he shakes his head like Fabio after a bath.

Spence: "Getting a jump on us, Cruz? Hear you like to do that. Shave a few seconds off your time. Any way that works for you."

Nic (deadpan): "Just more dedicated, I guess."

Cass (neutral): "How many drills did you do already?"

Nic (shrugs, like he's so fit it doesn't matter): "Some."

Cass: "A few more, then." (Glancing at Spence) "What do you think, Chan, crossovers? Or single-arm drill?"

Spence: "Single-arm, since Cruz has this entering too early problem . . . so he'll wind up driving down instead of extending forward and that'll increase his drag and slow the whole team down."

Impressive the way they can make drill techniques into insults.

"Boys," Vivien says to me, loudly enough for the three of them to hear. "We're so lucky we're not male, Gwen."

"At least two out of three of us agree with you, Vivien," Spence says smoothly, then winks at her.

Viv looks at Nic's somewhat thunderous face, makes a shooing motion toward the water, then claps her hands together briskly. "Get on with it, guys. I think you *all* need to cool off."

"Hang on," Cass says to the other two. He takes my hand and pulls me over to the corner of the pier, out of earshot of the others. Bends to my ear. "Let's declare the 'who's teaching and who's learning' thing a tie. You can one-up me in other ways."

"Hedge clipping?" I ask.

"Not my first choice."

"Come on, Romeo," Spence calls. "Vivien's got it. We all need to relax here and do this."

"Speak for yourself," offers Nic.

"I do, Cruz," he says flatly. "Always."

Viv clambers to her feet and I'm right there with her. At least we can still read each other's minds. She puts a comforting hand on Nic's back and I place mine on Spence's, and then Cass comes up next to us, and Viv and I shove all three of them into the water at once. I laugh. But Viv is pinwheeling, too close to the edge, eyes wide. She grabs at me—I flinch back—and we both go over in a tangle of arms and legs, until all of us are splashing and spluttering in the water, and it's almost impossible to tell which slippery body is whose until you see their laughing face.

Chapter Thirty-four

"Far too beautiful to go back indoors," Avis King says determinedly. "I propose we have our reading session on the beach instead of some stuffy porch.

A chorus of agreement from the ladies, although "stuffy" is the last thing anyone could call the Ellington porch.

"I personally am in favor of being rebellious and forgoing my nap today. My word, Henry is becoming fussier than any old woman. He called last night to make sure I was going to rest from one to three. I dislike being nagged," Mrs. Ellington says crossly.

But, since we didn't bring any reading material to the beach, I'm dispatched back to the house to fetch *The Sensuous Sins of Lady Sarah.*

When I get there, I am not at all surprised to see Henry's car parked in the driveway.

As I push open the screen door, I have a wave of weariness, then near fury. *Other people's stories,* I repeat to myself.

The door slams behind me and I shout, "Hello!" The way I learned to make noise coming home when Nic and Viv might be there alone. *Hello. I'm here. A witness. Don't let me catch you.*

Henry Ellington turns, startled, from the kitchen sink,

356

where he's standing, drinking a glass of water. He doesn't look well. His skin's pale, almost gray, and a sheen of sweat marks his forehead.

Spread out all over the kitchen table are silver bowls and all those complicated pieces of the tea set and these little cups with handles and engraved initials and silver bears climbing up them. Over the summer, they've become more than things to polish and wash. I know their stories. The powdered sugar sifter Mrs. Ellington's father used, "on Cook's day off," to top off the French toast, the only thing he knew how to make for Mrs. E. and her brothers. The ashtrays she and the captain bought at the London Silver Vaults. "They were so lovely. Neither of us smoked, but look at them." The grape shears. "We got five of these as wedding presents, dear Gwen. I enjoyed thinking that everyone, so proper, who danced at our wedding, imagined us dangling grapes over each other's mouths, like some debauched Greek gods."

So many moments of Mrs. E.'s are laid out on the table, like silver fish resting on ice at Fillerman's. I wonder if Henry even knows the stories. And if he does . . . how can he possibly sell them?

"Guinevere? Where's Mother?" His brow draws together. He straightens, somehow seeming to make himself taller. "I'd assumed she was napping, but there was no sign of either her or you."

"At Abenaki with the ladies," I say flatly. God, I'm suddenly so tired. I could sit at the blue enamel painted chair, rest my head on my arms, just go to sleep. Except that I'd have to move aside the silver first.

"You left my nearly ninety-year-old mother on the beach. With a bunch of eighty-year-olds to watch over her. This seemed like a responsible choice to you?"

He's peering over his reading glasses, literally looking down at me.

It isn't until I shove my hand into the pocket of my jean skirt and hear the crackle of paper that I remember what it is. Dad's had extra loads of laundry lately. This was my one clean skirt. I didn't think twice when I put it on this morning.

I pull out the check that Henry Ellington gave me, holding it out of sight.

I took it, that day Henry offered it. I don't need to open it again to see the amount, scrawled firmly in blue ballpoint pen. I haven't deposited it. But I didn't tear it up either. I never threw it away.

"Do you have an answer for me, Guinevere?" he asks.

Last night, I finally asked Mom why she named me Guinevere, after a woman no one admired. We were eating ice cream on the porch, passing the spoon back and forth, nearly over our heads to avoid the hopeful, slightly toothless leaps of Fabio.

"Really, Gwen, honey? I always liked her. She wasn't a wimp or a simp like that Elaine. Not helpless, asking someone to rescue her. Knew she loved them both. Mr. Honorable and Mr. Heroic. Arthur and Lancelot. I always thought she was the star of her own story. At least she knew what was really going on."

Which, of course I do.

So yes, I do, in fact, have an answer.

I smooth the check out on the kitchen table. Next to the fish knives. The silver ashtrays. All the stories. Henry Ellington looks down at it, his face showing nothing at all.

The day Dad gave me his "she's loaded and she's losing it" advice, I never thought it would actually apply to me, and definitely not like this.

I take a breath.

"Mr. Ellington," I say. "You told me you were giving me this because I deserved a little extra. I don't think you meant that. I don't think you admire my work ethic. I don't think you like me or value my service. I think you expect my silence."

His face crumples for a moment, the lines of his cheeks, his eyes, all contracting, freezing. Then he holds out a hand, palm outraised, like my words are traffic he's stopping. "I don't think you understand my position here, Guinevere. I'm protecting my mother. A helpless old woman."

Helpless old woman, my ass.

"Mr. Ellington." I close my eyes. Another deep breath. Open them. "Does she really want . . . does she really need . . . your"—I raise my fingers to form air quotes—"protection?"

Henry's face flushes crimson. "It's my job," he says. "My mother is . . . elderly. Not in full possession of her . . ." He darts a look out the window, as though making sure we won't be overheard, even as his own voice rises. "Damn it, why am I explaining this to *you*? Mother's getting older, times have changed, and she just won't make allowances for reality. When she goes, I'm going to have this entire estate to deal with, all of her promises, her debts of honor that don't matter anymore. Her special bequests to schools she hasn't been to for seventy years, to people like Beth McHenry, who cleaned the house— *cleaned the house*, scrubbed the toilets, and changed the sheets, while I was spending all my time working in a job to support

359

this summer home"—he says "summer home" as though it's an expletive—"a place I barely get the chance to visit, a lifestyle that's run its course. Yard boys and night nurses and summer help, cooks and cleaners, you, and that damned expensive end-of-the-summer party she always has. Her finances, *all* of our finances, have taken a hit in the market. But try telling my mother that! She's never even had to balance a checkbook!"

He crosses over to the bar, splashes some amber liquid into a glass, goes to the freezer for ice. Instead of taking the time to smash the pieces with his little hammer thing, he just drops them into the sink, hard, then picks up the shattered bits and dumps them into the glass, tips it back, swallows.

"All this . . . drama . . . would upset her," he mutters.

Don't upset your mother. Dad's refrain from that summer with Vovó.

"I can't tell her," he repeats.

Can't. Won't. Are afraid to?

I know all about all three.

"Have . . . have you tried?" The words seem to catch in my throat, it's so hard to say them. Just a job. Not my place. But . . .

He doesn't answer. Takes another sip.

There's a very long silence.

He watches me over the rim of his glass. And I stare back down at the check. Set my finger down on it, deliberately, slipping it across the table as though I'm passing him a napkin, just doing my job.

"Am I fired, Mr. Ellington? Because if I'm not, I'd better get back to the beach."

Mrs. E. has survived my neglect. She and the ladies are quite happily ensconced in their beach chairs, watching with a frightening level of appreciation as Cass rakes the sand.

They're in a circle, towels swooped around their shoulders, bobbed gray hair, permed white hair, long braids meant to be coiled up into buns, styles that went away generations ago.

"If I were thirty years younger . . ." Avis King says, nodding approvingly as Cass flicks seaweed into the tall grass.

Big Mrs. McCloud shoots her a look.

"Fine. Forty," she concedes. "Is this your boy, Gwen? He's adorable."

Adorable seems like a fluffy-kitten word, defanged, declawed— not Cass and all these feelings at all. He glances over at me, catches me looking, grins knowingly, then keeps raking.

"Ad-or-able." Mrs. Cole sighs. "Good lordy lord lord."

"Beach bonfire tonight, I'm hearing," Avis King says. "Isn't it nice that those still go on? Remember ours? Oh, that Ben Cruz. With his lovely shoulders. Always so tanned. Those cut-offs."

Okay, disturbing. I think she just referenced my grandfather as the hot yard guy.

"He'd get the lobsters. Who was it who brought the bread from that Portuguese bakery in town? Sweet bread and regular? Ten loaves each. We'd toast them on sticks, dip them in butter."

"Glaucia," Beth McHenry says. "She got her license first of all of us. Remember? She used to whip around town in that old gray truck, bring potatoes and linguica and malassadas from Pedrinho's out to the island."

Mrs. Cole nods. "I was always partial to the meringues."

"Remember when the captain brought the volleyball net down from the court and we decorated it with those tiny white Christmas lights?"

"Labor Day . . ." Mrs. E. says. "The final summer party. We all decided to dress in white because in those days you weren't supposed to wear it after Labor Day. It was our last hurrah. Our big rebellion."

"The boys wore their white jackets. If they had them," Big Mrs. McCloud reflects. "Arthur had too many, he loaned them out to Ben and Matthias and whoever needed one. He'd lend his tan bucks too. But then a lot of them went barefoot. That seemed so rebellious."

"We played volleyball in our long skirts," Avis King says. "I beat the pants off Malcolm. He proposed later that night."

"Was it easier then?" Mrs. Ellington asks. "I do believe so. Our revolts were so much smaller. Our questions so much easier to answer. There were rules to it all. *May I call on you after your European tour?* That was how I knew the captain cared for me. I don't believe that translates into texting."

They debate back and forth about it. Whether it should be one of those island rituals that sticks, the Labor Day party. Or whether its time has come and gone.

"We could do it again," Mrs. Cole says. "We're the entertainment committee on the board now. No rules to say we can't. Well, none like the rules we used to have, anyway."

From a distance, from the movies, I know these rules too—white bucks and blazers, don't wear white after Labor Day, wear this with that, go with that good girl, not this one. Strictly controlled social calendars, when all of that seemed as though it mattered . . .

We still have those, though. Not so much what we wear, but how we act and what we do.

Other customs, rituals, rules. New important things unspoken.

Will Henry say anything to his mother? More importantly . . . will I?

Chapter Thirty-five

Beach bonfire tonight.

As Cass drives us down the hill, I can see sparks crackling upward, flicking and fading into the darkening summer sky. Dom D'Ofrio is always overenthusiastic with the lighter fluid. The tower of flames shoots nearly ten feet high.

"That looks like something you'd use to sacrifice to the Druids, not toast marshmallows," Cass says as we near the beach, the sun sliding purple-orange against the deep green sea.

To my surprise, when Cass picked me up, Spence was slumped in the backseat of the old BMW, scowling.

"He had a bad day. Thought this might cheer him up. You mind?" Cass whispered.

"Yo Castle," Spence says now, a listless version of his usual cocky self. "Sundance stormed you yet?"

"Don't be a dick," Cass returns evenly.

"S'what I do best," Spence returns, then sticks his head out the window, taking in the scene.

This bonfire is a lot more crowded than the first of the summer. The summer people's kids have discovered it and are milling around, mostly in clumps, but sometimes venturing over to other clots of people, sitting down, feeling out the possibilities. Pam and Shaunee have parked themselves next to Audrey Partridge, Old Mrs. P.'s great-granddaughter. Manny's flicking his lighter for Sophie Tucker, a pretty blond cousin from the house the Robinsons rented. Somebody's dragged out a grill, and now Dom is enthusiastically pouring lighter fluid onto those charcoal briquettes too.

Cass backs the car into a spot with relatively low sand. We all get out.

Viv is standing near the water, arms hugging her chest, ponytail flipping in the wind, looking out at the distant islands. The sky's clear enough tonight that it seems as though you could reach out and touch them. Viv doesn't turn and see me. Manny comes up beside her, bumps her shoulder with his elbow, and hands her one of those generic "get smashed fast" red plastic cups. He walks back up the beach, catches sight of us, cocks his head a bit at the arm Cass has draped over my shoulder. "Nice shirt," he mutters as he passes me.

It's one of Cass's oxfords, loose and knotted at my waist, a flash of stomach over my rolled-up jeans. Not a look I would have tried before.

If I remember right, Manny was the one who welcomed Cass to the island because of his yard boy status. Now the causeway can't go both ways?

I head over to the cooler, pick up a beer I don't care about. No sign of Nic or Hoop.

"Who's the short fat dude, Sundance?"

"Manny. Good guy. Relax, Spence." Cass grabs my hand,

365

an aside to me. "Don't let him get to you. He's in douchebag mood today."

"You two are sweet together," Spence offers unexpectedly, sounding oddly sincere. "Nauseating as that is."

I mouth, "Is he drunk?"

Cass shakes his head. "It's not that."

"Feelin' sorry for myself, Castle. Just do it, Sundance. Cut me loose. Go back to Hodges."

"I'm not that guy," Cass says so firmly—convincing Spence? Or himself? "Forget it for tonight. Let's just relax."

For a while, relaxing works pretty well. Pam has the music cranking, good mix of old and new. It's a warm night and the sky is filled with a gold that rims the corners of the clouds, and shafts of pinkish light that slant down to the water. The charcoal heats up, the sweet burnt smell singeing our noses.

Cass and I are adding ketchup and mustard to our hot dogs when I see Nic, standing on the pathway that runs from the parking lot to the beach, staring at us, hands balled in his pockets. Hoop stands behind him, a small, badly dressed, angry shadow.

Nic's white-faced and stormy-looking, all his features frozen, angry, as though he's watching a nightmare come true.

"Yo, trouble at high noon," Spence tells Cass, scrolling mustard over his own hot dog so vigorously that the Gulden's squirts all over the sand.

"Don't make it worse," Cass says, shoving a napkin at Spence.

But immediately, it's worse.

It starts with Nic doing that slow clap-clap thing, guaranteed to annoy anyone. "Nice job, guys. Snagging both captain and cocaptain. What do they call that? A coup? Nice coup."

Cass doesn't say anything, focused on his hot dog. Spence is quiet too.

Nic walks over, chin raised. "Nice coup," he says again.

"You don't get it, man," is all Cass says.

"No?" Nic asks.

"No. This is no preferential thing," Cass starts. Vivie walks up then. Cass glances at her, back at Nic. "These last months . . . this whole last year . . . swim drills were all about you, Nicolas Cruz. Nothing about teamwork. You don't seem to know what that means. If you deserved to be captain or cocaptain, you'd be lining up behind us. Not acting like this."

"That's bullshit," Nic says. "We all know there's a fucking *I* in *team*. You're not swimming to make *me* look good. We're all after *I*. So I'm just gonna say it. *I* need this, Somers. You don't. Channing? Forget it."

"You want us to feel sorry for you now? *I* do. Sundance does," Spence offers. "Because this *West Side Story*, us-against-them crap and your shitty attitude is what keeps you stuck, Cruz. Nothing more, nothing less."

"*You're* lecturing *me*?" Nic shouts. "You're telling me to be fucking satisfied with what I've got? That's rich. You're the one who has to take *everything*."

Viv has her hand over her mouth. Spence steps forward, shoulders square. Cass grabs his arm.

Dom, Pam, Shaunee, Manny are moving away from the fire toward us now, attention snagged. Hooper assumes roughly the same stance behind Nic as Cass has behind Spence, but without the restraining hand. His is raised, placating. Or just unsure what's going on.

"Be honest with yourself. At least. I haven't taken a thing from you that you deserved to have," Spence says calmly. Cass yanks him back a little, jerking him to the side.

"Stop talking, Spence," he says.

Instead, Spence takes another step forward, pulling out of Cass's grip. "You don't deserve any of it," he repeats to Nic. "None of it. And for sure, not her."

Nic's fist shoots out so fast it's a blur and Spence's head snaps to the left. He staggers back for a second. We watch him stumble—a surreal, slow-mo movie. Nic charges forward, eyes blazing. Ready to hit him again. Cass moves in between them, fending Nic off with a forearm to his chest and grabbing Spence's arm tightly, yanking it back.

Vivien brushes past me. I try to clutch at her—don't want her to get in the way of Nic. He doesn't seem to be seeing straight. But instead of hurrying to him, she's wiping at the blood gushing from Spence's nose with one hand, the other cupped around the back of his head.

Nic stares at them, blinking as though he's just woken up, then shakes off Cass's arm, backing toward the parking lot.

"I'm good, don't worry about me," Spence assures Vivien.

Spence is assuring *Vivien?*

"You're hurt," she says, her voice cracking.

"Flesh wound," Spence tells her. And he smiles at her in a way I've never seen Spence smile at anyone. "Don't. God, Viv. Don't cry. Please. You know that kills me."

Hooper and I are gaping at them, as is pretty much everyone else.

"Yeah," Nic says. "This is just . . . Just . . . well . . . fuck this." He turns around, scrubs his eyes with the heels of his hands, starts to walk away.

"Holy shit," Hoop says.

"Go after him, Gwen," calls Vivien, still wiping away blood. She's crying. For Nic? For Spence? Not knowing which makes me flash white-hot furious.

"Me? What about you? And you, Spence? What *was* that? It's not enough to take his captain shot, you had to go for his girlfriend too?"

"This isn't like that, Gwen," Cass says. Spence just stares at the ground.

"This? There's a *this*? And you knew? When were you going to tell me? Ever? What happened to 'I'm not going to lie to you, Gwen'?"

He's ruffling his hand through his hair with that same expression he had the night after the Bronco.

Guilt.

Viv's still crying. Spence is wiping away the blood still running from his nose with the back of his hand. Hoop's muttering, "I haven't had enough beer to deal with this." Pam and Manny and the other island kids are standing around helplessly, murmuring.

And I can't stop my mouth. "So what did you two do to get this?" I ask.

"What did we *do*?" Cass asks, low and furious. "We swam. I deserve this. Spence does. This has nothing to do with money.

It's about teamwork. And you know it. Maybe Nic used to be able to do that. But he can't anymore. I don't know why, but you *know* it's true. He's a cheater."

"Nice, Cass. You've taken this away from him. And now you take his integrity too? Classy."

"I didn't take anything, Gwen."

I back up, move away from all this, everything, everyone.

"I didn't take anything," he repeats, turning away.

I scramble up to the parking lot. But there is no longer any sign of Nic.

"Come fly, come fly come fly with me," sings Frank Sinatra loudly, in his seductively snappy alto. Emory is swaying to the beat, doing his version of finger snapping, which involves flicking his pointer fingers against his thumbs. He's got the happy head-bobbing down, though. Grandpa Ben is cooking dinner, waggling his skinny old-man hips in time to the beat. I reach over to turn Frank's exuberance down a few notches, but still have to bellow when I ask if he's seen Nic.

Grandpa Ben shrugs.

"He didn't come back here? Where the hell did he go? Where's Mom?"

Ben clucks his tongue. "Language, Guinevere. He was not here when I got back from the farmer's market. Your mother, she is on a date."

A *what?*

Nic's pulled a disappearing act. Viv's consoling Spence. Cass knew. And I blew him off, even when I . . . I . . . And Mom's on a date. *Whose life is this???*

Grandpa shrugs again, points to the note scrawled on the dry-erase board on the fridge. *"Papi. On a walk around the island with a friend. If you see Nic, talk to him."*

"If you see him, keep him here," I say. "I'm going to look for him."

I grab Mom's car keys, clatter down the stairs, and am throwing the Bronco into reverse before it occurs to me to wonder how Grandpa Ben managed to translate a "walk around the island with a friend" into a date.

Chapter Thirty-six

They're walking side by side. Not holding hands or anything. But side by side is startling enough. Mom with any man but one on the cover of a book is a jolt. I jerk the truck to a halt. "Mom. Coach? Where's Nic? Have you seen him?"

Mom's frowning, worried. Coach's face looks, if possible, even ruddier than usual. He's out of his element, no whistle, wearing a baggy yellow windbreaker that somehow looks sadder, so much less official than his SBH jacket.

"We were hoping with you. He was headed to that bonfire," Mom says. "Wouldn't talk to me. He was wicked upset."

Wicked. Dad's word.

"I'll say," I snap, trying not to glare at Coach. Who's just doing his job and not actually responsible for this whole mess.

"Look, Gwen," Coach says, weary but resolute. "*Inches* from winning state this year. We need captains with nothing to prove. Gotta have that. Nic's a solid kid . . . but these days, he's no team player."

"I should have insisted he talk to me," Mom says. "I tried calling after he left, but I just got that damn voicemail. He never recharges his phone." She pulls out her own, punches in a number, shakes her head. "Stupid voicemail again." The creases in her forehead deepen. "Get Vivien," she tells me. "She'll know where he is."

He's not at Abenaki. I strain my eyes, looking way out beyond the pier, but there's nothing in the water but a flock of seagulls, and a lone kayaker way far out. The bridge by the Green Woods is still and deserted. Standing there, I feel a pang. What used to be Nic's and my place, years of memories, feels as if it belongs to me and Cass now. That thought leaves me feeling strangely disloyal. How did I not know about Viv? I'm so off balance, the way you are when you step off a rocking boat onto land, not sure how to find your footing.

I drive back to Sandy Claw, but the logs from the bonfire are just embers now, and no one's still hanging around. Nobody at Plover Point, not even the plovers, who have raised their eggs and moved on. I pull into Hoop's driveway to find him sitting on the steps smoking.

"Not here?"

"Nope." Hoop drops the cigarette, grinds it out with the heel of his flip-flop. "I was hoping you were him when I saw the Bronc. Not answering texts either. Dunno where he is, but he's on foot, since we hit the beach in my truck. Wanna beer?"

I shake my head, tell him to text me if Nic shows. He nods, lighting another cigarette, popping open another beer. As I drive away, I see him in the rearview, rumpled shirt, shoulders slumped. Will he still be sitting on those same steps, doing those same things, twenty years from now?

I find myself driving to Castle's.

It's ten thirty, a slow night, and it's shutting down. All the other workers have long since gone home. There's only Dad, tossing water on the grill, scraping off the last particles of grease and onions. Pulling out Saran Wrap to cover the tubs of ice cream in the freezer so they won't get freezer burn before he jams the lips on. Chopping onions and peppers for tomorrow's hash browns, knife flashing so fast it's a blur. Those jobs are so familiar. I've done them all. Dad's concentrating, never looks up to see me watching him.

This is the last place Nic would ever go.

I'm not even sure why I came. That "fix it, Dad" feeling? I can practically hear Cass saying, *"You get pissed off when I rescue you."* I swallow the lump in my throat.

We were doing so well there for a second.

I drive back toward Seashell, hitting the gates just as Cass's BMW roars up the other direction on Ocean Road, a little too fast over the speed bumps.

We both slow to a stop, our headlights picking out individual blades of grass on well-mown, carefully tended lawns on either side of the street, their brilliance turning the green into gray and white.

The passenger-side door of Cass's car opens, and Viv climbs out, crossing over to me.

"You gonna hear me out?" she asks.

"You gonna help me find Nic?" I return.

She walks around the front of the Bronco, opens the passenger-side door and slides in.

I expect Cass to zoom away immediately, but he doesn't, idling the BMW by the side of the road, waiting . . . for what?

Me to get out and talk to him? What am I supposed to say?

I stay where I am, and after a few seconds, he pulls forward and leaves us in the quiet of the night.

"I didn't mean to," Viv says, quickly, like she's accidentally broken a plate or something.

I slow to Seashell's only stop sign. Shift into park, because no one's behind us. No one's in any hurry this time of night. Ever, really, on Seashell. That's one of the promises that should be on the sign separating us from the causeway. *All the time in the world.*

Except that that's a promise no one can really make.

Forever.

"You got together with Spence by accident?" I ask, then hate the harshness in my voice. If anyone can understand that, it should be me. But Viv isn't supposed to have "crumble lines." Or not this kind. And if she did . . . why didn't she tell me?

She leans her head back against the headrest, eyes shut. "What do I say to you, Gwen? I hate that you know this. I'm glad you know this. I want to make excuses . . . I want to say they're enough. But they're not. I hurt Nic. You. If I didn't lie to you, I sure didn't tell you the truth, even when we said no secrets. Joke's on me. Because, let's face it, in my head I was all judgey about you and some of your choices. Alex, freaking Jim freshman year. Ugh. Cass, the first time around. Spence . . . I pretended not to be, but I was . . . smug. Like I couldn't get what you were thinking, so you must have been wrong. I guess you knew that. You had to have felt it. I guess that's why we couldn't really talk this summer. 'Cause I suddenly got it. And . . . and I didn't want to get it! I wanted Nic. Only. Ever.

Until . . . Until I didn't anymore. And I didn't know what to do with that."

Did I know, deep down? Maybe. This weird feeling I've had this summer . . . I thought it was because things were different—me the third wheel, not a threesome anymore. But maybe I somehow knew that we really were, *really*, not a threesome anymore.

I lean my forehead on the steering wheel. "But Spence, Viv? Why him—of *all* people?" I turn so I can see her, flipping my hair away from my face. "Did you do it to . . . to hurt Nic? Is that what this—Spence—is about?" As I ask, I feel an unwanted pang of sympathy for Spence, the handy weapon in someone else's war. Again.

"No. Not at all." She flushes. "But hell, Gwen . . . I thought Nic and I were . . . in this together. And then he's all . . . 'well . . . eight years from now, we'll' . . . Eight years! What am I supposed to do, while he's off having adventures, meeting girls who . . . I don't know. Dangle from tow ropes with their teeth? He's supposed to stay impressed with the girl who keeps everyone's water glasses filled? Screw that. I . . . can't compete. And I . . . don't want to. What's wrong with wanting to be here? If what I want is a little less big, less noble, than what he wants . . . does that make me a loser? That's the thing. I don't feel like a loser with Spence. He . . . I . . . Al got that contract to work with the Bath and Tennis Club late this spring . . . and it seemed like everything he did there, we'd run into Spence, because even though his dad owns it, his dad is kind of . . . out of it. At first I started talking to him just because of business. But then . . . he's not who I thought he was. At all."

I'm starting to wonder who is. But to be fair, I have to weigh the six or whatever girls in the hot tub against Cass's unflinching loyalty and those flashes of perceptiveness I've seen myself.

"I started feeling . . . really liking him . . . that's why I wanted the ring. I thought it would make me stop thinking about Spence and focus on Nicky."

"You do know that's incredibly messed up, right?"

She raises her hands in defense. "You don't get to be the only one who can be stupid and blind, Gwen."

"Yeah, welcome to my world." I'm laughing despite myself. But then I sit up and look at her, my lifelong friend, with the cartilage piercings at the top of her ear that Nic hated, but never told her because she wanted them, and I hurt so much for my cousin—what he had, what he lost—that I have to fold my arms against my stomach to keep the pain contained. "Viv? Did you ever really love Nic?" I ask it, and then wish I hadn't. I'm not sure I want to hear the answer.

"I'll always love him." She responds so quickly that I know it's true. "He was my first . . . everything. I never thought—I never planned—he'd be anything but my *only* everything. But these few months, and especially the last few weeks—it's not the same. He's . . . not the same."

"Maybe it's just that he's really tense," I say, "maybe . . ." Then I stop. Viv puts her hand on mine, clenched tight on the steering wheel, squeezes. Maybe I stop talking because I don't know what to say. Or maybe I stop because I finally get that sometimes we hold on to something—a person, a resentment, a regret, an idea of who we are—because we don't know what to reach for next. That what we've done before is what we have to do again. That there are only re-dos and no do-overs. And maybe . . . maybe I know better than that.

We can't find Nic anywhere. We try the same old places in another loop, but no luck. We text and call him. Nothing. Viv's eyelids begin to droop, and as I'm driving over the bridge yet again, she falls asleep, cheek pressed against the passenger door, so I carefully maneuver the car to the Almeidas' house, shake her awake and urge her into the house. Luckily, Al and her mom are out, so I just have to get her to her room, take off her shoes, and cover her up with the puffy green blanket she's had since we were little.

He has to be at the creek. He must have been walking through the woods before and now he's there. Of course that's where he'd go. Dangerous, but familiar. I pull the Bronco up, get out so fast I don't even shut the door, run to the bridge, looking out at the dark rushing water. But it's a cloudy night and there's not enough moon to see anything, so I pull the Bronco closer, snap on the headlights and run back.

The lights cast stark shadows. It's high tide. I stand at the place we always jump from, scanning the water, but there's nothing but the dark outline of Seal Rock and the gradual widening of the creek shore as it empties into the ocean.

When Nic and I were little, people who didn't know us would ask if we were twins, even though I was tanner skinned and darker haired than him. Now I wish like anything we were and had that twin bond you hear about. I wish I could reach out with my mind and know—just feel—where he is. But when I think . . . all I feel is scared.

Mom and Grandpa Ben both jump up from Myrtle when I come in, looking over my shoulder, faces falling when they see I'm alone. Emory's awake, cuddling Hideout, staring big-eyed at the television, which isn't even on.

"No panicking," Grandpa says sharply to Mom, despite the fact that he's reaching into the cabinet in the kitchen where he keeps his pipe, pulling it out and packing it with rapid, jerky movements completely unlike himself.

"I shouldn't have gone out with Patrick." Mom's twisting her hands nervously. "All we did was talk about Nico, but still, I knew better. You should have seen Nic's face when he told him. Like his last dream had died."

Sometimes the melodramatic phrases she picks up from her books are so not helpful. "Well, it didn't," I snap. "He's eighteen. He's got plenty of time to dream. He's still got the Coast Guard Academy."

But not Viv.

Which Mom and Grandpa probably don't even know. I'm not going to tell them because the rush of worry in my head is dark and loud as the creek water. They don't need to be there too, staring into the shadows, afraid to see what they're searching for.

I sit on our steps, looking up and down the road, waiting for Nic's broad-shouldered figure to appear out of nowhere, illuminated in the orangey glow of the porch light. But there's nothing except the dark road, the distant waves, the hulks of houses, the Field House rising a little higher than the ones before it.

Five houses down.

The Field House is five houses down. What, an eighth, a sixteenth of a mile? I could walk there. But I can't. Because my first instinct was to tell Cass he screwed this up for me. We finally had that conversation about what we were doing together. And doing this right. Is that gone now? Now that he kept something from me, and I left him without a word, or with all the wrong words, choosing my cousin's side without a second thought?

I let the screen door slam closed as I finally head inside.

"Anything?" Viv texts the next morning at five.

"Nicky Nic Nic!?" Em asks, throwing back the covers of Nic's bed as though he's sure to find him there.

Grandpa Ben frowns over his raisin bran grapefruit. Instead of leafing through the newspaper while he eats, highlighting the yard sales, he focuses on the food, only occasionally flicking a glance to the screen door.

I try Nic's cell again and again. It goes straight to voicemail every time. *He never remembers to charge that thing,* I repeat to myself, again and again. It's in his pocket, dead. It's not somewhere under water, somewhere where Nic jumped deep, somewhere he didn't swim back up.

Mom doesn't even ask. She gives me one swift look when she comes out of the bedroom, then, shoulders slumped, piles her supplies into her cleaning bucket, bumps it down the stairs to the Bronco.

Then she turns back.

"Shouldn't you be dressed to get to the Ellingtons'?"

"Mom. I can't go today."

Her gentle face turns as stern as it ever gets. "I didn't raise you to let people down. Abandoning an old lady who counts on you is out of the question. Get to work, Gwen. That's what we do when we don't know what to do."

So I go.

All morning I'm preoccupied, peeking out the front window, looking across at the Tucker house, waiting to see Hoop's truck, Nic hitching out of it, paint-covered, complaining, resentful, or sad or angry . . . just—alive

Or the flash of a pink shirt or the gleam of a blond head.

But Cass, who was everywhere at the beginning of the summer, and especially in my days and nights lately, is nowhere to be seen. Half a dozen times my fingers hover over the buttons of my phone to call him. Finally, Mrs. E. reaches out her hand, exactly like one of the teachers at school, and confiscates it, saying briskly, "You will get this back at the end of the day. We agreed from the start that you would not be one of those texting teenagers, and I am holding you to our agreement. Now, I'm in the mood for some hot tea, so please make me a pot. You look as though you could use some as well."

I go through the motions, the lemon thingie, the scalloped silver spoon . . . but the little silver creamer and the silver sugar bowl are nowhere to be found. Great. Somehow, from the moment I saw Henry and Gavin Gage doing . . . whatever they're doing, I knew that the person who'd be there when one of those itemized things turned up missing was me.

Mrs. E. taps her chin with a finger, brow crinkled. "I had it out just a few days ago to serve tea to dear Beth. I know Joy put them back in the cabinet afterward because she was so cross about having to do so. Really, that woman is unpleasant. I believe I should tell Henry to find another nurse."

I open my mouth to speak, shut it, open it again.

"You look like a codfish, Guinevere, and are most distracted today. Your young man was also supposed to be pruning the boxwoods and I haven't seen hide nor hair of him. Is there anything you need to speak with me about? I was young a thousand years ago or more, but I do remember. Sometimes better than I remember what happened yesterday, truth be told." She reaches over and pulls out the cornflower-blue painted kitchen chair, gesturing to me to sit down, then takes one of my hands in her soft, wrinkled one.

"Does everyone just keep secrets and lie all the time?" I ask at last, my voice loud in the quiet kitchen. "Is that just how it goes?"

She blinks, her gray eyelashes fluttering in surprise.

"Because remember how you told me there were no secrets on Seashell? There are nothing *but* secrets on Seashell. Everywhere. It seems like this big open place . . . I mean, no one has fences and there are hardly any trees, people leave their windows open, some of them don't lock their doors. But . . . but it doesn't matter. There are all these walls and . . . No one knows everything that anyone is doing or they know and aren't telling or they're telling the wrong people. I just . . . I just want to get away from this place to somewhere else. Somewhere nothing like that."

"My dear girl, I fear you will be hard-pressed to find such a place outside of the pages of a book. Even there, what are stories made of but secrets? Look at Lady Sylvia. If she had simply told Sir Reginald that she was the mysterious chambermaid with whom he'd spent that passionate night, the book would have been twenty pages long."

I don't want to think about Lady Sylvia and her sensuous secrets. I want what's true.

Mrs. E. examines my face. "I never thought I'd see you pout, Guinevere. You don't seem the type." She reaches for the china cup, takes a sip of uncreamy, sugarless tea, makes a face. "I expect my job at this point is to come up with some of the wisdom one supposedly gains with age." She taps her chin with her finger again. "This is difficult, as I seem to know less, and be far less sure of anything, in my late eighties than I was in my youth. Tea is dreadful without sugar, Gwen. Just add it from the canister, will you, never mind the silver service?"

"It's okay, Mrs. Ellington. You don't need to advise me."

"How about this, dear girl? It's about the best I have to offer. Yes, it's incredibly difficult for two people to be straightforward with each other. We get afraid, embarrassed . . . we all want others to think highly of us. I was married to the captain for five years before he confessed to me that he had never captained a boat at all. That, indeed, boats made him seasick. I'd thought he'd had a bad experience in the war and that was why he didn't want to go out on the water. But he was never in the Navy at all . . . but I digress. Perhaps, dear Gwen, you could think, instead of what a betrayal it is to be lied to, how rare and wonderful it is when two human beings can tell each other the truth." She pats my hand, gives me her most joyous smile and then says, "Don't pout, though. The wind may change and your face could be stuck like that."

"Mrs. E., your son is taking your things and selling them. That friend of his . . . he's looked through your silver and your paintings and your chairs and I overheard them . . ."

I trail off.

I wait for her face to darken with rage—at Henry, or more likely me, the eavesdropping bearer of bad tidings. The person who tells things no one wants to know.

But instead, she laughs, deep from the belly, patting my hand again, and leaving me completely confused. "Yes, dear," she says finally, practically wiping tears from her eyes.

"You know?"

"Yes, Henry and I had a conversation yesterday. But even before that . . . I'm not a fool, dear girl. Gavin Gage is an old friend of Henry's, but it was hardly likely he'd be popping by for a social call. Everyone on Seashell, if not all of Connecticut, knows Gavin is the man to go to when you wish to discreetly part with a useless family heirloom for a few useful dollars."

"But . . . But . . . he was always sneaking around and making sure you were napping and worrying about whether you'd notice something was missing."

"I'm so grateful I'm not a man," Mrs. Ellington says. "We women are proud, but honestly, men! Yes, Henry and I had a long discussion yesterday when I asked him to show me the balance books to see if I could give you a little something for being such a help so far this summer. I've never seen such hemming and hawing, and finally he had to confess that he'd made some unwise investments and that we are now, like half the families on Seashell, asset rich and cash poor. As if I'd rather he work himself into a heart attack than sell that hideous ring that belonged to my mother-in-law."

She tosses back the last of her tea, then says cheerfully, "It's chilly today. Too cold to go to the beach. The ladies will no doubt be wanting to hear more of Lady Sylvia's sins. Can you make some of Ben's sauce for them? He sent Marco to me last night with a perfectly cooked lobster."

Nic has been gone for a whole day of work now, edging into evening. Tony and Marco haven't even called to check on him. Manny must have said something. Mom goes to clean that office building in town. Because it's Thursday, and that's what she does on Thursday. Grandpa heads out to bingo night. Viv has a wedding rehearsal to cater for Almeida's. Emory had speech and occupational therapy and he's tired and wants to watch *Pooh's Big Adventure*. So I'm sitting here with my little brother, staring blankly at the screen, remembering Nic and me always trying to figure out why on earth Pooh had a shirt but no pants. I want Nic. I want Cass. I want the things I thought were sure things. The thing I was thinking, finally believing, would be a real thing. Rewind. Redo.

"Hideout loves you," Emory whispers, burrowing into my side, nudging his hermit crab into my armpit.

I'm crying over a stuffed crustacean.

I think this is what they call rock bottom.

"What in God's name is Emory doing awake at this hour?" Dad asks. I jolt awake. Myrtle groans. Dad is dragging in his laundry bag and tossing it in the usual spot.

I have no sense of time at all. It's dark. Emory's sitting beside me, eyes like saucers, still watching Pooh. Have I been asleep for minutes? Hours?

The digital clock reads 11:20. Nic's been gone now for more than twenty-four hours. We can report him missing, now, right? Or does it have to be forty-eight? The fact that I am even wondering about this makes my stomach hurt.

Mom and Grandpa are at the table, flicking out cards. Gin rummy? Really? We all start talking at once, including Em, who gets up, walks over, and puts his arms around Dad's waist, wailing, "Niiiiicky!"

Dad ruffles his hair absentmindedly, looking at Mom. "Luce, don't get yourself into one of your swivets. Gwen, I'd think you'd be smarter. Ben, he's fine. Calm down, all of you. I've got him. He's at my house. He'll be back tomorrow." *Tomarra.* Hard on the accent. Dad's not as casual as he sounds.

Our voices are still overlapping, asking if Nic's okay, telling Dad how worried we were, all about swim captain and "Why didn't you call and tell us, Mike?" This last from my mother, in such a loud voice that Emory murmurs, "Be nice to Daddy."

"It's fine, Emmie," Dad says. "I know all about the captain thing and the girl. He came over yesterday to Castle's wicked messed up, but I had a busload of tourists getting ice cream, so I told him to head to my house, get ahold of himself and take this the way a man does."

"How exactly is a man supposed to handle finding out that the girl he's loved all his life likes somebody else, Dad?"

Mom's and Grandpa's mouths drop open.

"Don't get all dramatic about this, pal. I expect better from you," Dad says, but then he gives me a grin that makes him look unexpectedly boyish, the eighteen-year-old Mom fell for. "Like a man takes everything. By drinking a beer, watching sports on television, feeling sorry for himself. For one night only. He was doing all three when I left him. He'll be fine. Christ, what a bunch of drama queens."

I grab Dad's sleeve as he's climbing into his truck, to thank him, yes, but also to ask why he let us worry for so long. Dad doesn't do the cell phone thing, but still . . . how hard would it have been to say it would all turn out okay?

"Don't worry about the kid, Gwen. He's a bit of an ass right now, but he'll be fine. Sometimes we all need to cut loose. I told him if he didn't knock off being such a hothead he was gonna wind up just like me." He gives me that young-boy grin again. "That should scare him straight."

He peers at me. "You look like you could use a drive, pal. Maybe a getaway of your own." He pauses, still squinting. Then leans over, flicks open the passenger-side door, tips his head to welcome me.

I climb in.

He backs up, screeching, zooms forward. The electric Seashell gate is primed to lift when you get close enough. But dad always barges through that. Every time I think he's just going to ram right through it, knock it down, but it lifts just in time.

I love that we're sheltered in Mom's and Grandpa's caring hands. But sometimes—like now—Dad's wildness is a relief too. Like jumping off a bridge. A rush.

I flick up the sound on his CD. In the Bronco, it's always soothing music Emory likes. Elmo, low-key Disney, more Sesame Street, Raffi. Grandpa's snappy, romantic songs from long ago.

With Dad, when it's not talk radio, you can count on the angry rasp of the Rolling Stones, or the frustrated yell of Bruce Springsteen.

"Tramps like us, baby we were born to run . . ."

"Dad. There's something I need to tell you about the Ellingtons," I start. "It's not good."

He turns down the music only slightly. "Jeez, you and Nic, disaster-wise . . . a mile a minute. What now, Guinevere?"

I explain about Henry Ellington.

Dad gets increasingly angry. Thank God, not at me.

"He said he was counting what? His lobster forks?" *Lobstah*.

"But that's what you told me to do, Dad. Keep an eye out for opportunity. That's what you said. 'My chance.' But I didn't take it. I would never. Couldn't. Did you want me to? Really?"

He pulls over to the side of the road, halfway to the causeway. Rakes his hands through his hair. Looks anywhere but at me.

"Pal," he says finally. "I was eighteen when your mom had you. We get to the hospital and she's screaming and she's crying and she's in pain and there's blood and there's just . . . I only wanted to run. It all seemed a million miles away from how it started, fun on the beach, a bonfire, cute girl . . . whatever. But . . . they hand us this kid—you, with your serious eyes.

This little worried crinkle thing you did with your eyebrows, like you already knew we aren't the best, and it's . . . like . . . like we're supposed to know what do with all that. How to fix that. And hell if we do. Luce knew how to clean stuff up. I knew how to fry stuff up. Gulia was already a disaster—pills, booze, dumbass boys. We knew what was coming our way there, and it was Nic. Another kid. We were his only chance. There was no other way. So, you know, we took it. Nic. You. Emory, with all his . . . whatever. I just want it to be easier for you guys. Something just a little bit easier. Maybe I picked a stupid way to tell you that. I just didn't want my way to be yours. 'Cause mine . . . well . . . I just want better for you. That's all."

Dad's starts the truck up again, heading to his house on the water.

He takes a deep breath.

Pause.

Another deep breath.

I'm waiting for major Dad wisdom.

"Pal."

"Dad . . . ?"

"So Nic's here. And you're here. Don't try to make the guy spill his guts. A time for talking, sure, but Mario Kart goes a long way."

Nic's crashed out in front of the TV, clicker outstretched in hand. Dad throws a blanket on him, too short for his long legs, pulls out the couch bed for me. I text Mom, Viv, and Grandpa before I fall asleep at like two in the morning. Grandpa has nothing to do with cell phones and Mom always erases messages while trying to retrieve them. Viv will get it, though.

Someone is shaking my shoulder, none too gently.

I bolt upward in bed, smacking the top of my head against Nic's chin. Both of us yelp.

Then, "C'mon, cuz," he says, his voice hoarse with sleep.

I slope off the couch, dragging the quilt with me, following him out the door to the slatted wide boards that run from the house over the salt marsh to dry land. Nic sits down heavily, wearing a pair of Dad's faded Red Sox boxers, dangling his feet over the edge of the small bridge, flicking his toe into the water, scattering ripples. He looks awful. Dark circles under his eyes, which are a little bloodshot, his hair rumpled. He's wearing one of Dad's plaid flannel shirts too, too tight on his wide shoulders, the front straining at the buttons. I wrinkle my nose. Beer and sweat. Ugh.

He clears his throat.

"Wanna hit the pier?"

"I want to hit *you*! I looked everywhere, Nic. I thought . . . We all thought you'd drowned yourself in the creek!"

"Seriously? I would never do that, Gwen."

"Nic—"

"Not here," he orders. "Come on."

He already has Dad's truck out in front, engine purring. So unlike Nic to premeditate. Everything is different now.

I slide into the passenger seat with the torn upholstery inadequately patched by duct tape. Nic adjusts the rearview mirror, fastens his seat belt, moves his seat back, doing all these safety checks as though he's about to take off in a Cessna rather than a battered Chevy.

Silence as we ride down to the bridge. Nic doesn't slow on Ocean for the speed bump, and the truck bounces hard as we go over it. Driving like Dad. He pulls in sharply, spraying sand, then turns to me.

"Did you know?" he asks, at the exact same time I blurt out the same question.

"About Vivie?" I press, because Nic doesn't. "Had no clue. I would have . . ."

I don't know what I would have done.

We slide out of the truck, pick our way down to the beach, the sand so cold and wet, I'm shivering. Cass would have grabbed a sweatshirt for me, offered me his. In this short time, I've gotten accustomed to these little things, little watchful courtesies, enough for their absence to feel strangely like a presence.

At the creek's edge, Nic sits down heavily. I fall into place next to him. He shifts sideways, reaches into his pocket, pulls out a flat rock, balancing it in the flat of his hand as though weighing it, staring at it as though he's never seen such a thing.

I reach for it, planning to snatch it from him, throw it into the rush of water, not to skip, just to get rid of it, wipe out the memories Nic must be leafing through, wondering what signs he missed . . . how what he thought was true turned out to be nothing like the truth at all.

But Nic curls his fingers around the rock before I can take it.

"So, I've been a douche lately," he begins.

"Well, yeah. You sure have," I say. "But that's not why Vivie—"

He opens his mouth to answer, then closes it, a little muscle jumping in his jaw. "I'm not talking about Vee."

"Nico—" I start, but he shakes his head, stopping me.

"Last year—even this spring—you never for a moment would have thought I'd offed myself in the creek. That's true, right?"

His brown eyes pierce mine. I nod.

"Did you know?" I ask. "About Spence?"

He shakes his head, kicks at the water. "Yes. No. Something wasn't right. She was . . . I was . . . I just figured I'd fix it later. I mean, she'd be there. Of course. Get the captain thing squared away, then deal. But . . . I mean . . . what happened on the beach. Pretty clear that ship had sailed while I wasn't even looking."

I wait, quiet. Dad said not to push.

"I . . . couldn't face you guys, after . . . Aunt Luce, Grandpa . . . you . . . You'd be all sorry for me." He rolls his shoulders as though shrugging off our imagined sympathy. "Knew Uncle Mike wouldn't be like that."

"Did you get the What a Man Does lecture?"

"Hell yeah," he says. "I knew you'd be freaking. Told him to call you. He said a man spoke for himself. If I wasn't ready to talk to you, he sure as shit wasn't going to do it for me."

Again I open my mouth, but he shuts me down with the wave of a hand. Or in this case a fist, since he's still holding the stone.

"Do you remember," he asks, "when Old Mrs. Partridge had that skunk under her porch, cuz? When we were, like, seven? And she called your dad to handle it? He threw a towel over it and tossed it to me and it bit me through the towel?"

I do. I remember Viv holding his hand in the clinic, crying the tears Nic would never let himself cry.

Oh Nic.

"And Vivien—"

"This is not about Vivien. I had to get rabies shots, 'member? And the nurse was standing there with this wicked big needle. Aunt Luce and Vovó were crying, and Grandpa Ben was praying, and you were asking if it would work if you took it instead. I asked if it would hurt . . . Grandpa and Aunt Luce started to say no and Uncle Mike said it was gonna hurt like a motherfucker. Do you remember that?"

I do, partly because I'd never heard that particular word before.

"Thing is, he was right. It did. But it helped. Knowing how I was going to feel. Can't deal with the truth if no one tells it, right?"

I nod.

"I've loved that girl all my life," Nic says.

"I know."

He weighs the stone in his hand, angles his wrist, flips it across the water. A double skip, not one of his best.

"And I'm more bummed about not getting the captain spot. Want to tell me what that means?"

That what you've always had doesn't mean that's what you'll always get. That what you've always wanted isn't what you'll always want.

I don't realize I've spoken out loud until Nic says, "Yeah. Exactly, cuz."

Mom's just pulling on her sneakers as I get home, sitting on the steps. I hear the shrill of Disney coming from inside the house. *Mulan. "I'll make a maaann out of you,"* Emory's voice wobbles, sweet and high.

"Nic okay?" Mom asks.

I nod. "He'll be fine."

She studies my face. "For sure," she says finally, firmly. "But if he isn't? For a little while? It's not your problem to solve." Mom picks up one of her Nikes, with an inextricable knot, tries to untangle it with the fingernails she has to keep short because of cleaning houses.

"Here, let me," I say, pulling at the shoe.

"Gwen. *I* can solve this." A pull and a jerk here and there and the shoelaces untangle. She slips it on her foot, reaches for her can of Diet Coke. Shuts her eyes as she drinks it, closing out the world, the way she does with the things that take her away, her books, her sodas, her stories.

A rattle of gravel and a flash of silver. Mom and I both look up in time to see Spence's Porsche flash by. His sunglasses pushed up into his hair, arm along the seat. He pulls into the Almeidas' driveway, slanted, the way the car was that first summer day at Castle's, taking up more space than it needs.

Viv runs down the short steps, climbs into the car, long hair loose and blowing.

"This is gonna take some getting used to," Mom says. "That boy sure looks out of place."

The paradox of Seashell. He does and he doesn't. Precisely the sort of car that belongs on the island, pulled into exactly the driveway where it doesn't. Not Viv in the place she's always been, all she ever wanted, or Nic in the place he was afraid would be all he had.

Chapter Thirty-seven

I stand on the steps of the Field House for a few minutes, working up my courage, raise my hand to knock but, before I can, it flips inward, so that I basically fall into Cass, who's opening it with a blue plastic recycling bin balanced on his shoulder.

"Hey," I say.

He sets the bin down on the steps, straightens. He's backlit from the indoor light, which picks out the bright of his hair, but leaves his expression in darkness.

Silence. Not even his ingrained politeness is going to get me in the door unless I talk fast. Which I do, so swiftly the words tumble over one another. "I have to tell you some things and ask you some things and you need to let me in."

He takes a step backward and raises an eyebrow. "Is that an order? Am I Jose here?"

"I'm asking. Not ordering. Can I . . . come in? Because . . . Cass, just let me in so we don't have to have this conversation on your steps. Old Mrs. Partridge probably has supersonic hearing."

He opens the door wider but doesn't move, so I have to brush past him going in, catching a faint whiff of chlorine, sun-warm skin.

I sit down on the ugly green couch. He sinks into the stained armchair across from me. I tug my skirt lower. He clenches and unclenches his hand.

"I need to ask you a question. No, three."

"Go for it," he says briefly.

"You knew about Spence and Viv, didn't you?"

"Yes."

One quick word. I was expecting an explanation, an excuse. It takes me by surprise for a second. I press on. "For how long?"

"Since the day after the boathouse. That night. At the B and T. I saw them," Cass says.

"Okay," I say. "Next one."

"Why I didn't tell you? I—"

"Shh, not that. Did you have condoms that day in the boathouse? Along with the towels and the Dockside Delight? Truth."

He shuts his eyes. "Yeah. Just in case. I mean, not that that was the goal or all it was, but—you know how things are with us—I didn't want to get caught off guard and not be smart. Again. And then, the next day, the next *day*, Gwen, I find out that there's this whole thing I can't tell you. That'll hurt you. When I've already said I'll be honest, when we'd finally gotten around the roadblocks and it was clear sailing."

"Mixed metaphor. But I know now. I got it."

A hint of a smile. "Okay, word girl, got what?"

"Your superpower."

"Uh—my what?"

"You can't lie. You don't lie. I just asked you about these awkward things that have gotten in our way before and you told the truth anyhow."

"I should have before. I just . . . didn't want Spence and Vivien—or anything—between us. I just wanted . . ."

"Me," I finish.

"Us," he says.

We haven't said everything we need to, but I have to kiss him now. I straighten up, he does the same, take a few steps, just as he does. Loop my fingers around his neck as he pulls my waist close. As always, he smells like everything clean and clear. Soap. Sunshine. The kiss starts carefully, his lips warm against mine, gentle and firm, knowing and calm, but then deepens, turns wild, because that is us too. He sets his hands at the back of my neck and I pull his shoulders closer, my hands on his back, breathing in Cass, this moment, all of it, all of him. I can't get enough, and, intoxicatingly, it seems as though he can't either. Not just of kissing me. Of me.

And we don't talk for a while.

Then . . . "How does this make you feel?" Cass asks, but before I can answer he groans, ducks his head. "I can't believe I asked that."

"Was there something wrong with it?" I inquire. "Because I thought it was nice. That you did."

"Mom's favorite phrase," he says, rolling onto his back on the rug. "The therapist thing . . . 'How does that make you fe-eel?' She's great, but I don't want to think about her right now. Much less sound like her. God."

He sits up, a little flush on his cheeks over the sunburn. I slip my hand into his hair, ruffle it.

"One last question, honest answer. How come you had

never—um—you say you aren't like Spence, and I get that. But what *were* you doing at those parties while he was collecting hot tub trophy girls? Recycling the empties?"

Cass snorts. "Hardly. I'm no saint. I just didn't go, um, the distance."

I start laughing. "The distance? A swim team metaphor?"

"Could you not laugh? This is awkward enough," he says, attempting a glare but half smiling.

"Why awkward?" I ask.

"Because . . . well, because . . . I'm thinking you're asking this because I'm doing something wrong or don't know what I'm doing or—" He winces, draws his hand quickly across his face, then says hurriedly, "I'm a fast learner, though. I mean, when I care. And I—"

"Cass." I rest my hand on his cheek. "If we're going to talk about me having some experience, a little more, than you, can I tell you what I know . . . from experience?"

He nods.

"That I would so much rather be with someone who cared what he was doing than someone who knew what he was doing."

And then we're kissing again.

Chapter Thirty-eight

The crash of thunder startles us apart, for a moment. Then he pulls me back as the rain begins, droplets spattering against the Field House roof. We get up off the couch, walk around slamming windows shut. More rumbles of thunder, lightning. Another stormy summer.

As I slam the front windows, the ones that look out toward the ocean, I catch sight of what I brought, set down in the bushes near the lawn mower before I climbed the steps. "Oh shit," I say, hurrying to the door.

Cass is behind me in an instant. "No running away."

"I'm not." I laugh. "Really. I'll be right back. Stay here. No, wait—go in the bathroom. Stay there until I tell you to come out. Maybe . . . maybe take a shower. Or something. Just give me five minutes."

Cass studies me, then asks warily, "I need a shower? Do I—"

"No, no, it's not about that. You smell delicious. I mean. Oh, God." I cover my eyes with a hand, lower it. "I mean—"

The dimples make an appearance. "Maybe just go in and wait? You are planning to let me out, right?"

The rain is coming down harder. "Yes, yes. Get in there."

And he does.

Mom's books, Grandpa's movies—I know all about the things that spell romance. Candles, roses, soft romantic music, gentle golden light coming through a window. All of it so carefully staged.

I can't do anything about the light through the window, or the fact that I left what I brought outside in the rain. But this is in fact, carefully staged. And yet still nerve-wracking. Even though I've thought about it, planned it, know it's right.

In Cass's room, I embellish his bureau with candles, set them on the nightstand, line them on the windowsill. Luckily, the yard boy hasn't been wielding his hedge clippers on the Field House shrubbery; the canvas bag I hid beneath the bushes was protected. Not much got wet in the downpour . . . except, of course, the matches. Great. I hurry back inside to the kitchen, adjust the sagging Dockside Delight bag I'd set on the counter. Then I light one candle at a burner, use that to light the next, then the next, and the next until the darkened room glows gently. I'm suddenly glad it's rainy out.

His bed's unmade, covers tossed around. Sheets . . . of course . . . pale pink.

I flip the comforter straight, fluff the pillowcases, then feel a little weird and want to switch them back to the way they were. I hover over the bed, unsure, when Cass calls out, "Can I—?"

"Not yet!"

The dress isn't even damp, thank God.

⌒

"Okay, you can come out now."

He opens the door, letting out a cloud of steam. He actually showered. And changed his clothes. His eyes flick to mine and he drops the towel he's rubbing through his hair to the ground.

"Hey," he says.

"Um," I answer, as if that *is* an answer.

He looks me over, my hair, my black halter top dress, my bare feet. I curl my toes, raise my chin, act like this is all easy for me.

But he knows, Cass knows me.

"Well," he says. "Wow, Gwen."

"I think we need to get this over with," I blurt out.

He starts to laugh. "Just what every guy wants to hear. We all want to be the Band-Aid you rip off fast."

"You're not. I want this. I mean . . . I . . . I . . . I brought candles," I say.

"And a Dockside Delight," he adds. He walks over slowly, sets his hands on either side of where I'm standing by the kitchen counter. I lean back against it. He just looks. "You planned this."

"Yes. I did. I . . . did."

He raises his hand, cups my face. Bends to tip his forehead to mine. Says the words I know he'll say. "Thank you."

"It's not about a jumbo box of condoms," I say.

"Never was," Cass says simply.

He slants his hand against my jaw, tips his mouth to mine.

EPILOGUE

Set up on the wide square green between Low Road and Beach Road, where Seashell weddings are always held, is a castle.

Well, the high-peaked tent *looks* like one, festive as something from my namesake's Camelot, with blue and white streamers—Stony Bay High colors—flapping in the wind from the tops of the canvas turrets, twinkling white lights wrapped in the rafters and looped around the poles, and blue and white flowers everywhere.

The "Congratulations!" banner droops crooked on one side, and Al Almeida is gesturing impatiently at someone to fix it. Not me, though. Not tonight. Or Hoop or Pam or Nic or Viv. Tonight we're guests, no clamshell T-shirts or rented tuxes.

It's an informal Stony Bay High tradition for seniors to leave graduation and drive to the lake near town, and dive in fully clothed. We all did it, Hoop, Nic, Spence, Viv, Cass, and me, piling into the Porsche and the Bronco, Hoop's truck, Cass's battered BMW, joining the lineup of our classmates for the plunge, screaming as we each hurtled ourselves over the water, and then driving across the bridge to Seashell for our own celebration—jumping off the pier at Abenaki in those same soggy clothes.

Hoop yelped that the water was freezing. Cass, already far toward the breakwater, called him a wimp. Spence paddled lazily, far from the fierce strokes that, combined with Nic's backstroke and Cass's flawless butterfly, made the SBH team state champions for the first time ever.

And now we have a party—not a tradition but something that will only happen once, celebrating all we are leaving behind, public and private, in school and at home. Spence's dad wanted to throw a big one at the B&T, but in the end, only Seashell seemed right.

"How'd that happen?" I asked Viv when she told me.

"I used my superior managerial skills," she said.

"You threatened to cry, didn't you? Spence can't handle that."

"No, I don't do that. When it's real love, no manipulation necessary."

"I still think you should get that job at Hallmark."

She shakes her head, "It would interfere with my college career."

Stony Bay Vocational has culinary courses, and Viv plans to take some this fall, picking up credits that, a year ago, she thought weren't important. If things go well, she can transfer to Johnson & Wales in Rhode Island in the spring. Spence will be at Harvard. Whether they can survive the distance is a page they haven't turned yet. They've already survived the school year, survived awkward family occasions at the B&T, where Viv was the girlfriend instead of the waitstaff, survived comments of Spence's like, "Wow. I've never been faithful this long. Or at all."

My high heels, another female torture device, like eyelash curlers and endless articles about how to "get a beach body," were killing me, so now I'm standing in the grass outside the tent, heels kicked off, absently rubbing one foot. Through the folded back tent flap, I can see Mom doing the same. She's spent the last few weeks opening houses on Seashell, shaking the sheets off the furniture, sweeping away the cobwebs.

Castle's opened last week, Dad grumbling over the tourist buses, everyone wanting their breakfast sandwiches made a certain way. Frustrated that no one wants smoked bluefish breakfast burritos. Now he's here, in a plaid sport coat I have never seen before, talking shop with Cass's dad, jabbing his finger toward the distant ocean, where a Herreshoff, one of Dad's dream boats, sails by, slow and majestic in the water as a king on procession.

Nic tilts against a table, sipping a Coke, but not morose. He got into the Coast Guard Academy, will go there in the fall. He watches Viv for a minute, then his eyes drift out over the ocean in the distance, out to his own horizon.

"You are not dancing, why?" Grandpa Ben demands, suddenly beside me with Emory in tow. He's actually in a tux, with Emory dressed in a scarily identical miniature, both of them complete with jaunty black bow ties. Grandpa found them in some classified listing in the *Stony Bay Bugle* a few weeks ago, and brought them both home as if they were that treasure he's been searching for with his metal detector. He insisted they both try them on immediately. "Fred Astaire, pah," he'd said. "Look at us, *coelho*. He should eat his heart out."

"Scratchy" was Em's response. "Want swimsuit. Now." All

winter, Grandpa—and sometimes Dad, freer once Castle's closed down—took him to swim at the Y in White Bay. Em can dive now, clean and clear into the water, coming up with a smile. And Hideout smells like chorine.

I edge out farther along the grass, looking back at the tent, the swath of lawn, the gray-shingled mansions and the low ranch houses. Seashell.

All the things that stay the same . . . and everything that's changed.

It was an uneasy truce for a while, all of us adjusting, our shifting alliances. But, in its way, it's all happened before, and it'll all happen again. Summer turning to fall, crisp breezes replacing warm salty ones. Corridors and class-rooms and indoor pools replacing sandy paths to the ocean, replacing the boathouse, fried clams at Castle's, the wide open sea. My grandfather, a young man, flexing his mus-cles as he mows the lawns, whipping up his special lob-ster sauce. My grandmother, the daring young woman who drove too fast into town, the distance between summer people and island people shorter than the causeway, only as long as it takes to step across the invisible line that only exists if you insist on it.

"Hey," Cass says, coming up next to me, jacket already off, sleeves already unbuttoned and rolled up. "I've been looking all over for you."

The B&T hired the jazz band (thank God not the barbershop quartet) and they're smoothly playing the lush old-fashioned songs I know so well from Grandpa Ben, the mellow music drifting softly into the night, out over low tide.

Cass is a better dancer than I am—not hard—but we know how, we know now, how to move together, so he dips and twirls me to the music, dance steps I never knew before.

"You're leading," he breathes against my cheek.

And I am. "Sorry," I whisper.

"S'okay," he says. And it is.

By chance, and maybe a little bit by design, we're going to the same university, State College. He to study cartography, me, thanks to a Daughters of Portuguese Fishermen scholarship (granddaughter, really, but Grandpa Ben talked his way around the logistics), to study English lit.

I love you, you know, I told him, that night at the Field House. Sort of fiercely, in this aggressive tone I immediately wished I could take back—a challenge more than an admission.

But Cass gets it. He gets me.

"I do," he said simply. And I knew he did. That that was true.

The old-fashioned music fades away, starts into something jangly and current. Cass pulls my hand and we head farther out into the grass, to the top of Beach Road where we can see everything—ocean, land, even a hint of the causeway far, far off. And I can glimpse it all, trace the path we've come along, like the lines on a map. Four kids lying on the sand, fireworks as bright as shooting stars. Two friends on the dock, looking out at the unknown. A little boy leaping for his life, an older one doing the same. A firefly glowing in the night, caught by a boy who shows it to a girl. This girl bending to that boy's kiss. An old woman who hasn't forgotten what it was like to be a young one, leaning back on her glider, rocking her feet against the floorboards, looks out over the water, the ocean that changes and never changes. Horizons that seem like endings but only bend farther into the sky, curving into something new, beginning all over again.

ACKNOWLEDGMENTS

Published Book Two is a whole different experience than book one. Most of all, this time around I am incredibly aware of how much talent, hard work, and goodwill go into making my manuscript into the book you hold in your hands.

Thanks beyond the scope of words to:

My family and friends. Father, the best of men, Georgia, the best of stepmothers, my brother Ted and sister deLancey, all my Thomas cousins, Patricia and Kramer, my Concord buddies and friends far and near, who gave me sailing tips, and Colette, Matthew, and Luke. Because because because.

Christina Hogrebe, my savvy, smart, and incredible agent, who works tirelessly to ensure that no one puts Baby (in the form of either my books or me) in a corner. And Meg Ruley, Jane Berkey, Annelise Robey, Christina Prestia, Andrea Cirillo, Danielle Sickles, and Liz Van Buren . . . all my friends at JRA.

To Jessica Garrison, whose story sense and editorial expertise are matched by her dedication and kindness, and who more than once worked over vacations and into the wee hours of the night (2:30 a.m. editorial letters, honest) to make this story as good as it could be.

To Vanessa Han and Jasmin Rubero, for making *WITWT*

beautiful outside and inside. To Molly Sardella, who threw her heart into promoting *My Life Next Door*. To Jackie Engel, Doni Kay (and the entire awesome Penguin sales team), Lily Malcom, and Claire Evans, for their support and enthusiasm for this book. Donne Forrest and Draga Malesevic, who work hard to send my books beyond borders. To Regina Castillo—fortunately my copyeditor once again, who ensures my grammar, my story logic, and that Cass's shirt won't change color—or cease to exist—mid-scene. And huge thanks to Lauri Hornik for her faith in me and my books. And Kristen Tozzo, who kept this baby on schedule.

Virtual bouquets and champagne toasts to everyone in CTRWA, the best friends any writer could ever have, who provided everything from computer savvy to handholding to plot suggestions at a moment's notice. And most especially to the plot monkeys: Karen Pinco, Shaunee Cole, Jennifer Iszkiewicz, and Kristan Higgins, who radiate imagination and general awesomeness, and who make me laugh until my stomach hurts on a regular basis. You all kept me from the looming danger provided by a certain dwarf.

And yeah, about that Kristan Higgins. You, my friend, get a double dose of thanks. I could not have gotten through this one without your suggestions, your reads, your advice, your borrowed bling, and your endless kindness: true friend, mentor, muse, fairy godsister, and just the person who, like her books, always makes me laugh. And cry.

Also my beloved Gay Thomas, a friend for life, and Jessica Anderson, both of whom read and counseled and calmed when I'd completely lost all perspective on this book.

The eternally awesome Apocalypsies, the talented team whose books, warmth, and wisdom rocked 2012 and kept me as sane as possible. The best club of all.

MLND, *WITWT*, and I owe the world to the bloggers, readers, booksellers, teachers, and librarians who so tirelessly read and recommend for the sheer love of a good story. Thank you for reading, for writing reviews and blogs and letters, and for caring.

Turn the page for a peek at
Huntley Fitzpatrick's first novel,

MY LIFE NEXT DOOR

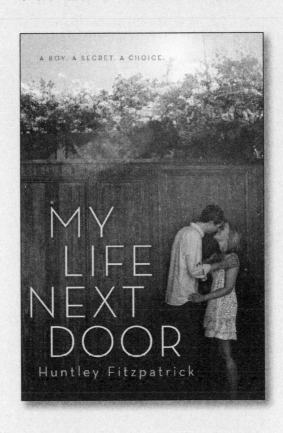

Chapter One

The Garretts were forbidden from the start.

But that's not why they were important.

We were standing in our yard that day ten years ago when their battered sedan pulled up to the low-slung shingled house next door, close behind the moving van.

"Oh no," Mom sighed, arms falling to her sides. "I hoped we could have avoided this."

"This—what?" my big sister called from down the driveway. She was eight and already restless with Mom's chore of the day, planting jonquil bulbs in our front garden. Walking quickly to the picket fence that divided our house from the one next door, she perched on her tiptoes to peer at the new neighbors. I pressed my face to the gap in the slats, watching in amazement as two parents and five children spilled from the sedan, like a clown car at the circus.

"This kind of thing." Mom gestured toward the car with the trowel, twisting her silvery blond hair into a coil with the other hand. "There's one in every neighborhood. The family that never mows their lawn. Has toys scattered everywhere. The ones who never plant flowers, or do and let them die. The messy family who lowers real estate values. Here they are. Right next door. You've got that bulb wrong side up, Samantha."

I switched the bulb around, scooting my knees in the dirt to get closer to the fence, my eyes never leaving the father as he swung a baby from a car seat while a curly-haired toddler climbed his back. "They look nice," I said.

I remember there was a silence then, and I looked up at my mother.

She was shaking her head at me, a strange expression on her face. "Nice isn't the point here, Samantha. You're seven years old. You need to understand what's important. *Five* children. Good God. Just like your father's family. Insanity." She shook her head again, rolling her eyes heavenward.

I moved closer to Tracy and edged a fleck of white paint off the fence with my thumbnail. My sister looked at me with the same warning face she used when she was watching TV and I walked up to ask her a question.

"*He's* cute," she said, squinting over the fence again. I looked over to see an older boy unfold himself from the back of the car, baseball mitt in hand, reaching back to haul out a cardboard box full of sports gear.

Even then, Tracy liked to deflect, to forget how hard our mother found being a parent. Our dad had walked away without even a good-bye, leaving Mom with a one-year-old, a baby on the way, a lot of disillusionment, and, luckily, her trust fund from her parents.

As the years proved, our new neighbors, the Garretts, were exactly what Mom predicted. Their lawn got mowed sporadically at best. Their Christmas lights stayed hung till Easter.

Their backyard was a hodgepodge of an in-ground pool and a trampoline and a swing set and monkey bars. Periodically, Mrs. Garrett would make an effort to plant something seasonal, chrysanthemums in September, impatiens in June, only to leave it to gasp and wither away as she tended to something more important, like her five children. They became eight children over the years. All approximately three years apart.

"My unsafe zone," I overheard Mrs. Garrett explain one day at the supermarket when Mrs. Mason commented on her burgeoning belly, "is twenty-two months. That's when they suddenly aren't babies anymore. I love babies so much."

Mrs. Mason had raised her eyebrows and smiled, then turned away with compressed lips and a baffled shake of her head.

But Mrs. Garrett seemed to ignore it, happy in herself and content with her chaotic family. Five boys and three girls by the time I turned seventeen.

Joel, Alice, Jase, Andy, Duff, Harry, George, and Patsy.

In the ten years since the Garretts moved next door, Mom hardly ever looked out the side windows of our house without huffing an impatient breath. Too many kids on the trampoline. Bikes abandoned on the lawn. Another pink or blue balloon tied to the mailbox, waving haphazardly in the breeze. Loud basketball games. Music blaring while Alice and her friends tanned. The bigger boys washing cars and spraying each other with hoses. If not those, it was Mrs. Garrett, calmly breast-feeding on the front steps, or sitting there on Mr. Garrett's lap, for all the world to see.

"It's indecent," Mom would say, watching.

"It's legal," Tracy, future lawyer, always countered, flipping back her platinum hair. She'd station herself next to Mom, inspecting the Garretts out the big side window of the kitchen. "The courts have made it absolutely legal to breast-feed wherever you want. Her own front steps are definitely fair game."

"But why? Why do it at all when there are bottles and formula? And if you *must*, why not inside?"

"She's watching the other kids, Mom. It's what she's supposed to do," I'd sometimes point out, making my stand next to Tracy.

Mom would sigh, shake her head, and extract the vacuum cleaner from the closet as if it were a Valium. The lullaby of my childhood was my mom running the vacuum cleaner, making perfectly symmetrical lines in our beige living room carpet. The lines somehow seemed important to her, so essential that she'd turn on the machine as Tracy and I were eating breakfast, then slowly follow us to the door as we pulled on our coats and backpacks. Then she'd back up, eliminating our trail of footprints, and her own, until we were outside. Finally, she'd rest the vacuum cleaner carefully behind one of our porch columns only to drag it back in that night when she got home from work.

It was clear from the start that we were *not to play with the Garretts*. After bringing over the obligatory "welcome to the neighborhood" lasagna, my mother did her best to be very unwelcoming. She responded to Mrs. Garrett's smiling greetings with cool nods. She rebuffed Mr. Garrett's offers to mow, sweep up leaves, or shovel snow with a terse "We have a service, thanks all the same."

Finally, the Garretts stopped trying.

Though they lived right next door and one kid or another might pedal past me as I watered Mom's flowers, it was easy not to run into them. Their kids went to the local public schools. Tracy and I attended Hodges, the only private school in our small Connecticut town.

One thing my mother never knew, and would disapprove of most of all, was that I watched the Garretts. All the time.

Outside my bedroom window, there's a small flat section of the roof with a tiny fence around it. Not really a balcony, more like a ledge. It's in between two peaked gables, shielded from both the front and backyard, and it faces the right side of the Garretts' house. Even before they came, it was my place to sit and think. But afterward, it was my place to dream.

I'd climb out after bedtime, look through the lit windows, and see Mrs. Garrett doing the dishes, one of the younger kids sitting on the counter next to her. Or Mr. Garrett wrestling with the older boys in the living room. Or the lights going on where the baby must sleep, the figure of Mr. or Mrs. Garrett pacing back and forth, rubbing a tiny back. It was like watching a silent movie, one so different from the life I lived.

Over the years, I got more daring. I'd sometimes watch during the day, after school, hunched back against the side of the rough gable, trying to figure out which Garrett matched each name I heard called out the screen door. It was tricky because they all had wavy brown hair, olive skin, and sinewy builds, like a breed all their own.

Joel was the easiest to identify—the oldest and the most athletic. His picture often appeared in local papers for various sports accomplishments—I knew it in black and white. Alice, next in line, dyed her hair outlandish colors and wore clothes that provoked commentary from Mrs. Garrett, so I had her down as well. George and Patsy were the littlest ones. The middle three boys, Jase, Duff, and Harry . . . I couldn't get them straight. I was pretty sure that Jase was the oldest of the three, but did that mean he was the tallest? Duff was supposed to be the smart one, competing in various chess competitions and spelling bees, but he didn't wear glasses or give off any obvious brainiac signals. Harry was constantly in trouble—"Harry! How could you?" was the refrain. And Andy, the middle girl, always seemed to be missing, her name called longest to come to the dinner table or pile into the car: "Annnnnnnnndeeeeeeeeee!"

From my hidden perch, I'd peer out at the yard, trying to locate Andy, figure out Harry's latest escapade, or see what outrageous outfit Alice was wearing. The Garretts were my bedtime story, long before I ever thought I'd be part of the story myself.

Chapter Two

On the first sweltering hot night in June, I'm home alone, trying to enjoy the quiet but finding myself moving from room to room, unable to settle.

Tracy's out with Flip, yet another blond tennis player in her unending series of boyfriends. I can't reach my best friend, Nan, who's been completely distracted by *her* boyfriend, Daniel, since school ended last week and he graduated. There's nothing on TV I want to see, no place in town I feel like going. I've tried sitting out on the porch, but at low tide the humid air is overpowering, muddy-scented from the breeze off the river.

So I'm sitting in our vaulted living room, crunching the ice left over from my seltzer, skimming through Tracy's stack of *In Touch* magazines. Suddenly I hear a loud, continuous buzzing sound. As it goes on and on I look around, alarmed, trying to identify it. The dryer? The smoke detector? Finally, I realize it's the doorbell, buzzing and buzzing, on and on and on. I hurry to open the door, expecting—sigh—one of Tracy's exes, daring after too many strawberry daiquiris at the country club, come to win her back.

Instead, I see my mother, pressed against the doorbell, getting the daylights kissed out of her by some man. When I throw

7

the door open, they half stumble, then he braces his hand on the jamb and just keeps kissing away. So I stand there, feeling stupid, arms folded, my thin nightgown shifting slightly in the thick air. All around me are summer voices. The lap of the shore far away, the roar of a motorcycle coming up the street, the *shhhh* of the wind in the dogwood trees. None of those, and certainly not my presence, stop my mom or this guy. Not even when the motorcycle backfires as it peels into the Garretts' driveway, which usually drives Mom crazy.

Finally, they come up for air, and she turns to me with an awkward laugh.

"Samantha. Goodness! You startled me."

She's flustered, her voice high and girlish. Not the authoritative "this is how it will be" voice she typically uses at home or the syrup-mixed-with-steel one she wields on the job.

Five years ago, Mom went into politics. Tracy and I didn't take it seriously at first—we'd hardly known Mom to vote. But she came home one day from a rally charged up and determined to be state senator. She ran, and she won, and our lives changed entirely.

We were proud of her. Of course we were. But instead of making breakfast and sifting through our book bags to be sure our homework was done, Mom left home at five o'clock in the morning and headed to Hartford "before the traffic kicks in." She stayed late for commissions and special sessions. Weekends weren't about Tracy's gymnastics practices or my swim meets. They were for boning up on upcoming votes, staying for special sessions, or attending local events. Tracy pulled every bad-teenager trick in the book. She played with drugs and drinking, she shoplifted, she slept with too many boys. I read piles of books, registered Democratic in my mind (Mom's Republican), and spent more time than usual watching the Garretts.

So now tonight, I stand here, stunned into immobility by the unexpected and prolonged PDA, until Mom finally lets go of the guy. He turns to me and I gasp.

After a man leaves you, pregnant and with a toddler, you don't keep his picture on the mantel. We have only a few photographs of our dad, and they're all in Tracy's room. Still I recognize him—the curve of his jaw, the dimples, the shiny wheat-blond hair and broad shoulders. This man has all those things.

"Dad?"

Mom's expression morphs from dreamy bedazzlement to utter shock, as though I've cursed.

The guy shifts away from Mom, extends his hand to me. As he moves into the light of the living room, I realize he's much younger than my father would be now. "Hi there, darlin'. I'm the newest—and most enthusiastic—member of your mom's reelection campaign."

Enthusiastic? I'll say.

He takes my hand and shakes it, seemingly without my participation.

"This is Clay Tucker," Mom says, in the reverent tone one might use for Vincent van Gogh or Abraham Lincoln. She turns and gives me a reproving look, no doubt for the "Dad" comment, but quickly recovers. "Clay's worked on national campaigns. I'm very lucky he's agreed to help me out."

9

In what capacity? I wonder as she fluffs her hair in a gesture that can't possibly be anything but flirtatious. *Mom?*

"So, Clay," she continues. "I *told* you Samantha was a big girl."

I blink. I'm five two. In heels. "Big girl" is a stretch. Then I get it. She means old. Old for someone as young as her to have.

"Clay was mighty surprised to find I had a teenager." My mother tucks a wayward strand of newly fluffed hair behind her ear. "He says I look like one myself."

I wonder if she's mentioned Tracy, or if she's going to keep her on the down-low for a while.

"You're as beautiful as your mother," he says to me, "so now I believe it." He has the kind of Southern accent that makes you think of melting butter on biscuits, and porch swings.

Clay looks around the living room. "What a terrific room," he says. "Just invites a man to put his feet up after a long hard day." Mom beams. She's proud of our house, renovates rooms all the time, tweaking the already perfect. He walks around slowly, examining the gigantic paintings of landscapes on the white, white walls, taking in the so-puffy-you-can't-sit-on-it beige couch and the immense armchairs, finally settling into the one in front of the fireplace. I'm shocked. I check Mom's face. Her dates always stop at the door. In fact, she's barely dated at all.

But Mom doesn't do her usual thing, glance at her watch, say, "Oh, goodness, look at the time," and politely shove him out the door. Instead, she gives that little girlish laugh again, toys with a pearl earring, and says, "I'll just make coffee."

She whirls toward the kitchen, but before she can take a step, Clay Tucker comes up to me, putting his hand on my shoulder. "Seems to me," he says, "you're the kind of girl who'd make the coffee herself and let her mama relax."

My face heats and I take an involuntary step back. Fact is, I usually do make tea for Mom when she comes in late. It's sort of a ritual. But no one has ever told me to do it. Part of me thinks I must have misheard. I met this guy, like, two seconds ago. The other part instantly feels chagrined, the way I do at school when I've forgotten to do the extra credit math problem, or at home when I shove my newly laundered clothes into a drawer unfolded. I stand there, struggling for a response, and come up blank. Finally I nod, turn, and go to the kitchen.

As I measure out coffee grounds, I can hear murmurs and low laughter coming from the living room. Who *is* this guy? Has Tracy met him? Guess not, if I'm the *big girl*. And anyway, Tracy's been off cheering Flip on at his tennis matches since they graduated last week. The rest of the time, they're parked in his convertible in our driveway, bucket seats down, while Mom's still at work.

"Coffee ready yet, sweetie?" Mom calls. "Clay here could use a pick-me-up. He's been working like a hound dog helping me out."

Hound dog? I pour freshly brewed coffee into cups, put them on a tray, find cream, sugar, napkins, and stalk back into the living room.

"That's fine for me, sweetheart, but Clay takes his in a big ol' mug. Right, Clay?"

"That's right," he says with a broad smile, holding the teacup out to me. "The biggest you got, Samantha. I run on caffeine. It's a weakness." He winks.

Returning from the kitchen a second time, I plunk the mug down in front of Clay. Mom says, "You're going to love Samantha, Clay. Such a smart girl. This past year she took all AP classes. A pluses in every one. She was on the yearbook staff, the school newspaper, used to be on the swim team . . . A star, my girl." Mom gives me her real smile, the one that goes all the way to her eyes. I start to smile back.

"Like mother, like daughter," Clay says, and my mom's eyes slide back to his face and stay there, transfixed. They exchange a private look and Mom goes over and perches on the armrest of his chair. I wonder for a second if I'm still in the room. Clearly, I'm dismissed. Fine. I'm saved from the distinct possibility I'll lose control and pour Clay's still-hot coffee from his big ol' mug onto his lap. Or pour something really cold on Mom.

Return to the world of MY LIFE NEXT DOOR in
Huntley Fitzpatrick's new novel,

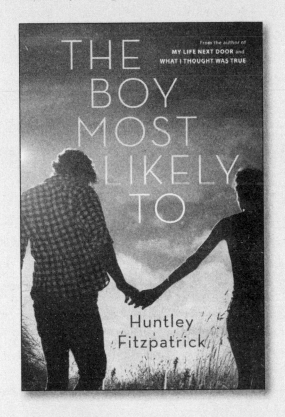

Tim Mason was The Boy Most Likely To find the liquor cabinet
blindfolded, need a liver transplant, and drive his car into a
house. Alice Garrett was The Girl Most Likely To . . . well, not date
her little brother's baggage-burdened best friend, for starters. But
somehow, they're drawn together like moths to a flame.

Then Tim's wild days come back to haunt him, and he finds
himself in a situation that he never could have predicted. And
Alice is caught in the middle.